THE HOUSE ON OCTAVIA STREET

THE HOUSE ON
OCTAVIA STREET

A Novel

JACQUELINE LA TOURRETTE

BEAUFORT BOOKS, Inc.
New York / Toronto

Copyright © 1984 by Jacqueline Gibeson

Library of Congress Cataloging in Publication Data

La Tourrette, Jacqueline, 1926–
  The house on Octavia Street.

  I. Title.
PS3562.A75895H6 1984   813′.54   83-22438
ISBN 0-8253-0194-7

Published in the United States by Beaufort Books, Inc., New York.
Published simultaneously in Canada by General Publishing Co. Limited

Designer: Cindy LaBreacht

Printed in the U.S.A.   First Edition

10 9 8 7 6 5 4 3 2 1

Foreword

This novel is based on a true story. Many of the events, which are really stranger than fiction, are on public record, revealed in numerous courtroom appearances, lawsuits, and an inquest. The sequence of these events has been altered in the interest of storytelling. Many things have been attributed to Mary Ellen Pleasant over the years; only those relating directly to her relationship with Teresa Percy have been explored.

The association of the two women, which lasted for thirty years, must have had love-hate elements beyond Teresa's dependent personality, her gratitude toward the older woman, and the blackmail by which Mrs. Pleasant bound Teresa to her. Mary Ellen Pleasant's oblique approach to any undertaking and the motivation behind her endeavors remain historically obscure. Her background certainly contributed to her secretiveness, but it also seems quite possible that her intellect and drive, which might have liberated her in a later age, had to be subverted in the time in which she lived and revealed themselves in an abnormal, furtive manner. That she exercised considerable power in San Francisco in her middle years without anyone's awareness of it seems more than possible. What she was actually working toward remains a mystery.

Thomas Bell's past in England is equally enigmatic. No specific crime has ever been ascribed to him, because to this day no one knows what type of crime he committed. Scotland Yard may have shared its file with an inspector from the San Francisco police, but there is no evidence of this; Bell's criminal record has been lost to history. Whatever Thomas Bell's youthful crime, he more than paid for it at the hand of Mrs. Pleasant during the last years of his life.

1

TERESA

I've never felt so sorry for
anyone. She was so fragile,
so beautiful, so utterly
helpless . . . so frightened.

—Thomas Bell
to a friend, 1870

Chapter 1

There had always been rumors. No matter how bizarre they were, they did not approach the truth. For over twenty years, the imposing gray mansion, more French than Victorian with its mansard roof, had stood on the corner of Octavia and Bush tantalizing San Francisco with its silence. A metal filigree fence, at once delicate and forbidding, enclosed the spacious grounds, which had fallen into neglect over the years. Shadowed by a row of peeling eucalyptus trees, its windows nearly overgrown by ivy, the place now deserved the appellation applied to it in the beginning: the House of Mystery. Few people could boast of having seen its magnificent interior; all social functions had ceased abruptly a long time ago. After its massive front door had slammed against society its hidden life had begun, and this caused eternal speculation. A journalist from one newspaper or the other could often be seen leaning against the eucalyptus trees, watching and waiting. The inhabitants had once provided spectacular copy.

At night, when the fog drifted up the hill from the Bay, only two dim lights could be seen, on the second floor, with darkened windows between them. The names of the two women who lived there were well known, though no one yet realized how remarkable each in her own way was. The mistress of the house was not its mistress at all: she was the prisoner of the other. In her solitude she kept a faithful diary that revealed a sensitive, educated mind tormented by fear, occasionally reacting to it with dark humor to release her tension. The other woman was also writing, working on her autobiography for the second time, confiding deeds so dark and plots so devious that only her complicated intelligence could trace its way through the maze. She had no intention of publishing the book, any more than she had the first one: she just

5

wanted certain people to know she was writing it. She was getting old, though, and most of her victims were beyond blackmail now, secure in their graves. Some things were so secret that she did not record them anywhere, depending instead on the keen wits and phenomenal memory that had served her so well in the past. She did not commit to paper the exact spot on the grounds where she had once buried a fortune in diamonds and sapphires; perhaps she had already forgotten the location of her treasure, and in the end it was her fate to outwit even herself.

An energy was growing between the two women that was not evident outside, a force so intense that, only a few years before the great earthquake, it would shake the house to its foundations, making it spew forth a story that would rock the city like a preliminary trembler.

Their story had begun nearly thirty years earlier, when a young girl traveling alone stepped off the ship in 1869.

Her fellow passengers on the steamer considered Teresa an adventuress, but she kept her own counsel, so they did not know her real intentions or how frightened she really was. An exceptionally pretty girl with abundant dark hair and deep blue eyes, she could not avoid attracting attention. In her crisp white blouse and full gray skirt, her figure was extraordinary, her waist small enough to be encompassed by a man's hands, which was a standard of the current fashion. Cynical, admiring gazes followed her as she descended the gangplank in the rain, clutching her pouch handbag tightly in one hand and maneuvering her battered portmanteau with the other. There was little sympathy for pretty girls disembarking alone in San Francisco. They were a common sight, and they usually ended badly, either in the dives of the notorious Barbary Coast, which were hazardous to their patrons, or in the cribs nearby, locally referred to as "cow barns." The growing city, which still retained its Gold Rush character, could accommodate an infinite amount of young flesh of all nationalities. If Teresa's wounded innocence elicited any sentiment from the financiers and businessmen traveling with her, they quickly suppressed it. The girl would get by, somehow, and they had no special charity for her type. She might have made a pleasant mistress, but a few minutes' conversation with her on the voyage was enough to appall them at her lack of education. If she had any schooling at all, it had been short, and her English was poor enough to discourage the most ardent man.

Filled with cold panic, she paused to survey the bleak Terminal

Building, a series of wooden sheds housing everything from bales of merchandise from the East Coast to livestock and chickens, drenched and woebegone in makeshift pens in the rain. Her first sight of the city from the Bay had been a shock. No one had misled her that the streets were paved with gold, but she had expected tall stone buildings at least, and not the tiers of crude wooden houses scattered over a series of barren, sandy hills. She had not come to make her fortune like everyone else, but a proper city was required to provide decent work in her new life, and she had a sinking feeling in her middle that the ship had brought her to the wrong place.

San Francisco was never a goal she had sought but, rather, the end of her desperate flight from New York; now that she was here she wished she could cling to the security of the ship a little longer. She had never before taken any action on her own, and she was ominously conscious of her friendlessness as she walked through the Terminal Building, dodging carts piled with the humpbacked trunks of the other passengers, noting for the first time why the trunks were constructed as they were: nothing could be placed on top of them without falling off. The porters and stevedores were all black, and she wondered how they had gotten here so quickly after the war. There were at least as many as in New York, and if they had brought their women with them, it might be difficult for her to get a job as a maid. The only other workers were a score of pigtailed Chinese scurrying about with unbelievable loads on their heads. She found them interesting but also confusing: she had other things to think about, instead of staring at a people she had never seen before and they made it more difficult to get her bearings.

As she stepped into the street, muddy water squelched through the worn soles of her only pair of shoes, and the misery spread up her legs to meet the unhappiness in her heart. She had wanted to be presentable on her arrival, and the betrayal of the shoes in which she had fled New York nearly brought tears to her eyes. She loved shoes, thin-soled and dainty, and hers were the most disreputable part of her scant wardrobe, which consisted of the articles she had snatched in the dark and stuffed into her old portmanteau, while Jim lay in a drunken slumber on the bed, menacing even in his unconsciousness. If she had spent less maintaining her clothing during the voyage, she would have more than the five dollars now in her purse. All her undergarments were on her back, and she had only managed to put two skirts and blouses and one light frock into her bag before she fled the rooming-house and found a ship leaving early the same morning. Her garments had to be laundered often in the heat off the coast of South America, and the porters just assumed that a girl in a first-class cabin could afford the necessity. Teresa did not have the nerve to confront the porters when they came for her laundry; besides, there was no way to wash anything but her underwear in her cabin.

Outside the Terminal Building, most of the horse cabs had already gone, and she was hesitating over taking the remaining one, wondering how much it would cost, when a man's voice spoke graciously beside her. "Miss Percy?"

She did not respond to the name as quickly as she should, and when she realized he was addressing her she glanced at him with alarm. Mr. Fletcher, one of the gentlemen from the ship, was gazing at her with level dark eyes.

"My carriage is here," he offered tentatively. "May I drop you somewhere? This weather's really foul. Not the best introduction to our city, I fear. I assure you it isn't always like this."

She was forced to check the rush of relief she felt at the offer. "Thanks a lot, sir," she flushed, "but my uncle's gonna collect me."

"Your uncle ... of course. I'd forgotten," he nodded, as though he experienced some relief himself. "Well, good-bye, Miss Percy, and good luck to you."

Her face continued to burn as he moved to his waiting vehicle. He did not believe the story about her uncle any more than the other shrewd men on the ship. Strange that he should approach her so politely now, after the general avoidance of all of them. No, probably not that strange, she decided, the others aren't watching him now. The flush in her cheeks increased, assisted by an element of anger. She knew she was an ignorant girl, but she was no fool, and the insult inherent in his offer was like a slap across her face. She had created her uncle in order to stave off such ugly suspicions about herself. The passengers had learned nothing about her, and she intended to keep things that way with everyone she met. The fewer people who knew Teresa Percy, the safer it would be for her. She wished now that she had chosen a name other than Percy, because it still linked her with the past. But when she boarded the ship with the first-class ticket purchased by Jim's gambling money, she could not think of any other name quickly enough, and she could not use her own.

The only transportation left was a decrepit wagon hitched to a bony horse, the straw hat on its head sagging as wretchedly as her own. The red-faced driver stirred from under his black umbrella to assist her up onto the seat beside him, and, between making noises and lightly applying his long whip, encouraged the horse to turn up a wide, cobbled street flanked on both sides by ugly brick buildings with advertisements painted on their second stories in letters three feet high: OWL CIGARS, 5¢, and WEILAND'S EXTRA PALE LAGER. To Teresa, feeling as she did, the advertisements proclaimed open and clearly that this was a man's town and there was no safe niche in it for her.

"Where to, Miss?" the driver asked amiably. "Reckon you just came in on the boat. This here's Market, the main street . . . cuts right across town. From here, it's a dollar to the Barbary Coast and two bucks to Van Ness. Should be the other way around. The big spenders are on the Coast."

Teresa's cold fingers tightened on her purse. Lord o' mercy, she thought, a dollar! I only have five. If everything's this dear, I'll have to move fast. "A hotel," she whispered and cleared her throat to speak more normally, "nearby and cheap. A decent place. I'm gonna start lookin' for a job tomorrow."

He considered the request in silence for a moment; then, he clicked his tongue and turned the horse up a side street. "I think I know just the place. It ain't Mrs. Pleasant's highfalutin boardinghouse, but nobody'll bother you there."

They stopped before a two-story gray clapboard building with a ROOMS TO LET sign in front of the torn curtains in the bay window. She paid the driver the requested "two bits," which turned out to be a quarter, and ran up the steps into the dark entry, which smelled of cooking and mothballs. A heavy, middle-aged woman entered from the back of the house, wiping her hands. For some reason, she regarded Teresa with displeasure through her metal-rimmed spectacles, but she finally pushed the register toward her grudgingly.

"Staying long?" she asked. "I'm Mrs. Bolton. My rooms are clean and only two dollars a night. No visitors are allowed in the rooms."

"I just got here . . ." Teresa smiled wanly " . . . from Maine. I don't know nobody here, so nobody'll visit me, ma'am. I'm looking for work. You don't happen to know somebody that needs help? I want to be a maid in a big house. . . ."

The woman shrugged her ponderous shoulders and angled herself to look at Teresa's cramped signature. "No work like that in this city. No one hires white domestics. Mrs. Do-good has that all tied up."

Teresa looked at her expectantly, but the woman did not contribute

9

anything more. "I don't get it," Teresa said at last. "Who's Mrs. Do-good, and what's she got to do with hiring maids?"

The proprietress grunted and wiped her face against her sleeve. Dressed in a house dress in a print of tiny flowers on a field of gray, she looked to Teresa like a sack of flour tied in the middle, because her only association with such a fabric was the flour bags on the farm. "You'll find out, I reckon," the woman finally conceded. "I don't have nothing against Negroes, you know. But the war set everything on its ear in that respect, didn't it? She's made them her special charity, like some people collect dogs and cats. Started bringing them here even before the war, when it wasn't legal. Escaped slaves, most of 'em, from what I hear. You can bet your boots she finds work for every one of 'em, too. Your skin's the wrong color to be a domestic in San Francisco, girl. If I was you, I'd look for something else. And just remember, I don't have any special charities. I have to make a living, too."

Teresa groped for the key to her room, attempting to hold back the tears that were finally welling to the surface. The day had brought disappointment and humiliation, and she wanted to be alone. The information that someone had actually imported black help for the kinds of jobs she sought was the realization of her worst fears. Her room was small and chilly and damp, and she took off only her wet shoes before slumping across the bed. She knew she should change her wet clothes, too, but she was too cold to do so. The tears that had threatened did not flow immediately. She had to coax them gently by remembering things that had hurt her in the past. She did not have to search far before she felt the heaviness behind her forehead and dampness on her cheeks. There had never been a girl more unfortu-nate than she, and the black cloud appeared to have followed her all the way across the country. She had left the farm and married Jim to get away from the beatings of her foster parents; then, to save her life, she had had to flee from his jealous abuse and threats. Now she was on her own for the first time, and everything looked hopeless. At least she was alive, she decided at last, and no one would ever beat her again. Since she had left the ship, she had been increasingly conscious of a feeling like a yawning void somewhere in her middle, which made her help-less, as though she had to depend on other people to get by. Look where it's all landed me, she breathed with her hand pressed to her lips, alone in a strange city, with two nights' lodging money if I don't eat, and the possibility of finding work dimming by the minute.

She wanted a hot cup of coffee badly, but the thought of venturing out of the hotel again was so ominous that she had to abandon the idea. The first thing to do, she decided with some determination, is to get out of these wet clothes and make a fire. *If I get sick into the bargain, everything's lost.*

In the morning, white sun attempted to penetrate the gray clouds, and Teresa found a coffee shop not far from the hotel. She had bought a newspaper called *Alta California* from a boy on the corner, and perusing the want ads over her breakfast of toast and coffee made it easier to avoid the bold stares of the rough-looking men in the restaurant. She had hesitated upon entering, but had finally lifted her chin and, looking neither left nor right, sailed past the interested men to a small table in the rear. Secure that she appeared quite proper in her clean skirt and blouse, she was relatively certain that no one would approach her at this time of the morning. She had even managed to coax her straw hat back into shape. No lady went out without a hat. She was wrong about the behavior of the men, but she managed to get through her breakfast by ignoring their heckling.

Not surprisingly, there were no ads for female help, and Teresa decided she would have to overcome the barrier against her sex if she were to survive in the city. She managed to find the paint store and tobacconist who had advertised for help and bore up under the ridicule and rejection of their proprietors before becoming hopelessly lost in the maze of strangely laid-out streets above Market. She had approached a policeman for directions early in the morning, but the representatives of the law seemed few and far between, especially when she needed them. After walking for a while, she concluded that she had never seen a less disciplined, more untidy place. Saloons and gambling halls abounded, and men too drunk to proceed further were sleeping in doorways. When a white-faced woman with swollen eyes leaned out of a window in her camisole to hail a fruit vendor pushing his cart between the wagons delivering barrels of beer, Teresa began to walk more quickly, realizing she had wandered into the wrong part of town. She went over the policeman's directions in her mind quickly. She should have turned left instead of right on Montgomery, she realized; he had stressed that. "If you turn right after Union Square, you'll be in trouble," he had said lightly, swinging his nightstick. "The bogeyman and the devil always approach from the right here, instead of the left, like most people think."

She attempted to retrace her steps to get out of the seamy section,

11

conscious that this was the sort of place a girl without work might wind up and trying to flee it quickly. When she reached Jackson, she bore left, because, she remembered, there was an opening for a grocer's clerk on that street, and she proceeded with confidence for a few blocks. Then the streets became narrower and dirtier, and she began to see more Chinese. After another block, she might have stepped right off the boat into the back streets of any city in China, and terror began to set in for the first time. The odors from the food stalls and garbage heaps made her put her handkerchief to her face, and the faces on the street appeared sinister and hostile. She had heard stories of opium dens and white slavery and, had she dared to look, she was certain there would have been evidence of them in every basement window. There was a rumor in the periodicals that there was a complete underground city in San Francisco's Chinatown, and during her short stay there, Teresa was willing to believe anything. When something horrible squashed beneath the open sole of her shoe, she could no longer retain even the semblance of dignity and broke into a run until she regained the small park called Union Square just beyond the area. She still did not feel safe.

She finally found the grocer, and she was reduced to pleading with him for a job. Though he seemed sympathetic, he shook his head. When she returned to the hotel in the early evening, she was convinced that there should be signs stating NO WOMEN WANTED on all the businesses—except in the section she had blundered into in the morning, where *only* women were wanted. The cheap stew she ate in a place called The Eatery made her stomach burn, and she was not prepared for another interview with Mrs. Bolton in the entry of the hotel.

"Any luck?" the hotel manager confronted her; when Teresa shook her head, she appeared almost triumphant. "I told you, didn't I? Lordy me, you look done in, girl. You must have been all over town."

"I got lost," Teresa stammered, moving toward the stairs and the safety of her room, aware that she had money for only one more night's lodging, wondering whether she would have to sneak out of this place at night without paying, as Jim was practiced in doing. She did not want that to happen. This was supposed to be a new life, and she did not want to start it employing the old ways of survival. "I'll find work tomorrow.

But in the morning she had to forgo her toast in the interests of economy, and she did not seem to hold up well on just heavily sugared coffee. Her knees felt weak and she was a little confused when she

walked to the fabric shop that was her destination. She did not understand the way she felt at all. She was young and strong, and she had
gone without food before. Her hands were trembling, too, and she
wanted to cry. Surely, the manager of the fabric shop would be merci-
ful and see what she had to offer, she told herself. She loved beautiful
things, and she would be happy selling material for pretty dresses and
underthings. She knew she made a good appearance, and she could
even sew a little. She would have to convince him it would be in his best
interest to employ her.

The shop was quiet when she entered, with only one customer, a
young woman like herself, browsing through the remnants of folded
satin, taffeta, and lawn stacked on a table a short distance from the
counter, where the proprietor was doing book work in preparation for
the day. He was a slight man in his midthirties, with a thin face and
neatly waxed mustache, and the dark eyes behind his spectacles were as
courteous as his manner—until Teresa asked him, almost in a whisper,
so the patron would not hear, if he would consider employing her, and
began to ennumerate the reasons for doing so. His clipped reply was
not as discreet as her request had been.

"I don't employ clerks. My customers require my personal attention.
It's inconceivable that I'd hire a woman, anyway."

"I know how to sew," Teresa assured him, not quite truthfully, the
note of pleading creeping into her voice in spite of her effort to control
it. "It wouldn't be no problem helping the ladies with what they need. I
just love pretty things, sir, and I'd work very hard. I—"

His features tightened with distaste. "Perhaps you don't understand
the English language, young woman. You certainly don't excel in
speaking it. I said no. Even if I were employing a woman, you'd be
altogether unsuitable. Good day."

Teresa clung to the length of fabric he was attempting to reroll. "I
know I don't talk very good right now, but I want to change that. I'm
smart, sir, I really am. It won't take long, as soon as I get a job and find
someone to teach me. But I've just gotta get a job. . . ."

By her very insistence, she realized, she was botching things badly.
She could not see his expression through the blur of tears she could not
control, but she imagined it was one of disgust. Without waiting to be
turned out of the shop, she turned and fled blindly into the street,
where she had to lean against a wall for support. Her legs were as weak
as water, and her face, hot with shame. Unable to cope with the real
problem of still not having work, her mind turned angrily toward the

owner of the shop and all the people like him she had known. Why do they think that you're less human and without feeling, just because you don't talk right? she asked herself. I never asked to be born. I didn't ask to be dragged up by ignorant foster parents who pulled me out of school as soon as the law allowed. I guess there isn't no hope in the world for a girl like me, she wept. I wish I'd fall down and die, right here in the street, and it would be all over then.

"Lousy stuck-up bum," a female voice said, echoing her thought. Teresa pressed the tears from her eyes to observe the young woman from inside the shop. "I heard the whole thing. Are you all right?"

The girl, whom she had not seen closely until now, had a freckled face and clear, pleasant eyes. She wore a hat tied with a wide pink ribbon over her dark curls, and her buxomness increased the impression of good humor.

"Look, if you don't have nowhere to stay, you can come home with me," she pressed, proffering Teresa her wadded handkerchief. "I know what it's like to be down on your luck, believe you me! I'm Lizzie Walters. What's your name?"

The time passed so quickly and pleasantly in Lizzie's small frame house that Teresa did not think about the future for a while. She contributed to the household by doing all the chores, and she thought she had never been so happy. She had a friend, at last, and she would do anything for her. Lizzie appreciated her domesticity, because she was as untidy as Teresa was meticulous.

When Teresa had first arrived, the dishes had not been done for days, Lizzie's bed had been unmade for at least that length of time, and her nice clothes were scattered from one room to another, but Lizzie's cheerfulness more than compensated for her faults.

"I clean it up when my boyfriend's coming," she smiled, pouring coffee into chipped, heavy cups like those used in restaurants. "Barney's a miner in Virginia City. He pays for all this." Then, sensing she might have said the wrong thing, she added, "He won't be back for weeks. How'd you like to try on some of my frocks? I swear, you're about the prettiest girl I've ever seen! With a little powder and rouge and some curls, you'll be a real beauty, Teresa."

They were like little girls playing grown-up with their mother's clothes, giggling and laughing in their experimentation, until Lizzie finally felt she had found a hairstyle that suited Teresa. She open-handedly gave Teresa a blue taffeta dress, and when she let her look in the full-length mirror, Teresa touched the neckline with awe at what she saw.

"Is that really me? I've never seen all of me at once before," she said with delight. "I never had such a pretty dress, either. You're awful good, Lizzie."

"There's more where that came from," her new friend shrugged. "I've never had it so easy. You stay with me, Teresa, and you won't have to worry about anything."

"I still have to find a job," Teresa said quickly, having already assessed Lizzie's situation. "I came here to start a whole new life, Lizzie." Then, her native sense of humor, which had been dormant too long, bubbled to the surface. "I sure didn't start off very good. Yesterday, I blundered right into the red-light district and ran from there straight into Chinatown! It nearly scared the britches off of me. All those slant-eyed people starin' at me like they wanted to eat me alive. It was dirty there, too. Shoot, it was as bad as the pigsty on the farm, but I didn't nerve up to run until I stepped into a rotten melon or something in the street. The soles are plumb out of my shoes," she laughed, admiring herself in the mirror.

"We'll get you some," Lizzie smiled. "Where is home, anyway? If you want to start a new life, there musta been something wrong with the old one."

Teresa's happiness was so expansive that she nearly told Lizzie her story, but she checked herself just in time, for her own security. "Nothing *bad*," she assured her friend. "I never did anything wrong. I come from Maine. There's lots of farms there, and I don't like farms at all. You work from morning to night, summer and winter. Did you ever milk a cow in a cold barn in the winter? I can tell you, you'd leave, too, with the milk still frozen on your fingers."

"No men?" Lizzie inquired with disbelief. "With your looks, you can't tell me there haven't been men."

Teresa shook her head, observing her own disillusioned blue eyes in the mirror. "Hell," she said, adjusting the ruffle at the neckline of the blue dress, "who'd want to marry a farmer's daughter anyway? People just make jokes about them. Some of the farm boys had ideas, but I sure wouldn't marry them, and there's nothing else down in Maine."

She was not really sure where Maine was, but she had always heard it referred to as someplace south of New York. She sensed that Lizzie did not accept her story, but her friend was too polite to ask where she had gotten the passage money. She decided to volunteer only the information asked of her, and she knew how quickly she could come up with a story. She did not like to lie to such a good friend, but it was her life that was in danger if she were found, not Lizzie's. She would maintain her silence, fabricating as little as necessary, as she had determined to do on the ship.

The two young women spent several hours of the day window shopping, and Teresa soon became familiar with most of downtown San Francisco in Lizzie's company. She learned how the streets fanned out above Market, instead of running straight, as in most towns, which explained how she had lost her way that first day. She learned which places to avoid at all cost, one of the worst being a small alley off Union Square called Morton Street, which Lizzie said was the vilest two-block area in the whole city. Lizzie discussed hangings and shootings with her quite calmly, as though they were the most natural events in the world, and the far west began to appear like the other side of the moon to Teresa, but it was strangely exciting, too.

"This place is a little scary," she told Lizzie, impulsively squeezing her hand. "I don't know what I'd do without you. I won't ever be able to pay you back."

"Forget it," Lizzie smiled. "Why, the house has never looked so good. I won't have to lift a finger before Barney comes next weekend."

Teresa's heart skipped a beat: *next* weekend? She didn't want to be in the house when Lizzie's lover was there, but she could think of no way to avoid it. If she were not in the house, she would be back out in the street, and the perils had been brought home to her clearly, now. Still walking in stride with her friend, she fell silent.

"That's Mrs. Pleasant's boardinghouse," Lizzie remarked, pointing to a building across Washington Street, an unimposing clapboard structure with a tracery of wooden lace on its overhanging entrance. "They say she practically owns the whole town. She must be loaded with money, the way she helps people out. I don't know how she gets it just by serving fancy food."

"I've heard of her somewhere," Teresa replied, studying the building. "What do you mean, she helps people out?"

"Oh, if someone dies or gets shot, she takes care of everything. Widows and orphans and all that, too." Suddenly, she pulled Teresa closer and lowered her voice. "I know something most folks don't about her. I shouldn't tell you this. I promised Ann I wouldn't say a word. But," she glanced surreptitiously across the street, "Mrs. Pleasant took my friend, Ann, right off the street and made a lady out of her. She married her to a banker! Annie said there were others, too."

16

"She . . . *what?*" Teresa asked in a small, incredulous voice. "Why would anybody do a thing like that?"

"I don't know . . . just nice, I guess. If you ever tell anyone, I'll deny I said it. People married to bankers don't like anyone to know about their past. Look! There she is now! The tall lady in the dark dress and poke bonnet."

The white bonnet obscured the woman's face, but she carried herself like a queen—tall, graceful, and commanding—and the modest dark dress emphasized the fineness of her figure. She paused for a moment to speak to a young Negro man entering the establishment as she was leaving it, and Teresa studied her wistfully. If someone would only take her off the street and make a lady out of her, she would be forever beholden, she thought. But with her background, it was too much to hope for. Besides, she was still legally married and could not oblige anyone by marrying a banker. The realization made her ache inside, and a sigh escaped her lips.

"Do you want to meet her?" Lizzie asked eagerly. "She don't care for me much, but I know her to speak to. Come on!" She dragged Teresa by the arm with a grin. "She's probably the most mysterious woman in the city, and you'll be able to say you met her. Besides, it never hurts to renew old acquaintances."

Mrs. Pleasant would have nodded and passed on when Lizzie spoke to her, but something suddenly arrested her in her progress and she lingered. Her face was the most remarkable Teresa had ever seen, and she stared openly, because the older woman's attention was not on her. The bone structure was the first thing one noticed, strong and fine beneath her clear, light skin, the tone of which suggested some Spanish blood, perhaps. Her nose was narrow and perfect, as were her lips. It was not a sensuous face, but an intelligent one. And her eyes were peculiarly mismatched, one dark and the other blue, a defect that did not detract from her appearance; indeed, it mysteriously enhanced it.

"This is my friend Teresa," Lizzie blurted out in her usual cheeky way. "She's new here, and she's living with me. Teresa, say hello to Mrs. Pleasant," she urged, nudging Teresa in the ribs. "Has the cat got your tongue?"

"Pleased to meet you," Teresa managed, conscious of the woman's antipathy to Lizzie. She could not think of anything else to say to such a fine lady, and she fixed her wistful blue eyes on Mrs. Pleasant's incredible face again, totally unconscious of herself.

"I suppose you have another name?" Mrs. Pleasant asked softly, and Teresa had to recall herself from her wishful thinking that she could ever be such a lady.

"Percy," she flushed. "Teresa Percy, ma'am."

Mrs. Pleasant nodded and turned her attention to Lizzie. "Some things never change, I see," she observed in the same soft voice. "Wherever did you get that dress, child? One more ruffle, and you'd be hidden completely from view. I suppose you're still with the miners?"

"You bet!" Lizzie said enthusiastically. "I never had it so good. You can see how wrong you were, Mrs. Pleasant. I didn't wind up on the Barbary Coast like you said."

"I suppose that's something," the woman said without interest and, with a curt nod, dismissed the young women before proceeding down the street. Lizzie stared after her angrily.

"Damn her! She never has a good word for me, no matter what I do. She's really pretty stuck up, even if she does some good things. You stared at her like a fool, Teresa. She must have thought you were daft. Come on, let's go home. I'm sorry I bothered."

They had walked only a short distance before Lizzie put her arm through Teresa's and giggled. "Do you know what people call her, behind her back? *Mammy!* Isn't that a caution? I bet she'd spit nails if she ever heard that."

"Why Mammy?" Teresa asked. "She isn't a Negro. I think she's about the most beautiful woman I ever saw."

Lizzie shrugged carelessly. "I don't know. I suppose it's on account of all the Negroes she's brought here. Just about surrounds herself with black people, from what I hear. Now, *that's* a hobby I find mighty peculiar. I wonder if she likes black *men. . . .*"

"Lizzie!" Teresa exclaimed but, even as she did so, the connection between Mrs. Pleasant and the Mrs. Do-good the hotel proprietress had mentioned struck her mind. The woman she had been admiring so wholeheartedly was the reason for all her trouble in finding a job. "Well, maybe it is a little strange," she conceded, "but there are people in New York who act the same way. They got a lot of slaves out of the South to freedom. Some people admire that kind of thing."

"Well, I don't. Let's forget about old Mammy, the stuck-up bitch. There's something I've been meaning to ask you. Now, don't get mad at me. I wrote a letter to Barney and told him all about you. I'm not sure, but he just might bring someone with him this weekend. What do you think about it? We could have a real good time, and he would buy you lots of things. . . ."

18

Teresa was silent. She had feared something like this, but she did not know how to respond without alienating her only friend. "I don't want to hurt your feelings," she said at last, "but I'm not like that, Lizzie."

"You aren't a *virgin?*" Lizzie asked with astonished interest. "If you are, you must be about the last one around."

Teresa had to bite her tongue to keep from responding that she was not a whore, either, and she maintained her silence again. The matter was still not settled when they reached the house, and Teresa thought it best to let things rest awhile. Lizzie was not too insistent, and she needed time to think. Mrs. Pleasant's remark about miners had not escaped her, and she realized that not only Barney contributed to the upkeep of Lizzie's little house. Teresa knew that she had gotten herself into trouble again, but she was helpless in dealing with it for the moment.

"I think I'll take a nap," Lizzie said, yawning and stretching her plump arms. "What's for dinner?"

"I don't know yet. I'll see to it now," Teresa replied as she walked into the kitchen, anxious to be alone. Lizzie closed the bedroom door, and Teresa took a leftover roast out of the cooler, sniffing it for freshness. Then, she stood for a long time next to the table staring at it. The fact that she was treated like a maid did not bother her. Her ambition had been to be a maid, and she wanted to do her share toward her support. But Lizzie had gone beyond herself when she wrote to Barney about her. The stupid girl probably thought that everyone's morals were like her own. Teresa wondered vaguely if she could remain in this capacity, cooking the meals and cleaning while the miners were here, but even she was not that naïve. She reflected that she might have been a really proper maid by now, if Mrs. Pleasant were not so enthusiastic about helping colored folk, and she could not forgive her for that.

No amount of resentment toward Mrs. Pleasant was going to solve her present situation, though, and to dissipate her feeling of helplessness, she put on a white apron and began to stoke up the fire in the old iron stove. Standing with the stove lid suspended above the opening by its detachable handle while she added more coal, at first she did not hear the light tapping on the front door. When the sound finally reached her, she wiped her hands on a cloth as she went to open the door. A large black man was standing on the porch, and Teresa's first reaction was one of alarm. But his benign, friendly smile and slight bow reassured her, and, without speaking, he delivered a folded slip of paper with her name written on it into her hands and lingered while she read it.

19

Dear Miss Percy,

You are in bad company, and I think I can help you. Pack your things and come to my boardinghouse at 920 Washington Street. My man Billy Beaumont will assist you.

Mary Ellen Pleasant

Chapter 2

Stepping over the threshold of the boardinghouse was like entering another world to Teresa. A large, gilt-framed mirror faced the entrance, reflecting the candelabra and small marble statue on the table below it. The walls were not papered, but covered with a richly textured dark red fabric that matched the upholstery of the two chairs flanking the walnut table. She barely had time to study an umbrella stand that looked like an Oriental vase, or the painting on the opposite wall, before Billy Beaumont, who had not spoken during their short walk, turned both Teresa and her portmanteau over to a colored maid named Blanche, who escorted her up the thickly carpeted stairs to an even more extraordinary room off the second-floor hallway.

"Madame's cookin' the dinner," the maid told her. "She want you to make yo'self comfortable here. She join you soon as she done."

"She does the cooking herself?" Teresa asked, surprised, and the colored girl, who had probably been a slave until recently, smiled condescendingly.

"Course she does! She don't let nobody near her kitchen after the peelin' and parin's done. She the best cook in San Francisco—the best in the world—an' she don't want nobody messing with her recipes. She the nicest lady alive, too, an' don't you forget it. You show respect."

Teresa had more questions, but the maid left abruptly, as though on instruction, so she satisfied some of her curiosity by examining the small sitting room. Moving about seemed to relieve some of her tension while she waited. When Billy Beaumont had brought the note, there had been no question in her mind about whether she should come, and she had begun covering her tracks immediately. With Lizzie's confidences about her friend Annie still in her mind, Teresa had scratched a short message that a chance for a job had come up and had left it on the kitchen table. While Lizzie slept, she quickly packed her bag to flee, an activity in which she was becoming expert. Upset and dissillusioned by Lizzie, she felt she did not owe her more. To make the break as honest as possible, she left the blue taffeta dress behind, with some regret. If Mrs. Pleasant's note meant what Teresa hoped it did, her recent past was effectively erased.

She followed the taciturn Billy almost happily in the hope of getting some education, trying to push her concern about where all this would lead from her mind. If Mrs. Pleasant intended to marry her off later, she would just refuse. With her new accomplishments, she would secure a good job and pay the woman back whatever the training cost. Anyway, Mrs. Pleasant owed her something for having deprived her of honest work in the first place. An opportunity had come to better herself, the first chance in her life, and Teresa vowed to take it. She did not like to deceive anyone, so she would say as little about herself as possible. Her only deception would be a sin of omission, to achieve the basic education she had never had.

Now, walking about the sitting room, touching the pale blue brocade of the small sofa and matching chairs, and running her hand across the tea table to satisfy herself that the floral pattern in varying shades was really inlaid and not painted on, Teresa felt any lingering sense of guilt fall away before the actual evidence of Mrs. Pleasant's wealth. Mrs. Pleasant began to take on the outlines of a fairy godmother in Teresa's mind. A black man in livery entered briefly to light the candles in the crystal chandelier. Teresa did not know whether to speak to him or not; before she decided, he was gone, and she sat down carefully on the delicate-looking sofa. This must be the way kings and queens live, she thought, feeling slightly subdued. I have an awful lot to learn.

When the ormolu clock on the mantel chimed six, Blanche entered quietly, bearing Teresa's dinner on a silver tray. She removed the covers of the china dishes to show their contents and turned the thin-stemmed glass upright beside a carafe of wine. "Madame say she won't be long. She worried you was hungry. That's the kind o' lady she is. Bet you ain't never tasted nothing like this befo'."

Teresa waited until the maid had left to shake out the napkin gently and put it across her knees. Using her knife and fork European style—or farm style, for she knew no other way—she tasted each serving delicately before slowly consuming the meal. The maid was right. The mixture of sauces over the tender meat and fresh vegetables was like nothing she had ever tasted; she finally understood the expression that something melts in the mouth. She decided against the wine, though; she needed all her senses about her. Like a child with a prism, she lifted the crystal glass to watch the light play on it, but she had a sudden feeling that she was being watched and put it down again. She glanced over her shoulder and arched her neck to see into the hallway, but there was no one there. Her nerves were really playing tricks on her, she decided. If she had any intuition at all, it was when she sensed she was being watched; but obviously there was no one around. She folded the linen napkin carefully and returned it to the tray, hoping she would not have to wait too long if she was getting so edgy she was imagining things.

Blanche had hardly removed the tray before Mrs. Pleasant walked gracefully into the room in her dark dress. "I apologize for the delay, Miss Percy. Everything's ready in the kitchen, now, and the gentlemen will be arriving for their dinner soon." She settled into the chair across from Teresa and smiled warmly. "We have plenty of time for a friendly visit before I have to put in an appearance. I hope you enjoyed your meal."

"Yes, ma'am," Teresa said, more conscious of the older woman's charm than she had been in the afternoon. In her own surroundings and without her poke bonnet she was a different person, relaxed and expansive, and one could not resist being drawn to her. "I never tasted anything like it. You're sure a good cook."

"Cooking's a talent as much as hard work." Mrs. Pleasant smiled. "And I was trained by the very best cook in New Orleans. When I arrived here during the Gold Rush, men wanted a good meal more than anything else. I was able to write my own ticket and cooked for the most influential gentlemen in the territory. California wasn't even a state, yet. Little by little, I accumulated a small nest egg, and, with the kind help of my financier clients, I've done pretty well. I prefer that skirt and blouse to that blue tafetta thing with its fuss and furbelows that you had on this afternoon."

"Lizzie gave it to me, but I left it at her place, ma'am. I shouldn't ought to have accepted it at all. I didn't know much about her then. She told me she had a boyfriend," Teresa said awkwardly, dropping her gaze and finishing almost in a whisper, "I didn't know there was more than one. . . ."

"I suspected as much," Mrs. Pleasant nodded sympathetically and sighed. "There are too many girls like Lizzie. It's a pity, really. No talent, no education. There's little else they can do. But let's not concern ourselves with them for the moment. Your coming here indicates you share my views. I suppose Lizzie told you that I take an occasional protégée and help her rise above all that."

Teresa flushed, unable to answer, because Lizzie had sworn her to secrecy over the confidence. For the first time Mrs. Pleasant laughed, not openly but deep in her bosom, a companionable and understanding laugh. Teresa found it difficult not to join in, and she suppressed a smile.

"Of course she told you," Mrs. Pleasant said, "and that's why you're here. You're anxious to improve yourself, and I approve of that. Would you mind telling me a little bit about yourself, my dear?"

Teresa was grateful she had not drunk the wine. It was difficult enough to resist Mrs. Pleasant's personality and keep from telling her everything. She was the sort of woman a girl could confide in very easily, but Teresa had too much at stake for that. "There's not much to tell," she said quietly, meeting the benign gaze of those mismatched eyes. "I'm a farm girl, that's all. I don't have much schooling. I know I'm awful ignorant, but I could learn if you give me the chance. They always said I was quick enough."

"Who did, my dear?"

"The folks on the farm that raised me." Teresa decided not to go into the matter of her foster parents. She must say as little as possible about all that, she reminded herself, gazing evenly into Mrs. Pleasant's face.

"How old are you, Teresa?" Mrs. Pleasant asked, and Teresa answered without hesitation.

"Twenty-one." Some truths were safe enough to tell. "I turned twenty-one on the boat, off the coast of South America."

"The trip around the Horn's a long one to take to get away from the farm," Mrs. Pleasant considered indulgently. "It took a lot of egg money, too, I imagine. Do you mind my asking, how you *did* get the fare?"

"A legacy," Teresa said without thinking about it, her quick mind coming to her aid. There had been a lot of talk about legacies on the farm, her foster parents believing some bequest was their due. "Not much," she added without blinking her eyes. "I only had five dollars when I got here. They charge an awful lot for doing laundry on a boat. But I like to be neat and clean, ma'am. I like pretty things. My clothes aren't much, but I keep them good."

"I like pretty things, too," the older woman smiled, acknowledging

24

that they had something in common and abandoning the embarrassing questions. "I don't wear them, because I'm in business, and it wouldn't be appropriate. You should have pretty clothes, though. I'm offering you the opportunity to improve your station in life. Before you decide anything, you should know exactly what you're getting into, Teresa. You'd have to work very hard at improving yourself, and you'd obey me completely. I have no time for pouting and tantrums. When I tell you to do something a certain way, you'll do it. And, with you, it may take a lot of time. Not because you need help more than anyone else, but because I want you to be perfect. Are you willing to submit to such strict education and training?"

"I want to be a lady," Teresa told her earnestly. "A girl can't get nowhere without learning. I want to do it, ma'am. Would I be staying on here?"

"No. You'll have a house of your own. It may take a few weeks to arrange that, and you'll be here until then."

"A house of my own?" Teresa breathed in disbelief. "My very own?"

"Your very own," Mrs. Pleasant smiled, "in your own name. Everything will be provided for you. You won't have a care in the world while you're studying. You won't leave the house, either, unless I tell you to. Eventually, you'll be allowed on outings under supervision. Will it bother you to remain cloistered . . . to stay in the house all the time?"

Teresa shook her head, fighting a feeling of unreality. Surely all this was too good to be true. "I'll do whatever you say, ma'am."

Mrs. Pleasant rose, glanced at her lapel watch, and stood staring down at Teresa with a contemplative gaze. "Good. You'll do. You'll do very nicely." Then, as though recalling herself to the present, she said, "Blanche will take you to your room. Please wash all that powder and rouge off your face. A pretty girl like you doesn't need it. I must find someone to tutor you in English." She turned to leave, but paused in the doorway. "By the way, does Lizzie know you've come here?"

"No, ma'am. She was asleep, and I wrote her a note saying I got a job."

Mrs. Pleasant nodded her approval. "You're a bright girl, Teresa Percy. We'll get along nicely."

If she had any lingering doubts about her benefactress, they were dispelled during the time she was at the boardinghouse. The house of her own had worried her a little, because it brought Lizzie to mind; but apparently Mrs. Pleasant's largesse was unbounded, and she did not ask for anything in return. The presence of a young widow, Mrs. Barrett, and her small daughter, Amy, in the boardinghouse, along with several other unfortunate women, put Teresa's mind completely at ease. With the freedom to visit back and forth between the exquisite rooms, Teresa got to know Mrs. Barrett better than the others, and she sympathized with her predicament.

She met her through the little girl, who was standing quietly by the open door of Teresa's room one morning after Blanche removed the breakfast tray. Aware that someone was watching her dress her hair, Teresa was relieved to find that someone was really there. "Hello there," she said, smiling at the pale, pigtailed child, "what are you doing here?"

Without taking her finger out of her mouth, the child told her, "My papa's dead," and Teresa experienced a shock of compassion.

"I'm sorry to hear that. What's your name, honey?"

The child's black-clad mother appeared behind her at that moment, apologizing for her daughter's intrusion. "I'm sorry. I hope she hasn't bothered you. Amy, dear, you mustn't bother people."

"It's all right," Teresa said. "Blanche left the door open. Why don't you both come in for a spell? I've seen folks around when I'm in the sitting room, but nobody's talked more than to say hello."

"Thank you," the subdued young woman said, leading her little girl into the room by the hand. "I'm afraid most of us have a lot on our minds. I'm Etta Barrett, and this is my daughter, Amy. Mrs. Pleasant has been so kind to us. We're waiting to take the train back to St. Louis."

"Please, go ahead and sit down," Teresa said, indicating the polished bench at the foot of her bed. "The *train*? I heard something about it linking up, but I didn't know it was making regular trips so far."

"Oh, yes." Mrs. Barrett smiled wanly. "The trouble is that they aren't very often. I suppose it'll be a while before there's regular service. But, considering the last spike was driven only five months ago, I guess that's to be expected. Are you one of Mrs. Pleasant's homeless too?"

Teresa did not know how to answer, so she smiled. "In a way. I won't be here long. Your little girl said—"

"Yes, I heard. It's all she talks about. Her father's death." She paused to overcome the break in her voice. "My husband's death was a terrible shock to both of us. We've only been here a few months. We waited two years for him to send for us, and then . . ."

"I'm sorry," Teresa said with feeling, but it sounded hollow, a stupid thing to say, and she sat at her vanity staring uneasily at her hands.

26

"Mrs. Pleasant's going to get you home? You must have been friends of hers."

"No. That's the incredible thing. I don't think I've ever really believed in Christian charity, before, Miss . . . ?"

"Teresa."

"Bill came West to look for silver, you see. Up in Washoe. That's where I thought we'd be living when he finally sent for us, but he said he'd meet us in San Francisco. He'd never been a gambling man. You can imagine my surprise when we got here and found . . ."

Teresa could imagine it only too well. She had firsthand experience with a drunken gambler and confidence man. "Well," she temporized, "it takes some men like that. I suppose he lost all that he mined."

"Worse," Mrs. Barrett almost whispered. "He was a professional gambler in that terrible place they call the Barbary Coast. Do you know why they call it that? It hasn't anything to do with Barbary pirates, as I'd always thought. It's because the people there are *barbarous*, barely human. One night, someone shot him to death."

"Shot him?" Teresa asked incredulously. "I've heard of people threatening things like that, but . . ." She wondered whether Mrs. Barrett's husband had been dealing an honest game, but it did not seem appropriate to introduce the subject.

"It happens here all the time," the young widow sniffed, covering her nose with her handkerchief. "Shootings and stabbings, and the good Lord knows what all. I wish we'd never come. I wish Bill had stayed at home in St. Louis. He would be alive today."

Teresa considered the information and was more thankful than ever to be where she was. "How did Mrs. Pleasant come into it?" she asked hoarsely.

Mrs. Barrett wiped her nose with determination and stuffed her handkerchief in her sleeve. "It was like a miracle," she said firmly, "she was a godsend. I didn't even have the money to bury him. I was nearly distracted. Then, suddenly, this wonderful woman dressed like a Quaker came to my flat. She'd heard about the shooting, somehow, and my inability to pay the undertaker. She not only took care of that, in the kindest possible way, she took Amy and me in, as well, and she's going to send us home. We have relatives there."

"That was awful nice of her," Teresa agreed, without knowing what to make of it. "Mrs. Pleasant's a good lady for sure."

"Oh, she is!" Mrs. Barrett exclaimed passionately. "I've found out since that we're not the only recipients of her good work. It's difficult to believe, but she only happened to find us because she sees that all indigents are buried properly. Sometimes, she takes up a collection from their friends, but, mostly, I think she does it on her own. She has a huge plot at Laurel Hill Cemetery just for that reason. She even installs headstones." The young woman fell silent a moment while she reached for her handkerchief again. "Most people don't like to think about death. We just shove it under the table, so to speak. But Mrs. Pleasant assures some dignity, even to the lowliest drunk who passes away in the gutter. And, more importantly, she cares a great deal for the living."

Teresa happened to be one of those people who did not like to think about death, and she suppressed a slight shudder. She did not question Mrs. Pleasant's charity, but it struck her as slightly morbid. Still, someone had to do it, she reasoned. If the city's as bad as Mrs. Barrett indicated, the alleys and gutters would be crowded with corpses in no time at all if someone did not come forward to help.

"The other ladies staying here," she could not refrain from asking, "how'd she find them?"

Mrs. Barrett shook her head. "I don't know. Their need must have cried out to her. Some are waiting for relatives who did not meet them on their arrival, and Mrs. Pleasant's assisting in finding them. She's very efficient, you know; it's amazing how quickly she can locate a lost relative. She seems to know a great deal about this city, God love her."

What with the excitement of being measured by a seamstress, the arrival of several pairs of lovely shoes, and Mrs. Pleasant's visits, which usually took place in the evening, Teresa found herself in a state of pleasant excitement that sometimes made her pace her room. Unable to share her good fortune with the other temporary roomers, whose situations were less happy than her own, she longed for some expression of what was happening to her, and she finally found it in a delivery of books and notebooks that took place during the second week of her stay at the boardinghouse. The English primers did not interest her particularly; she knew how to read, at least. But the notebooks with their pure, blank pages beckoned with a sudden fascination, demanding to be filled. Never having heard of a diary, she finally settled down with one of the notebooks on her vanity, entitling it TERESA PERCY . . .HER BOOK, and proceeded to recount her experiences since encountering Mrs. Pleasant, in unpunctuated, run-on sentences that relieved the fullness of her heart. In cramped, childish handwriting, she began:

28

There was never a girl as lucky as me and its all because of Mrs
Pleasnt the finest lady I ever met Some times I think some bodys
watching me but it dont worry me no more becuz I no its my Gardian
Angel now Mrs Pleasnt is so good that I think my Gardian Angel
who forgot me so long finally has come back to stay. She brot me 3
pares of new shoes today 3!!! Not my Gardian Angel but that other
Angel Mrs Pleasnt . . .

She made no attempt to conceal the notebook, because there was
nothing in it to hide. And if Mrs. Pleasant noticed it on her evening
visits, she made no comment. There were always too many other things
to discuss. Teresa looked forward to the appearance of her gentle,
practical friend and the discussions they had over tea served in thin
china cups shortly after dinner. Always cheerful, her delicate but
strong features benevolent and kind, Mrs. Pleasant became more
friendly every day, sharing small confidences and jests that Teresa felt
were reserved for her alone.

"I swear, men are all little boys at heart," she considered triumphantly, during the second week of Teresa's stay. "Give them a
good meal, and they'll practically eat right out of your hand. Mr.
Hanlon, one of the most important gentlemen of the board of the Bank
of California, is a sour old party, but I got this out of him!" She took
some folded papers out of a long envelope. "This is your bungalow,
Teresa, all signed and sealed and legal. You can move into it
tomorrow."

Teresa regarded the papers without comprehension, though her
spirits rose at what she had just heard. "He *gave* it to you?" she asked in
amazement, and Mrs. Pleasant's warm laughter filled her room.

"Mr. Hanlon's never given anything away," she said happily, "but he
gave me an unsecured bank loan at very low interest. All you have to do
is sign right here, and the house is in your name, my dear. This is just to
register the property. It has nothing to do with the bank."

Teresa scratched her name on the line indicated, but something
about the transaction tugged at her mind. "I don't like to think of you
borrowin' money on account of me, Mrs. Pleasant. It don't seem right."

"You mustn't trouble yourself about anything. And for goodness
sake, please call me Mary Ellen. We're friends, aren't we?"

"More than friends . . ." Teresa said with awe, " . . . Mary Ellen. But I
could stay right here. That way, you needn't borrow . . ."

"My dear, in business," Mrs. Pleasant smiled equably, "a bank loan boosts your credit. I didn't *have* to borrow the money, I wanted to. The more people know about your good credit, the better. And," she added comfortably, "the less they know about your real holdings, the better, too. That little house at 19 Tehama Street is yours as long as I say it is. If you're a good girl, that could be forever. I think we're going to have a long, happy friendship, Teresa. This is just the beginning. I have great plans for you."

She does mean to marry me off, Teresa thought guiltily, feeling sick over her deception, but not letting it show in her face. "You're very good," she breathed helplessly as Mary Ellen turned to leave. "Thank you."

When her friend was gone, she drifted miserably over to her looking glass and studied her face. Why me? she wondered, not for the first time. Lots of girls are prettier, and I must be the most ignorant one around. She touched the aquiline nose that she had always considered her worst feature: a pretty nose should be straight and short. Her deep, pansy-blue eyes with their long lashes were difficult to fault, except for their reserved hurt expression. The rest of her face was pretty enough, she allowed. Her skin, at least, was exceptional, as clear and creamy as the day she left the farm, and she stroked it with her fingertips to confirm its smoothness. Yes, she means to marry me off, but she said my training would take a long time; that's on my side, anyway. She wanted nothing more than plenty of time to remain hidden from the world while she worked on her education. And enough time, she sighed guiltily, to figure out what to do when the day finally came when she would have to tell Mary Ellen she could not marry anyone.

Chapter 3

She had only one morning to get accustomed to her house and try on some of the clothing awaiting her there before she was faced with her first trial of obedience. The colored girl, Maggie, who did all the household chores without talking much, was in the kitchen washing up after lunch, when Mary Ellen arrived in high good humor, carrying a package from a pharmacist in her hand. She chatted amiably as she removed her damp bonnet and shawl, for it was raining again.

"Well, what do you think, Teresa? Is the house comfortable enough? If there are any changes you'd like, just tell me and I'll take care of them. That braided frock fits you perfectly. You look wonderful in it, but you'll have to take it off for a while."

Teresa was particularly fond of the pale blue woolen creation with its ornamentation of matching braid, but she went into the bedroom, and Mary Ellen followed her to undo the fastenings down the back. When she stepped out of the full skirt in her new camisole and petticoats, her friend observed her so carefully that she blushed and reached for the velvet robe hanging in the wardrobe.

"No, don't put that on," Mary Ellen said. "You really have the most marvelous skin, my dear. You hardly need the corset. Let's get you out of it. You'll be more comfortable during this afternoon's chore."

The light corset was dutifully unlaced and discarded, and Teresa felt not only naked but cold, and hugged herself with her arms. Mary Ellen left the room for a moment and returned to drape her in a sheet, taking particular pains to ensure that it was tight around her neck. "We're going to make you a blonde," she announced to Teresa's dismay. "It's an untidy business, but you'll have to learn how to do it."

Teresa did not want to be blonde. She found the idea repellent, but

31

she remained silent as Mary Ellen undid the string on her package. If she objected now, Teresa realized, it would be bothersome to Mary Ellen, in complete violation of her demand for obedience. So she swallowed hard and submitted to the process, assuring herself that no one would see her anyway, since she was bound to stay in the house. Mary Ellen wore a wraparound apron that completely covered her black dress as they worked for a couple of hours over the kitchen sink, with the taciturn Maggie handing Mary Ellen what was needed next. The room smelled so strongly of ammonia that tears ran down Teresa's face and she coughed periodically.

"We're almost finished," Mary Ellen reassured her. "My goodness, you do have a lot of hair, don't you? It's longer than I expected it to be, and there's some natural curl, too."

Teresa thought of her thick, dark hair, which had never been cut, and real tears joined those caused by the chemicals. "I'm scared," she admitted through the fumes, "I don't think I'll look good with blond hair, Mary Ellen. And what about my eyebrows and eyelashes? If there's one thing I'm proud of it's my long dark eyelashes. People have always talked about them. . . ."

"Don't worry about a thing," Mary Ellen soothed her, as Maggie pumped more water for rinsing. "We may have to touch up your eyebrows a little, but your lashes will stay as they are. I've admired them, too. There. Maggie, wrap her head in a towel and we'll dress her hair."

She did not allow Teresa to look into the mirror until she was finished, the hair dry and fashioned with a curling iron. Then, Mary Ellen removed the sheet with a flourish, like a sculptor unveiling his masterpiece, and Teresa faced her reflection in stunned silence. At first, she hated the voluminous, carefully curled blond hair. She even experienced a moment of disorientation, as though someone else were staring back at her from the looking glass. Only when she was able to look at it more objectively did she realize the depth of Mary Ellen's insight into how a girl should look.

"I shoulda been born this way," she finally admitted with enthusiasm. "Lord o' mercy, it's beautiful! Shoot, nobody back home'd know me at all. Nobody would know me . . . *nobody*."

"That sounds important to you," Mary Ellen smiled, folding the damp sheet, "as if there were someone you wouldn't like to recognize you."

Realizing that her words had been incautious, Teresa smiled at her own reflection, noting that nothing revealed itself in her eyes, as blue and deep and mysterious as they had been before. "I don't care about nobody back there," she said easily, "and they don't care about me. Why should I be scared that they'd know me? I just think my hair's beautiful, Mary Ellen. I never would have thought of turning blond."

"I'm pleased with the result myself," Mary Ellen said, contemplating Teresa closely in the mirror. "You don't talk about your parents much. Where is this farm you've mentioned? Upstate New York?"

The expression in Teresa's eyes did not change. "Maine," she lied. "I'm from down in Maine."

"Really?" Mary Ellen smiled. "You certainly don't have the accent. I'd never have known. Why don't we try on that black velvet ballgown in the wardrobe, so you can see how wonderful you really look?" And, as Teresa moved toward the wardrobe with excitement, she interjected, without pressing the point, "I should think your parents would worry about you, my dear. It would be nice to drop them a line to let them know where you are, that you're all right."

"Not likely!" Teresa exclaimed without thinking and dispensed with the subject by focusing all her attention on the black velvet gown crushed against her camisole. "One of the snaps in the back's all loose. I was scared to put this one on before, because I thought I shouldn't ought to. I'm sure glad I didn't, since one of the snaps got broke somehow."

Mary Ellen was a marvel of patience. She abandoned her interrogation with a sigh. "I'm only thankful that the English teacher will be here tomorrow morning."

The following weeks were so full of activity that Teresa abandoned her trepidations about the past. The opportunity to exercise her considerable intelligence for the first time brought results that surprised even her. Her tutor, Mrs. Hastings, a schoolteacher before her marriage, was so gratified by her student's rapid progress that she began to bring her classic English novels and history books to read. And once Teresa discovered the joy of books, nothing was lacking in her life any longer. After a whole morning of tutoring and Mary Ellen's instructions about caring for her person, instead of falling into bed with exhaustion, Teresa read late into the night, writing down the words she did not know in one of her notebooks for full explanation by her teacher. After a short while, Mrs. Hastings asked her to request a dictionary of Mrs. Pleasant. When it was in her hands, she was filled with so much excitement that she read it like a novel.

"You're a born scholar," Mrs. Hastings said one morning. "I'm surprised you've had so little opportunity to develop your talents until now, Teresa. Mrs. Pleasant explained that you were a young relation of hers, but she said nothing about your background."

Teresa was slightly surprised at Mary Ellen's fabrication, but she quickly rationalized that there was no other way to explain her presence in this house. "It's a long story," she temporized, "and, I'm afraid . . . I *fear*, a very sad one, ma'am. I'd rather not speak about it."

"I'm terribly sorry," Mrs. Hastings said quickly. "I had no intention of distressing you. Teresa, you must stop calling older women ma'am. It makes you sound like a servant. When you address me, you should call me Mrs. Hastings, because that is my name."

"Yes, Mrs. Hastings," Teresa smiled happily. "I'm so happy that you've come. I can't imagine what I was doing with my mind before I met you!"

"That's probably the highest praise any teacher ever received," her tutor said, smiling affectionately. "But few teachers have had such an engaging and enthusiastic student, either. Your diction's improved amazingly, and I don't think there's any way to stop your vocabulary now. I know how well you work in the morning and that you read well into the night. What do you do with your afternoons, young woman?"

"I read then, too," Teresa said with the same calmness and steady eyes she employed when speaking to Mary Ellen. Her teacher was curious about the whole situation; she had recognized that for some time. If Mary Ellen realized that Mrs. Hastings was intrigued by her household, she would probably dismiss her, so Teresa determined not to mention it. There were some things she could handle on her own now, and keeping her tutor was one of them. Even in her little cloistered house, an intuition had reached her that people were extremely curious about Mary Ellen Pleasant; but it was not until a few months later that the extent of that curiosity, and some of the reasons for it, were revealed to her in quite an unexpected manner.

Billy Beaumont's taciturnity during their first meeting, when he took her to the rooming house, had left Teresa with the impression that the husky black man either had little to say or acted entirely on Mary Ellen's instructions. So when he arrived one Saturday morning to repair a faulty flue in the parlor fireplace, she looked up from her book only long enough to nod in recognition. She felt vaguely uneasy in his presence, for reasons she did not attempt to analyze, though the fact that he knew about her coming from Lizzie's did come into it. He was also handsome, strong, and young, and, like every other white girl in

34

America, Teresa had heard that Negro men favored white women. As he crouched before the hearth, gazing up the chimney, an unnerving thought crossed her mind, one that was not beneficial to her nervous nature. What if he came at me, all alone here, with Maggie out shopping? After reading the same paragraph four times without understanding a word she had read, she resigned herself to pretending she was interested in the book, while she was really keeping a cautious eye on him.

"Ain't no real problem," he suddenly concluded, standing up and brushing his hands on the sides of his trousers. "Billy can fix it in no time at all. You got yerself a nice little house here," he observed, surveying the parlor. "A whole lot nicer than Mammy's other pro-tégées have come by."

She had determined to speak to him only in curt monosyllables, but her displeasure over hearing him refer to Mary Ellen by that name forced a reprimand from her. "I'm surprised at you, calling Mary Ellen that, Billy Beaumont. She's your friend, and she looks after you very well."

"Course she do," he replied, nonplussed. "That's why all us black folk call her Mammy. She's like our own mammy to us. There ain't no one like her. I don't know what that woman's up to most of the time, but she do get by, don't she? With a little help, here an' there. I bet everybody in this town knows who Mammy Pleasant is."

His sudden loquacity interested Teresa, but she remained quiet, staring at the open book. Now at least she knew where the appelation that Lizzie had considered derogatory came from. People had repeat-ed the Negroes' affectionate term for Mary Ellen, giving it a shading of their own. The young black man's voice was heavy with innuendo regarding Mary Ellen, and Teresa was interested, but she felt he was trying to impress her and declined to encourage him in any way. She would feel more at ease when Maggie, who was really taciturn, returned in half an hour. In all the months she and her maid had been together, Maggie had revealed nothing about her employer, behaving in a methodical, self-effacing manner that Teresa found completely acceptable in her race.

"The walls in all them big houses have ears, I can tell you," Billy Beaumont continued conversationally as he knelt to fix the flue. "She got her spies *everywhere*. The white folk think they know who Mammy is, but she know *all* about them! Funny thing about people with ser-vants, Miss Teresa. They just don't pay them no never mind. But them servants got eyes like saucers and ears like big bowls."

Disquieted by what she was hearing, Teresa did not rise to his bait.

35

What if Mary Ellen had sent him to test her loyalty, she considered, to see if she was as intrigued by her friend's comings and goings as everyone else appeared to be? The implication that Mary Ellen had placed her Negroes in wealthy houses to spy was too incredible. The idea made her smile slightly behind her book. She had never known any black people and had no idea until now that they were so imaginitive.

She did not hear him move from the fireplace. Only when his shadow closed out the light and fell over her was she aware of his proximity. She tried not to react to his nearness, held down her fear, and said with as much dignity as she could gather as she glanced up at him, "Is it all repaired, Billy?"

"Miss Teresa," his deep voice fell to a confidential whisper, "I been tryin' to tell you something, and there ain't much time. I can judge people, and I knew you were a good girl when I came to fetch you for Mammy. You ain't like the other ones, and you don't belong here. I don't think you know what you got yourself into. I been tryin' to tell you, but you ain't listenin'. You just keep reading that book."

Teresa put the book aside and regarded him with her impenetrable blue gaze. "If you have something to say, why don't you come right out with it, Billy?"

"It ain't that easy," he said, glancing nervously over his shoulder. "You gotta promise you won't let on you heard anything."

"All right, I promise," Teresa said, maintaining her calmness with an effort. "I can't imagine what you're—"

"Do you know what she got planned for girls like you?"

"You make it sound . . . sinister," Teresa replied. "I understand that it's . . . marriage . . . eventually. There isn't anything wrong with that, is there?"

"Not if it turn out like that." His dark eyes stared down at her with sympathy. "Sometimes it do, and that's all right, I suppose. But there's some mightly peculiar men in this town, Miss Teresa. Some of the girls don't take to them much." He looked around again to make sure that Maggie had not crept on silent feet into the house. "Two of them been murdered, Miss Teresa."

"*Murdered?*" Teresa cried with a shudder. "Two of Mary Ellen's protégées have been—?"

"Yes, ma'am! The men wanted them more than they wanted the men, an' not just for wives, you understand? The men woulda' married them to get what they wanted, sure enough, but those girls didn't want

36

no part of them, no how. Miss Caroline got herself strangled, and Miss Bertha, well, we don't know what happen that time, but she was sure dead, the day after a dinner at the Cottage. You gotta leave, Miss Teresa, before it comes to something like that. And I don't mind tellin' you that Mammy'd have my hide on the barn if she found out I told you this."

Teresa found that she could not discount Billy's story entirely, but she felt unnaturally calm about it. She had no intention of letting anything go as far as marriage or introductions leading to it. She was safe enough for the time being. She would not leave her pleasant, peaceful life and her studies, yet—in fact, she would find it difficult to do so. She had never been so happy. Whatever had happened, she decided, Billy had probably embellished it, just as he had his other stories. If two girls had been murdered, Mary Ellen could hardly have covered it up. No, the story as he told it was ridiculous, a drunken attack and a beating, perhaps, magnified by the servants. She heard the back door open and Maggie rattle her parcels in the kitchen.

"Don't worry about me, Billy," she said softly enough not to be heard outside the room. "I can take care of myself. Tell me, if you can, how things like that could be kept from the newspapers and the police?"

Maggie's presence in the house unnerved him completely, but he replied in a whisper, "What she got that big plot in the graveyard for? An' her own undertaker, too." Then, straightening himself to his full height, he took a deep breath and spoke loudly enough for Maggie to hear, "Well, Miss Teresa, I don't guess that flue will give no more trouble. If it do, you just tell Maggie. She knows how to get me."

Teresa did not mention Billy's warning in her diary that night, and as she was writing about her uneventful day, several things fell uncomfortably into place in her mind. Who would be more appropriate than an undertaker to inform Mary Ellen about Mr. Barrett's untimely death? His wife had mentioned the plot in Laurel Hill Cemetery, too, where her husband had been buried so charitably. And when Billy mentioned that "the walls have ears," a peculiarly receptive chord had been struck in her. If Maggie was spying on her, there was little that she could report to Mary Ellen, so that was not what bothered her; but she recalled the sensation of being watched in the boardinghouse when no one was around, as though the walls had eyes instead of ears. The thought was preposterous, of course. She was, indeed, growing as fanciful as Billy Beaumont. Poor Billy, of whom she had initially been frightened, had only tried to hold her attention for a while by almost maligning the woman he called Mammy, because she treated him like his own mother—the woman who, when Teresa really considered it, had shown her more kindness than she had ever known, filling the empty space in her own motherless life.

"You've come a long way in seven months," Mary Ellen said, shaking her head, her attractively mismatched eyes glowing with admiration as she studied Teresa in the new black silk ball gown she had brought with her in a large box tied attractively with a wide ribbon. "The days of walking with a book on your head are over, my dear, though we'll continue your education. You care for your hands and hair beautifully. I've almost forgotten that you aren't a natural blonde. And, just to prove I always keep my word, I have a nice surprise for you."

"Oh, Mary Ellen," Teresa objected softly, "you've already done so much for me."

Her objection was honest. She felt she could not accept anything more from her friend, and she had learned to anticipate Mary Ellen's moods, respecting them when she appeared to have some troubling business on her mind and recognizing the joy in that perfect, aristocratic face when it was moved by generosity. Sometimes, it seemed unfair to accept such lovely things from a woman who worked so hard and wore only gabardine herself. Considering the new ball gown, Teresa reflected that Mary Ellen was very fond of black; both of the gowns she had received, the velvet in the wardrobe and this luxurious one, were black. She had not worn the velvet since the day she tried it on for Mary Ellen, because she had not been out of the house nor had occasion to wear it. It seemed a terrible waste. Velvet was for winter, and she could not wear it now.

"I mean it, Mary Ellen," she smiled. "You're too good to me. I've never been happier in my life, and I don't need anything more. I can never repay your kindness."

"Perhaps you repay it with your appreciation," Mary Ellen said graciously, "and by your hard work. I told you that you'd have a bigger house if you did everything I told you, and you deserve that house."

Teresa was speechless for a moment, and when she replied, her eyes were earnest. "But I'm perfectly happy here. You're a dear woman, and I have a deep affection for you. Heavens, you don't have to keep your word about something like that!" Mary Ellen was sitting in her favorite burgundy velvet armchair, and Teresa leaned to embrace her

38

and kiss her on the cheek, catching the faint odor of the rose and patchouli scent she used. "Another house! What will you think of next?"

Mary Ellen shrugged and waved one long hand in her lap. "Financially, it's no problem," she assured Teresa, "and I've already selected the house. My second boardinghouse is doing very well, and my investments have soared since I met you. Perhaps you're my good-luck charm. I insist you accept the house, my dear, as a showcase for the way you've turned out, surpassing even my expectations. You're still supposed to do as I say."

Sensing that they were reaching a new stage in their unwritten contract, Teresa wanted to raise a further objection. She did not want anything to change, but Mary Ellen's word was still law in their relationship. "All right," she whispered uncomfortably, "of course I'll do what you say."

Mary Ellen rose and took both of Teresa's hands in her own, smiling reassuringly. "You'll like your new house. Tomorrow morning you'll go to the Bank of California and draw out this sum of money from your account." She withdrew one hand to extract a piece of paper from her apron pocket. "Then, you'll meet the estate agent at 719 Sutter Street and pay him in cash."

Concentrating on her inner confusion, Teresa hardly took in the instructions. The suggestion of leaving the security of her little house filled her with panic. She did not want to go out into the streets where, after all this time, danger might be awaiting her.

"You aren't listening to me," Mary Ellen said, lifting Teresa's chin to observe her face; and before Teresa could control her expression, the fear in her eyes revealed itself. "What's the matter, child?" Mary Ellen asked with concern. "You're afraid to go out, aren't you? If there's any reason for fear, you must tell me. You should know by now that I'll look after you."

"No," Teresa gasped, "there's no reason at all. I guess I've been inside too long. Forgive me, what were you saying? Something about a bank."

Patiently, but still observing Teresa closely, Mary Ellen repeated the instructions, pressing the paper into her hand. "The funds are in an account in your name; all you have to do is withdraw part of them."

Teresa studied the record of her bank account vaguely, barely noticing the number of figures in the columns, "But this says . . . *Mrs.* Teresa Percy," she frowned, and her heart raced in her chest. Had Mary Ellen discovered that she was married? But it was impossible, she recalled, drawing a deep breath, she had covered her past too well. "They must have made a mistake at the bank," she added lamely.

"It isn't a mistake," Mary Ellen replied, leading Teresa by the elbow to the sofa and sitting down with her in a warm, companionable manner. 'You're an elegant young lady, now. I think you don't realize how attractive you really are. And even with servants, it isn't suitable for an unmarried young woman to live alone. A young widow, on the other hand, is in another category altogether, as far as society is concerned. I'm only considering your welfare and your good name. Surely, you can understand that."

"Of course," Teresa nodded, "it makes very good sense. But, Mary Ellen, do I really have to go to the bank and everything?"

Nothing was more reassuring than Mary Ellen's deep-throated laughter. "Good Lord, you have to go out sometime!" she encouraged. "You'll be appearing quite a bit from now on. You'll be able to do your own shopping. Now, don't tell me you won't enjoy that. Of course, you'll never be alone, my dear. John Willis is a very good driver, and he'll accompany you everywhere."

"I didn't know you had a carriage," Teresa said distractedly, preoccupied by the problem facing her. The more she thought about it, the less she wanted to go out in the streets. "You've always walked when you came here."

"I don't use it much," Mary Ellen admitted. "I doubt if anyone even knows it's mine. From now on, we'll just consider it yours," she said lightly. "That poor horse needs exercising anyway. I like to walk. When I go anywhere, it's usually by shank's mare," she smiled, patting her thigh. "It keeps me young and active."

The first day out was a nightmare for Teresa, and she concealed herself deeply in the shell of the one-horse carriage, fixing her gaze on the back of the liveried black driver. In the cocoon she had woven about herself for so many months, she had not allowed herself to think of the past; but now that she was expected to be a butterfly, the hidden fears crashed down on her all at once. In seven months anything could have happened, she reflected, cautiously glancing at the streets, which were as full of men as usual. No one had to take the long trip by boat anymore: the train schedule was almost regular. And how, in that sea of male faces, could she pick out the one intent on harming her? She began to feel as if someone was watching her again, only this time right out in the open and not in the confines of the boardinghouse. Indeed, when she was assisted from the carriage in front of the Bank of

40

California, she had no doubt that she was being watched. Gentlemen in fine suits with gold watch chains across their vests paused to look at the blonde beauty in widow's weeds, and two of them nearly collided in attempting to open the door for her.

Inside the bank, she did everything according to Mary Ellen's instructions, speaking little and withdrawing the required amount from a thin-faced young teller who blinked as if a strong light had shone into his eyes. The amount of the transaction required the approval of the manager, as Mary Ellen had predicted, and a portly, side-whiskered gentleman attired like other men in the financial district proved to be most gallant, though his words made Teresa wonder why Mary Ellen had not advised her better about the transaction.

"My dear Mrs. Percy," Mr. McAllister smiled, "this is a very large amount to carry about in cash. May I suggest a bank draft?"

"I prefer the cash," Teresa told him quietly, fastening her level blue eyes upon him.

"Of course, if you wish," he demurred. "But if you have another transaction of this sort, indeed, any business at all, please come to my office. You'll find it much more convenient. We're always happy to accommodate ladies, and we like to make it as comfortable as possible for them." He glanced at the signature Teresa had just made on the withdrawal slip and the one the clerk had on file and bowed slightly. "It's a pleasure to do business with you, ma'am."

Feeling that needless attention had been called to her, Teresa accepted the valise she had given the teller, now heavier than when she had entered the bank. "Thank you very much, Mr. McAllister," she said, ignoring the teller, as she prepared to leave, and the bank manager snapped his fingers at a guard standing nearby.

"He'll accompany you to your carriage," he explained with a courteous smile. "Please, do be careful on your way home."

She collapsed back into the private shell of the carriage with the valise on her lap, thankful to be rid of the guard, and upset that the incident had occurred. Mary Ellen knew better. She also knew how to duplicate her signature to perfection on the file card, which Teresa had seen in the teller's hand, and this surprised her in a woman of Mary Ellen's stature. Where I come from, she considered, still lapsing in thought into her former speech pattern, that'd be a crime. But her friend had only done it to deposit large sums to her account so that Teresa could draw them out when needed, and there was no crime in that, she supposed, though an intuition of some sort of wrongdoing persisted.

41

She did not have to tell her driver, John Willis, where to go next. He prodded the horse gently with his whip the moment she returned to the carriage. And, lost in thought as they made their way to Sutter Street, Teresa did not notice the groups of men by the saloons and moving along the sidewalk. Only when the rocking of the carriage stopped did she come out of her reverie to observe the narrow, two-storied house with all its bays and gables, a remarkably sumptuous dwelling from her viewpoint.

"Are you certain this is the right place?" she inquired of John, who turned only slightly to reply.

"Yes, Ma'am. Seven-nineteen Sutter, Mrs. Percy, an' the real estate gent'man right there on the porch."

Afterward, everything else remained a blur in her mind—touring the house, paying the agent with the cash in her valise. When she was home safely in her little cottage, the only impression she retained was that, large as it was, she had not liked the house much and that it was devoid of furniture.

More reluctant trips to the comfort of Mr. McAllister's office at the bank, furniture stores, and drapery shops were required over the next two months, before she was forced to move into the house. Mary Ellen gave her a free hand in decorating it, and it should have been a happy, enthusiastic time for Teresa. But her emotions were flat, until it was necessary to venture out again on some errand connected with her dwelling. Then, the cold fear soared again, making her feel weak and vulnerable. Against Mary Ellen's objections she began wearing only hats with veils or long chiffon ties under her chin, which partially concealed her face.

Her intuition that trouble had followed her from New York grew stronger with every excursion into the city.

"Stop fidgeting, my dear," Mary Ellen told her as she put the final touches on Teresa's hair in the boudoir in the new house. "For heaven's sake, don't go peculiar on me now. Your whole problem is that you haven't done anything enjoyable for a long time. I can assure you you'll enjoy both the dinner and the company tonight. There, that's very nice. Your shoulders are like cream," she said with admiration, stroking them with her long fingers. "A necklace would look lovely, but it isn't really appropriate to mourning. A black ribbon with a small brooch might be suitable, though."

"The neckline seems too low for mourning," Teresa remarked, attempting to pull the black silk up higher on her bosom, but finally abandoning the endeavor. "I suppose it doesn't matter. Mary Ellen, where's this dinner being held? Who's going to be there?"

As she tied the ribbon around Teresa's neck, Mary Ellen's voice, always warm and soft, took on a purring quality. "Geneva Cottage, a nice little place I have on the old San Jose Road. When the Spanish had this territory, they called it the King's Road, *El Camino Real.* The Cottage is out in the country in a lovely spot, and it's almost become a private club, because the same gentlemen keep coming there. I save my best recipes for their dinners, once a month. All you have to do tonight is relax and enjoy yourself."

The prospect sounded agreeable to Teresa, who had been too tense to concentrate on her music and French lessons since she moved into this house. "Who are the gentlemen?" she inquired, conscious that Mary Ellen was showing her off for the first time and remembering Billy Beaumont's warning. "Do they always have ladies at their dinners?"

"Only occasionally," Mary Ellen said, standing back to observe her creation. "They just happen to be some of the most influential gentlemen in the financial world, my dear. You'll be seated beside Mr. Thomas Bell, an old and dear friend of mine, a wonderful man. I'm sure you'll enjoy his company."

So this must be the man she expects me to marry, Teresa considered, and her wicked sense of humor, which seldom let her down when she was tense, once again came to her aid as she recognized the absurdity of the whole situation. "He may enjoy mine," she announced, studying her regal beauty in the mirror as though she were observing a portrait. "I imagine he's pretty rich?"

"Indeed he is," Mary Ellen said, gathering up her own gloves and shawl to leave for the Cottage early and prepare the meal. "He's my own financial advisor, but it wasn't always that way. When I met him, he was no more than a meek little clerk. The ship I was on coming out here put into some country in South America, because there was a revolution going on there. We picked up the foreigners who'd been trapped there, and that's when I first met Thomas Bell." Her voice had grown almost wistful, and she stared with uncustomary reflectiveness at the wall. "He's a Scot, though there's only a faint burr in his voice now. Sometimes he's slightly dour, but he does love a good time too. He's very relaxed when he comes to Geneva Cottage with his friends. I must hurry now, Teresa. I sent my kitchen staff there to get things ready, but I've a considerable meal to prepare."

"Mary Ellen," Teresa cried, turning suddenly to observe her more closely. Until now, she had been too concerned with other things to notice the subtle change in her friend's apparel. Instead of the plain black dress and Quaker bonnet, she was wearing a taffeta gown that outlined her bosom and waist tightly and flared into a skirt many yards wide at the hem. The ornate black voile hat, which had initially attracted Teresa's attention, was fastened into place with a long pin over her smooth, well-coiffed, dark hair, and the brooch at her neck and sparkling pendant earrings appeared to be real diamonds to Teresa's unpracticed eye. "You look wonderful!" she exclaimed, "I've never seen you really dressed up before."

With her clear features immobile, Mary Ellen pulled on her black kid gloves. "Perhaps I've reached a point in life where I can indulge myself a little," she said. "Yes, perhaps I have, and I'll do it more often in the future. Don't wrinkle your gown while you're waiting, my dear. Remain still, reading a book or something. John Willis will return for you at seven. And remember to put on your white gloves. If you feel nervous, you can drink one small glass of my homemade wine. No more. It's very relaxing. I really must go now." She moved across the room to give Teresa a quick embrace and held her at arm's length for a moment. "If I don't miss my guess, the young widow Percy will create a sensation this evening."

Chapter 4

Perhaps, it was the homemade wine, or just the enveloping dusk, but Teresa left her trepidations behind that evening as the carriage wound its way along a country road to Geneva Cottage. I might even have a good time, she considered as she watched the lights go on around the Bay below. One of Mary Ellen's finest meals and compatible company might be just what she needed, even if it meant an introduction to the man she was supposed to marry. I must enjoy this life as much as I can, she thought wistfully. If marriage is the next step, all the fine living could end very abruptly.

The summer night was just falling when they approached the edifice desginated as a cottage. Surrounded by trees and lighted from within, the low stone building, which appeared to cover a considerable space on the rolling green property, had charming mullioned windows and beams extending from the roof. Already, the sound of genteel merriment rose cheerfully from within, with subdued male laughter echoing into the warm night. As John Willis handed Teresa down from the carriage, she took a deep breath, more out of habit than need. She was actually looking forward to joining the company within and enjoying herself like a normal human being. She knew she looked her best. Indeed, probably for the first time she knew she was beautiful, thanks to Mary Ellen's training and grooming. Not a golden hair was out of place under her black net stole, and the silken skirt rustled slightly, almost snapping with electricity as she walked to the door. Like Cinderella, for one night I am perfection, she told herself, and I must behave that way, too, so I won't let Mary Ellen down.

At first, when the tuxedoed manservant took her wrap, the low, beamed rooms inside seemed to be filled with people, but a quick estimate numbered the men at only twelve. She had not expected an equal number of girls, though, and for a moment her trepidation returned. They were all beautiful, their pastel gowns as colorful as flowers; a soft odor of many light perfumes mixed with cigar smoke hung in the air. Surely Mary Ellen did not have this many protégées. But if she didn't, where on earth had she recruited so many lovely creatures to attend the dinner?

"You must be Mrs. Percy," a sweet-faced girl said as she approached Teresa in greeting. "I've been asked to look after you and introduce you. I'm Melba Granville. Perhaps you'd like to come to the lounge and freshen yourself a bit first."

"Yes, thank you," Teresa smiled faintly, conscious that she was a grieving widow. The honey-skinned Melba was overwhelmingly lovely in her pale yellow gown, and Teresa regretted having to play widow in such a bright company as the rest of the girls. The lounge into which she was led had Mary Ellen's special touch of French Provincial elegance, the chairs and vanity touched with striped pastel satin and not too much gilt. Teresa dutifully checked herself in the looking glass, more interested in her companion, who seated herself gracefully on the chaise lounge to watch. Yes, Melba had Mary Ellen's touch too; she must be another protégée. But how did the woman find the time to train so many girls? In repose, Melba's pretty face was dejected, and there was a shadow in her hazel eyes, which Teresa observed in the mirror.

"Have you been here before, Melba?" she asked courteously. "It appears to be a charming place."

"Several times," Melba said, looking hopefully at Teresa. "It can be nice, I suppose. Yes it would be, if a girl could choose who she sits next to at the table. But you know Mammy, as stubborn as she can be. Things may get lively, later, when I face up to her. I won't be near that man. He gives me the horrors. I find him repulsive. I'm sorry," she said quickly, "I don't want to ruin your evening, Mrs. Percy. I didn't mean to run on like this...."

Teresa noted that Melba called Mary Ellen Mammy, though she was not a colored girl; apparently it was not that uncommon to do so, though it seemed overly familiar to her. She was more concerned about Melba's reluctance about her suitor, because she remembered Billy Beaumont's implausible and unpleasant story. "I'm sure that if you took the matter up with Mary Ellen again, really explained your feelings, she would understand, Melba. It would be better than making a scene in company, wouldn't it? After all, it's just for the length of the meal."

The glance Melba gave her was almost one of pity, as though Teresa was an innocent from another world. But she shrugged her shoulders and regained her cheerfulness, as if on cue. "You're right, of course. Forget all about it, Mrs. Percy, and for goodness sake don't mention it to Mammy. Come along, now, and I'll introduce you to the gentlemen and . . . ladies."

The pause in her voice before uttering the last word and the light irony attached to it startled Teresa, and she dwelled on it as she accompanied Melba into the parlor. What's happening here? she wondered, studying the face of each young woman as she was introduced. They didn't look the sort who might stay on after dinner; but if they didn't stay overnight, why were there so many rooms in the cottage? She realized that this was not the first time her mind had hovered on the edge of wondering about Mary Ellen's lucrative activities, but she had never actually been conscious of these thoughts before. Not for a moment did she believe that Mary Ellen had trained her for anything but marriage. She was not in personal jeopardy. And if Mary Ellen had chosen this time and place to introduce her to a candidate for marriage, she would not plunge her into some sort of pleasure palace, tainting her reputation at the onset. Still, there was more taking place than she knew, if not in this particular company, then in others, and her suspicion unnerved her, draining away all her carefully practiced poise as she met one whiskered or mustachioed gentleman after another without remembering any names. Were they courteous or predatory as they stared at her with interested gazes? She found that she could not speak, so she kept a fixed little smile on her lips, inclining her head as she was introduced.

"Mrs. Percy," Melba said formally, "I'd like you to meet Mr. Thomas Bell."

Teresa found herself staring into a pair of merry blue eyes set in a clear-skinned, slightly ruddy face. It was a kind face, the only one besides Melba's that she had encountered this evening, and she was much in need of kindness in this confusing company. Before she could think of something to say to the sympathetic ginger-whiskered gentleman, Mary Ellen swept into the room, and the magnetism of her personality drew everyone's attention, with the possible exception of Mr. Bell's.

"Mammy's made her entrance," he commented wryly to Teresa, "and they're all at her mercy, God help them."

"She's a generous lady," Teresa defended Mary Ellen, almost to herself, "She's a generous, beautiful lady. . . ."

"That she is," Mr. Bell agreed sardonically, "if you happen to like your ladies too clever by far, with more rabbits up their sleeves than you can imagine. Well, good evening, Mammy," he greeted Mary Ellen heartily. "You've changed dressmakers, I see. That's a fine creation, and the earrings are a nice touch, too. Still fond of diamonds, eh? And what sumptuous repast have you planned for us this evening?"

"You won't be disappointed." Mary Ellen smiled, putting her long hand on his arm in an almost proprietary manner. "I see you've met dear Mrs. Percy. I'd hoped to introduce you myself, but the construction of my dessert was too delicate to abandon, as you'll see when it's served."

"Yes, we've met," he said almost curtly, "and I'm certainly not disappointed. For the past few months, I've heard nothing but the praise of Mrs. Percy everywhere I go." He smiled gently at Teresa, belying the brusqueness of his tone. "You're not to be intimidated, my dear young lady. News of the arrival of a beautiful woman in this city does seem to pass from circle to circle. May I have the pleasure of taking you in to dinner?"

Mary Ellen disengaged her hand quickly so Teresa could take his arm, but she did not return to the kitchen. If Mr. Bell was the host of the party, she fell quite naturally into the role of hostess; she did not join the others at the table, which sparkled with crystal and silver under the large candelabra, its delicate floral arrangement complementing the hues of the ladies' gowns. Teresa recognized the small statue of dancing maidens in the center of the flowers and realized that both the statue and the candelabra had been brought from the boardinghouse. Mary Ellen did know how to do things correctly, she marveled, suddenly wondering where she had acquired her expertise. But there was little time to think about that as she concentrated on selecting the proper spoons and forks during the six-course meal. At her side, Mr. Bell grew more jovial with each wine that was served, lost all of his dourness, and proved a most amiable table companion. When he learned that Teresa had traveled by ship, a flood of reminiscences was unleashed.

"I was plucked from Valparaiso in the middle of a revolution by a ship like yours, shortly after my twentieth birthday. Good thing it was, too. Instead of sweating out my life as a clerk in the mines, I came here and bought some. There were endless opportunities in those days. Still are, for those with their heads on straight."

Teresa estimated his age to be about forty and realized he must have come here during the gold rush. She did not like to ask if he had owned gold mines, so she said ingenuously, "You have silver mines, then?"

He shook his head. "Mercury, ma'am. I'll wager you don't even know what that is," he smiled, "but it's an important element, nonetheless. You've probably heard of quicksilver? The gold's nearly closed down, and the silver's going fast, but there's a wealth in mercury from here to South America."

Teresa nodded with interest, though she did not have any idea what he was talking about. She would have to look up quicksilver in the dictionary when she got home. "I'm afraid I know little of mining," she apologized, observing Melba's set white face across the table and the man sitting next to her. His black mustache was waxed so that the ends turned up, and he had a heavy face with damp, red, sensual lips. She suppressed a shudder, and Mr. Bell was immediately aware of her distress.

"Are you chilly, Mrs. Percy?" he inquired with concern, "I'll have Mammy fetch you a shawl. I find it almost stifling in here, but I'm afraid I've drunk more wine that I should."

"No, thank you," Teresa smiled. "I'm fine, thank you. Is the gentleman across the table a friend of yours, Mr. Bell?"

He shook his head vaguely and blinked his eyes at the subject of her attention. "Not likely," he muttered. "That's Harvey Benvue, and I find his dealings questionable, to say the least."

"But I understood that you were hosting the party," Teresa said with a frown. Had that been a lie, too? she wondered, her spirits falling.

"I am," he replied with joviality, "but sometimes the wrong people get in." His gaze met Mary Ellen's, where she stood by the sideboard supervising the service. "One endures, my dear lady," he said to Teresa, "one endures."

His conviviality faded after that, though he allowed his champagne glass to be refilled several times. Teresa, suspecting that he had reached the point in drinking where joy turns to moodiness, did not attempt to communicate further. After a while he turned to her suddenly to apologize for his silence and in so doing spilled champagne on her skirt.

"I'm terribly sorry," he said, attempting to remedy the situation with a crumpled white napkin from the table. "So clumsy of me . . . your beautiful silk gown. I'm afraid it's ruined."

Teresa rose with a gracious smile. "Please don't concern yourself about it, Mr. Bell. I'll take care of it in the lounge."

Actually, she was grateful for the respite. The dinner had gone on far too long, and the gentlemen had drunk too much. She was alone in the lounge, pressing her tiny handkerchief to the wine stain, when Mary Ellen entered quietly, closing the door carefully behind her.

"Are you all right, dear?" she inquired. "Don't bother about the stain: I know how to remove it. Just don't try to wash it out with water."

"I'm afraid things didn't work out very well," Teresa sighed, overcome by the strain of maintaining her role, her eyes smarting from cigar smoke. "I didn't think men smoked cigars around ladies, Mary Ellen. They don't in the novels I've read. No one that I noticed even asked if it would bother us. I really don't think I can go back there."

"You aren't." Mary Ellen said. "That's why I followed you. Mrs. Percy wouldn't remain at such a party. Get your things together, child, and I'll have John Willis bring your carriage to the door."

"Shouldn't I apologize, say good night or something? Is it polite to just up and leave?"

"No one will notice at this point, Teresa. You did very well tonight, and I'm proud of you. Now, you may go home."

"Mary Ellen?" Teresa ventured cautiously, "The other girls . . . will they remain much longer?"

"Of course not," Mary Ellen emphasized. "They're my protégées too, Teresa." A frown appeared over her thin nose. "What are you implying? Surely you don't think the girls are prostitutes?"

Teresa shook her head, feeling guilty. "I guess everything's been too much for me. You arranged everything so beautifully, Mary Ellen, the table . . . everything. And one of these days, I'm going to talk you out of some of your recipes."

"Most of them are in my head." Mary Ellen smiled. "I keep a lot of things in my head, where people can't get at them, dear."

The cool air revived Teresa as her carriage made its way back to the city, and she leaned forward to observe the gaslit streets, which after midnight were still teeming with activity. The darkness protected her like the warm cape around her shoulders: she felt safe and invisible. It was the first outing in the carriage she had enjoyed. As soon as Geneva Cottage was a few miles behind her, all the small concerns about its inhabitants dissipated like smoke, and the only impression that remained with her was that of lights and music and laughter and the kind face of Mr. Bell. He was a most attractive man, she reflected with some regret; if things were otherwise, she would consider marrying him. He

50

had drunk too much at dinner, but not more than the other gentlemen, and he'd been lucid enough after he spilled wine on her gown. When he was drunk, his Scottish burr was thicker. He was gentle and considerate, and she had known little enough of either quality before. The only puzzling thing about him was his attitude toward Mary Ellen. If they were old friends as Mary Ellen proclaimed, he did not appear to like her very much. His attitude was ironical out of her presence and almost comedic in his gallantry when he spoke directly to her, as if he knew her very well, shared the fascination everyone felt for her, but had no illusions left. What had he meant, for instance, about "rabbits coming out of her sleeves"? He could not have been referring to her matchmaking, because he was too charming to Teresa all evening.

Swaying slightly with the motion of the carriage as she leaned from beneath the shell to watch the activities of the downtown area as she neared home, she was struck with amusement at the sidewalk vignettes, which ranged from an accordion player with his monkey to tipsy, improvised barbershop quartets singing off-color ballads, to lusty hoots of appreciation for streetwalkers with their inevitable feather boas, who were pert enough to give as much as they took. She wondered if this city ever slept. Surely some of these people had to work in the morning. Everyone was so much livelier than in New York, and the streets, though not all paved yet, seemed cleaner, too. Perhaps the city was so young that the fingers of dirty alleys and encroaching slums had not yet touched it; and there was no doubt that the weather also had something to do with its liveliness. A few rainstorms in the winter and blue skies the rest of the time, with the fresh air blowing in from the Bay. Of course, there was the fog, but Teresa preferred even that to the heavy, humid air of Manhattan in the summer, when people moved around in a torpor, like fish stewing alive in their own juices.

She was grateful that she had come to San Francisco, though her destination had not been one of choice. She had boarded the only ship leaving the harbor that night, and San Francisco was as far as she could afford to go. Her mood tonight was so mellow that she could easily put all that behind her, resolving never to think of it again. She was safe, and she was rich, at least for the time being. The city was alive and full of fun, even after midnight, and she could observe it with her new sense of invisibility.

Later, she couldn't remember which she saw first, the sign NEW YORK HOTEL or his face—they ran together in her mind in a flood of icy horror. Her paralyzed mind rejected the recognition: he could not be

51

here. But the identity of the pale face and the cold blue eyes beneath the gaslight in front of the New York Hotel could not be denied, and, almost in a faint, she cringed beneath the shell of the carriage, unable to speak but gasping breathlessly, "go faster, John Willis! Oh, my God, please go faster!"

The driver did not hear her and continued on to Sutter Street at his own easy pace, unconscious of the distress of his trembling passenger, who stared at his shoulders with wide, unseeing eyes.

She did not sleep that night. After pulling down every window shade in the house and dimming most of the lights, she spent the hours remaining until daylight either slumped on the sofa or furiously pacing the Oriental carpet. He had come to kill her, and she could see no way out of her predicament; her worst fear had been realized. No one could help her, not even Mary Ellen, who would have no more to do with her if she told her who he was. Maggie looked into the parlor once, her black face almost invisible over her white cotton nightgown.

"You all right, Mis' Percy?" she inquired with concern. "If you can't sleep, I can bring you a glass of Mammy's wine."

Teresa shook her golden curls violently and motioned her maid to bed with her hand. What she didn't need, right now, was anything that would dull her wits. She wept until the hot tears scalded her cheeks, and when the first gray light appeared behind the blinds and a sparrow chirped, she realized that she was completely vulnerable with the cloak of darkness gone. In a frenzy of terror, she ran to the doors and windows to check the locks again and collapsed to her knees with her hands held against the front door with all her strength to prevent it from opening, as it had so often done in her imaginings during the night. She was kneeling there, tense with hysteria, when the sensation of a pair of hands on her shoulders brought a scream to her throat.

"Teresa, dear," Mary Ellen asked softly, "what are you doing there? Maggie told me you were behaving strangely, but what's it all about?"

Teresa buried her face in the dark folds of Mary Ellen's skirt and rasped out, "Mammy. He's *here*. He's here to kill me! I didn't think he'd find me, but I saw him on the street last night."

Putting her arms beneath Teresa's, Mary Ellen coaxed her to her feet with soothing words. "Come, child, I'll help you to the sofa. You're really in a state, aren't you? You should know that you haven't anything to fear with me here to help you. Together, we can take care of anything. Now, who's this man who has you frightened silly?"

"James Hoey!" Teresa shuddered, staring with blank blue eyes at Mary Ellen. "James Percy Hoey. He said he'd kill me if I ever left him! And he meant it, Mary Ellen. He's here to do it. I couldn't stand the beatings anymore, and I thought if I got far enough away. . . ."

"Did he see you, last night?" Mary Ellen asked calmly.

Teresa shook her head slowly. "I don't know. I went out of my mind with fright. Mary Ellen, I think I'm having a nervous collapse." She began to weep helplessly. "And even you won't want to help me when you know everything."

"I think I do," Mary Ellen considered. "James *Percy* Hoey. You kept part of his name, didn't you? The man's your husband, Teresa." Her voice was matter-of-fact, her face inscrutable. Teresa realized how much she was losing by this confession, but she wanted Mary Ellen to understand why she had deceived her.

"I told myself I'd pay you back for everything, Mary Ellen. I wanted to be a lady so much! I wanted more education, everything you were offering me. I knew I couldn't marry anyone. I was going to tell you, if it came to that, honestly I was. I was afraid he might find out, somehow, where I'd gone, but the chance was so small. He's mean and bad and jealous. I know he'll kill me if he can. But I don't blame you if you wash your hands of me for living such a lie. . . ."

"Hush," Mary Ellen entreated her softly, "I'm thinking. Nothing's as bad as you imagine, child. It's a slight inconvenience, nothing more. No one has to know about it. God knows, Thomas Bell won't be won overnight; he's a cagey old devil, and he's managed to remain a bachelor this long." Then, with more decision, she took Teresa's trembling hand. "I'm not angry with you, and I'm not throwing you out in the street, be assured of that. I knew you had a secret, and you kept it well enough to intrigue me, Teresa. Now it's out in the open, and I can deal with it. Tell me everything you can about this James Percy Hoey."

"He was in our area selling from door to door, when I was on the farm. He seemed nice enough, and he's rather good-looking, or I thought he was at the time," Teresa said, twisting her handkerchief in her hands. "I wanted to get away from that place so bad, you can't imagine, Mary Ellen. He was attracted to me, and I saw my chance. I was only seventeen."

"You ran away with him," Mary Ellen surmised without much difficulty. "Were you legally married, Teresa?"

"Oh, yes," Teresa said quickly, but her voice dropped when she added, "I insisted on that. How foolish can a person be? We'd hardly gotten to New York City before he started to gamble, and I didn't know from day to day if I'd have anything to eat or not. The rent had to be paid, and we'd have to slip away in the middle of the night to avoid landlords. But that wasn't the worst of it. He was so jealous that he'd beat me if another man glanced in my direction."

"There are men like that," Mary Ellen assured her calmly. "They never strike you in the face, though, so the neighbors never know."

Teresa nodded miserably. "He told me he'd kill me if I ever tried to leave him. When things were going well for him, things weren't too bad. He wasn't just a gambler, he was a confidence man, and he's very clever. One night, after a terrible beating, I decided I'd had enough. He'd won some money and fallen down on the bed so dead drunk he was helpless. I decided it was the only chance I'd ever have. I threw some things in a bag and took the roll of bills. The only ship leaving that morning was coming here. I didn't think . . . I hoped that he wouldn't find me, but he's pretty smart. He has to be in his line of work."

"Some people are smarter," Mary Ellen reassured her, leaning to kiss her cheek. "If I don't miss my guess, Mr. Hoey will take up his old ways for a living, if he hasn't already. And he hasn't found you, yet. He probably didn't even see you, and wouldn't recognize you, if he did. Don't you worry about a thing, honey. Mammy will see that he leaves town, post haste."

"I didn't mean to call you that," Teresa apologized weakly. "I was nearly out of my mind, Mary Ellen, and Melba called you that last night. God, was it only last night? It seems a hundred years ago!"

"I liked to hear you call me that," Mary Ellen smiled faintly. "Most people who like me do. And I guess we're just about as close as two women can be. I have great plans for you, Teresa, and nothing's going to get in their way. Do you feel better now?"

Teresa embraced her warmly. "You can't imagine. I'm tired, and I'm still shaking all over, but everything seems better than I thought it would be all night. I'm sorry I deceived you. I'll never do it again, I promise. You're so good and straightforward that you deserve better than I've given so far. I'll do anything to make it up to you."

"We're friends, my dear," Mary Ellen said with sincerity in her eyes, their mismatched colors more obvious than usual in the sunlight coming through the window blinds. "Friends help each other. If you become the lady I see in you, it'll be enough for me. You called me Mammy a while ago: I liked that. It's a term of affection many people use. Are you afraid to stay in this house?"

54

Teresa nodded vehemently, and the fear returned to her eyes. "I don't think I can! Not after last night. . . ."

"Put that black stole around your face, and come along with me," Mammy said with decision. "Maggie can bring some of your things later. You'll be safer at the boardinghouse for the time being."

Unable to concentrate on the books that were sent with her clothing, Teresa spent a lot of time peering from behind the lace curtain hanging at her window, observing the small segment of street and alley the view encompassed, watching nervously. No one in the city knew she was at the boardinghouse, except a few faithful black servants, but she could not settle down until she knew that Jim had left San Francisco forever. Unlike her previous stay, she now had the full run of the second floor. There were no charity cases in residence at the moment, and, as she had in the past, she ventured as far as the sitting room in the evening to break the monotony of her vigil. Though she carried an open book with her, she hardly glanced at it. She sat on the damask sofa lost in her own thoughts, speaking occasionally to Byna, one of the maids, who was a light-colored Negro, when the girl took short rests from her work.

Teresa had been vaguely curious about the slaves Mammy had helped, but until now she had been too busy with her studies to question even her own maid, Maggie. But as she became more familiar with Byna, she found herself pursuing her curiosity, just to get her mind off the one thing that occupied it.

"I'm a New Orleans gal," Byna told her, touching her feather duster to furniture that already shone like glass, "jest like Mammy. Most of the slaves she helped sailed outta Loosiana, 'cept the ones that took the Underground Railway North. Lawd, those were times! I was never so scared as the night I sailed outta that bayou. We was all cringin' underneath a big piece o' canvas, an' I swear you could hear our bones a-rattlin'. We wouln't a done it, if it wasn't for Mammy. In them days, a runaway slave got her hide lashed off with a whip!"

Even Teresa had heard of the Underground Railway, but she had to interject questions when she spoke with Byna, because she was unfamiliar with anything Southern. Over a period of days, both in the sitting room and in her own room when Byna brought her meals, a picture of the South began to emerge which she found both intriguing and appalling. Her admiration of Mary Ellen's efforts, which she had resented on her arrival in San Francisco, began to grow. Saving so many people from a degrading life was like her, she thought. She is the most benevolent woman I've ever known.

One evening, Byna lingered in Teresa's room longer than usual, remarking that Mammy was out and probably would not return until late. "I was wonderin' Mis' Percy, if there's anything you need. Can I brush your hair? You have the mos' beautiful blond hair I ever did see."

"Thank you, Byna, but surely you have something you'd rather do?"

"No, ma'am, and Mammy say to look after you." Byna smiled, picking up Teresa's hairbrush. "You must be just *lost* without Maggie around. She goin' to stay at your house long?"

"Only for a little while," Teresa said evasively as she took the pins out of her hair. "Someone has to watch the house while I'm away. Where did Mammy go tonight? I've hardly seen her in the past few days."

"She ain't been around much, 'cept to cook dinner for the gentlemen. She a busy lady, you can bet. Sometimes we think she's here, an' she's gone out by the private stairs to her rooms."

"Private stairs? I didn't know she had a private entrance, Byna. Perhaps, she's still here. How do you know she left?"

"She took her gig, piled full o' things. An' she was dressed up *fit to kill*, I can tell you. She won't come back tonight."

With all of Mammy's slightly mysterious comings and goings, Teresa wondered with despair if she was working on her problem at all. The long stroke of the brush through her hair was soothing, and Teresa closed her eyes for a moment, giving herself up to enjoyment of the sensation. When she opened them again, a trick of the gaslight beside the mirror made Byna's reflection look almost like that of a white woman, and Teresa considered it thoughtfully for a moment, wondering if it would be polite to make the inquiry taking shape in her mind.

"Byna," she said cautiously, unable to restrain her curiosity, "your skin's so light. It isn't like that of the others at all."

"Yeah," Byna agreed with a serious face, "but I could never pass, even if I wanted to. Not many mulattoes can."

"Mulattoes?"

"Half-breeds," Byna smiled. "You don't think the massah kept to his own bed all the time? I s'pose most of us have a drop o' his blood in our veins, Mis' Teresa. You don't know 'bout all that, do you?" Teresa shook her head under the firm bristles of the brush.

"You mean pass as white?" Teresa clarified, and Byna nodded, her smile betraying the enjoyment she was experiencing over playing instructor.

"Well, depends on how much of the massah's blood you got. If it only a quarter, it makes you a quadroon, and they can pass pretty easy, sometimes.

"An octoroon, now, that's something else," she chatted amiably. "Some of them gals is real fine lookin', honey-color gals, like my friend Melba. . . ."

Melba! Teresa could hardly conceal her surprise; but when she thought about it, it seemed possible that Melba had a little black blood. She had even noted Melba's honey-colored skin when she met her. "Melba's a very pretty girl," she said. "So are you, Byna. I'm a real Yankee, I suppose. I don't know anything about such things. Where I lived, I didn't even see a colored person until a couple of years ago. It didn't even occur to me that some of them have varying degrees of white blood."

"I could tell you some stories," Byna said, twisting the shining length of Teresa's hair into a coil and experimenting with a French twist instead of the usual curls. "Lordy, that's pretty! Golden hair look so pretty in a twist. But it make you look older, I think. Some of them girls with a 'touch of the tarbrush,' as they call it down South, are real good-lookin' an' so smart there ain't no keepin' them down. Some of them even married planters, would you believe that? And some of them are good enough to help the colored folks, because they know they're part colored, too. I could tell some stories," Byna intimated slyly, " 'bout Melba an' her kind. But I think I better keep my mouth shut."

Teresa's stillness must have betrayed the faint repugnance she was feeling about miscegenation, because Byna finished doing her hair in silence. The idea of a white man and a black woman together bothered Teresa more than she might have expected. As a Northerner, she had some reservations about the South, because of the war, but she had always thought it was fought for a good reason. No one should be anyone else's slave. But the thought of blacks and whites cohabiting in the South was new to her, and she was having trouble accommodating it in her view of the order of things.

Chapter 5

Billy Beaumont owed everything to Mammy Pleasant, who had brought him out of the South as a runaway slave at fifteen, but he did not agree with some of the things she did, though he heard of most of them from other blacks who worked for her. He had always been too close to her to see much. The closer a person was to Mammy, especially in daily proximity, as he was in his work at the boardinghouse, the more he fell under her spell. As a free man working for real pay, he was happy with his lot, and he had never tried to find fault with the bountiful lady who had saved him from the cane fields.

San Francisco was as different from New Orleans as any place could be, and in the years he had been there Billy had learned the city by heart. No matter where she sent him on an errand, he was able to get there by the most direct route, usually on foot, because he did not drive a carriage like his friend, John Willis. When they had any time off, they spent it together casting a line in the Bay near the Presidio for perch, as they had done for catfish in the Mississippi, though the activity was the only point of similarity. Instead of sweating in the humidity of Louisiana on a levee, they were more likely to be dampened by fog or fine, cool rain here. Of course, there were those fine days in the summer when everything in the Bay was visible, and Billy could see the big guns on Alcatraz island that even before the war had been positioned by the Army to defend the city. The pretty little island was a military prison now, and Billy wondered what kind of view the offending soldiers had from their small stockade.

He and John Willis never spoke of Mammy when they were fishing, but they often discussed Mis' Teresa and some of the other protégées, when John Willis was not talking about the piece of land he would like to buy somewhere near the water. He saved every penny he earned to get a little place of his own, with a wife to go along with it. The one time they did mention Mammy, it was on one of those clear, sunny summer days when they were relaxing with their fishing poles in the surf. There had been a strained silence between them all morning, and John Willis was the first to break it.

"I wish Melba wasn't mixed up in those dinners out to the Cottage," he said. "She's about the prettiest little gal I ever did see. Too highfalutin for me, I guess. Mammy spoils them girls too much."

"Those girls like to be spoiled," Billy told him. "Besides, Melba's too white for you, John Willis. She has all the dreams of a pretty octoroon, an' she probably won't come to any good, like most of them." He considered his words carefully before he added, "I don't like this protégée thing much. If any of those gals got a husband, I don't know about it. I had half a mind once to warn Mis' Teresa about it . . . but of course I didn't," he lied. "Now that's a lady with class."

"She too white for you," John Willis grinned, knowing that Billy did not aspire to her. "She's doin' jest fine."

"She sure did a lot of improving," Billy nodded. "I wish I could learn to talk the way she has. Why, the first time I met her, she was nothin' at all. She's got some brains in that pretty head of hers, I guess. Mr. Thomas Bell is it?" he asked with a sigh. "He's rich enough, but God, man, he's old!"

"She been to Geneva Cottage," John Willis said heavily, touching on the subject on both of their minds. "She sure acted strange on the way home, too. If she had a whip, I think she'd have used it across my shoulders to make that carriage get home faster. She was scared."

"Something's goin' on," Billy mused, "or she wouldn't be back at the boardinghouse. John Willis," he said, taking a deep breath, "I know I shouldn't say nothing, but I don't like what Mammy's doin' out there tonight."

John Willis remained silent for a moment. He had a certain dignity when he was not speaking as a friend. "I don't, either," he said, unable to hold his opinon to himself any longer. "Some things shouldn't be made a mockery of, Billy. It ain't the way we was brought up."

"She says it won't be no different than the rich Creoles comin' to Congo Square. It won't be no real ritual. Just somethin' for the gentlemen's entertainment. That's what she says. I don't know nothing about Congo Square, do you?"

"Only what I been told. I was a plantation slave just like you. I don't know nothing about the city. The way I heard it, there was a big ritual at

Congo Square out by the lake once a year, an' sometimes the rich white gentlemen came for some kind of thrill. Lordy," John Willis said, shaking his head, "they don't even know it's a religion. They don't know nothin' about us, only what they want to think."

"Do you think Mammy should do it?"

"Who am I to take offence with her? She knows more than we do 'bout such things. She knows everything, Billy. I just wish you and me wasn't involved in what she doing tonight."

Billy had been to Geneva Cottage often, carrying supplies with Mammy in her gig, but he had never seen it at night before with its windows blazing with light and sleek carriages waiting outside. There was a sense of excitement and luxury in the air, and he almost forgot his apprehensions as John Willis maneuvered the gig they had come in to the rear of the house. Mammy's was already there, still dusty from her drive; though the vehicle they had come in was worn and rusty, John Willis exclaimed aloud at the sight of the dust on Mammy's. He jumped down from the driver's seat and began to polish his mistress's rig with the red handkerchief he carried for that purpose.

"There ain't no time for that," Billy cautioned him. "It must be close to midnight, and that crowd in there's pretty noisy. Where are we supposed to change our clothes?"

"The stable," John Willis said, indicating the direction of the building as he put the finishing touches on his polishing. "An' don't forget them drums."

They pulled off their work clothes in the hot darkness of the stable and bound red cloths around their loins without speaking, knowing that they were sharing the same thoughts. Even if they did not wear their sacred amulets, this did not seem right at all. John Willis put his head in a bucket of water and shook the drops away, his ebony body gleaming in the light reflected from the house. The ride had been long and hot, and Billy followed his example, feeling naked in the loincloth without his amulet.

"Where?" he asked, gazing towards the music-filled cottage and listening to the raucous laughter. "John Willis, those gentlemen are pretty drunk."

John Willis shrugged, picked up the drums, and gave Billy some of them. "Mammy say midnight. Maybe she didn't know they'd be so drunk by then. We're supposed to go to that garden on the side. The one with the stinkin' honeysuckle."

"No real music . . . no *chants*?" Billy asked carefully.

61

"Hell, no," John Willis said with irritation over their predicament. "Just pound the drum any old how so some of the gals can dance around a little."

They both laughed suddenly to relieve their tension. "Just so the little gals can dance," Billy said ironically. "Well, whatever the rich white folk want."

At the sound of the clock chiming twelve inside the house, they began to pound their drums in the dark garden in the sickening odor of honeysuckle; and a scantily clad girl ran out with a torch to touch it to other torches that had been placed around the area beforehand. The gentlemen in tuxedoes, with cigars in their hands, nearly fell over each other to get outside to watch.

"Just like Congo Square," Billy grinned at John Willis, picking up the beat of the words on his drums, *Con-go Square, Con-go Square*, varying it with *Mis-is-sip-pi*; he enjoyed improvising on his drums, when they were not being used for religious rituals. Perhaps this would be fun after all, he thought. It's only a show they want.

But that was before the girls came out, dressed only in skirts and revealing colored blouses—no different than they might have worn in the South, but far from proper here. Melba was among them, and Billy heard John Willis's drums go silent for a moment at the shock of seeing her this way. He regained his composure soon enough, though, and seemed to enjoy the music and dancing as much as Billy. One of the girls began to sing a Creole song in a chanting voice, though it was not religious; and before Billy realized what was happening, he was beating the rhythm for the *calinda*, a wild, secret dance banned long ago in New Orleans, and the astonished girls were attempting to dance to it with abandon. He caught sight of Mammy for a moment through the sweat pouring into his eyes; she was clapping her hands as she attempted to explain something to the gentlemen around her; she laughed when some of the men began reaching for the pulsating girls, though she reprimanded them by shaking her finger at them. Billy did not like to see the white men reaching for the colored girls either, though he could hardly blame them. He was excited himself.

He did not know exactly when things began to go wrong. There was a scuffle near the honeysuckle vine, a tuxedo and a red blouse clashing, but the gentleman involved, who was dark-haired and sensuous-looking like some Creoles Billy had seen, was subdued by the other men and went into the house. Neither Billy or John Willis, still beating their drums, recognized that the girl was Melba, and a semblance of order returned to the party for a while. He looked for Mammy and saw her still beside the door with the same group of gentlemen, who were relatively controlled and appeared to be just having a good time.

Suddenly, the same man rushed from the house with a carving knife in his hand. The drums stuttered to an alarmed silence, and Billy and John Willis hardly had time to get to their feet before the screaming started.

"It's Melba," John Willis said, as they rushed with the others toward the sound in the darkness behind the bushes. Someone in the crowd had the foresight to grab a torch as he ran, but what it revealed made John Willis cry out and Billy get sick to his stomach. Melba lay sprawled on the grass with dark liquid bubbling from her slashed throat. With the stained knife still in his hand and blood on his tuxedo front, the man whirled to confront Mammy and the other gray-faced gentlemen.

"She wouldn't have me," the man said, "she wouldn't even sit at the table with me! The little bitch had it coming. . . ."

Mammy stepped forward, tall and dignified in her dark satin dress. "Give me the knife, Mr. Benvue," she commanded, "you don't need it anymore."

Several of the gentlemen attempted to stop her, but she approached the blood-stained man intrepidly, holding his gaze with her hypnotic mismatched eyes and showing more courage than anyone else present. He dropped the knife with a sob, and she bent to pick it up, wrapping it discreetly in her lace handkerchief. After feeling her limp wrist, she placed her own black lace shawl over Melba and arose with decision. "Let's return to the house, gentlemen. The party's over. It appears to have been too much for some of you."

John Willis lunged at Mr. Benvue as he passed with Mammy, but she arrested the action with a quick flash of her eyes and spoke softly and rapidly in French. "That isn't necessary, John Willis. I'll take care of him."

Both Billy and John Willis knew what she meant, so they stood aside as the procession of men followed her into the house. He heard some of them protesting, "I don't want to get involved with the police. I'm sorry I came" and "Good God, this is awful! It'll be all over the papers tomorrow." And he heard Mammy reassure them that there was nothing to worry about: she would take care of everything.

John Willis was sobbing on his arms at the rig when Mammy came out of the back of the house later. Not knowing what to do, numb with shock, the two men had gone back to the stable to dress before they began their wait, knowing she would come to them. She was always there in times of trouble.

"This is terrible," she said, patting John Willis on the shoulder sympathetically, "such a lovely girl. There's no way I could have foreseen such a tragedy. I'm more upset than you are. The man's unstable, but I didn't realize how bad he was until tonight. I'll fix his wagon, never fear, boys."

"I could kill him with my bare hands," John Willis said tearfully. "That little gal never hurt no one in her life."

"I need your help," Mammy said. "I'll take care of that man later. Hitch up the horse to that low-bedded farm cart over there. I want you to take Melba to the usual funeral home, boys. Carry her gently, poor girl. I'll follow in my gig to make the arrangements. I want everyone at the service, tomorrow. *Everyone* . . . you understand."

The funeral home that Mammy used to bury indigents and black friends at her own expense was small and not too clean, but it accommodated the forty black mourners, even though some of them had to stand. Billy and John Willis, who had given their folding chairs to women, stood in the rear, where they could oversee the whole congregation: some people were in their Sunday best, others were dressed in livery or maid's uniforms in preparation for returning after the service to the houses where they worked. Most of the women were mourning noisily, but the men remained as poker-faced and silent as Billy and his friend. An injustice had been done to one of their race, and they were waiting to see what would be done about it. In the past there would have been no justice, but they were not in the South anymore.

The coffin on the dais at the end of the room was surrounded with white candles and flowers, all tributes from Mammy. The funeral had been held at such short notice that the mourners had not had time to send tributes of their own. Billy and John Willis had already filed past the coffin, and Billy was amazed and touched by what the undertaker had done for the poor, bleeding body he had delivered the night before. Melba appeared calm and peaceful, as pretty as she had been in life, in a white satin dress with a lace scarf wrapped around her neck. He wondered if the others knew how she had died, because it was impossible to detect it under that scarf. John Willis had nearly lost control of himself again, and Billy had had to guide him away from the dais with a strong arm around his shoulder.

They were both red-eyed and drawn from lack of sleep and the shock of the murder, and Billy half supported himself against a dingy gray pillar behind the mourners while he waited for Mammy to appear. He had tried to put last night out of his mind, but even in his weariness everything kept going through his head over and over again as he attempted to rationalize his own inaction. The scuffle in the honeysuckle should have alerted him, he told himself, but he had never seen a white man act like that before; he had not expected what followed. No one at the party had expected that, so how could he have foreseen it? What he kept trying to push out of his thoughts was his displeasure with Mammy for putting on that phony show to begin with. A woman with her power shouldn't abuse it that way.

"John Willis," he said hoarsely, softly enough so that no one else could hear, "was that Mr. Thomas Bell there last night?"

Almost stupefied from lack of sleep and weeping, John Willis shook his head. "They was a group of rich business folk," he replied almost inaudibly, "not high class like Mr. Bell. I never seen most of them men before last night."

Alert for the sound of Mammy's rig through the distance of the small lobby behind him, Billy sighed deeply when he finally heard it. He was curious how she would go about handling this affair without compromising her position among these people or driving them to fury.

"She's here," he said aloud, and the murmured information spread through the whole congregation. The women stopped sobbing and turned their heads to look, and even the men glanced toward the aisle when Mammy appeared at the rear of the room. She stood very tall in her black frock and white Quaker bonnet, and Billy saw immediately that she was wearing her red cord of power over her shoulder and carrying something in her outstretched hands. He experienced a jolt when he recognized what was in the small black box, and he turned to assess John Willis's reaction. John Willis had a thin smile on his lips, and his red eyes were narrowed with vengeance: he approved of what he saw.

Billy had never seen a real wax doll before, though he had heard about them all his life. And this one was particularly frightening to him, because of the large, dark Louisiana thorn thrust into the genital area, marking the method of revenge that Mammy had chosen. He shuddered slightly and perspiration appeared on his upper lip. That man wasn't going to die easy, he thought. He's going to suffer something terrible in the place that hurts the most.

As Mammy proceeded down the aisle, appearing almost to float instead of walk, she held the small box low enough for everyone to see, and a murmur of approbation went through the room like a hum. When she reached the dais, she turned three times in front of the coffin and gently placed the box beneath the lace shawl around Melba's throat. No words were spoken, no other gestures made. The rituals of their religion were secret, performed only at the proper place and time. Then, without looking to one side or the other, Mammy retraced her steps to the rear of the room and disappeared through the lobby. She had made her statement, and the whole gathering let out its breath at the same time, as if they had all been holding it in her presence. A woman near the dais began to sing a spiritual, and everyone joined in. Though there was no minister, the funeral took on all the trappings of an ordinary black funeral in the South, for, after all, they shared several traditions that they had brought along with them.

"John Willis, are you sure that Mr. Bell don't go to parties like that at the Cottage?" he asked uneasily.

"I told you, he got too much class," John Willis responded without turning his head. "What you got on your mind, boy? Mis' Teresa hardly gives you the time o' day."

"It ain't that," Billy said slowly. "I don't feel anything like that for her. I just like her. I don't think she's had an easy life. I got a funny feeling about her, John Willis. Like there may be bad trouble ahead. I don't want nothing to happen to her."

"Forget it," John Willis told him. "I see her 'most every day. I won't let nothing happen to her, Billy."

Chapter 6

Teresa realized that there were things she had no right to ask Mary Ellen. She was so grateful to her for getting Jim out of the city that nothing else mattered. Teresa did not find out many details, but she knew that Mammy, with the help of a friend, had managed to outfox him, and that was no small attainment in itself. Someone Mammy referred to as Walter, undoubtedly a white man, had befriended James Hoey in the saloon he frequented; when Walter learned that Mr. Hoey was looking for his wife, Teresa, he told him that he knew the lady, but she had moved on to Washington or Oregon, he was certain. He even allowed Hoey to cheat him in a card game so he would have the money to travel, and Jim had left San Francisco to go north the following day.

"There was nothing to it," Mary Ellen told Teresa complacently in the parlor of her house, after she helped her move back home. "We shouldn't see any more of him for at least six months, when he returns to go back to New York in discouragement. No, don't be alarmed, honey; I'll know the minute he hits town. You have nothing to worry about. I've been so busy, I've neglected you, and there's one thing I've wanted to tell you. You had a note from Mr. Bell right after you moved out of here. You were so upset at the time that I took care of the matter. I hope you don't mind."

"Of course not," Teresa said, still concerned about her husband's eventual return. "What did he say?"

"It wasn't so much what he said," Mammy smiled, "but what he did. You remember that he spilled champagne on your gown. He sent an apology and a check to buy a new one. A rather large check. Take it from me, Teresa, Thomas Bell's not a generous man. He'd never have done it if he weren't interested in you."

The check interested Teresa, who would have liked to have some cash of her own. "Where is it?" she asked. "I think that was very gracious of him, don't you?"

"Maybe. I returned it with a very ladylike note: 'My dear, Mrs. Percy is independently wealthy, and she would never accept money from a man.' Don't look so disappointed, child!" she laughed. "Things are going just the way they should. You've been cooped up too long, under too much strain. You haven't even seen what spring is like in California. I have some things to take care of out at Geneva Cottage. Would you like to come along?"

"I don't know. . . ." Teresa hesitated, recalling the dinner party there. "I'm really not up to any company, Mammy. I just couldn't face anything like that right now."

"We'll be alone there," Mary Ellen said encouragingly. "Every year I spend a couple of days there, putting up preserves and gathering herbs. A little sunshine would do wonders for you."

"I'd like that," Teresa smiled, her spirits rising. "I'd like it very much! Why, I could even help you, Mary Ellen. If there's one thing I know how to do, it's jarring preserves!"

"I do all the kitchen work myself. You should know that by now," Mary Ellen laughed. "But I can find something else for you to do. We'll relax and have a good time and come back to the city with our whole outlook changed."

Wildflowers covered the rolling green hills around the Cottage, and a fresh, cool breeze rustled the boughs of the trees near it. The sky was almost unremittingly blue, except for a few gauzy clouds that reminded Teresa of the thin white veils streaming from a lady's hat. She found herself taking deep breaths of the clear air, almost as if she were on the farm again and happily aware that she was not. There were no cows to milk, no chores from morning until night, just the beauty of the countryside and no obligations. She could wander through the high grass, or read on the veranda as she pleased, while Mammy sang in the kitchen over the clink of her glass jars and the odor of boiling strawberries. Teresa was not even allowed the guilt of knowing how hot it was in there, because she had been barred from Mammy's sanctum sanctorum. The secrecy that Mary Ellen maintained regarding her kitchen amused Teresa, who knew of only one recipe that had been so closely guarded, that of Mrs. Williams's peach cobbler in upstate New York. And, not much interested in cooking herself, she had never comprehended the identification of a woman with her favorite recipe.

She was reading under a fragrant tree in the garden, when Mammy finally emerged in the afternoon, wiping perspiration from her face with her white apron and pushing strands of dark hair back under the new frilled cap she had recently adopted, which reminded Teresa of those Queen Victoria wore.

"Everything in jars?" she inquired lightly. "How many did you put up this morning?"

"Enough," Mammy said cheerfully, "but the day's work isn't finished yet. Maybe, after lunch, you'd like to accompany me when I gather a few herbs that aren't in my garden. One of the amazing things about California is that you can just collect what you need from the countryside."

"If you know what you're looking for," Teresa joked. "I wouldn't know an herb from a weed."

Mammy reached up and broke a twig with leaves from the tree Teresa was sitting under and crushed a leaf between her fingers under Teresa's nose. "Bay," she said, "you've been sitting underneath an herb all morning!"

She filled her apron with bay leaves before they entered the house, where the table was already set and their meal awaited them in a covered dish.

"Mammy!" Teresa exclaimed in awe. "You really are a caution. When did you find time to do all this?"

"Just sit down and enjoy it," Mary Ellen said as she bore her bounty of leaves into the kitchen. "I'll join you in a second."

The fluffy omelette was so delicious that Teresa did not speak as they ate it with crisp homemade French bread and butter. Only when she was almost surfeited did she lean back in her chair with a sigh. "I know why you keep your recipes so secret," she exlaimed. "Anyone else could start a restaurant using one dish alone! That was marvelous, Mammy, but I ate too much, I think."

"Coffee?" Mammy offered, lifting the silver pot. "It's freshly ground. That's the real secret, child: freshness. As for the omelette," she smiled, "it's hardly a recipe, at all. Just fresh eggs and fresh basil and a little salt and pepper, that's all. No mysterious ingredients."

Hot coffee was exactly what was needed to finish the meal, and Teresa shook her head. "Where did you learn to cook, Mammy? Everything's always just right, at the right time."

"New Orleans," Mary Ellen said, obviously enjoying the praise. "There's no one like a New Orleans cook, child. Whether it's French or

Creole, the food has to be perfect there. I wish there were an old French Market out here."

"What's . . . Creole?" Teresa asked cautiously, baffled by what seemed another racial designation, but unable to stop herself in the congenial setting.

"That's New Orleans–born," Mary Ellen said, beginning to clear the table. "Very high class, whether you're French or Spanish. If you're a direct descendent of the early settlers, then you're a Creole, honey. Some of my cooking's Creole, but I don't make common dishes like gumbo very often, because I have to send for my filé powder, so I conserve it. Now, if you haven't stuffed yourself too much, we'll take our baskets and go for a little hike in the fields, where the really secret ingredients grow."

"You'll have to show me which ones to gather," Teresa said, following Mammy to the door of the kitchen with the coffee tray and noting that her friend walked differently when she was pleased with herself. Instead of moving like an upright Puritan, as she usually did with some grace, Mammy unconsciously allowed her hips to sway in a languid and most seductive manner. I wonder if that's the real Mary Ellen Pleasant, Teresa considered with gentle amusement. Perhaps we all betray ourselves with our gestures and walk at times, just as Mammy said I might regress to my former speech pattern under stress. If I'm more observant, there are probably many things to learn. She handed the tray to Mammy, who was already at the kitchen door with two flower baskets over her arm. "Left to my own devices, I'll only pick flowers," Teresa jested, "or put something in my basket that might poison someone."

As they picked their way through the high grass harboring wildflowers, Mammy paused occasionally to pull up a plant for her basket, so intent on what she was doing that Teresa wondered if she was gathering the ingredients for her famous cowslip wine. Surely, all the weeds she was gathering were not ordinary cooking herbs. Teresa was able to recognize a few of them from the farm in New York, but she had never before seen the spring glory of California poppies blooming in golden blankets over the hills, interspersed with flushes of blue lupine, and she paused to admire the sight with her empty basket hanging from her fingers.

"It's pretty, isn't it?" Mary Ellen said, coming back from her collecting to join her. "This is the best time of the year out here."

"It's beautiful," Teresa said softly. "The whole world seems to be in bloom. I've never seen anything like it."

"Enjoy it while you can," Mammy said as she shook the earth from the roots of a plant. "It's like youth, honey. It doesn't last long. By the end of June, these hills will be burned yellow, as tawny as sleeping lions. You'll be glad enough to be in San Francisco, then, where the temperature's always just right. The grass is high this year, because of the wet winter," she observed, scanning the area around them. Then, noticing Teresa's basket, she smiled. "You haven't even picked a wildflower. Some assistant you are! See that plant over there, the one with the small white flowers? Put that in your basket. Mine's full."

Teresa did as she was instructed, tugging hard at the roots. "It's an ugly thing, except for its flowers," she said over her shoulder. "The leaves remind me of a potato plant. These berries won't stain my dress will they?"

"No. They aren't ripe, my dear," Mammy reassured her. "Come along, now. I think we have everything."

"What is this thing, anyway?" Teresa asked. "Potato plants are poisonous, did you know that? If you eat any part of it except the tubers, you can get sick and even die."

"It isn't a potato plant," Mammy chuckled. "Some plants can be good for you, dear. My herbal medicines cure better than any of those patent ones. They're all opium and alcohol."

"You know how to make medicines, too?" Teresa asked as she trudged after her. "I swear, there isn't anything you can't do! A woman near the farm was an herbalist, but all her remedies did was cause the flux."

"That's what most herbalists' remedies do," Mammy said with a laugh. "If you don't know what you're doing, you could hurt someone. Teresa, dear, I'd appreciate it if you didn't use that expression 'I swear' again. It's a dead giveaway that you're from the farm."

They sat out on the veranda after dinner, drinking glasses of cool peppermint tea, and in close companionship watched the dusk give way to darkness. Teresa had never had such a dear friend nor known anyone so clever, and she felt completely relaxed in Mammy's company. She had not realized how lonely she really had been, until the void was filled by a friend. Mammy was old enough to be her mother, and her presence filled a need that had always been with her. Mary Ellen must have been thinking something very similar.

"It's nice to have someone to talk with," she said, her voice lazy from the day's work she had accomplished. "Not just anyone, Teresa, but someone like you. You're feeling better now, aren't you?"

"Yes," Teresa said with a smile. "I suppose I made a fool out of myself, but I was so frightened, Mammy. Now that Jim Hoey's gone, everything's all right again."

"You'd be a fool not to be frightened, if someone's threatened your life, my dear. You behaved as anyone would, probably better than I would under the same circumstances." She paused thoughtfully, rubbing the moisture from the outside of her glass with her long forefinger. "Teresa, I don't want to alarm you, but I think you should be able to protect yourself. He may never come back, but transportation goes two ways. Do you know how to shoot a gun?"

Teresa experienced a thrill of apprehension. "I used to shoot a rifle on the farm," she said tightly. "I was a pretty good shot. Do you really think he might return?"

"No," Mammy smiled comfortably, patting her on the knee. "But one should always be prepared for the worst. It's better than being caught unprotected. I have a small derringer, the sort that's made for a lady to carry in her handbag. Shall we do a little target practice tomorrow? It might be fun. I need a little relaxation after all I did today."

When Teresa was able to shoot several bottles off the fence at a distance of about twelve feet, Mammy was enthusiastic in her praise. "You're a better shot than I am," she said with a smile. "Here, you keep the pistol, my dear. You deserve it more than I. I'm sure you'll never have to use it, but San Francisco can be a wild town, and you'd be surprised at the confidence having it in your purse gives you."

The weapon was a pretty, pearl-handled little thing that fit in the palm of Teresa's hand, and she was flushed with excitement over the success of the morning's game. "Thank you, Mammy," she said breathlessly. "My goodness, I'm surprised at how well I did, after all these years! I guess there are some things one doesn't forget."

Mammy appraised her with pride. "Not after one learns them by heart," she smiled. "It's well to remember that, honey. It applies to everything you do. Put that thing away, now, and let's take a short hike over the hill before it gets too hot."

Teresa accompanied Mammy happily, filled with pride over her accomplishment and the praise she had earned for it. The day was clear and cloudless, and she wanted nothing better than to walk at Mammy's side in companionable tranquillity, listening to her name the wildflowers and reminisce about the convent school she had attended in New Orleans and her arrival in San Francisco during the gold rush.

"I didn't have any more money than you did when I arrived, Teresa," she smiled. "I've done pretty well for myself, don't you agree?"

"Remarkably well," Teresa agreed warmly, remembering her own helplessness and panic on her arrival. "You have a strength I can hardly imagine, Mary Ellen. I think you're the strongest, most intelligent woman alive. No one else could have achieved what you have."

She could tell from the tone of Mammy's voice that she was pleased when she said, "There's quite a way to go yet, Teresa, but we'll make it. We're an unbeatable combination."

Teresa was gratified to be included in Mammy's master plan, whatever it was. In her mind, Mammy was her protector, her mentor, her friend, almost her mother, and she felt happiest when she was pleasing her.

The two days in the country went by too fast. When they returned to the city Teresa did not see Mammy for a while, and her absence left Teresa dispirited. She knew that her friend had returned to her busy schedule and tried to excuse her on those grounds, while she went back to her studies of music and French—partly out of interest, but more specifically to impress her mentor.

The loneliness returned, and as the summer wore on she became aware that it was not associated only with Mary Ellen. In her daily routine of caring for herself to enhance her beauty, she started to realize that she was very beautiful, and the knowledge that she was desirable and had something fine to offer inevitably made her think of men. She tossed and tumbled in the sheets in bed at night, tormented by her fantasies, which did not leave her completely during the day. She was surprised at herself. During her brief, unhappy marriage, she had dreaded the intimacies of her marital duty, cringing under Jim Hoey's touch. Now, suddenly and shamefully, she felt like a bitch in heat and tried to force the thoughts from her mind. If she was destined to marry Mr. Bell, she found herself wishing that it could be soon. But James Hoey still stood in the way of that consummation. Once, she found herself wondering if Mary Ellen would allow her to become Mr. Bell's mistress before their marriage and flushed with shame over the thought. It was not as if she loved the gentle, kind-eyed little man, because she felt only a vague affection for him. She just wanted any man, preferably one as handsome as the one she imagined making love to her in her fantasies.

She was practicing at the piano in the parlor, attempting to get into a more peaceful frame of mind, when Billy Beaumont startled her by entering with his bucket and stepladder, making her hands go silent on the keys.

"Go on playin', Mis' Teresa," he said, "it sounds real nice. I won't make no noise."

"Mammy didn't say you were coming," she said, abandoning the piano and moving to the sofa. Of course, I haven't seen her for some time, she thought, so she could hardly let me know that Billy was coming to clean. She watched him as he set the stepladder in place beneath the windows, conscious that she had no trepidations about his company now. She must have grown more accustomed to black people.

"That's a lot o' high windows!" he exclaimed. "Reckon I better polish yo' chandelier first, before I use that smelly ammonia."

"Whatever you like," Teresa said, picking up her French book to study the endings of French verbs. "It's been quite awhile since you were here last, Billy."

Once again, he had come when Maggie was doing her errands, Teresa observed. She sensed that he wanted to tell her something from the way he kept glancing toward the kitchen, but he could not come out with it, so she determined to show her former lack of interest as she had done before.

"Mammy keep me real busy," he said as he moved his ladder beneath the chandelier, only a few feet away from her. "Here an' there, this an' that. There's enough to do at the boardinghouse. Of course, I don't mind," he added quickly. "That lady's done a lot for me."

"She's an amazing woman," Teresa remarked, "so full of energy. She seems to have a lot of control over her servants."

He was silent for a moment, and Teresa heard the clink of the prisms he was polishing. "White folks like to think that slaves was lazy," he said at last, "but that was because they worked us so hard. Just bein' free makes a man work harder. What you earn on your own makes the difference."

Why didn't he just come out with it, instead of worrying about Maggie's return? Had Mammy really sent him today, or had he come on his own to tell her something? "I'm very ignorant about the South, Billy. I don't know anything about colored people. Are you from New Orleans, too?"

"With a name like Beaumont, you have to ask that?" he laughed harshly. "I didn't get to town much from the plantation. Couple times, I went to market with my pappy, though. That were some town!" He stepped down a rung on the ladder so he could speak to her directly.

74

"Mis' Teresa, I got something to say to you. Just 'tween us, you understand? I tried to warn you once befo', an' you gotta listen this time."

Teresa felt her heart race a little, in spite of her attempted calm; there was something frightening in his lowered voice. "Yes, Billy?" she breathed expectantly. "What is it?"

"A couple o' months ago, another one of Mammy's protégées got killed. An' just between us, Mammy was to blame. Melba was a real sweet little gal. She didn't want to have nothin' to do with that man. Mammy gave the wrong kind of party at Geneva Cottage one night, and he cut her throat. . . ."

Melba! She nearly exclaimed the name aloud. The beautiful girl who had shown her around that night had been murdered? And at Geneva Cottage, where she and Mammy had recently spent such a peaceful time? Mammy had said nothing to her. She felt as though the color had drained from her face, but she knew she would get more out of Billy by not overreacting to his statement.

"To my knowledge, Mammy doesn't give the wrong kind of parties," she said, clearing her throat to prevent herself from whispering. "I attended one at Geneva Cottage, and everything seemed all right."

Everything but Melba's aversion to one particular man, she recalled, the one with an unpleasant face and waxed mustache and red, sensual lips. She could not recall his name, but she knew he must have done the deed.

Billy Beaumont clambered down from the ladder and faced her directly. "Mis' Teresa, you could be in danger, too. So could I, if Mammy found out I been talking to you. She gave a party for the wrong kind o' gentlemen. I know, 'cause I was there. Nobody should mess around with religion, even with a pretended ritual, not even a priestess. . . ." He checked himself, realizing he had said too much. "The dancin' and music was too much for them gentlemen. Some of them just turned into animals, Mis' Teresa. The *calinda* ain't for everybody."

"The *calinda*?" Teresa managed weakly, struggling with her confusion. "What are you talking about, Billy?"

The young black man looked abashed, weighing how much he should tell her. "A kind of music and dancing," he finally brought out, "from the West Indies an' beyond. A long time ago, the people in New Orleans decided it weren't good for white folks. They even made a law. The slaves had to find secret places to dance it."

At first, Teresa could not imagine how music and a dance had whipped the man Melba disdained into murder. But, when she added an element of alcohol to what must have been a frenzied exhibition, she was able to correlate the events in her mind.

"What is your religion?" she heard herself saying in an attempt to clear all the confusion. "The dance is connected with your beliefs, isn't it?"

Billy Beaumont was silent for a moment. "I go to the First Baptist Church," he lied. "Most black folk go to the Baptist Church. But that ain't important, Mis' Teresa. What I been tellin' you *is*. You gotta be real careful, so nothin' bad happens to you."

Teresa knew that the Baptist church did not embrace wild dancing: quite the contrary. She watched Billy ascend his ladder again with the realization that he had said what he intended to tell her and he would offer no more information. Abandoning her former tactic of reserve, she decided to pursue the matter for better understanding. She was so distressed about Melba's terrible death that she required some answers.

"It wasn't a Baptist ritual that provoked that girl's murder," she said. "What sort of dance would make a man do something like that?"

His voice did not waver, and his face revealed more concern than fear. "Mis' Teresa, I like you. I like you a lot. You made something out of yourself. You're a smart lady. I wish I could do the same thing, readin' books and all. You don't mean no harm, I know that, but harm's something you could find if you ask too many questions. Don't go pryin' where you don't belong. Don't ask questions like that no more. I forgot how smart you were when I told you about Melba. You got on to somethin' you never could understand. The next thing you know, you could find a *wonga* on your doorstep an' that'd be the end of you. Stay in your own world, where you safe an' sound."

"Maybe I'm not safe," Teresa said, playing on the protectiveness he had revealed. "Perhaps I should know what's going on around me for my own protection."

"Just be careful about the men. What you talkin' about now don't have nothin' to do with you, as long as you keep out of it. You playin' with fire, now, Mis' Teresa, an' you don't have no *gris-gris* to protect you. I ain't sayin' nothin' more. You wasn't born dumb, so you just do what I say. I'm goin' to wash the windows now."

As soon as he left, Teresa tried to look up *gris-gris* in her French dictionary, using several different spellings, but the single word *gris* meant only gray or drab, which told her nothing. Frustrated, she wrote the word, along with *wonga* on a slip of paper and concealed it in her hidden diary. Billy's right about one thing, she told herself; I wasn't born stupid. If I can maintain some detachment and keep my eyes and ears open, I'll get to the bottom of this yet.

Was Mammy innocent or evil or something in-between? She wondered as she made her entry in her diary that night, hesitating for the first time about putting her thoughts in writing. She had abandoned making entries for the past few weeks, and she deeply regretted not recording fully the dinner party she had attended at Geneva Cottage. The name of the man Melba had feared was lost to her forever. Try as she might, she could not recall it, although she had recorded Mr. Bell's conversation about mines at the table, before she asked who that man was. The time had come either to keep a full account of everything or to abandon the diary altogether. She would have to conceal it safely if she wrote everything, she realized. Mammy already knew she had kept a diary at the boardinghouse, when she first stayed thee; she had left it in plain sight to prove she had no secrets.

Unaccustomed to real duplicity, she was surprised by the idea that came to her mind, though it was simple enough. She could keep two diaries, one to relate ordinary everyday events and to practice her penmanship, as she had been doing, and another to record the mysteries springing up around her. The regular diary could be left casually on her writing desk so no one would suspect that her real diary was hidden.

With a faint smile of satisfaction on her lips, she began to write in detail everything that had transpired since Mr. Bell's party.

A few days later, when Mammy finally visited her carrying a dressmaker's box under her arm, Teresa observed her closely, carefully masking her scrutiny with her faint, ambiguous smile. Mammy made no mention of Melba, of course, just as she had kept silent about the tragedy when they were together at Geneva Cottage. If anything was still upsetting her, she hid it well under a flood of trivial remarks about Teresa's wardrobe, which she had evidently decided was due for a change.

"No one knows how long Mrs. Percy's been in mourning," she said over a cup of coffee in the parlor. "Well, the year's finally over, Teresa! I've instructed Mrs. Bouchard to make some pretty dresses for you. If you'll open that dressmaker's box you'll get an idea of what I mean."

Teresa untied the wide ribbon without enthusiasm. "I wish we could go back out to Geneva Cottage," she suggested. "Do you think Mr. Bell will give another dinner there?" She held the pale ecru gown up by the shoulders and smiled dutifully. "It's lovely. Thank you. I'm tired of black. I'm tired of being in the city, too."

Mary Ellen dismissed the idea of returning to the Cottage. "It's too hot out there at this time of year. You'll be attending some social events before long, Teresa. I can understand your getting restless, you spend so much time alone."

"I had such a good time at the Cottage," Teresa pursued like a willful child. "I don't mind the heat, Mammy. Just for a few days, please?"

"I said it's too hot out there," Mary Ellen said, rising. "I'm not serving dinners there anymore, either. I always stay in San Francisco during the summer. I told you that, Teresa." She walked to the mantel, half turning so Teresa could get the full effect of her charming smile, and Teresa could not imagine her being anything but the lovely woman she knew. "How would you like to go shopping with me? You need some underthings. We could go to the lace shop and. . . ."

"Is it safe?" Teresa asked quickly, recalling James Hoey for the first time since she heard of Melba's tragic death, realizing that she was still in a vulnerable position herself. "I don't want to go out and run into Mr. Hoey, Mary Ellen."

"He hasn't returned," Mammy assured her with confidence. "If he does, I'll be the first to know. You mustn't worry yourself about such things. Well, I can see you really don't want to go shopping. You aren't even able to offer a lady a small sip of wine," she smiled. "What if a gentleman called, child? I'll send a little something for your cupboard around from the boardinghouse."

"What gentleman?" Teresa asked, wondering if Mr. Bell was finally coming to see her.

"Who knows?" Mary Ellen smiled in a teasing manner. "One should always be prepared."

As she prepared to leave, Teresa mustered her courage to find out if Mammy, indeed, had sent Billy Beaumont or if he had come on his own as she suspected. "Isn't it about time for Billy Beaumont to come to do some cleaning?"

"I suppose it is," Mammy said. "The house looks so clean, I didn't think of it. I'll send the wine along with Billy in the morning."

Chapter 7

She was gratified when an invitation to luncheon at Mr. Bell's house arrived, almost at the same time as her colorful new wardrobe. She selected a periwinkle-blue frock and a straw bonnet with an open weave that revealed her hair and wove a blue ribbon through it to coordinate her outfit, taking great care over every aspect of her appearance on the day of the engagement. She was putting a last-minute buffing to her already shining nails, when, to her surprise, Mary Ellen appeared at her bedroom door.

"Are you nearly ready, child?" she asked. "John Willis is waiting for us outside in our new phaeton. I know you're going to like it. The top lets down, so everyone can see how pretty you look."

"You're invited to the luncheon too?" Teresa asked in bewilderment. She had thought this was Mr. Bell's first step in courting her.

"Invited?" Mammy laughed. "I wouldn't call it that exactly. I'm *cooking* the meal. I do that sometimes for bachelor gentlemen who want something special. Oh, by the way, I brought you a book." She put a worn, paperbound book on Teresa's vanity. "You seemed interested in herbal medicine when we were at the Cottage, and I thought you might like to look at it."

"Thank you," Teresa said as she pulled on her gloves and picked up her folded parasol. "Do I look all right, Mammy? I did the best I could without you here to assist me."

"You look beautiful. I think you're actually developing a flair for color and texture, dear. The ribbon on your bonnet is a nice touch. Yes, you're coming along very well. Get a move on, now, though, so you'll be there when the gentlemen arrive."

"Gentlemen?" Teresa asked. "I thought only Mr. Bell would be there."

"That would hardly be proper," Mammy explained as they descended the front steps to the open carriage. "He's invited a few of his financial friends. They always spend a long time over lunch anyway. So why not at Mr. Bell's house?"

Teresa did not like riding in the open phaeton without even the security of a veil. She was relieved to find the ride short, only as far as a fine, large house on Stockton Street. The gentlemen rose to greet her as she entered the room, and Mammy disappeared like a shadow into the realm of the kitchen, from which delicious odors were already emanating. She must have been here already, Teresa thought as she sat down gracefully in the chair held for her by Mr. Bell. She started the meal, and then came to fetch me.

"It's nice to see you again, Mrs. Percy," Mr. Bell said pleasantly, his merry blue eyes as appreciative as before. "I promise this time to refrain from ruining such a lovely dress."

And that was all he said to her during the entire meal, which the gentlemen used as a business session. Instead of being affronted, Teresa pretended she was invisible and watched and listened, without understanding much. She was interested to note several things, however. The servants were colored, and the house was decorated in Mammy's unmistakable manner. The men were respectful toward Mammy when she came into the room to see if they had everything they wanted, and she joked with them discreetly, but with the camaraderie established between old friends. She was unmistakably the hostess, just as she had been at Geneva Cottage. Well, Teresa thought, I'll enjoy Mammy's excellent cooking, at least. I wonder what I'm doing here?

She found out later from Mammy that the men were all wealthy and influential, "good people to know," and that Mr. Bell was terribly shy around women, though he was very attracted to her.

"He told me yesterday that he'd never seen a more beautiful woman than Mrs. Percy," Mary Ellen confided the following day in the phaeton, when they were on their way to a similar luncheon at Mr. Bell's fine house. "You must remember, Teresa, he's a cagey one and he'll move at his own speed, when he feels more comfortable around you. In the meantime, just continue to be proper and self-effacing. You did that very well, dear. Everything will work out just the way we want it."

"I didn't know what else to do. I don't know anything about mines and railroads, Mammy."

"Nor should you," Mammy said, patting her gloved hand. "Things like that are the domain of gentlemen, not ladies like you."

"If he's that shy, I'm surprised he doesn't have someone speak for him," Teresa said with faint irony, "a John Alden to his Captain Smith."

The remark was lost on Mammy, who reacted to it with some asperity. It was the first gap in Mary Ellen's education Teresa had detected. "You're just getting too educated for your own good," she said. "But that's all right. It's what I wanted, isn't it?"

Teresa attended the luncheons for three weeks, straining the variations of her wardrobe and eventually wearing the same frock twice. She was always greeted with great gallantry, properly seated, and ignored for the entire meal. Some of the same guests attended regularly, and occasionally other gentlemen came. She was politely introduced to them by Mr. Bell, before he forgot she was there. She decided she must have met every "wealthy, influential" man in San Francisco, some of whom were more attractive than Mr. Bell, and it crossed her mind that he might be trotting her out for their opinion. This made her uneasy, until one afternoon she accidentally caught something that Mary Ellen was saying in a low tone to one of the financiers.

"She's lovely, isn't she?" Mammy was saying. "He—" she indicated Mr. Bell with a tilt of her head "is so in love with her, and you can hardly blame him. He wants to marry her, but she can't make up her mind. There's the age difference, you know."

Teresa did not reveal that she had heard, but she felt as if a light had been turned on in her skull. Thomas Bell was not interested in her in the least, except as a pretty presence at his table. Mammy was behind the whole thing, as usual. She was trying to make Mr. Bell's friends think he wanted to marry her, but to what end, she could not comprehend.

Her watching and listening had paid off, but she was left with another puzzle to unravel in her diary that night.

She had to admit that she found Mammy's machinations and unpredictability compelling. She forgot about her research into what had taken place at Geneva Cottage on the night that Melba died as she attempted to understand what was taking place in her own life. Everything was as interesting as in a novel, but she had no idea of the ending. One night, she made a list of possibilities in her diary:

1. *She knows I'm married. How does she expect to work that out? Surely, she is opposed to bigamy.*

2. *She wants everyone to know Mr. Bell is interested in me. Does she think that cautious old bachelor will succumb to public opinion and capitulate?*

3. *Why Thomas Bell? Others are as wealthy and more attractive. They would be easier to win, too. This question is of the utmost importance; it should be #1. Why Thomas Bell?*

4. *What does she get out of all this complicated matchmaking, anyway? Probably just the satisfaction of manipulating people. I can't think of anything else.*

5. *Must attempt to understand the way Mammy thinks. What drives her? Why is she so generous? Does she have some kind of hold on the blacks she has helped, as Billy once implied?*

All of Teresa's speculations were made more complicated the following afternoon. Most of the gentlemen left Mr. Bell's house to return to their work, only a few remaining behind at the table, which the colored servant quickly cleared. Teresa was rising to leave, when Mammy entered from the kitchen and motioned her to remain seated. Then, to Teresa's surprise, Mammy drew up a chair to join the gentlemen over a sheaf of papers one of them produced from his case.

"There's going to be a merger between Consolidated Silver and Mr. Wallace's firm," she informed them. "I suggest we buy now. Consolidated has a lot of power behind it. We buy as many shares, under different names, as we can without attracting attention, just as we have in the past."

"Inside information?" Mr. Bell asked mildly, regarding her with affection.

"Right from the horse's mouth," Mammy smiled. "Do I ever give you anything else?"

The astounded Teresa listened for the better part of an hour, not understanding the financial manipulations taking place, but recognizing that Mary Ellen was not only part of them—she was the advisor. The gentlemen hung on her every word, as if they were getting an inside tip on a horse. Teresa had observed that rapt, unquestioning expression on people's faces before, when she had been married to a gambler and con man who was not above illegal bookmaking, keeping the take and running. But these men were not gullible betters; they were shrewd financiers. And Mammy, she realized with amazement, was their *partner*, with Thomas Bell as respectful and easily managed as a child at her side.

She did not question the legality of their operation until much later, but she wondered where Mammy got her inside tips, which went far beyond what could be conveyed by a network of black servants in wealthy homes, as Billy Beaumont had implied. To get a reliable inside tip on a horse, one would have to talk to the trainer, practically be in the stall, Teresa considered. She could not imagine financiers sharing inside information with anyone. One would have to be a fly on the wall to come by the tips Mammy was giving her avid, admiring circle.

Her respect for Mary Ellen had never been grudging, but now it was overwhelming. She was certain there was nothing the woman could not do. Teresa observed her from the end of the table with a faint, affectionate smile on her lips. Mammy might be just a little crooked, she conceded, but she was not involved in cheap confidence tricks like Jim. Everything that was taking place here was probably quite legal, she decided. Men of such status would not take chances with their reputations. She felt warm and secure in the friendship of such a remarkable woman, realizing that Mary Ellen had taken her into her confidence by allowing her to remain during the meeting.

Teresa was so impressed that she considered Mary Ellen's gesture an honor bestowed upon a trusted friend, to whom she would eventually confide everything. There was a master plan somewhere, but it still eluded Teresa completely.

She was mildly surprised and almost disappointed when, shortly before they would have left, a message from Mary Ellen informed her there would be no luncheon at Mr. Bell's the next day. Teresa had spent the better part of the morning grooming herself and thought the white lawn dress with its matching parasol and hat looked particularly well on her. She removed the hat with a feeling of flatness, as if the whole day had leveled off before her, without any highs or lows. She had become accustomed to the two-hour break in the afternoon in the company of gentlemen, and she found the time difficult to fill. She played a few notes on the piano and finally settled down to catch up on the practice she had been shirking. The day was fine and clear; her gaze wandered from the music sheet to the window, and she wished she were riding in the phaeton in the warm sunshine.

She was not aware that Maggie had entered the room until she spoke. "You all right, Mis' Percy?"

"Of course I am," Teresa smiled, turning gracefully on the stool. "Why do you ask that, Maggie?"

"I dunno," her maid said helplessly. "I just got a message from Mammy to keep you inside. I thought you might be ailing . . . like before."

Teresa was instantly alert. There was only one reason Mammy would send such an instruction. Her fingers felt icy on the warm ivory keys. "Did she say anything else?"

"Byna brought the message. She say Mammy'll come here as soon as she can."

"Lock all the windows, Maggie. I'll take care of the doors!"

"Lawd o' mercy, it *is* jest like before! What you want to close the windows for, on a nice day like this, Mis' Percy? Why don't you jest sit down and calm yourself?"

"You heard me!" Teresa said stridently. "Do as I say! I'm in danger, Maggie. You can't possibly understand."

"Yes, ma'am," Maggie sighed, dutifully closing the windows and securing them at the sills. "You want the blinds pulled down again, too?"

"Yes!" Teresa cried from the door, before she ran to the kitchen to turn the key in the latch there. When she returned to the entrance hall, Maggie was descending the stairway from the second floor. "Are you sure everything's locked?" Teresa asked.

"Yes, ma'am," Maggie replied, observing her with distrust. "I jest hope Mammy gets here, soon. I don't like you when you're like this, Mis' Percy. You ain't never had fits, have you?"

"No, but I'm cold all over. Please fetch my shawl," Teresa said with a shiver, realizing that she must appear insane to Maggie. She must control herself more. But the very thought of Jim looking for her with his cold, blue, cruel eyes was nearly enough to throw her into a fit. When had he returned, she wondered. Did Mammy hear about it at once, or had he started to make more inquiries? She wished desperately that Mammy would come, soon. Mammy could take care of everything, she felt sincerely—Mammy had told her she could.

84

The sound of several people coming up the wooden stairs made Teresa peer carefully from behind a curtain, and she was heartened by what she saw. Mary Ellen was accompanied by Billy Beaumont, who looked taller and stronger than ever, and a white man equal in height and size. She ran to unlock the front door and nearly collapsed into Mammy's arms as she entered.

"Thank God!" she cried. "Where is he? When did he come back, Mammy? What . . . ?"

"My goodness, child," Mammy said cheerfully, "you've really gotten yourself into a state again. Everything will be all right. I've brought two strong men and another decanter of brandy, so we're just fine. Oh," she said, remembering her manners, "Mrs. Percy, I'd like to introduce my friend, Mr. Ben Willard."

Teresa nodded quickly, noticing even in her overwrought state Mr. Willard's handsome, craggy features and friendly eyes. "Please come into the parlor," she said breathlessly. "You too, Billy . . . please. I wish you'd brought some of your homemade wine, instead of brandy," she told Mammy. "I could use it right now."

Mary Ellen put the decanter next to the one Teresa had never opened on the sideboard by the fireplace and took off her dark shawl, indicating to the men that they might sit if they liked. Ben Willard settled his long frame into an armchair, but Billy Beaumont preferred to stand, leaning his back against the wall near one of the windows and remaining so silent and inconspicuous that he seemed to blend into the dark pattern of the wallpaper.

Teresa could not sit, either, though she accepted the snifter of brandy from the tray Mary Ellen handed around, passing over Billy. The warm liquor in Teresa's chest steadied her nerves somewhat as Mary Ellen answered her questions one by one.

"He got back last night and checked into the New York Hotel at ten o'clock. From there, he went to his customary saloon, probably looking for Ben, here, who'd given him such a bum steer. At least, he used a phoney name. The report I received said that Hoey's drinking quite a bit and asking questions again. He's angry, Teresa. More than he was before he went off on that wild goose chase. The question now is, what shall we do about him? As pleasant as your company is, the three of us can't keep watch here forever, in the chance event that he might come."

"I could return to your boardinghouse," Teresa suggested. "I could go there, right now, with all of you."

Mary Ellen relaxed against the cushions of the sofa and sipped her brandy thoughtfully. "No. We must reason with him to rid ourselves of him, once and for all. You aren't going to like this, Teresa. I've invited him here to see you."

"*No!*"

"It'll be safe enough, with all of us here, my dear. I think I can offer him enough to make up for losing you. It's the only way, Teresa."

In her agitation, Teresa poured herself another brandy and gulped it down, though she was not accustomed to drink. Terrified, she hardly heard what Mammy was saying. If Jim gets into this room, he'll kill me, she thought. No one can stop him. Her pouch bag was lying on the piano, and she did not stop to wonder what it was doing there, though she never left anything laying about so untidily. To rid herself of some of her fear, she quickly extracted the small gun from her bag while the others were talking and concealed it in the folds of her skirt with her finger on the trigger. She considered taking another drink to give herself courage, but she decided against it. Her senses were already slightly clouded by alcohol, and her fear was still intense.

When Mammy rose to pour more liquor into the bottom of Ben's snifter, Teresa sank down on the piano stool and stared toward the door, listening for the expected knock on the door. She was not prepared for its opening quietly and Jim Hoey's sudden appearance in the arch leading into the parlor. His ice-blue eyes were narrowed menacingly, his face pale with hatred.

"You little whore!" he said through clenched teeth, taking a step toward her. "What the hell are you doing here, fancied up like a harlot? I warned you not to leave me, Teresa. . . ."

The gun came from his pocket so quickly that she barely had time to respond. If shots rang out, she did not hear them, though her arm was extended in front of her and she pulled the trigger repeatedly, aiming once again after he slumped to the floor. She was conscious only of the ringing in her ears and of standing alone in the middle of a room that seemed to dissolve at its edges around her.

"Well, that's done it," Ben Willard said, his words coming from a distance as he knelt to examine the heap of clothes on the floor. "Christ, Mammy, why didn't you tell me that the little bitch had a gun? Get it away from her, before she kills someone else, if there are any bullets left."

"Teresa," Mammy said evenly, close beside her with one hand touching her shoulder, "Teresa, give me the gun, my dear. That's a good girl.

86

Now, come over here and sit down on the sofa. You're as white as a sheet."

A glass was placed to her lips and small sips of sweet homemade wine forced between them. She began to relax inside, and the haze cleared miraculously. She did not remember what had happened and stared with calm curiosity at the body on the Oriental carpet. "Is he dead?" she asked, feeling nothing. "I didn't hear any shots, Mammy. Is he really dead?"

"I'm afraid so," Mammy confirmed with a sigh. "If you'd only listened to me, Teresa! I'm sure we could have handled things another way."

Ben Willard's tall, handsome figure loomed up before Teresa, and there was an expression of distrust and disgust on his face. "What do we do now? Call the police? I've always said no woman should ever be given a gun. Mammy," he said, "we have a corpse in the middle of the carpet. What do you intend to do? I don't want to get involved with the police. They know I'm a gambler who can use a gun. I'll be damned if I'm going to play the gentleman and take a rap for *her*."

"She didn't know what she was doing," Mammy defended Teresa, "the poor girl was out of her mind with fear, Ben. We won't report this to the police," she considered. "If anyone had heard the shots, there would be people here by now. Billy," she said, summoning Billy Beaumont from his position against the wall, "come here."

The young black man moved closer, his eyes white and round in his handsome face, and Teresa felt a twinge of compassion for him. Billy Beaumont had always liked her, made up stories to amuse her, but he was too shocked to look at her now. Her head began to whirl in an alarming way and she grasped the arm of the sofa against the wave of dizziness. Surely this could not be happening, she told herself; I'll wake up and find it is only a bad dream.

"We don't want the police," Mammy was saying. "I don't want a scandal. Teresa's my friend. She was unbalanced by the fear of this man, who mistreated her badly. I don't condone what she's done, but he was a really bad man. We'll just have to cover the whole thing up, somehow. Of course, everyone here will have to swear to remain silent about it. Billy," she addressed the crestfallen young man, who avoided looking at Teresa, "do you swear that you'll never mention what happened here today?"

He hung his head and shuffled his feet, but he answered in a deep mumble, "I swear, Mammy. I didn't see nothing."

"Ben?"

"Of course, darling," he said quickly. "I don't want it known any more than you do. But what about the coroner?"

"I asked you to *swear*," Mary Ellen emphasized, and he appeared embarrassed.

"Sure, honey," he muttered, "I swear to God I won't say a thing."

"Maggie, come here." Mary Ellen summoned the maid from the archway, where she stood twisting her apron anxiously. She did not have to be asked to swear, because she babbled hysterically, "I didn't hear nothing or see nothing Mammy! I swear by the Great Snake I won't ever say a thing."

"The *Great Snake*?" Ben laughed shortly. "What in the name of God is that?"

"There won't be a coroner," Mary Ellen said swiftly, "he isn't a doctor, anyway. Dr. Mouser will sign a death certificate. He owes me that much. That won't be a problem. . . ."

"Getting the body out of here might," Ben observed ironically. "Billy and I could do it, I suppose, but we'd have to wait until dark."

"Move him to the edge of the carpet," Mary Ellen said, and the two men did as they were commanded, though Billy Beaumont showed little stomach for the job. "Now, Billy, you just roll that carpet up as if you were taking it for cleaning. You do it all the time, and no one will question it." He did as he was told, and Teresa observed the grisly maneuver as if she were still dreaming. "Good," Mary Ellen said, "now, just throw it over your shoulder the way you always do and march right out the front door to the carriage."

"Where am I suppose' to take it?" Billy asked uncertainly. "I can get it to the carriage, Mammy, but what do I do then?"

"Have John Willis drive to Mr. Gunther's mortuary and go up the back alley there. Tell him I sent you. I've sent him enough itinerants to bury."

Sitting as if she were frozen into stone, Teresa watched Billy hoist the rolled carpet over his strong shoulder and carry it out of the house in broad daylight. Then, the room began to spin around her, and she lost consciousness.

"Wake up, dear," Mammy's voice said kindly, "Teresa, wake up. It's evening, and you must accompany me."

She did not know how long she had slept, or who had carried her to her bed. For one hopeful moment, she believed the whole thing really was a dream as she rolled her head on the pillow to meet Mammy's gaze.

"You've been asleep for hours," Mammy smiled, brushing the hair back from Teresa's forehead. "How do you feel?"

"I don't know. My head's heavy, and I can hardly keep my eyes open, Mammy. What were you saying?"

"You must get up and accompany me to the mortuary, dear. It's only a formality, so Dr. Mouser can fill out the death certificate."

Teresa frowned and closed her eyes. If she could only sleep again, perhaps things would be different the next time she woke.

"I've laid out a black dress," Mammy told her as she helped her out of bed, "and I bought a black hat with a heavy veil this afternoon. Not even the doctor would recognize you if he should see you again. You're a widow anyway, and people are always uneasy around the newly widowed."

Jim must be dead, Teresa considered, more concerned about her aching head than the fact that she had probably killed a man. She had never felt this way before. If she did not know better, she'd almost think she had been drugged. Something was very wrong with her reactions.

Mammy dressed her as if she were a mannequin, with about as little assistance as a mannequin could give, and Teresa would have put her head down on the vanity while her hair was being touched up if Mammy had not jolted her back to consciousness.

"For the love of God, child, you've shot a man! I'm doing everything I can to cover it up for you. The least you can do is cooperate a little, Teresa. It isn't much to ask."

"I'm sorry. It's my head, Mammy. I feel as if I'd had chloral hydrate. . . ."

"What do you know about chloral hydrate, Teresa?" Mammy asked, stepping back from the vanity. "Where did you hear about anything like that?"

"From Jim. He told me it was used in bars to shanghai sailors. There wasn't anything like that in your wine, was there?"

"Of course not," Mammy reassured her, bustling across the room to get the black hat. "A little relaxant, perhaps, but nothing from the chemist's shop. It'll pass off in no time, dear. You were in a frightful state."

Teresa decided that the effect of the homemade wine must still be with her as the carriage drove through the dark, gaslit streets. She had killed Jim, and she should be feeling something, but she was tranquil as if it were a Sunday drive. The mortuary was located between two storefronts in a part of town that did not seem very respectable. She had no idea where she was as she stepped out of the carriage and was hurried inside by Mammy. The place was definitely run-down, she observed fastidiously, refraining from touching the dusty seats in the foyer. Even the potted palms were brown at the edges, unable to flourish in such an atmosphere, and to hide the disreputable appearance of the place, the minimum of gas was used for the lighting.

She had hoped that they would not have to go inside the parlor, but she was not spared even that. As they walked into the pool of darkness, she saw that two pine coffins were on the dais. They were lighted by candles and covered with floral offerings. The heavy, spicy odor of carnations turned Teresa's stomach as Mammy led her toward the man waiting for them at the end of the aisle. He could only be Dr. Mouser, Teresa concluded with a bubble of hysteria rising in her chest, because his appearance matched his name so perfectly. Short and rather plump, in a mouse-gray suit, his most conspicuous feature was two large teeth beneath his mustache, and she had to suppress the laughter struggling to dominate her emotions. He doesn't look well, she thought, staring through her veil at his pale, pasty face and bright little eyes. He doesn't look well at all. He should see a doctor. And the inappropriate laughter trembled near her lips so strongly that she put her handkerchief to her face to smother it. I'm very near the edge of insanity, she realized; one more push and I shall be carried laughing and screaming from this place. She avoided looking at the doctor as he wrote out the death certificate, using the coffin lid as a writing surface.

Although she was the widow of James Hoey, she was able to provide very little information about him, except his age. She did not know where he was born, and she was grateful that the question was not asked. The doctor assisted her to a seat beside the dais with obvious concern, because she still held the handkerchief to her face and her shoulders were moving as though she was sobbing. She managed to control herself when he returned to Mammy for the rest of the ritual, which consisted first of a large wad of bills passing into his hands. What followed really made Teresa fear for her sanity, because it was totally incomprehensible to her. The floral offerings were removed from the other coffin and then, Mammy on one end of the coffins and Dr. Mouser on the other, the coffins' positions on the dais were switched, and the floral offerings were put back where they had been. Teresa had not realized how strong Mary Ellen was until she observed her lifting half a coffin, and she allowed her amazement to carry her through the following minutes.

She had hoped there would not be any sort of service; it would have been too much of a travesty. To her relief, there was none. With their business attended to, Mary Ellen and the doctor parted; he left by the back door of the mortuary, and Mary Ellen took Teresa's arm and they groped their way to the carriage, which Mary Ellen had driven herself.

She handled the reins adeptly, as if she had driven carriages all her life, and Teresa remained silent beside her, lost in confusion over what she had witnessed, but too unstable in her reactions to inquire about it for the moment.

"You're probably wondering what that was all about," Mammy said at last, as she prodded the horses forward with a click of her tongue. "It was all for your protection, my dear. It's unlikely that any of the witnesses will ever talk, but if one of them does, you're quite safe. In the event that Mr. Hoey's grave is ever exhumed, the body in it will not have a bullet in its skull. He'll really be buried in the other person's grave. Only you and I will know where your husband's body really is, Teresa, and of course, neither of us will ever tell. I've gone to a great deal of trouble to protect you, but I know it will be worth it in the end."

"Who was in the other coffin?" Teresa asked, her emotions switching dangerously between anxiety and guilt. "What about his family?"

"He didn't have one. He was one of Dr. Mouser's patients, who passed away from an infection yesterday. He isn't the best doctor I know, but he can be bought for the price of the morphine he requires."

"Perhaps the doctor will tell someone."

"He does what I say," Mary Ellen said. "We don't have to be concerned about him." When Teresa remained silent after this information, Mammy asked, "Are you all right, honey? You've had a terrible day."

Teresa nodded, trying to dismiss her apprehension about what Mary Ellen had revealed and the conspiratorial tone of her voice. "I'm very grateful, Mary Ellen," she sighed. "I don't know how I can ever repay you, though."

She told herself that she must not have any bad thoughts about Mary Ellen. She was good; she was her friend. She did not know what she would do without her. All of her fleeting suspicions were a sign of ingratitude. She must not listen to the servants' gossip, and she must stop attempting to penetrate the smoke screen of mystery Mary Ellen inadvertently created by everything she did. Only a very good person would be so kind to her. She had never known kindness or affection before, and she must learn to adjust to it. Deep in her heart, in spite of her good looks and determination to better herself, Teresa knew she had always thought of herself as unlovable.

The effect of the homemade wine was wearing off now, and she was more conscious of her feelings. The pang in her chest was just the beginning, she realized, the beginning of the awful knowledge that she had killed another human being.

Chapter 8

All in all, it was not a bad day's work, Mary Ellen concluded when she returned to the boardinghouse and the luxurious suite to which only her personal maid was admitted. She had lavished funds from her assorted accounts on the decoration of her boudoir and felt that only she was able to appreciate its elegance. Most of the Louis XV furniture had come around the Horn from New Orleans, though the rose silk wall covering with its ivory stripes and scattered flowers came all the way from France, copied from the queen's chamber at Versailles. Her bed was that of a queen, too, its cone of drapery fanning out above her when she lay down. The Austrian crystal chandeliers gave her unlimited pleasure, though no one seemed to appreciate the ones downstairs very much. Only here in her private world could she be herself, discarding the pretense necessary beyond these walls. And the first thing she did after returning from the funeral parlor was stand before a gold ormolu mirror, which caught the tint of rose from the room, and unfasten her demure white collar and the bodice of her black dress until her breasts gleamed in the light of the ornate oil lamps on her vanity.

With a bemused smile, she poured herself a glass of her homemade wine from a shining crystal decanter and sipped it slowly as she observed herself in the mirror. She had not left any of the dulling wine with Teresa, who would now have to work through the implications of today's action without the help of sedatives. She must understand the magnitude of what she had done and appreciate who had saved her from the police. There was no doubt in Mary Ellen's mind that Teresa would transcend murdering a man, though she had not shown much spunk so far. Teresa was young, and she liked her comforts more than she revealed. She would do almost anything to keep them. Within a month or so, she will have buried the whole episode, Mary Ellen calculated, even her guilt about it. It was important that she retained a measure of guilt.

Today had been a coup of sorts. In the space of a few hours, she had freed Teresa for her own purposes, bound the young woman to her forever through the witnesses she had skillfully brought along when she engineered the shooting; and, as an added touch, she had made Teresa watch the switching of the coffins, so she would know that Mary Ellen was the only person on whom she could depend. She was satisfied that there would be no rebellion from Teresa later, not with this secret between them.

Thomas Bell was inordinately fond of this homemade wine, she reflected, sipping it with caution. It's strong and full, like me, and, perhaps also like me, its subtle effect can dull a man's alertness. He had gotten hopelessly drunk on it several times without recognizing that the effect was not of alcohol alone, and any clever person could take advantage of him in such a state. She did not want him when he was drunk, though, or for only an occasional night together, like the ones they had enjoyed in the past. She wanted him forever, along with his considerable fortune, and she would have him yet, because his caution was no match for her subtle mind.

She stretched contentedly and let her dress drop to her feet as she reached for a rose satin robe, which she slipped into with sensual enjoyment. The fabric was as smooth as her own skin. Teresa is singularly passive, she considered, enigmatic and beautiful, but a leaner if ever I knew one. She would find out everything about her in time, just as she had about Thomas. She had her methods. She enjoyed people who challenged her intellect with their secrets, whose reticence kept her wits honed. At least, after today, part of Teresa's past was settled; there would be no more husbands coming out of the woodwork. That quiet little girl had really fooled her about that in the beginning; and she felt the young woman was still holding something back. That distant smile of hers nearly drives me mad. She smiled slowly, ready to exercise her wit against anyone else's.

She loosened her long hair in front of the mirror and studied it for any sign of crimping, the only legacy from her quadroon mother, wondering if she should treat it again this month. Perhaps she had another legacy, she mused, a blue eye from her planter father and a dark one from the slave he had used. But her eyes were not unattrac-

94

THE HOUSE ON OCTAVIA STREET

tive. She would not have had them any other way. After the first curiosity wore off, people seldom noticed it, she thought. She was an octoroon and had very little black blood. Just enough to stigmatize her in the South and keep the slaves she had freed under her control here. She knew her blacks served her as much out of fear as gratitude, and that is the way she wanted it. Gratitude tended to fade or turn into something else against the giver, but fear was a potent persuader that, at least in her experience, did not lessen in intensity until the one who caused it was removed. And she had no intention of allowing that to happen.

She could now hold Teresa with both emotions, gratitude and fear, play her like a musical instrument to do her bidding. A life of luxury seemed to suit her most important protégée just fine, and she could be induced to desire even more. Strangely enough, she really liked Teresa and sometimes thought of her as a friend. She was more intelligent than the other girls and had such an incredibly well-bred beauty, something of which she herself was not aware. Mary Ellen was particularly suited to judge good blood in both humans and horses, and she recognized that this young woman from a farm in New York was almost a freak of nature. Teresa had told her she was part Irish and God knew what else, but she was endowed not only with beauty, but every feature of an aristocrat. Mary Ellen had noticed it that first day in the street, even beneath all the rice powder and rouge. She was a born lady who had only needed to be groomed as one. And Mary Ellen had also noted in a flash that Teresa was the only girl to use as bait to get Thomas Bell.

She scrupulously surveyed her own beauty in the mirror, comparing it to Teresa's in spite of her own forty-five years. They could not have been more different, but Mary Ellen considered herself superior in many ways. She felt no envy of the girl, who lacked the most important female endowment in attracting men, the almost musky sensuality that emanated from her own image. She enjoyed dressing Teresa in gowns that she herself dared not wear in public for fear of weakening her humble, philanthropic image. It was almost like playing with the doll she had never possessed as a child, but something else was involved, too, and as she began to brush her long, dark hair she puzzled for a moment over what it was. When the answer came to her, she laughed shortly and shook her head. What a wonderful, mysterious thing the human mind was. Without being completely aware of it until now, she had made Teresa an extension of herself, enjoying through her not only the sumptuous wardrobe, but the position Teresa was beginning to gain in the eyes of Mr. Bell's fellow financiers at his luncheons.

Her relationship with Teresa was a murky area, one that she would explore more thoroughly sometime. She was not certain she liked it; her own personality was too strong. In the meantime, she must consider the next step in the conquest of the reluctant Mr. Bell. She had already thought it out, so she had only to satisfy herself about its timing. Yes, it was time that Mrs. Percy and Thomas Bell had a child to cement the impression that they were lovers. Several of her protégées had been successfully married this way before, but things would be slightly different this time. The thought of Thomas Bell sleeping with Teresa pierced her heart with jealousy. She did not mind about the other girls he had, but Teresa could be a force to be reckoned with if his affection inclined toward her. She would have to alter her previously successful paternity scenario in his case, so Teresa would not be the actual mother of a child that was his. God knew, he slept with several different young women a week, and it would not be difficult to slip one in who was already pregnant, without his knowing that she, Mary Ellen, had anything to do with the encounter.

Thomas loved children, she reflected sentimentally. It was really a wonder he hadn't married for that reason alone. Giving him a child now would be killing two birds with one stone again. She could give him the child he thought was his own, while advertising to all of San Francisco that he was intimate with Mrs. Percy. Teresa would care for the baby, of course; there would be no problem there. He had laughed off the gossip that he and Teresa were lovers—he did not care much about public opinion—but once a child was involved, some of the barriers would crumble for the sake of the infant, she was convinced of it.

She hummed a Creole lullaby as she buffed her nails, feeling complete contentment. Nothing satisfied her more than taking care of more than one thing at a time in the advancement of her plan. She had one more task to attend to this evening, though. The gentlemen who attended the fake "voodoo ceremony" she had staged at Geneva Cottage were just about ripe for picking, now. The ceremony alone, which appealed to their jaded appetites, would have been enough to hold over them for small contributions to her "charities." But Melba's death had been a bonus, upping the price she had intended to ask—they were all so grateful to her for keeping the police out of the matter. She was becoming quite expert at that. Now they could show the depth of their gratitude, and most of them would not even recognize it as blackmail.

96

Aware of her many little charities, they would be happy to contribute after all she had done for them. The curse she had uttered at Melba's funeral was just to appease her black followers.

She sat down at her writing desk and extracted several sheets of buff-colored stationery and some envelopes from the drawer. The first name she wrote was that of Mr. Harvey Benvue, and she penned it with a flourish. He would know what was happening at least, and the amount of his contribution would reveal how much he was under her power for Melba's murder. As she wrote the ladylike note asking him to contribute, she was aware that he was a different breed than the other men, though he was just as wealthy. Ruthless in business, he had already revealed his violence, but her insight into his personality did not bother her particularly. She had dealt with worse in the past twenty years without having to use the tiny pistol in her purse, which was close to her at all times.

She stacked the ten identical envelopes neatly and began to apply the stamps, estimating that this mailing alone might bring in as much as ten thousand dollars, the down payment on her design to capture Thomas Bell for herself.

If he was disconcerted when Emma Anderson joined them at their next monthly dinner in an apartment she kept in the boardinghouse for such purposes, he hid it well and turned his attention to entertaining the pretty girl, instead of dwelling on financial matters. He always was a fool for a pretty face, Mammy reflected, as she poured him another glass of her potent cowslip wine. Emma Anderson isn't really that pretty, she decided with a tinge of jealousy. She's just blonde and wholesome-looking, six weeks pregnant, and more than a little awed by the circumstances in which she finds herself. Mary Ellen had never used her own apartment for anything like this, but these rooms were elegant enough to entertain Thomas or an occasional lover like Ben. Her suite was sacrosanct.

"Miss Anderson's been alone so much, lately," she told Thomas smoothly while they were dining. "I hope you don't mind her joining us. I know there are business matters that need our attention, but I thought we could go over them later."

"Mind?" he smiled, his blue eyes already sparkling with the wine. "I consider it a great privilege to have such a charming young woman dine with us."

The drug was taking hold of his mind, she thought ironically. Emma had shown no more charm than the well-upholstered bed in the next room which she was not going to share with him. That sacrifice she would not make. The other pregnant protégées destined for marriage to certain high-placed gentlemen had done their sleeping at the homes of those gentlemen, but Thomas was too careful to allow a woman to spend the night at his house on Stockton. Everything considered, Thomas was a difficult man to conquer, a formidable challenge equal to her wit. But Thomas knew hardly anything about her, so she had the advantage to a degree.

He did not know about her house for unwed mothers, for instance, which she never visited in daylight and which was not associated with her name. Several protégées had come from there, pretty enough to turn a man's head and early enough in their pregnancy to convince any man he had fathered their child in one intimacy with him. In such cases, Mary Ellen had only been openly involved in seeing that the men married the girls or paid vast sums for the care of the child, only a fraction of which went for their actual care, though both mother and child lived decently enough and were grateful for what Mammy did not withhold. If a pregnant girl married well, however, she was an unending source of revenue, contributing grandly to Mary Ellen's "charities" out of fear of losing her high position if Mammy revealed what she knew. The beauty of all these arrangements was that Mammy's involvement either was not known or, in the event of marriage, only came out on the side of righteousness.

When she began to consider a child for Thomas Bell, she went immediately to her house for unwed mothers one night and studied the cards on file for the current inhabitants, which never numbered more than four or five. The girls gave all information gladly in the hope of finding a hospice, without even wondering why the physical characteristics of their child's father were required, but not his name. Emma, fair and of Swedish descent, had been the only choice; the father of her child was equally Nordic in appearance, with blue eyes and blond hair. Thomas was shrewd enough not to accept a dark-eyed, black-haired child as his own, even if the mother had light coloring. Mary Ellen had been slightly disappointed when the girl was sent to her the next day. She was anything but an overwhelming beauty, though her skin and bosom were good. But within two days' time, as the business meeting approached, she had worked one of her miracles, she congratulated herself. Emma looked almost pretty tonight, if a little uncertain, not knowing what might be expected of her. But, then, she would never know. Having already agreed to give up the child when it was born, she would not connect its adoption to anything that occurred this evening.

"We mush' do something 'bout the shliv—silver stock," Thomas said in a slurred voice, valiantly holding out until the end. "Shee what you can find out, Mammy . . . tha's a good lass."

"I think you've had enough to drink, Thomas," Mary Ellen smiled indulgently, as he proffered his glass again. "This homemade wine is pretty potent, you know."

"Nonshence! I've had it before, my dear. I can dhrink any man under the . . . the table, an' then dhrink myshelf sober again! Fill it up, lassy."

A few minutes later she and Emma half carried and half dragged him into the bedroom and deposited him on the bed, and Mary Ellen observed his almost innocent, clean-shaven face with sadness. Curious, she thought, the way he lapsed into his Scottish accent under the effect of the drug.

"What do I do, now?" Emma asked uncertainly. "I don't have to sleep with him, do I, ma'am?"

"Of course not, my dear," Mary Ellen reassured her, putting an arm about her shoulders. "I would never countenance such a thing. Sleep with him, indeed! The room next door's all made up for you, and I'll have to sleep somewhere else, too, it appears. Men really think their capacity for drink is bottomless, don't they?"

"I guess so, ma'am," Emma said, unable to disguise her relief about sleeping alone, but not completely trusting her good fortune. "Is that really all I have to do for what you paid me?"

Mary Ellen accompanied her into her sitting room and closed the bedroom door behind them. "How would you like to have a place of your own to live in until the baby's born and adopted, Emma? I think it would be nicer for you than staying in that dreary house with the other girls, don't you?"

"Oh, yes! I don't really like it there, ma'am, though I'm grateful enough to have a roof over my head."

"Well, you shall have it, if you'll do one more small service for me. I'll awaken you early in the morning to return here. Mr. Bell will still be sleeping, and you'll get into bed with him, just until he awakes. At that point, I'll come in immediately."

The girl was reluctantly silent for a moment. "How will you know when he wakes up?" she asked.

"Trust me, my dear. I'll know. Nothing will happen to you, Emma, and you'll have your little house."

The girl sighed heavily. "Yes, ma'am," she agreed, unable to turn down the bait, too concerned with her own circumstances to question Mary Ellen's actions. "Anything you say."

"You won't be sorry, I promise you," Mary Ellen told her. "You'll go to your new house right after breakfast, Emma."

Disrobing the unconscious Thomas and slipping into bed beside him naked would have been almost necrophilic if his body were not so warm and smooth against her own. He had wanted her once, Mary Ellen thought as she caressed his shoulders stealthily, but she had always been proud, and the penniless, uncertain clerk her ship picked up in South America had not interested her then. The wealth and position she had helped him gain were only indirectly responsible for her attraction to him now; other influential men did not hold the same interest for her. Some men improved with age, beyond all imagining, and Thomas Bell was one of them. The pale, shy clerk had miraculously become a British gentleman over the years, relaxed and self-sufficient, impervious to her charms. And, though Mary Ellen was not introspective, she knew one thing about herself for certain; she wanted what she could not have, and she usually got it, too.

We're partners, darling, she whispered into his unhearing ears, we've been partners for years. You may not realize it, yet, but we're going to be partners for life, you stubborn little man. The web I'm weaving is already beginning to adhere to you, and before you know it, you'll be encased in a soft cocoon; you won't know how it happened. With your wealth and mine combined, we'll be powerful, and we'll enjoy our lives to the fullest, making up for all those years in between. Your only fault now is lack of imagination, Thomas, the inability to dream and make your dreams a reality. But it doesn't really matter. I have the capability of two people in that direction.

At the first sign of light, she rose carefully and dressed in her black dress and bonnet, returning to the bed to observe the sleeping man for a moment and brush a single dark hair from the indentation in the pillow beside him. She had a little difficulty waking Emma, but the girl accompanied her without protest and quickly fell back into a deep sleep beside Thomas. When the scene was set to Mary Ellen's satisfaction, she went to her own dressing room and closed the door, smiling to herself. Emma might well wonder how she would know when Thomas awakened, she thought. She found it incredible that so few people were conscious of being secretly watched. Teresa had been one of the few exceptions, when she was at the boardinghouse—Mary Ellen had to be careful with her. But others, including financiers discussing business after dinner, were so unaware of her observation that she had a sense of invisibility from her vantage point.

She walked into her dressing-room closet and pressed her hands against the far wall, which gave beneath her touch to reveal a narrow passageway. She did not have to walk more than a few feet to see into the bedroom where Thomas was sleeping from the small hole, which was worked so discreetly into the flowers of the wall hanging that it was difficult to observe it from the other side. This private passage was a secret, because Mary Ellen had shared knowledge of it with no one, and in all the years it had been here, not one servant had stumbled upon it accidentally. This was hardly surprising. There were only two entries to it: the one in her dressing room and another hidden deep in the basement, permitting her to come and go as she pleased. More often, she used the passage to observe and listen at any room on the dining-room side of the building, and her eavesdropping had made her a fortune from inside tips on the stock market, which baffled Thomas Bell and his friends, who did not know that they, too, were under observation when they dined here.

The passage was dark and stuffy, but Mary Ellen was too intent on watching the bed to notice. As the room grew lighter, Thomas stirred and groaned, and she smiled. He would have quite a headache from her homemade wine, and he would be slightly befuddled, which was to her advantage. When he raised himself on one elbow with his attention directed toward his bed companion, she moved quickly and silently to enter the rooms from the hallway. Smoothing her skirt, she opened the bedroom door as if she expected no one to be there, and stood gaping with surprise in her bonnet.

"Thomas Bell!" she exclaimed with outrage, her raised voice breaking the heavy sleep of Emma, who rubbed her eyes as she sat up in bed. "How dare you! With one of my protégées in my own bed! When I was called away after dinner, I didn't expect anything like this!"

Thomas shook his head groggily, protesting incoherently, "I don't remember a thing. Can't imagine what happened. . . ."

"That's pretty obvious!" Mary Ellen said sharply, assisting Emma out of bed and putting a dressing gown around her. "You poor child," she commiserated, "go to your room, now. I'll see you shortly." And, as Emma left the room, "Thomas! I'm really ashamed of you. You're a real old goat, after all the pretty girls."

"I'm sorry," he said, blinking his bright blue eyes and holding the sheet over his chest. "Damn it, Mammy! I must have got drunk on your wine. . . ."

"You were halfway there when I left," she sighed hopelessly. "I don't know what to do about that girl. She should have known better, at least. I don't know how I can marry her to anyone now."

"I've never been under the impression," he said wryly, recovering some of his wit, "that your blessed protégées were virgins, anyway."

"Who knows?" she said wearily, shaking her head, "some are and some aren't. I suppose no real harm has been done." Then, with an understanding smile, she said, "You *are* the limit! I suppose you're hungry. I'll bring you some breakfast."

"Just coffee," he said, searching her face helplessly. "I have a god-awful headache. I'm sorry, Mammy, really I am. It's damned good of you to be so understanding. I'm surprised you don't have me tossed out. I'm not a man who expresses himself well, you know, but . . . you really are my best friend. We go back a long way, don't we?"

"A long way," she said with a smile, "a long way, Thomas. And, God willing, we aren't even halfway there yet, if I can manage to put up with you."

Teresa's state of mind had not improved in the six months following Hoey's death, and Mary Ellen recognized that she had grown thoughtful, a state of mind that could not be allowed. Thoughtfulness in an intelligent person made Mary Ellen feel threatened, and she needed Teresa too much to lose her support now. The young woman had stayed closeted in her house until now, and that had fit in with Mary Ellen's plans. She had coddled her and tried to cheer her on her weekly visits, but the time was coming when Teresa must either remain in her house for several months or dress in a way appropriate to a pregnant woman if she did go out. On her next visit, in one of her more dramatic attempts to kill two birds with one stone, Mary Ellen arrived with a large box from the furrier.

"You're looking really peaked, dear," she told Teresa when she found her moping in the parlor. "You just can't go on like this. I never worry about anything I can't do something about, and you should look at things the same way. Besides, there's nothing to worry about anyway."

"Maggie didn't think so," Teresa said listlessly. "She was afraid to live in the same house as a murderer, wasn't she? I was never really fond of her, but her leaving was like a slap in the face."

"Nonsense! She just wanted to work back at the boardinghouse with her friends," Mary Ellen explained calmly, stroking Teresa's hair and observing it suddenly with interest. "You're letting yourself go, Teresa. Your hair needs touching up. I just can't allow you to do this to yourself. You like Byna, don't you? She's a pleasant little thing."

"I've always liked Byna," Teresa said. "Actually, I'm glad she's here. She's better company than Maggie ever was. I'll do my hair tonight, Mammy. I'm sorry, I just can't seem to concentrate since . . ."

"It's in the past; forget it," Mary Ellen said, lifting the large box and putting it across her knees. "I've brought you a little present, dear. If this doesn't perk you up, I guess nothing will."

Teresa was fond of surprises, and if her hands did not move quite as quickly as they used to in removing the ties on the box, there was excitement in her fingers. She gasped at the sight of the sealskin cloak and stood up at once to put it over her shoulders, running her palms over the soft fur. "Oh, Mammy, you shouldn't have!" she whispered. "I've never seen anything so beautiful. You're such a dear. I want to see it in the full-length mirror."

Mary Ellen followed her into her bedroom and lifted her blond curls over the dark fur to show the cape to advantage. "I didn't want you to be cold this winter," she smiled. "This will keep all the rain and fog away. Sealskin repels moisture like a duck's back, so you'll be cozy when you go shopping."

Teresa turned suddenly and kissed her on the cheek. "Thank you, Mary Ellen. You're so good to me."

"You must promise you'll go out, so you can wear it," Mary Ellen said. "There isn't another lady in the city with a fur like this."

"I promise," Teresa smiled. "Why, I'll go out just to wear it!"

"Good. Do you embroider, Teresa?"

"No, Mammy. I'm afraid all I ever learned was how to mend. I'd like to learn embroidery, though. I can't seem to get into my books lately."

"I'll teach you. If there's one thing I learned well in the convent, it was embroidery. We used to make all or own underthings out of white lawn, and I've never seen anything like them since. You could start on your trousseau."

"My trousseau?" Teresa said with astonishment. "Do you really think I'll need one? I haven't thought about Mr. Bell in the last few months, I'm afraid, Mammy. Do you honestly think he'll ever propose to me?"

"Stranger things have happened. I'd work on a trousseau, if I were you, my dear. Sometimes, a girl needs it most unexpectedly. You go to

103

the lace shop tomorrow and buy everything you need. You have an account there, you know."

"You do think of everything," Teresa said, laying the cloak across her bed and running her hand across it again. "I don't know how to thank you. I can never thank you for all you've done for me."

"Why don't you do it with a cup of coffee? That's one thing Byna makes well, and it's chilly outside. My hands are like ice."

When they were settled by the fire in the parlor with the coffee tray, Teresa rewarded her with one of her radiant smiles. "This is fun, isn't it? I guess I have been too gloomy lately. I promise not to dwell on it anymore. Tell me about the convent school, Mammy. I should love to have gone to such a school. Tell me about New Orleans."

"New Orleans?" Mary Ellen asked lightly. "I really wasn't there very long. Just a few years. It's a lovely city on the Mississippi Delta, almost underwater, really. All the tombs are aboveground, in St. Louis, because of the water. And the wealthy people have courtyards in their houses, with intricate wrought-iron gates."

"Is there Spanish moss on the trees? I read a book that mentioned it."

"Oh, yes. It flows from the trees like lace. I always found it rather gloomy, except when it was in bloom. Once a year it has tiny yellow flowers, did you know that?"

"Really?" Teresa said widening her blue eyes. "I didn't know that. There's so much I don't know, Mammy. Reading about things isn't the same as seeing them. I suppose you speak French much better than I. They do speak French there, don't they?"

"Some of them," Mary Ellen laughed at her naiveté. "I had a little at school, and I can read any menu that's put before me, but I think you've studied it more."

"Oh," Teresa said with disappointment. "I was hoping you could help me with a word I can't find in the dictionary."

"If it isn't in the dictionary, I might know it," Mammy smiled. "It also might be very rude."

"I don't think so," Teresa said with her enigmatic smile, her long dark lashes veiling her eyes. "It sounded more like an . . . amulet, a charm. *Gris-gris*. I'm not even certain of the spelling, and I couldn't find it anywhere."

Mary Ellen's shock was well concealed, but she wondered if her pause was too long, perceptible. "I can't imagine what it means," she said evenly. "I told you my French isn't much. Where did you hear it, anyway?"

Teresa thought for a moment with a tiny frown between her eyes. "I don't know," she said at last, "I must have heard it somewhere. Perhaps, I read it," she said with relief, but shook her head. "No, I couldn't have, or I'd know how to spell it. It doesn't really matter." She shrugged amiably without taking her gaze from Mary Ellen's face. "What's one word more or less? There's so much I don't know."

Mary Ellen's face was frozen like a mask, and she met the blue-eyed gaze with attempted amusement. "There's a lot none of us knows, Teresa. I'm proud of how much you've learned in such a short time. Next week, we'll see if you can learn embroidery as well."

Clever girl, she thought as she sipped her coffee, perhaps too clever by far, but not too clever for me. One does not hear a word like that by chance, and I can assure you that you'll never hear another like it.

Chapter 9

When she bound the bright yellow *tignon* around her head in the dimly lit dressing room in the boarded-up laundry she owned, her blood began to pound even before the sound of the drums was heard. This was the *véritable Vaudaux*, not the silly show she had put on for the white men, and she was its queen, with power of life and death over every slave she had brought to San Francisco. Whether she believed or not did not matter on a night like this, for it was not the ceremony but the feeling of power that made the pulses beat in her neck. As she secured the heavily decorated belt around the narrow waist of her simple, clinging, bright blue dress and looped the red cord of her station over her shoulder, she sensed the silent padding of bare feet into the great, empty hall outside the dressing room, and closing her eyes she began to think in French, rehearsing one of the chants.

> *Héron mandé, héron mandé,*
> *Tigul li papà.*

The gourd drums began to beat under the hands of Billy Beaumont and John Willis on the open laundry floor. She picked up the sacred box with hanging bells that contained the Great Snake and a dark bag. It fluttered at her side as she approached the altar with its red candles, bowls of Obi charms, herbs, and small cakes. With ritual ceremony, she placed the sacred box on the altar, and the drums ceased abruptly as she turned to face the worshippers, almost invisible to her in the darkness. With the moving bag dangling from one hand, she raised the

other hand before her, standing perfectly still, conscious of her imposing presence and the nakedness of her splendid body beneath her
dress. After saying the opening prayer in French and Congolese, she
fell silent a moment, staring into the darkness where the candlelight
picked out the red scarves around the heads of the men and the yellow
dresses of the women and some eyes that had widened in suspense over
the burden hanging from her hand. She silently allowed the fear to rise
until she could almost smell it before issuing her proclamation.

"We have been endangered by one among us," she said melodiously,
powerfully. "The *loa*, the great spirit, on the altar rattles his tail with
displeasure, demands the reinforcement of the blood oath which, until
now, none of you has taken here. Once the oath is taken, it will be
enforced. Anyone who opens his lips about the Voodoo will by seized
by *mauvais sang* and the bad blood will rise in his throat and strangle
him."

She enjoyed the power to evoke a calculated response from so many
people and waited until the murmur died down to raise the fluttering
bag high, bringing moans from the darkness. She began a rhythmic
chant in French as she reached in to grasp the white chicken by the feet
and waved it over her head as she drew the knife from her belt.
Holding it over an empty bowl, she decapitated it with one slash. The
body continued to flutter as the blood poured out of it. Continuing to
chant until the body was still, she grew silent as she raised the bowl in
both hands, proffering it to the congregation.

"So shall the bad blood rise and pour from any who speak again.
Venez!"

They approached cautiously, with round white eyes, and she took
note of every face, assuring them that she would remember as each of
them smeared his lips with the blood from the bowl. They were completely under her control, and she rejoiced in such power. She could
have ordered them to do worse than this. Voodoo was not without its
revolting aspects, and she knew them all, but this would suffice. They
were no longer slaves, direct from Africa or Haiti, though the old
religion still held them. In their new free and civilized state, the blood
alone was a penance. When all had participated, she smeared her own
lips and emptied the last drops on the altar before raising the sacred
box with its ringing bells for the next part of the ceremony.

Standing on the box, only a few inches from the dry, rattling death
within, she listened to the supplications of each person in turn. She
found this part of the ritual wearisome, though she was able to bring

about the desired results for most of the supplicants. Malvina loved a man she could not attract; the queen would make her a charm (and a financial arrangement with the desired lover). Billy wanted more responsibility and pay in his job; the queen could take care of that, too. The requests were concerned with fear or jealousy or petty malice; the queen could grant or withhold anything according to her caprice. What Billy Beaumont would really like, she thought with amusement, was to be king, but she knew that would never happen.

The time finally arrived to give them some enjoyment, and raising the sacred box with some relief, she jingled its bells to start the *calinda*, crying,

> *Eh! eh! Bomba, hone! Hone!*
> *Canga bafio tay,*
> *Canga do keelah.*

The drums began to beat rapidly, the bodies moved in a frenzied dance of nervous twitching and writhing, and there were cries of "Aie! Aie!" and "Voodoo magnan!" from the darkness. She joined the dancers swooning and raving around her, the *véritable* queen orchestrating the hysteria but mating with none of them as they fell together in couples on the laundry floor. She would deal with her own sexual excitement later, in her pale rose French Provincial room with her surrogate lover, Ben Willard.

"I'll never be the gentle lady you are," Teresa said with despair as Mary Ellen assisted her with her embroidery. "A real lady would learn faster than I, and she wouldn't begrudge all the hours spent over her embroidery frame. She'd be calm and peaceful inside, the way you are, Mammy. To be perfectly truthful, I'd rather read a book."

"You have time for both." Mary Ellen smiled patiently. "French knots take a little practice, Teresa, but you'll learn, my dear. This white lawn you bought is very fine. I hope you enjoyed your outing?"

"Yes. I love beautiful fabrics. I didn't go the lace shop, Mammy. I went to a fabric store where I once tried to get work. The proprietor didn't recognize me, and I gave him a terrible time." She smiled secretly. "You should have seen him, bowing and scraping and climbing his wooden ladder to get the bolt on the top shelf. That's another reason I'll never be a real lady," she sighed. "Sometimes I'm mean. You don't have a mean bone in your body, Mary Ellen."

"I hope you wore your fur cloak, so you won't catch cold," Mary Ellen said, completing the knot and reversing the needle as expertly as a little girl in a convent school.

"Of course!" Teresa smiled brightly. "Why, I'll never go anywhere without it, after yesterday. Fur seems to bring out the groveling instinct in mean-minded shopkeepers, and it has a curious effect on the wearer, too."

"Dear me, what sort of effect?"

"I felt like a sleek and splendid animal, as if it were my own skin," Teresa teased, and then grew more serious. "Not really, Mammy. I felt as if I were hiding behind someone else's skin, as though Teresa Percy was quite invisible."

"You've mentioned your invisibility before," Mary Ellen said with interest. "Why would a beautiful young woman like you desire not to be seen?"

"I don't know," Teresa pondered, "I really don't. I was very shy once, but I'm not like that anymore. Perhaps I don't like myself much, but I can't imagine the reason."

"Perhaps, you haven't been liked properly at some time in your life. You are very well liked now, my dear," Mary Ellen assured her. "You must never feel that way again."

Teresa concentrated on her embroidery, her aristocratic profile and long dark lashes turned to Mary Ellen. "I've never told anyone this," she said quietly, "but sometimes I think there's something wrong with me. I don't know if you can understand. You're so strong, Mary Ellen. You don't really need anyone. But with me . . . well, it's as though there were a great void inside of me, which makes me unable to survive on my own. I imagine it sounds odd."

"Yes," Mary Ellen agreed, studying her seriously. It did not sound odd at all to her, and she was relieved that Teresa had finally given her a key to her personality. "I don't understand such feeling, especially in someone like you. But it really doesn't matter. I suspect many women feel just as you do, Teresa, and that's what makes them so attractive to men. If a woman's too independent, it frightens men. Men have a high opinion of themselves, and like someone to care for to justify their 'manliness.' "

"That's probably true," Teresa agreed. "Mr. Bell seems like that to me, but not in a derogatory way. I think he'd be very kind to the woman he married . . . if he ever decides to marry at all." She smiled. "I miss going to his luncheons a little. Isn't he giving them anymore?"

"He's spent a lot of time at his mercury mine down in San Jose. No, it isn't you, Teresa. There you go again! You don't seem to think that anyone could care for you. Mr. Bell will come around. He's having a little personal problem right now. I suspect he's too ashamed to face you."

"What sort of problem?" Teresa asked with interest. "He's been kind to me, and if there's anything I can do to help. . . ."

"We'll see," Mary Ellen said, putting her embroidery hoop aside and glancing at her lapel watch. "Dear me! Four o'clock already. I must get back to the boardinghouse or dinner will be a disaster. I'm so glad you like your cloak so much, Teresa," she said as she tied the ribbons of her bonnet. "We must keep you nice and warm."

"I feel guilty," Teresa said earnestly, her gaze sweeping the dark gabardine cape Mary Ellen had come in. "You're so good to me, and you care nothing for yourself. If anyone needs a fur, it's you, with all the running about that you do. You should pamper yourself a little, Mary Ellen."

"That's sweet of you," Mary Ellen said, bending to kiss her protégée's flawless cheek. "I've told you before, I'm a businesswoman, my dear. It wouldn't do for me to stalk around like some sleek, splendid animal."

She was selective about the groups of diners she listened to from behind the wall. When some minor notables in the financial world came to dine at the boardinghouse one evening, she was tempted to forgo any eavesdropping and retire to her bedroom after the meal was served. She was on her way up the stairs,when a familiar feeling began to nag at her, one she had learned to trust, though she was not ordinarily very intuitive. She did not know just what had alerted her to the fact that something was taking place—whether it was a word that had been spoken in her presence in the dining room, or a look that had passed between some of the men.

Locking the door of her drawing room behind her, she hastened to the closet in her dressing room and pressed the panel. The secret corridor was completely dark, but she knew it by heart, without having to extend her hands to touch the walls, and she did not slide the cover from a peephole until she reached the dining room. Her view from the middle of a gilt scroll in the center of the mirror's frame was excellent, as the men relaxed with cigars and brandy after dinner. She knew them

111

all by name, though none of them were connected with anyone as high as William Ralston, the founder of the Bank of California, or Thomas Bell, one of its trustees. One of them, however, Walter Meredith, was connected in a minor capacity with the Bonanza Kings, Fair and Sharon, and Mary Ellen decided he was the one to watch tonight. Quite apart from the fact that he had just consumed one of her marvelous meals, he looked like a cat with cream on its whiskers, and he had recently returned from Virginia City.

The diners appreciated the Napoleon brandy so much that they drank more than usual, under her scrutiny. She estimated that, along with the wine at dinner, they were at least half inebriated, and that was always to her advantage, though they said nothing very interesting until one of them rose for an extemporaneous toast.

"To the gold of Ophir!" he said, referring to an already spent mine in the Comstock. "We'll never see its like again."

The gregarious diners thumped the table and cried, "Hear! Hear!" All except Walter Meredith, she noted. She focused her attention completely on him as another man rose to toast the "lost silver from the Gould and Curry mines," to which the financiers responded more morosely.

"It's like watching the end of an era," a muttonchopped gentleman next to Meredith sighed. "What a miracle the old Comstock was! But everything's petering out now, and we're left with railroads, which aren't nearly as exciting as a gold or silver boom."

The room fell silent as they remembered the glorious and not too distant past. Meredith was bursting to say something, but he clipped the end of a cigar instead and worked it nervously in his mouth, removing it only to sip his brandy.

"Well," his companion considered, "they were good times, and good friends were made. They were times for younger men than we are now. I wonder how often we've helped each other over the bad times? It'll never be like that again, but at least we have each other."

Meredith was nearly twitching in his chair. Finally, unable to restrain himself, he said in a low voice, "It may be like that again," capturing everyone's attention. "Don't let it get beyond this room, do you understand?" He was given effusive assurances, and, relishing the attention, he drew his revelation out as long as possible. "I've only heard rumors, you understand. But, perhaps not too far in the future, Con Virginia will be the one to watch."

The Consolidated Virginia Mining Company, owned by Fair and

MacKay, had been valueless for years, but Mary Ellen considered the statement and took it seriously. If two of the Bonanza Kings were up to something for themselves, they would keep it quiet as long as possible while they bought up shares. They might be mining silver again right now, stockpiling the ore before making an announcement. And that would involve the bank, Thomas's bank, where all their money was invested. It could cause a crash that would close many banks.

"Con Virginia?" one of the men said incredulously. "Mackay and Fair have been trying to get more ore out of it for years. You have to be joking, Meredith."

Meredith shook his head importantly. "Hang on to your Con Virginia stock, and remember all the shares old Sharon's kept! Have you ever heard of a vertical shaft?"

He would say no more; perhaps he had said it all. Has the shaft been sunk, Mary Ellen wondered, or is it just being considered? She must speak with Thomas and, perhaps, take a little trip to Virginia City. James Fair had dined at her boardinghouse, and he was a gracious man. He would be happy to see her, perhaps give her a tour of his mine.

"Is that all I have to look for?" she asked Thomas Bell in his office at the bank the next morning. "It sounds like something anyone would notice, particularly mining men."

"They'd notice if they had access to the property," Thomas said, "but Mackay's always been a tricky bugger." He studied the drawing he had made for her on his desk. "I think Sharon must be involved, too. You should go. We'd better keep on top of this, Mammy. If you hear anything more—anything, whether it makes sense to you or not—keep me informed."

"I always do," she said, studying his face with affection, marveling at the way he accepted her advice and turned things around so it would look as though the ideas came from him. "How much do we have invested in the Bank of California right now?"

He had to unlock a drawer of the desk and take out a small battered ledger, while she had the answer, within a few hundred thousand, in her head. "Eleven million, before returns this month," he said. "Interest-wise, it was a good idea to combine our assets."

"That's a powerful amount of money," she said thoughtfully, wishing it were all hers. "What would happen if we protected it, and there were still a crash?"

"There'd be a recession. Our money wouldn't be worth as much. But we can't cover everyone's tail. We'll keep what's happening to ourselves."

"And buy up Con Virginia if I find the shaft?"

"No, we don't want to tip our hand."

"Well, maybe some other people will buy it. Mrs. Percy, for instance. Someone should profit from all this."

"Mrs. Percy?" he chuckled. "I'm sure that if that lovely, innocent lady bought a lot of stock, she would only be considered daft. How is the lady, by the way?"

"Fine. She manages to keep busy all the time. If it isn't her house, it's sewing or becoming wildly enthusiastic about a new book."

"A charming woman."

"Mm," Mary Ellen grunted her agreement. "Oh, speaking of women, Thomas. I suppose you remember Emma? I hate to be the bearer of bad tidings, my dear, but she's four months pregnant. I suppose you'll make some arrangement, such as marrying the girl?"

He stared at her aghast and, when he finally recovered, said faintly, "I don't even know if it's mine."

"It must be, Thomas, since she didn't sleep with anyone else. Oh, I'll take care of it for you! I'm surprised it hasn't happened with one of them before now. I can't really see you married to Emma, though she's a nice enough girl."

"You're sure it's mine?" he asked, his blue eyes gazing intently into her face. "No mistake?"

"No mistake. How do you want me to handle it?"

"I don't know," he sighed. "Put the girl up someplace until the child comes, of course. I'll write you a check." He took his checkbook out of a pigeonhole in his desk and paused a moment before filling in the amount. "I'm sure if you think about it, we can make some arrangement later."

Mary Ellen put the check into her reticule without looking at it, knowing it would be generous. "I suppose congratulations aren't really in order?" she said, smiling, and he groaned aloud. "It's all right, Thomas. Perhaps what you need is someone of your own to care for. You might enjoy having a son."

"Nonsense," he said gruffly. "If I'd wanted that sort of thing, I'd have married. I'm too old to think about it now. Mary Ellen," he said softly, taking her hand, "I do appreciate all you've done for me. I don't know what I'd do without you."

"We're partners, Thomas," she assured him gently. "What sort of friend would I be if I abandoned you when you needed me? Now, don't worry about a thing, dear. But I think you should consider what I've said. Even if you just think of it in a business light, you'll find it makes sense. What's the use of working so hard to amass a fortune if you've no blood relative to leave it to?" She patted him on the shoulder as she prepared to depart. "I'll take care of things before I leave for Virginia City. Take good care of yourself while I'm gone."

"You'll be back in time for the governor's inauguration, won't you? You haven't forgotten about that?"

"That isn't likely," she laughed, "since Newton Booth's having his inaugural dinner at my boardinghouse. I'm going to put on a feast that no one will forget!"

The celebration of the inauguration, carefully orchestrated and pre-sided over by Mary Ellen, brought some of the prestige that Mary Ellen had sought for so long. Though she arrived back from Virginia City just the day before, she had the servants clean and polish everything on the ground floor, while she planned the menu in her room in prepara-tion for the sideboard meal that would be served. Her new gown was laid out on her bed. For one night, she would give in to her impulse for luxury, and though she could not wear her diamonds, her black jet necklace and earrings would go well with the maroon velvet gown.

This evening was a welcome reward for all her years of planning, and she did not attribute it to mere luck. When Newton Booth was still a senator, he had maintained a room in her boardinghouse for his frequent visits to San Francisco. Her ability to help him in a domestic matter had given her the idea of providing Thomas Bell with a child to draw him closer to her. Emily Putnam, one of her protégées, a genuine young widow whom Mammy had saved from distress, became the senator's mistress and gave him a child. Though Booth was inordi-nately fond of Emily, he could not bring himself to marry her; because she had attended some of the dinners at Geneva Cottage, he feared her reputation would not hold up to the scrutiny a politician's wife must face. As always, Mary Ellen was up to the challenge, was on the spot to give assistance, and she had bound Booth to her as closely as many other men by housing his mistress and looking after Emily and the child. His choice of her boardinghouse for his celebration was not a happy accident, she considered with satisfaction. If you want some-thing, you must go after it, using as many connections as possible along

115

the way. That Booth had been elected governor was the only surprise to her, the bonus she would savor tonight as she entertained Mr. Ralston of the Bank of California and William Sharon, one of the Bonanza Kings, under her roof at the same time.

Of course, Thomas would be here too, she reflected, drifting over to her vanity and staring into the glass. He had never really seen her in her secret finery, and she tried to anticipate his reaction. She was forty-five years old, but she still looked thirty. Another bonus, she thought ironically, the only one of my heredity. The strong, youthful bone structure inherited from her mother would never change. She recalled as well that Marie Laveau, New Orleans's notorious voodoo queen, had appeared youthful well into her fifties. Of course, she had more black blood than I, Mary Ellen considered, but the good bone structure is there, even if I am only an octoroon. Without doubt, I'll be the handsomest woman at the party, though I'll be dressing only for Thomas.

She was relieved that Teresa would not be here. Under ordinary conditions, this would have been a perfect showcase for her blonde beauty, an invaluable opportunity to tie Mrs. Percy's name with that of Thomas. But, fortunately for herself, if detrimental to her immediate plan, Mrs. Percy would not be attending tonight. Teresa was being kept under wraps to give the illusion that she was pregnant, for future entrapment of poor, dear Thomas. Mary Ellen would bring her to the boardinghouse this evening so she could enjoy the fireworks and the band from upstairs.

She spent the better part of the afternoon in the kitchen, preparing the dishes suitable for a sideboard that she knew her gentlemen liked most, while her black servants heaped generous servings of her relishes and sauces into silver dishes and arranged the flowers under her careful supervision.

When everything was ready, she surveyed the sideboard and assured herself that there had never been one more lavish: oyster gumbo replete with shallots, garlic, and thyme, which the gentlemen persisted in calling "chowder"; a *daube glacé* the like of which none of them had ever seen before, consisting of beef round cooked slowly in its herbed gravy and moulded in gelatin with green parsley and a few brilliant carrots; caramel sweet potatoes, glazed to perfection; and white potatoes beaten until they were fluffy and stuffed into their shells with slivered pecans. For dessert, she had created what she considered a masterpiece: a mountain of small puff pastries filled with *crème patissière* with sherry and a light caramel sauce trickling down the pyramid. The service set off the food to perfection, from the silver epergne of bright fresh fruit to the heavy candlesticks at either end of the groaning buffet. The sight of the candlesticks made something click in her mischievous mind. With deep satisfaction she placed the statue of the dancing maidens between the polished silver candelabra, just behind the floral centerpiece, so that the half-draped figures appeared to be dancing among the flowers. Once again, she had furthered her schemes by killing two birds with one stone, and she felt almost gleeful over her cleverness. The statue would almost go unnoticed by most of the party, but a few gentlemen would observe it with a sinking sensation, connecting it with Geneva Cottage and the night Melba was murdered. They had been contributing regularly and generously to her "charities," but there was no harm in reminding them of what they still owed her.

The first cloud shadowed her triumphant evening when she went to Teresa's room after dressing. She was relieved that Teresa would not be allowed downstairs, for she had never seen the young woman looking more radiantly beautiful and excited. Clothed in a simple oyster-colored satin gown that set off the soft tone of her skin to advantage, her golden hair tumbling in curls over her shoulders, she reminded Mary Ellen of a watercolor she had once seen of Marie Antoinette. All the good breeding was there, the fine aquiline nose and smooth, poreless skin. It was enhanced by Teresa's pansy-blue eyes that, usually so serious, were dancing with excitement and were quite irresistible beneath her long dark lashes. Before Mary Ellen could compliment her on her appearance, Teresa flew across the room to admire her.

"Mammy, you look marvelous!" she exclaimed. "Oh, I'm so happy you've finally dressed up! Why, you're as regal as a queen in that shade of velvet. You must be very proud tonight. I had no idea you knew a senator, let alone the new *governor*."

"I've known Newton a long time," Mary Ellen said, observing the sealskin cloak draped over a chair. "You look very nice yourself. I hope you understand why you can't join the group downstairs, Teresa. It wouldn't do to have you the only unmarried young woman there."

"I wouldn't be comfortable with them anyway. I'll be quite happy here, observing their arrival from the window. Thank you so much for inviting me, Mammy. I've never been so close to something like this before."

117

Not only would she fit in very well with the party, Mary Ellen realized grudgingly, she would overcome every man present, probably including the governor himself. How could any young woman be so intelligent and so stupid at the same time? The only problem she might ever have with Teresa was if she suddenly recognized her potential. "I must go now," she said. "I'll see that a tray's sent up for you."

"Thank you. I suppose Mr. Bell will be here?" Teresa asked wistfully. "I'd like to see him again. He's such a friendly, gentle man."

"He'll be too busy," Mary Ellen said quickly, surprised at the stab of jealousy she experienced. "He's coming with Mr. Ralston, and he won't even know you're here."

The guests were beginning to arrive when she descended the staircase, conscious of the drag of her velvet train on the thick carpet runner, but her visit with Teresa had distracted her momentarily from her triumph. She might have to alter her plan, she considered, as she smiled and nodded at a group of gentlemen in tuxedoes. She had not bargained on Teresa's caring for Thomas or the eventuality that he might respond, any more than she had prepared herself for the pain the thought might give her. She could not keep them apart altogether and still further her goal, but barriers could be thrown up between them quietly and insidiously that might stay in place even when they were alone.

"Mammy!" a tall, florid, and triumphant man cried out as he entered, rushing to her side to kiss her on the cheek. "I bet you didn't dream of tonight ten years ago, when we first met, dear lady. You've really outdone yourself tonight, and you look absolutely marvelous too!"

"Congratulations, Newton," she said wholeheartedly. "No, I didn't think you'd ever bring us so much glory. We're very proud of you."

"We? Do you mean that. . . ." He glanced toward the stairway hopefully without finishing the question and smiled broadly at her nod. "You really do think of everything, Mammy. Thank you."

He was almost immediately engulfed by his supporters, and Mary Ellen followed his progress through the crowd from the buffet, where she would eventually be able to greet everyone. There were not as many ladies present as she had anticipated, but it did not trouble her unduly, since most of her dinners were attended only by men. Standing in queenly grandeur, she surveyed the crowd in the hope of catching sight of Thomas, but if he was here, he was too short to be seen among the larger men.

"Ah, you've made your heavenly chowder!" William Ralston said from the far end of the sideboard, taking her by surprise. "You promised to give me your secret recipe one day, Mammy, and I'm holding you to it."

"It might be wine," she smiled at the banker, "and then again it might not. William," she lowered her voice conspiratorily, "I made it just for you."

Thomas was supposed to come with him, and she was faintly perturbed by his absence, but she could not ask about him or reveal any particular interest in him. No one knew they were partners, and they were considered no more than casual friends, though she did business with him at the bank. She observed Ralston quietly as he ladled his soup from the silver tureen. He was Thomas's friend, but he was handling the bank badly, overextending himself on his grandiose new project, the Palace Hotel. He would be hurt the most when the crash came, but Thomas had instructed her about keeping silent, even to Ralston.

"How is your fine hotel coming along?" she inquired at last. "From the plans in the newspaper, it will be the best in the country, if you ever get it built."

"Time, my dear lady," he cautioned. "An enterprise like this takes time. No one has conceived an eight-story hotel on this scale with a glass rotunda over the carriage entrance. Will you allow me a couple of years?"

"Perhaps," she said with a smile, "if you'll invite me to the opening."

"Consider it done," he said. "I couldn't by any chance lure you away from this place to supervise the dining room?"

She shook her head slowly, just as she caught sight of Thomas moving in their direction. "I only supervise what is mine," she said, vaguely wishing she could get her hands on the new hotel. "Good evening, Mr. Bell."

"Have the chowder, Thomas," Ralston advised, moving away with his buffet meal to join the governor in the dining room. But Thomas, after nodding agreement, worked his way to the roast beef and relishes next to Mary Ellen.

"How did it go?" he asked, selecting a lean piece without looking at her. "I thought you'd contact me when you returned."

"It's vertical," she said to his surprise, jolting the fork in his hand from the beef and making him look at her. "High-grade, too," she added, slipping a sample of the ore into his waistcoat pocket. "Everything's just as I told you."

His excitement was so great that he put down his plate and examined

119

the small sample surreptitiously by the light of the candelabrum. "The scoundrels," he whispered, concealing the rich sample in his pocket again. "The scoundrels. Well, we know what this means. I say," he exlaimed suddenly, staring at her, "you look very fine tonight. You should dress that way more often. You're still a good-looking woman, you know. Why aren't you wearing your diamonds? You'll never have a better occasion, Mammy."

"Perhaps, I will someday, Thomas," she said, disheartened by his lukewarm praise. "If not, I'll be buried in them."

His blue eyes twinked. "I believe you would," he considered with humor. "Once you acquired something, you'd never let it go, would you? You're a mystery, Mammy." He shook his head. "The most mysterious female I've ever known. A beautiful woman who conceals her charms beneath black alpaca and a scuttle bonnet, when you should advertise your wares. Aren't you interested in men at all?"

"I've never said that," she corrected him. "I may be more interested than you imagine. Someone's coming, Thomas, so let's be quick. I want all the Con Virginia you can buy, and you should buy, too, if there's any left on the market."

"We'd better discuss this in my office," he told her, moving away from the buffet. "I'm surprised that Mrs. Percy isn't here tonight. I was looking forward to renewing our acquaintance."

Teresa and Thomas might have been conspiring to ruin her evening, but she was determined to have her night of glory, listening to the band outside with the governor's friendly arm around her and, later, watching the fireworks, with the water wagons from the fire department standing by to prevent a fire. She did not see Thomas again during the evening; she would avoid Teresa until tomorrow and savor what she had worked so hard to attain. When the party finally broke up, she and Newton Booth ascended the stairs together so he could see his mistress and his child; indeed, he would probably spend the night in the room he maintained here, she thought. Well, she did not need anything more against him to ensure his contributions, and she was too excited to concentrate on business anyway.

When they reached the top of the stairs, Emily cried out from Teresa's room, "We're in here, darling! The view was better from Mrs. Percy's room."

Mary Ellen felt sick inside at the thought of Emily's spending so much time with Teresa without her knowledge. As Booth embraced Emily and their child in an affectionate hug, she stood in the door to assess how much damage the governor's friendly, candid mistress might have done. Teresa avoided meeting Mary Ellen's eyes for a few minutes, but the tension between them was so high that she finally turned from the window to face Mary Ellen with quiet dignity. Her serious blue eyes and compressed lips give her face a rebellious quality that troubled Mary Ellen.

Chapter 10

"First, one of your protégés is murdered, and now I've met one who's living as a man's mistress, after having their child," Teresa confronted her, when she called at her house the following afternoon. "Have any of them really *married*, Mammy? I liked Emily when I met her last night, but her life's practically ruined. It's been so long, and Mr. Bell's paying less attention to me than ever. He doesn't care for me even a little, and I want to know what you really have in mind for me."

"Teresa," Mary Ellen said, attempting to calm her, "what happened to Emily has nothing to do with your situation. I can't help what people do behind closed doors. I didn't know they'd become lovers until she confessed she was pregnant. As for the other girls, several have made good matches. You must understand why I hesitate to give their names. Once a marriage is accomplished, the young woman and her husband must be immune from gossip, and are no longer connected with me. You've nothing to worry about, my dear. Mr. Bell's very busy right now, and he has some personal problems as well. He has a good deal on his mind."

"Obviously, it isn't me," Teresa snapped petulantly. "Did you know that the reason Newton Booth can't marry Emily is because she attended some dinners at Geneva Cottage? I attended one, too. How do I know that my reputation isn't too questionable for Mr. Bell? You shouldn't have insisted that I go."

Mary Ellen smiled and folded her hands calmly in her lap. "Teresa," she pointed out ironically, "Mr. Bell was the *host*, if you recall. He asked me to bring you, when I told him about you. You left very early, and I'm certain your reputation isn't tarnished in his mind. I told you a long time ago that marrying him wouldn't be easy. He's too wrapped up in

123

his financial dealings and his mines to spend much time with anyone. He probably thinks he's too old to marry, too."

"Why Mr. Bell, then?" Teresa asked earnestly. "Why did you choose him, Mammy? There appear to be a lot of unattached, well-to-do gentlemen in this city."

The question took Mary Ellen by surprise. Apparently, Teresa had been giving serious thought to the situation, but Mary Ellen's quick wits permitted only a brief pause before she answered. "I think you're right for each other, Teresa. I've known Mr. Bell for a long time, and under my supervision you're perfect for him now."

"You puzzle me," Teresa responded thoughtfully. "You seem to think nothing of manipulating other people's lives. Some things are either meant to be or they aren't, Mary Ellen, and whom one marries seems to be one of them."

"I don't agree. People have married whom they wished only in fairly recent times, and it doesn't always work out as well as marriages that are arranged. You should know that. You haven't asked me about Melba. You mentioned her earlier. We might as well have everything out in the open."

"I liked her," Teresa said. "I spent just one evening with her, but I liked her very much. And, in that short time, I could see how much she disliked that man with the full lips and sensual eyes, even if you couldn't. I think you forced a situation that was potentially volatile, with disastrous results, Mary Ellen. Where was your insight into the compatibility of people in Melba's case? I wish I could have attended her funeral service."

"That isn't what happened," Mary Ellen said quickly, alarmed that Teresa remembered the man's face well enough to recognize him, though she did not appear to recall his name. She had to protect her contributors. "It was a different man altogether, and I didn't know him well. I'd already separated Melba from the gentleman she didn't like, and he wasn't there that night." She paused thoughtfully, contemplating how she might use Teresa's affection for Melba to her own advantage. "It was tragic. Such a pretty girl. I was very fond of her myself. I didn't think you knew about the incident, my dear, and I wouldn't upset you for the world. If I had known, you certainly could have attended the services. How did you hear about it, anyway?"

Teresa shrugged her shoulders. "I don't remember," she lied. "One of the servants weeping, I believe. I was terribly upset. She was so lively and sweet, and she was one of your protégées, too. The whole thing was covered up, Mary Ellen, and that troubled me as well."

124

"It's important that we talk about things," Mary Ellen sympathized. "If something troubles you, please discuss it with me, Teresa. It's very dangerous to draw your own conclusions, which may be erroneous. We suppressed it to protect some very important gentlemen who were there that night but had nothing to do with it. Reputations are important in a community of this size, as we've already mentioned. I have a wonderful idea. As soon as the weather clears, I want to take care of poor Melba's grave. I thought I'd plant some flowers. Since you missed her funeral, perhaps you'd like to help me. You don't have to," she added gently. "You must do what you think is right for you."

"I'd like that, Mammy," Teresa whispered with tears in her eyes. "She's been on my mind so much."

The spring of 1871 was a gentle one, and when the flowering almonds began to blush in the sandy cemetery, Mary Ellen loaded trays of forget-me-nots and lilies-of-the-valley, which she had started indoors, into the open phaeton. John Willis started to drive up Bush Street with his mistress and Teresa sitting solemnly behind him. When they reached the low crest of a sparsely populated hill, Mammy leaned forward suddenly.

"John Willis, stop here for a moment. I want to show Mrs. Percy something."

Teresa had been gazing toward the sand flats reaching to the ocean and the blank, watery horizon between the two points of land where the Bay met the sea, but she came out of her reverie when the carriage stopped. "Why are we stopping, Mammy? I thought we were going to Laurel Hill."

"We are. I don't think you've been out this way before, have you?" Mammy asked with a smile. "We're on Bush Street, the main route to the cemetery, but I want to show you something. Do you see that corner lot across the street? It doesn't look like much right now, but I'd like to build a house there."

"Right on the route to the cemetery?" Teresa jested, but she was impressed by the size of the property and the view from the hill. "Surely you don't need another house, Mammy. You must own half of San Francisco as it is, with all the papers I've signed. What sort of house do you have in mind?"

"Only the finest one in the city," Mary Ellen said, picturing it as though it were already there. "Not a great pile of stone like those of Crocker and Flood or that turreted monstrosity of Hopkins on Nob Hill, but something almost Louisiana-style on the outside, which would

125

underplay the richness of its interior. Would you like to live in a house like that?"

"I don't know." Teresa laughed shortly. "I'm content where I am. I don't know what Louisiana-style is, Mammy, but I do like the view toward the ocean. I've never seen such a large expanse of sand. One can hardly call it all a beach, especially with some houses in between, but it's clean and has a sort of lonely quality about it that I find curiously relaxing."

Mary Ellen motioned John Willis on, and as they descended the hill, she noted that another house had been constructed near her coveted property. If she did not buy the land soon, she might lose it, and the prospect was frustrating. She must figure some way to get it, regardless of her certain knowledge of the coming crash.

"Where's the Cliff House, Mammy?" Teresa interruped her thoughts. "I've read about it in the newspaper, but of course I haven't seen it. I tried to get John Willis to drive me there once, and he said it was too far away."

"It's near that point you saw extending into the Bay," Mary Ellen told her, "right on the edge of the ocean, and it's a long, sandy drive."

"Could we dine there sometime?" Teresa asked, her cheeks full of color from the outing. "I'd love to see it."

"Ladies don't dine there alone," Mammy said. "I wouldn't go there at all. There are rumors of some pretty wild parties there, Teresa, and you've expressed some concern about your reputation."

"Oh, dear! I didn't know." Teresa sighed. "I really don't know very much, do I, after all the time I've been here? I suppose it's because I haven't any friends to discuss things with."

"I'm your friend. And when it comes right down to it, dear, the less a lady knows about what goes on in this town, the better. It's still a bit shady and rough, though it's growing rather fast. When you have a man of your own, he'll be able to see that you only go to the right places. I think I'd better put a deposit on that property tomorrow."

Teresa gave her a bemused glance. "You weren't really listening to me, were you, Mammy? It doesn't matter," she added with resignation. "Is that the cemetery?"

Only the headstones and tombs in the rolling sand hills distinguished it from its surroundings, and Mary Ellen was forced to admit that Laurel Hill, from a short distance, was a rather sorry sight. The trees had already lost their blossoms, but their green leaves were not yet visible, and she felt a twinge of disappointment. The flowering trees were the best thing that could be said about the place. The carriage drew up to the metal arch, inscribed LAUREL HILL CEMETERY, and Mary Ellen began to hand the flats of plants down to John Willis. "You'll have to carry some, too," she told Teresa. "There's still a bag of loam and moss to come."

"Will anything grow here?" Teresa asked, delicately accepting one of the trays into her white-gloved hands. "There isn't much foliage. Who'll water them?"

"There's a caretaker, believe it or not," Mary Ellen replied ironically. "If he's let my graves go to wrack and ruin over the winter, I'll take care of him."

But when they reached her extensive plot, they saw that either the caretaker or the Northern California rain had provided a solid green carpet around the small marble headstones, and Mammy nodded with approval as she appraised the area. "Things do grow in sand if you bed them properly," she remarked, handing Teresa a trowel from her bag. "That's Melba's grave there, second from the end, my dear. You can plant a flat there. Which would you prefer, lilies-of-the-valley or forget-me-nots?"

"Forget-me-nots," Teresa said with sober blue eyes.

"That's nice," Mary Ellen said with approbation. "You take this flat, dear. I'm going to start at the other end."

She glanced over her shoulder under her dark bonnet as she moved away and observed with satisfaction that the trip had been worth the time. Teresa picked her way carefully through the grass to Melba's grave, but she stopped suddenly and nearly dropped the flat of plants when she saw the headstone of the last grave in the plot:

JAMES PERCY HOEY
1840–1871
REST IN PEACE

She was obviously shaken, but she straightened her shoulders and knelt down to work at Melba's grave with her back to that of her husband. Mary Ellen continued walking to the far end of her plot with an almost jaunty spring to her steps. There's no harm in a little reminder, she thought, especially when the time has come to further your plans. The way Teresa had carried on about Emily and her child, she was doubtful about her acceptance of Thomas Bell's infant, but what the young woman had seen today would take some of the starch out of her opposition. Whatever her feelings, she could not refuse.

127

In a spirit of sudden magnanimity, Mary Ellen decided to prolong the excursion after they had washed their hands in a bucket and brushed away any sand and soil that had stuck to their clothing.

"Since we're out this far, we might as well go on so you can see the Cliff House," she said, noting Teresa's pallor and thoughtfulness. "You do want to see it, don't you, dear?"

"Yes," Teresa said with abstraction, "that would be nice, Mammy."

They spoke very little as they rode on the narrow road through the endless dunes, but the fresh salt air from the ocean brought the color back to the young woman's cheeks, and she once again began to take notice of her surroundings. John Willis guided the horses to the right in full view of the crashing waves of the shoreline, and the horses labored up the hill toward the flat-roofed building identifying itself in large letters across the front. Teresa put her hand to the blowing ribbons of her bonnet and observed, "It really is far out, isn't it? And it isn't as grand as I imagined, Mammy."

"That's because you can't see the crystal and linen and silver service from the outside. Pull up over there, John Willis. Mrs. Percy and I are going to walk for a while."

She led Teresa down the wide concrete steps at the side of the restaurant to a platform overlooking the cliffs and the gray ocean, the view broken only by a small group of high rocks rising from the water a few hundred feet from where they stood. Teresa shivered and drew her pale blue gabardine cape around herself for warmth, remarking, "It's a fine view, Mammy, though I've never enjoyed the ocean much. It's so big and . . . boundless. I was rather frightened on the ship coming out here."

"I share that view," Mammy chuckled warmly. "The truth is, I've wanted to discuss something with you, my dear. I feel I should do it today. Mr. Bell's gotten himself into some difficulty; it was really he who asked me to come to you."

Teresa turned to her with interest. "You've mentioned he was having some kind of trouble several times over the past few months. What is it?"

"It's all been the same problem," Mammy sighed. "I don't know how you're going to take this, Teresa, though I'd consider it a compliment if he called on me for assistance. It shows he's been thinking of you." She paused long enough for the words to have their effect, though she appeared to be feigning reluctance to speak of the matter.

"I don't know how I can possibly help him," Teresa said eagerly, "but I'd be happy to do anything I can."

"I felt he could depend on you. It's a rather sordid little story, really. But just because a man's a bachelor, it doesn't mean he has to be celibate, does it? He had an . . . encounter . . . with a young woman last year, a very short one, you understand. She's had a child, and she was demanding that he marry her. Of course, he couldn't. She's a very common girl, not his sort of woman at all. Actually, she's a tart."

The expressions that crossed Teresa's lovely face ranged from surprise to disapproval and, finally, to loyalty to the man who had been kind to her and whom she hoped to marry. "Of course, he couldn't marry anyone like that," she agreed, "but what does he want from me?"

"A good home for his little boy," Mary Ellen said, almost entreatingly. "Mr. Bell loves children, and this is the only one he has. He wants to see him brought up properly, Teresa, and he thought of you. 'There isn't a finer lady in San Francisco,' he told me," she lied. " 'My son would be safe with Mrs. Percy.' Little Fred is only two months old."

"A baby," Teresa considered with a gentle smile. "Oh, Mammy, I'd love to have him! A child in the house is just what I need . . . lacking a husband," she added ironically. Then, humor welled in her eyes and touched one corner of her lips. "Perhaps, there's hope for Mr. Bell, yet," she said. "I'll confess, I'd begun to wonder if he was natural."

"He's that, all right," Mary Ellen replied drolly. "I'm glad you can be so broad-minded about it. He'll appreciate this and provide for all of little Fred's needs, of course. I'm sure he'll be generous toward his son." If she had realized Teresa would be so amenable to taking the child, she would not have taken her to the cemetery and this chilly, uncomfortable promontory. The young woman was still able to baffle her. "Mr. Bell will undoubtedly want to visit the child. I guess we have no objection to that, have we?"

"None at all," Teresa smiled. "I'd like to see him again. How soon can I have the baby, Mammy?"

Registering the child's birth and suppressing any public announcement was not difficult for Mary Ellen. She had handled such matters before, and she kept Dr. Mouser on her payroll for just such contingencies. As long as a morphine addict was provided with what he needed, he could be depended upon; curiously, the numbing drug interfered only marginally with his practice of medicine. He delivered the baby in the little house Teresa had once occupied and made out the initial certificate without question under Mary Ellen's supervision, just as he had filed James Percy Hoey's death certificate. The birth certificate would never be flaunted, but in the years to come, it would be there for the very curious, without even Thomas Bell's knowledge, listing him as the father and Mrs. Teresa Percy as the mother of the child. Emma, the real mother, was relieved to be rid of the baby and grateful enough for her small share of the ten thousand dollars Thomas gave Mary Ellen to "take care of the matter and find someone to care for the baby."

Thomas Bell's paternal nature could be played on later. In the meantime, everything was going exactly as she had planned. When he returned from a tour of his quicksilver mines, she called on him in his office at the bank, a discreet if well-known figure in her drab dark dress and Quaker bonnet; Mrs. Pleasant brought smiles to the faces of the bank personnel whenever they saw her come to make her small deposits directly to one of the bank's officers. They considered her no more than a colorful character, and that was just the impression she desired to make. She shed her Quaker manner as she entered her partner's office.

"How many Con Virginia shares have you bought?" she asked, removing her bonnet and seating herself across from Thomas. "I've managed to secure a few for Mrs. Percy."

"They've just about cornered it, Mammy, but I've picked up as much as I could. You're very businesslike today. You haven't even asked about my trip," he said with a smile.

"South America probably hasn't changed," she sighed. "I couldn't abide the place when my ship put in there twenty years ago, and don't care about it now. You didn't acquire anything interesting, like malaria, I trust?"

He laughed. "You're truly a heartless woman, Mammy," he said good-naturedly. "You can't imagine how ill I was with the usual complaint down there. I didn't drink the water, so it must be in the food. It isn't my favorite place, either, but I picked up a new mine."

"Gold?"

"No, not gold, or silver, either," he smiled, "so you can't possibly have any interest in it. You aren't at all impressed by my being called the Quicksilver King, are you? I'm almost afraid to ask, but what have you been up to while I've been away?"

"Nothing much. I haven't heard anything more about the Con Virginia, and the silence worries me. I attended the birth of your son, and Mrs. Percy's been kind enough to take him on. I named him Fred."

He considered the information in silence for a moment. "A boy, is it?" he said at last. "Why in God's name did you call him Fred?"

She shrugged. "It's as good a name as any for an orphan. I didn't give it much thought."

"He isn't an orphan, Mammy," he said almost severely. "He has a father, and I shall look after him. Mrs. Percy, eh? That was very gracious of her. Does she know he's mine?"

"Of course. She wasn't seeking the care of a child. She agreed to care for him because she's fond of you. She thinks you're kind."

"And so I am, more often than not," he said amiably. "Please assure Mrs. Percy that I'll more than recompense her for the boy's care. In fact, I'd better do it right now." The familiar checkbook appeared, and he paused with his pen. "Would thirty thousand be right?"

"Whatever you think is right," she said with no apparent interest, though she was so astounded by his generosity that she had to hide her excitement. The payment would buy the property on Octavia and Bush she had been dreaming about, and she had Teresa's power of attorney. The young woman did not know what she was signing when a stack of papers was placed before her, and she knew so little about legal and financial matters that she would not know what a power of attorney was if she saw it. Mary Ellen made a strict rule of never touching the investments she held with Thomas, no matter how desperately she wanted something, such as the Octavia property. She was constantly on the move to acquire extra capital to finance all her charities and schemes, and a windfall like this was a great relief.

He rolled his blotter over the wet ink and handed her the check. "Do you think Mrs. Percy would mind if I stopped by, sometime in the future, Mammy?" he inquired. "I'm too busy right now, but I'd like to have a look at the boy."

PART II

THOMAS BELL

He's a gentleman in every
way, but he's difficult to
understand. . . .

—Teresa's diary

Chapter 11

"I have some bad news," one of Thomas Bell's mining partners said when he arrived at Thomas's house on Stockton Street the day after the Bank of California crashed in August 1875. "I think you'd better have a drink first, Tom. It's been a bad week."

"I've managed to survive it," Thomas said, scrutinizing his partner's face closely. The man was too emotionally upset for the news to be anything about their mining ventures, he concluded. Besides, if it were the mines, he would have been the first to know. "I think you're the one who needs a drink. Please help yourself."

"I know how close you and William Ralston have been, in spite of your disapproval of his hotel," the man said, taking a gulp of Scotch. "There's no easy way to say this. He's dead, Tom. He drowned this morning while he was swimming."

"Suicide?" Thomas asked, turning his back and walking to the window. Of course it was suicide, he thought—it was the only honorable way out. He had liked Ralston, an amiable, handsome man, but he was a bad banker, and the crash brought all his manipulations to light. Thomas felt no guilt at having withheld the knowledge of the Con Virginia bonanza from him.

"I guess no one will ever know, but it certainly looks that way," his mining partner said. "If I'd diverted nearly two million dollars in stock and bullion to my own account to build that crazy hotel, I think I'd do myself in when it was discovered. I'm sure you want to be alone, Tom. I'm sorry to be the one to bear this kind of news."

After the partner left, Thomas poured himself a glass of Scotch and savored it slowly. Thanks to Mammy's advice, he had gradually withdrawn their funds from the bank and bought up Con Virginia over the

135

past year, so the crash had not affected him. Quite the contrary. His assets, combined with Mammy's, had skyrocketed to thirty million dollars. Warning Ralston would have served no end; his finances were already hopelessly muddled, a mess just waiting to be discovered. The man was a dreamer. And, in Thomas's opinion, dreamers should not be allowed to handle finances. The hotel he had built was a marvel, but it would go to that bastard, William Sharon, now. He could not explain his antipathy toward Sharon, which went beyond Sharon's strange appearance and sharp, avaricious mind. His big, bulging eyes and domed forehead were certainly unattractive enough, but there was something else about the little man that repelled, even frightened, Thomas. He reminded him of a bug-eyed fish with a large mouth, just waiting to gobble up all of his competitors. And he had done as much to ruin Ralston as poor Ralston himself had done. Someday, he mused, with the liquor warm in his chest, I'm going to get that man. I don't know how, yet, but I'm going to ruin the little son of a bitch.

In the meantime, there were other things to do until the bank regrouped and he could go back as one of its officers. Perhaps he could afford to allow himself some leisure for a change. The new house he had built had been completed for several months, but he had not had time to have it furnished. Mammy usually took care of such things, but she had been strangely evasive, almost disapproving of the new house. Jealousy? he wondered. She had always seemed happy enough at her boardinghouse, though. It was impossible to tell what went on in any woman's mind, and Mammy's would be the ultimate challenge for anyone who cared to bother with such things.

He always thought of her with mixed emotions. She was too intelligent by far, but she was also the most exciting woman he had ever known. During his early years in South America, where he had slept with both Indian and Spanish girls, he had developed a taste for dark, exotic women. When he first met Mammy, he knew she was the epitome of what excited him most. But he was just a little Scottish clerk, and she had shunned his advances at first. She was ambitious, even then. She must have seen something in him, though, because she had not severed their connection, after that brief love affair, and he owed everything he had today to her sharp mind. Just as she had so recently saved him from ruin, along with herself.

I think it's time for another little gift of diamonds, he thought, smiling to himself over the idea. She won't wear them, but Mammy does love diamonds, even if she does keep them in a bank vault. She's

THE HOUSE ON OCTAVIA STREET

always childishly elated by any gift from me. I suspect I'm the only one who's that thoughtful, when it comes right down to it. With all she does for other people, she doesn't get much in return. At least I pay my debts, if only in cold, hard stones.

He had often tried to analyze his feeling for her. He knew it was not love, though he had never really loved anyone. Perhaps it sometimes came close to love when he was in her presence, but he would never risk letting her know that. She was his friend and a pleasant companion, and he treated her almost like his male friends, in spite of the desire that was always just under the surface. When he was away from her these emotions disappeared, and he reflected on her as ruthlessly as he did on his other acquaintances. She was one of those rare individuals who charm one so completely while one is in their presence that they appear to have no faults; only later, when deprived of the glow of their personality, does one become judgmental.

When Mammy was not with him, he could not explain the feeling, almost of antipathy, that seized him regarding her. It was not really unlike what he felt toward William Sharon, his worst enemy, but to a lesser degree, and there was absolutely no foundation for it. She had been completely honest with him. She had brought nothing but good into his life. He was aware of her tireless work among the less fortunate and even had some of the Negroes she had rescued from slavery as servants in his house. He was one of the few people who knew about the "touch of the tarbrush" in her heredity, and he knew that she was still married to a former slave, whom she kept far from the city, working on a riverboat on the Sacramento River.

He also knew why she had married the ex-slave; and perhaps therein lay the problem, for this move on her part had revealed her enormous patience and the extent to which she would go to gain what she wanted. She had told him all about it years ago in an unguarded moment, while discussing her two marriages.

"My white father's name was Pleasant," she told him, "and I always wanted to bear his name. As a slave girl, I had no name except Mary until I married Mr. Smith, a Virginia planter, who didn't live very long. You can imagine my surprise when I discovered that his plantation overseer was named Pleasants. His parents were from Santo Domingo, like my mother, and his family had been the slaves of someone named Plaissance there, before they were bought by my father. The names were so similar that his family named him John James Pleasants out of respect for both of their masters. I wanted that name, Thomas, and I

137

wanted it legally. The first thing I did when I was widowed was give John James his freedom; the next thing I did, after we went to Boston, was marry him. It took me twenty-four years, but I finally got my father's name; all I had to do, then, was drop the *s*. John James and I worked on the Underground Railway, getting as many slaves out of the South as we could, before he started drinking so hard and I came here."

That she had gone through the inheritance from her planter husband in assisting slaves Thomas had no doubt, because she had no money when he met her on the ship and she quickly hired herself out at high wages as a cook when she reached San Francisco. There was much about her besides her beauty that was admirable, but he could not shake the feeling in recent years that she was closing in on him. She obviously did not have marriage in mind, since she was still married. And the only other attraction he might have for her was his money, combined with hers. But now she surely had enough to please even herself, so perhaps he could be less on guard about her. If their thirty million were split right down the middle, she finally would be a multimillionairess, though she had given no indication that she wanted to separate their new assets.

She was a good woman, he told himself as he poured another Scotch, a brilliant woman when one considered her beginnings. She had been honest with him all along, candid and forthright. The pity was that he could not be the same with her. No one knew what was behind his reserve, and as long as he lived, no one would ever know. Mammy's past was colorful and extraordinary, but his must remain secret. If it were ever revealed, he would lose everything.

"Diamonds," he decided, nodding his sandy head. "I'll see about them tomorrow. I really should buy Mrs. Percy some bauble, too, for all she's done. But I doubt that she's the sort of lady who'd accept an expensive gift."

Mrs. Percy's house was well ordered and peaceful, but that was not what drew him there increasingly often. He was completely enthralled by his growing son, Fred, and almost as completely baffled by the emotional hold the child had on him. At first, when Fred was just a baby, Thomas's visits were less frequent, though the tiny blond and blue-eyed bundle in Mrs. Percy's affectionate arms fascinated him, because he seemed to be an unexpected extension of himself that tugged curiously at his heartstrings. Actually, the boy resembled Mrs.

138

Percy more than himself, though, as she pointed out, his eyes were a more brilliant blue, exactly like his father's. She was a contented, orderly young woman, who seldom complained about anything, except right at the beginning, when she felt she was not allowed to take enough care of the baby.

"The nurse that Mammy brought with him is really formidable," she said with a shiver. "Sometimes I only see him to kiss him good night. If it's all the same to you, Mr. Bell, perhaps you can induce Mammy to dismiss Ophelia. I'm perfectly capable of caring for Fred myself."

"*Ophelia?*" he said with amusement, recognizing the connection with Ophir mine. "Are you absolutely certain that's her real name?"

"Oh, yes," she said, sharing his amusement, "Mammy said so. They do have colorful names, don't they? It would be difficult for me to imagine Shakespeare's Ophelia as dark complexioned. As I was saying, though, Mr. Bell—"

"If there are any servant problems," he said mildly, "you'll have to consult Mammy. She's really very good about that sort of thing. Besides, you have your own life to lead, my dear. You mustn't devote all your time to my son."

She had accepted his words calmly and without any petulance over his decision, but then, Mrs. Percy was probably the calmest and most even-natured young woman in the world. She was pleasant to be with, and out of consideration for his privacy she did not hover when he wanted to be with his son.

She had not changed over the years; if anything, her cool beauty had increased. She reminded him of an Englishwoman, and whenever he took tea with her, he felt slightly nostalgic, though his days in London were something he usually attempted—successfully—to forget. Fred was three years old now, a hardy youngster who still resembled Mrs. Percy in everything but temperament, and he wondered if he had made a mistake in not allowing her more closeness with the child. That Fred was spoiled was quite obvious, but he was probably more responsible for that than the black nurse. He never arrived without some toy, however small, in his pocket, and the one time that he came during a break in his busy schedule without a gift, the chubby child went into a raging tantrum. But he continued the practice, probably out of a sense of guilt, disregarding Mrs. Percy's suggestion that he really should not bring something every time he came.

When he arrived at the house one afternoon in mid-December, a few months after the crash and the recession that ensued, he could not believe the aroma that met his senses as he discarded his wet overcoat and rubbers in the hall. It evoked more than a little nostalgia for the British Isles.

"Can that be plum pudding I smell cooking?" he inquired when Mrs. Percy met him at the door of the parlor. "Good Lord, I haven't smelled anything like that for years!"

"Fred and I thought you might enjoy it on Christmas Day," she said, smiling her shy, distant smile. "I'll tell Ophelia you're here, Mr. Bell. Please make yourself comfortable. You know where everything is."

A fire was burning in the hearth, and the whole room smelled of the fresh evergreen tree, gaily decorated and garlanded, standing between the windows. All that would be required to take him right back to Scotland was to light the candles. At the sight of the tree, his eyes misted in spite of his attempt to hide his feelings, and he quickly took his handkerchief from his pocket to hide his weakness and blow his nose. No sooner had he done so than Fred roared into the room with all the subtlety of a runaway locomotive.

"Papa! Papa!" the rosy child cried eagerly, but when Thomas tried to lift him in his arms, he squirmed away. "Which pocket is it in? What did you bring me today?"

"Guess!" Thomas smiled, opening his suit coat. "Perhaps there's nothing at all. It's very close to Christmas, young man."

"I hope you'll spend it with us," Mrs. Percy said, as she prepared to leave the room. "Be a good boy, Fred, or Santa won't come. You might give your papa a kiss, instead of tearing at his pockets."

Thomas spent a happy hour or so with his son, mostly helping him spin the top he had brought, but when the little boy made up his own game, he was relieved to get off his knees to sit back and watch him. I'll be in my sixties when he's ready for college, he considered, but at least he'll be well provided for, with the trust I've set up if anything happens to me. The bank had reopened, and he was back in his old position, with no one the wiser about his financial manipulations. But if he was to keep what he and Mammy had recently made and add to it, he needed her advice. She had left town to live in the country the week after the crash, and he had not seen her since. Blast the woman, anyhow. She had never behaved irresponsibly before. He needed her more than ever, right now, with the market all over the country dipping and a general recession eating into their funds. He had responsibilities, if she didn't. He must look to the future of his little son, leave him with an empire worth inheriting. He really must have a word with Mrs. Percy tonight about Mammy's behavior, though he'd hesitated to bring up the subject until now.

A few minutes later, the impressive nurse, Ophelia, took the boy away for an early supper. She was very rigid about his schedule. Fred was removed bodily, screaming and fighting in her strong arms, and Thomas was unable to kiss him good night while he was having such a tantrum. He poured himself a Scotch from the sideboard, which Mrs. Percy always thoughtfully kept stocked, though he had never seen her drink anything but a small glass of wine herself. Perhaps she really would have been a better person to care for Fred, but he knew little about the rearing of children. To console himself about Ophelia he recalled that his parents had been very severe with him, but the recollection had the opposite effect. Full of silent rebellion, he had run away to London before he came of age, and what he had done there was not easy to forget. He was still haunted by it, and the fate that would meet him if he ever tried to return.

"I thought you might like some coffee," Mrs. Percy said in a clear, sweet voice, as she carried the silver coffee service into the room herself. "It's so wet and cold outside, it'll keep you warm until you get home."

"Thank you," he said, finishing his drink in one gulp and sitting in his usual chair by the fire opposite hers across the low table. "I've been wondering, Mrs. Percy, if you've heard anything from Mammy. I'm worried about her. I haven't seen her for a long time."

"I was concerned, too," she said as she poured the hot coffee into delicate china cups and handed him his without sugar, the way he liked it. "So concerned that I finally went out to Geneva Cottage the other day. I'm afraid it did nothing to reassure me, Mr. Bell, though she seems happy enough. She's always liked to putter about there, jarring preserves and feeding the chickens, you know, but I still felt a little sorry for her. She's never been gone this long before and . . . well, I suppose I shouldn't say anything."

"You can tell me, my dear. I'm her oldest friend."

"I think she lost a lot when the Bank of California folded," she said cautiously. "She told me the boardinghouse wasn't doing well enough for her to remain there for the present. And," she hesitated, "she brings eggs and butter to the Washington Street Market once a week, dressed in shabby men's clothing. After all she's done for so many people! I begged her to come stay with me, but she wouldn't hear of it, Mr. Bell."

141

"She hasn't visited you when she comes to town?"

She shook her head sadly. "No. I didn't know about it until I saw her preparing to drive in alone before I left. Surely, something can be done about her situation? I rather suspect she's even lost what little real estate she had to cover her losses."

The sly old fox, he thought, suppressing a grin. Who but Mammy would think of covering her sudden, if ill-gotten wealth, by pretending to be a pauper? He had managed to do it by liquidating everything and keeping their funds in a bank deposit box in another bank. Sometimes, he had wondered if Mrs. Percy was one of Mammy's creatures, and he had avoided her because of this suspicion. But she was so obviously innocent of what was taking place, so genuinely concerned about her friend, that such an assumption was permanently laid to rest. Mammy had never touched their combined wealth, and she might actually be suffering somewhat from the general recession, but to assume that she was poor was ridiculous. She had taken out a loan for her boarding-house about five years ago, and she had not defaulted on that, though he had wondered at the time why she needed so much money in cash.

"The bank can advance her something to keep the boardinghouse running," he said, trying to keep a straight face. "If you see her again, please tell her I'd like to speak to her."

"She's considering closing the boardinghouse," Mrs. Percy said sadly. "She said it isn't paying for itself. She has only two boarders, now, and the gentlemen don't come to dinner as they once did. I guess everyone's suffering a little, except myself, and it just isn't fair. Of course, I offered her everything I made with the Consolidated Virginia stock she purchased for me, but she's very stubborn."

"She can't close the boardinghouse," he said suddenly, the panic he experienced at the notion putting more harshness in his voice than he intended. What Mammy overheard at the boardinghouse had kept them ahead of the market for years; indeed, it had saved them from the crash. What the devil was the woman really up to, anyway? First, cutting him off entirely, and now, talking about drying up the very source of their inside information. "What I mean is that the boarding-house has been her life for a long time," he said, modifying his tone. "She'd be lost without it."

I'd be lost without it, he thought angrily. Has she decided to scuttle me? But that was not reasonable, either, since she'd go down with him. His agitation was so great that he rose to leave in order to conceal it. "It's been verry nice," he said, the Scottish burr in his speech revealing

142

his emotional state. The bloody thing always returned when he was under pressure, as Mammy had noted a long time ago. "I'll be delighted to spend Christmas with Fred, Mrs. Percy. As always, you've been most gracious."

He was walking to his carriage with his head bent against the pouring rain when he remembered the diamond he had given Mammy the day after the crash. The goddamn diamonds! Forty thousand dollars' worth of stones. What in the name of God had she done with *them* when she went to the country to play pauper? He knew how she loved to look at the flash and sparkle of perfect stones under the light, turning them in her long fingers and watching their fire like a child with a crystal prism. If he knew anything about her at all, she had her fortune in diamonds out there with her and was admiring them at night after churning her butter and gathering those goddamn eggs.

Without Mammy to guide him, Thomas Bell began investing small sums, carefully, and he soon found that he could trust his judgment in small investments, but he had to fight the impulse to throw everything into his mining ventures, as month after month passed without his silent partner's putting in an appearance. He was too close to his mines, so involved in them, that he could not be objective; if he lost all his and Mammy's money financing his mines, he would one day have to face Mammy, and that was a sobering thought. Without putting their money into something as quiet as his own mines, though, he was forced to keep it frozen in the bank deposit box, because he was as anxious as Mammy not to have anyone know he had tripled his fortune at the expense of his friends. And the recession was cutting into the money's value while he sat on his hands and waited.

He was alternately angry with her and frightened of her, but most of all, he missed her. Some of the brightness had gone out of his life when she left. Except when he was traveling, they had not been separated for any long period for over twenty years. He had not realized how important she was to his well-being. Uncomplainingly, indeed enthusiastically, she did so many things for him. His new house stood empty of furniture without her decorative flair. He could not give a dinner at his home without Mammy to cook it and see that everything went smoothly, right down to the table service and flowers. But most of all, he missed her charm and ageless beauty, he admitted grudgingly.

She's probably just going through the change of life, he decided, and her absence has nothing to do with me. Women did not discuss something like that, least of all one as vain as Mammy, who was sensitive about her age. But married friends had shared their experiences with him. Their wives were subject to giddiness and burning flashes and quick changes of mood that left their husbands baffled and on edge most of the time. Sometimes it was even worse than that, he thought, recalling Martin's wife, who had gone insane and had had to be put away. The idea of Mammy experiencing such unpleasantness alone in the country while he tormented himself over their funds gratified him curiously. She was at the right age. She's probably crawled away like a dog into a dark place so no one would witness her discomfort and know her real age. He had no conception of how long such things took to pass, but he was confident that when she returned, she would be in top form and able to take on the world singlehandedly again.

When he came to his office one morning early in the spring, he began to find out how much her life really had changed.

She was sitting in his chair behind the desk, dressed in her dark dress and Quaker bonnet, with a happier expression on her face than he had ever seen there. He nearly rushed to embrace her in his relief at seeing her, but something about her sitting in his chair made him cautious, and instead, he put his hat on the rack and studied her shrewdly.

"You're looking well," he commented dryly. "Is it your delivery day for butter and eggs? You haven't seen fit to call on me during your busy rounds before."

"That's all finished," she said with a smile that seemed to pervade the room and engulf him in its warmth. "I know what I want to do now, Thomas. I needed some time to think."

He would not sit on the chair across from his desk, so he remained standing with his thumbs thrust into the pockets of his vest. "You must have done some soul-searching," he commented gruffly. "It took you nearly a year."

"You're upset with me," she said with understanding. "I've thought about you a lot, Thomas. You seem to have managed very well without me, though."

"No real problems. Aside from thirty million dollars losing value through not being invested. We've managed to break even, I guess, with the portion I channeled back into the market. But I couldn't use a free hand without consulting you, so the rest has just sat there."

"It's still a lot of money," she responded, rising gracefully and moving to the window to look down over the financial district. "I've decided to use some of it, Thomas. I want to build a house."

144

"No problem. It might as well be invested in real estate," he said, regaining his chair of authority and clipping the end of a cigar. "In fact, it wouldn't be a bad idea to throw a lot of money into real estate. San Francisco's growing, and we're still pretty much on the ground floor."

"The house I have in mind will take quite a bit of money," she said, without facing him. "I picked up a lot on Octavia and Bush a few years ago. I thought we might invest in the mansion together."

"Mansion? A few moments ago it was just a house."

"I think Fred should have a proper place to grow up. He should be able to mix with the best society, Thomas. After all, he'll probably be your heir."

"Don't you think I've considered his future?" he said acidly. "Why do you think I built a new house? Which, incidentally, still isn't furnished."

"Oh, that!" she said, dismissing his house with one hand. "You don't think on a large enough scale, Thomas. You never have. What I have in mind is a mansion suitable for the Quicksilver King and his son. I've put my boardinghouse on the market to start it."

He observed her silently for a moment without drawing on his cigar. "Who's going to live in this house of yours?" he finally inquired. "It seems ungrateful to remove Fred from Mrs. Percy's care, after all she's done for him."

"Oh, of course Mrs. Percy would live there," she reassured him. "I hadn't considered anything else. I thought I'd run the household. As you know, I'm reasonably good at that. And you could live there too, Thomas, if you liked."

"I wouldn't like," he said crisply when she confirmed his suspicion. "You can have your bloody house, Mammy, and expense is no object. But I'll never live there. My part of the investment will be for Fred."

He was surprised at how much the suggestion unnerved him. The thought of dwelling under the same roof as Mammy, falling completely under her power, was frightening. He was his own man, and he would live in the house that was waiting to be decorated, even if he had to have someone else do the decorating. She remained silent, still not looking at him, but he thought he saw her shoulders straighten.

"You must understand," he said more gently, "that I couldn't live in the same house with Mrs. Percy and you, Mammy. Good Lord, it'd cause a worse scandal than openly recognizing Fred as my son, which I don't intend to do until I die. He'd have few advantages as Mr. Bell's bastard, you know. As Mrs. Percy's ward, he's better off. Her reputation is impeccable, as far as I know."

"I understand," she said, turning to smile at him. "We certainly don't

145

want a scandal. I'll just go ahead with the house. I've thought about it for years, and I'm very excited over the prospect. Things will work out, somehow."

"I suppose you'll be very busy," Thomas considered, wondering if she was abandoning their investments completely. "And, without the boardinghouse, there won't be any more inside information."

"No one's been coming there anyway. I'll never be too busy to make more money, Thomas, and I hear of things in other ways. As a matter of fact, why don't we just sit down right now and plan a new strategy."

His relief was so great that he took her hand. That's my Mammy, he breathed with rising hope. I know I can do some things well on my own, but I need you, more than you know. "Well, I suppose we could go over a few things," he said, feigning reluctance, as though he had everything under control. "I've a half hour or so before the board meeting."

The warmth of her smile as she pulled a chair over next to his brought him under her spell again. He felt normal for the first time in months. He even chuckled when she drew a deep breath and joked, "There must be something we can do with thirty million dollars, Thomas."

"I shouldn't be surprised," he said happily. "It's a damned sight more than we arrived here with, isn't it, old girl?"

She laughed, putting her hand on his shoulder and patting it. "A damned sight more, indeed. You know, Thomas, I never could figure out what you were doing as a company clerk in that steamy jungle, my dear. No one would go to such a place if he had a choice, in my opinion. A man like you should have had more foresight. The seeds of ambition were in you, even then."

"I suspect I knew a ship would save me and bring me here," he said lightly, "and I'd meet a very remarkable lady on board."

"Mm," she considered, squeezing his shoulder affectionately, "you've never believed in intuition before. By the way, do you know Captain Leighton of the San Francisco Police?"

The mention of the police after their previous remarks made him stiffen slightly, and he hoped she did not feel it with her hand. "No, I don't believe I do, Mammy. Why do you ask?"

"No particular reason, I guess," she said with a smile. "For some reason, he's making a trip to England to talk to Scotland Yard. I thought you might like to send a message to your people or have him take them a little gift."

His chest and abdomen felt as if they had been filled with cold concrete, and he was not certain he would be able to speak. But after a short pause, he rejoined heavily, "You know I don't have any family there anymore. My parents in Scotland must have passed away years ago, and there was never anyone else."

He controlled the impulse to ask why this Captain Leighton was traveling so far to speak to Scotland Yard, and he had to touch his handkerchief to his upper lip to blot the perspiration he felt there. He could not conceive of the motive for the captain's journey, but the chance that it had anything to do with him was preposterous. He would not give it any more thought. Why the devil did Mammy have to mention it to him, anyway? he considered unhappily. And how did she know about the comings and goings of a single officer on the police force?

But within the next half hour she revealed that she knew a great deal about what was going on in the city and as far away as the mining fields, as she calmly and incisively made her recommendations for the investment of their fortune.

PART III

THE HOUSE ON OCTAVIA STREET

The circumstance in which
I find myself surely could
not have happened to anyone
before.

—Teresa's diary,
1880

Chapter 12

Teresa had been grateful for Mammy's return to the city, but during the following year, she did not see as much of her as usual, and this was a disappointment. Mammy was her only friend, and Teresa had grown accustomed to her daily visits in the past, which brought some warmth and excitement into her life. She always greeted these visits with interest and amusement. No hint of wrongdoing or exotic rites had reached her ears in the past few years; with these suspicions allayed, she could enjoy Mammy's company completely, recording her observations of her unique benefactor carefully in her diary at night. That Mammy Pleasant was a remarkable woman she had never questioned, and as she became more comfortable with the older woman, Teresa's sensitive observation quickly appreciated that Mammy's personality was more than remarkable—it was extraordinary. If one did not try to see mysteries where there were none, Mammy was a warm and colorful friend. One friend like Mammy made up for a score of less interesting associates.

She had lived well under her friend's gentle domination for over ten years, and she seldom questioned Mammy's long-term plans for her. She did not believe that Mr. Bell would ever marry her, but Mammy's faith in the outcome of their relationship did not waver. Teresa no longer felt pressured to marry anyone. She had everything she had ever desired in comfort and luxury, and her least whim was quickly gratified. She did not ask for much. Aside from her carriage rides with little Fred, she had become almost a recluse in her Sutter Street house.

She had always been shy, and her reading continued to open up new vistas for her imagination and kept her indoors most of the time. Without leaving her parlor, she could go anywhere in the world and associate with every class of person. This saved her from exposing her self-consciousness to anyone. Without noticing it, she had gradually become sensitized to mingling with crowds and communicating with strangers. She played with little Fred when his taciturn black nurse allowed, and a short time with Fred was quite enough for her. He was not the most endearing child. Aside from not having a husband to please, her life was probably little different than that of most housebound mothers, except that she had no social life. She was almost relieved when Mammy sold the boardinghouse, and cut off contact with everyone besides Mr. Bell and herself.

Her thirtieth birthday took her by surprise in the even flow of her life. Surely, she could not really be thirty years old, she thought, subtracting the year from her birth date on paper in disbelief, and going to look into her mirror. She had not changed at all, not a single line had touched her face. The bone structure was more defined, perhaps, but that gave it greater beauty. But life was really passing her by, she considered unhappily. By thirty, a woman should have children of her own instead of caring for someone else's. She should have a man of her own to love, someone besides herself to care for, someone who would love her in return. Mammy had Ben Willard, whom she had taken to the country with her last year. She had not told Mr. Bell about that, after her visit to Geneva Cottage, because the situation had embarrassed her. She had surprised them in an embrace in the kitchen; after taking one look at her, Ben had stalked out of the room, and she did not see him again during her short visit. He could not forget that Teresa had killed her husband and could not abide being in the same room with her. His behavior had upset Teresa, and Mammy had tried to soothe her, claiming she would eventually bring him around.

Yes, Mammy and Ben had spent nearly a year in the country together. And Mr. Bell, she was certain, continued to sleep with girls as often as possible. She was not sure how often that would be at his age. She alone was celibate, and, on her thirtieth birthday, unwillingly so. She wept a little, feeling alone and forgotten. She even considered leaving her house, Mammy, everything, to live a more normal life. But she only considered it briefly. She was so accustomed to living in this style, without any cares and with everything she wanted that she doubted she could trade it for any man's embrace, even that of the fantasy lover she had created from imagination, who kept her company in bed at night in her dreams. Of course, her imaginary lover was rich and titled, along with being more beautiful than any man she had ever seen. If he appeared in her life, she would not hesitate to go with him. But she knew he would never appear, because he did not exist, except in her mind.

Mammy must have a natural sensing device, she thought later, like the whiskers of a dog or the antennae of some insects. Teresa had not seen her for weeks, because she was so fanatical about finally building her house on the hill. But just when Teresa was feeling at her lowest, her old friend appeared, flushed and excited, discarding her bonnet and shawl as she spoke.

"I have the most marvelous idea," she said breathlessly as she embraced Teresa. "I'm certain you'll love it, my dear. But, first, a little birthday present."

As Teresa took the small black velvet box in her hand, Mammy studied her soberly but with anticipation, and Teresa wondered if she noticed that her eyes were faded from weeping. "Earrings," she said, attempting a smile, "Diamond earrings. They're very lovely, Mammy. Thank you."

"Is that all you have to say?" Mammy asked sardonically. "Each one is a full carat and the stones are perfect. Maybe the rest of your gift will cheer you more." She handed her a train ticket. "You're going to the Centennial Exposition in Philadelphia, Teresa! And you're going to buy the most beautiful furniture there. Now, get your hat and parasol, honey, because you're going to see our new house."

"But, Mammy," Teresa said with a dry mouth, "I've never been on a train, and Philadelphia's so far away. I feel light-headed and a little faint even when I go shopping here."

"I'm not sending you alone," Mammy said with a smile. "I've selected exactly the right man to accompany you as a . . . bodyguard, if you will. He'll take care of everything. A trip's just what you need. You'll have a wonderful time."

"You started to say 'keeper,' didn't you," Teresa said wryly. "I'm not quite that bad, you know."

Mammy laughed softly. "No, that isn't what I started to say at all," she reassured Teresa. "Wait until you see him. Come along, now. You're in for the experience of your life. You want to see the house you'll be living in when you return, don't you?"

A large gray house with bay windows extending three floors on either side of the columned, porticoed entrance occupied the corner third of the leveled lot, which was unrecognizable compared to the way it had looked the time she saw it on the way to the cemetery several years before. Mammy kept up a steady account of her plans for the rest of the immense property as they circled her dream house before going inside.

"I plan a large Italian garden, perhaps with a fountain," she said with a sweep of her hand, "and stables at the rear, with a high wall encircling the grounds, except in the front. There'll be a wrought-iron fence there and large trees. You'll see that I've already planted them, and they'll grow fast."

As they picked their way through the dry grass that was to produce a miraculous fountain in the near future, Teresa observed that the side of the house duplicated the front in everything except the narrow Greek columns: bay windows climbed to the deep red roof here, too. She was surprised to see that, for no apparent reason, the rear of the house was built on an incline, and the back rooms extended to the edge of the property in that direction, but she did not remark upon this odd feature, because Mammy was so obviously proud of her creation.

"Why's the roof red?" she finally ventured. "I mean, that vibrant shade of red Mammy. I've never seen it on a house, before."

"It's my favorite color," Mammy replied blithely, and Teresa noted that she was swinging her hips as she walked, the way she always did when she was pleased with herself. "Well, what do you think?"

"It's . . ." Teresa hesitated, "big, isn't it?"

"Thirty rooms, including the servants' quarters. Wait until you see the interior, Teresa. You have marvelous taste. I know you'll love it."

So far, Teresa hated the house and hoped she would be able to have a more positive response when they went up six steps and through the arched portico to enter by the two recessed front doors, which contained high, etched-glass windows. Teresa gaped at the size of the marble entry hall and the circular stairway to the right, which wound all the way up to the third floor, uninterrupted by the landings she knew must be there, beneath the dome of colored glass. The sunlight pouring through the stained glass sent prisms onto the frescoed walls, which for an instant she thought were tapestries. The ceiling was paneled with gold, and, of course, there were the inevitable huge, crystal chandeliers—two of them. Mammy adored crystal. The only really discordant note in the hall was the huge figure of a half nude woman carved, like the stair railing, out of walnut and serving as the newel post. The statue provided extra light by means of a bronze candelabrum. Teresa suppressed a smile at the sight of it, trying to decide which it reminded her of more, the Statue of Liberty or the figurehead of a ship.

"It's like a palace," she said truthfully of the rest of the hall. "Really magnificent, Mammy. I had no idea you'd envisioned anything like this. May I see the rest of the rooms?"

"They aren't finished yet," Mammy said, obviously pleased by her friend's reaction. "But they'll be every bit as grand, I assure you. You'll be buying some of the furniture." She squeezed Teresa's arm affectionately. "And you know what I like. I've already purchased a clock for this hall. It's almost eight feet high, and I guess I paid nearly a thousand dollars a foot for it."

Teresa gasped at the price. "Surely, you aren't going to put the responsibility for that kind of expense on my shoulders? I'd be terrified if I had to pay that much for furniture. Suppose you didn't like it?"

"I know which antique shops you'll be browsing through, my dear, and everything will be purchased on a previously sent letter of credit. You won't have to concern yourself with money. Come up to my rooms, now. They're the only ones that are finished. I had to have someplace to live, and I wanted to be right here on the spot. The workmen, especially the Italian artists, haven't always appreciated my presence," she said as they ascended the red carpeted stairs. "When I make an investment, I expect full value, though."

Teresa wondered if the remark was an oblique reference to her own inability to land Mr. Bell, and she remained silent until Mammy opened the door of her quarters. She had never been inside Mammy's apartment at the boardinghouse, and she had expected something simple. But what she stepped into might have been in an Italian palazzo; for the first time during their tour, she was really stupefied. The ceiling and paneled walls were decorated with frescos of blue skies and cherubs and garlands of roses that were circled by ornate gilt borders, and the rose-colored carpet was so thick that Teresa's thin-soled shoes seemed to sink into it. Mammy's sitting room was furnished in the French style she preferred, the dainty gilt chairs upholstered in rose and pearl-gray brocade. Teresa was not admitted to her bedroom, the cream and gilt doors of which remained closed to her.

"This will give you some idea of what I have in mind for the other rooms," Mammy said, as she poured two glasses of wine from a crystal decanter more elegant than any Teresa had ever seen. "You prefer pale blue, I know, and you can select your own furniture, my dear. I want you to pick up as many auction catalogues as you can, too, especially of English furniture. What's the matter, Teresa? You look as if you'd been struck by lightning. I'm fond of nice things. All the furniture in these rooms is from my suite in the boardinghouse."

155

"I had no idea," Teresa said with a laugh of relief. "I thought your rooms were as plain as your clothing. All this really makes me feel so much better. You've been living like a queen, just as you should." She sat on the satin sofa and put her wineglass on the table. "Where did you find the artists to do all this?"

"Someone's coming," Mammy said, and though Teresa had not heard any footsteps on the carpeted stairs, there was a light tapping at the door. Dear God, she thought, don't let it be Ben. I'm not up to facing him again. I was beginning to enjoy myself. She did not look up when Mammy opened the door. She sat rigidly in her chair, fearing the worst, and the sound of a man's voice was not reassuring. Maybe Mammy will send him away, knowing how he feels about me. I can't bear to be looked upon as a murderess. She did not look up until Mammy spoke her name, and she was grateful she was not holding the fragile wineglass when she did so.

The young man at Mammy's side was nothing like Ben. He had gentle gray eyes, and his features were right out of her fantasy. Tall and athletic-looking in his well-tailored suit, he moved with an easy, confident grace when he bent to take her hand at Mammy's introduction.

"Teresa," Mammy said with a smile, "I'd like you to meet your traveling companion, Mr. Anthony Ward. Mr. Ward, this is Mrs. Percy."

"It's a pleasure, Mrs. Percy," he said with a crooked smile, assessing her with open admiration. "I can assure you that no harm will befall you while you're in my care."

She wrenched her gaze from his with an effort and looked at Mammy, who stood beside her with a benign smile on her narrow lips and an expression in her mismatched eyes that confused Teresa. She had worn the same expression earlier, when she gave Teresa the diamonds, and Teresa was more than a little nonplussed.

"Your help will be appreciated, Mr. Ward," Teresa said with as much composure as she could gather, wondering if she sounded cold and haughty, almost hoping that she did. Where had Mammy found this handsome, well-spoken man to send on such an assignment? she wondered. Judging from Mammy's expression, he almost appears to be part of my birthday present.

Mammy did not come to see them off on the ferry to the Oakland railway station, but there was a familiar face there that dampened Teresa's spirits considerably. Billy Beaumont approached them upon their arrival at the ferry slip and, with a closed, hangdog expression on his face, announced that he was accompanying them, too. He handled the disposition of her humpbacked trunks and other luggage with dispatch but kept his distance on the ferry, and Teresa felt her whole body grow tense in his presence. If Mammy had appeared to give something with one hand, she had certainly taken it back with the other by sending along Billy, one of the people who had seen her shoot Jim Hoey.

After the short ferry ride she found herself comfortably settled in a private compartment on the Central Pacific train, which was still boarding passengers after their arrival. She wondered if Mr. Ward had similar accommodations, but she hesitated to ask, distracted by the presence of Billy Beaumont. Overwhelmed by Mr. Ward's masculinity and good looks, she cautioned herself about appearing too friendly, especially with Billy here to report everything to Mammy later. She must have misread Mammy's intention, she decided. The idea of her selecting a lover for Teresa was preposterous, anyway. She still wondered where Mammy had found her companion, and she asked him about it during their first meal in the well-appointed dining car. Mr. Ward laughed shortly, discreetly covering his mouth with his linen napkin.

"Talk about a stroke of luck!" he exclaimed with candor. "I've been trying to get a job on the *Alta California*, without any result. I want to be a writer, and the *Alta* is the paper that gave Mark Twain his chance. My situation was just this side of desperate, when I met a fellow in a bar. Ben Willard was his name. We talked for awhile, and he suggested that I apply to Mrs. Pleasant for the job of accompanying a widow lady on a trip to Philadelphia. Your housekeeper's a very acute lady, Mrs. Percy. She seemed to like the idea that I wanted to be a writer. She said you liked to read and would enjoy my company."

Teresa was impressed. She noted that the only black men in the dining car were those serving the meal, and she wondered distractedly where Billy Beaumont ate. "Are you really going to be a writer?" she asked at last, fixing her serious blue eyes on Mr. Ward. "I think that's very interesting. I read everything I can get my hands on. Tell me, where is Billy Beaumont, Mr. Ward? Are you sharing your quarters with him?"

"You might say that," he smiled. "We're in the same sleeping car together. Oh, it's quite comfortable, I assure you, ma'am. He's a quiet one, isn't he?"

Teresa hoped with all her heart that Billy was, but she was not reassured by the fact that the two men were in such close proximity.

157

"Tell me about your writing," she said, taking a sip of water to relieve the sudden dryness in her mouth.

"It's something I want to give a whirl," he said with a smile, delighted to be talking about his aspirations again. "I have nothing to lose, have I? Of course, I haven't had a fancy education like yours, Mrs. Percy. But Mark Twain didn't go to college, either. It's the way you see things and write them down that counts. I'm interested in the new mystery books: I like to untangle things in my mind. Sort of like Mr. Poe's Auguste Dupin, you know?"

Teresa did not know, not having read much of Edgar Allen Poe, and she almost corrected his impression about her degree of education, but she thought better of it just in time. She did not want to interject a note of familiarity into their relationship. Besides, she enjoyed having someone believe she had attended a good college. "I think reading a lot is more important than a formal education," she said. "And traveling is important, too. I can see why you decided to take this trip."

"Oh, I've traveled a lot," he assured her. "I was in the Navy for a while. I've practically been around the world. We sailed the whole Mediterranean from Spain to Constantinople. I've seen a few things in my day, Mrs. Percy."

He had Teresa's complete attention, and she leaned forward slightly to hear him better over the sound of the metal wheels on the track. "That's very interesting, Mr. Ward. You must tell me all about the places you've seen. Philadelphia probably won't be very interesting to you after all that. I haven't really traveled much, myself, but I'm fascinated by accounts of foreign places."

"There's plenty of time for that," he smiled, staring at her intently. "I think Philadelphia's going to be just fine. And all the places in between. We'll be stopping over at the Brown Palace Hotel in Denver to break the trip, you know."

"Stopping?" Teresa asked with a frown. "I thought we were booked straight through. I've unpacked most of my things."

"I thought your housekeeper told you. She said a long train trip was too hard for a lady like you. We'll be stopping in Denver and St. Louis, Mrs. Percy. You shouldn't look at it as an inconvenience, you know. It'll give us time to explore both cities before we move on."

With Billy Beaumont at our heels watching everything, Teresa thought unhappily. "I'd never dream of doing anything like that on my own," she said timidly. "I'm glad you agreed to accompany me, Mr. Ward."

"It's my pleasure, I assure you," he said softly, holding her gaze with his. "I'd appreciate it if you'd call me Tony, though. Everyone does, and I might not answer to 'Mr. Ward.' We'll be spending a lot of time together, Mrs. Percy, and you might want me to respond in a hurry sometime."

In the confines of the train, it was impossible to avoid some closeness, but Teresa attempted to do so at first. The table in the dining car proved the most difficult problem. There was very little space beneath it, and Tony Ward was so tall that his knees touched hers unless he sat sideways, a solution he did not seem to consider. Night after night the pressure of his body through her skirt haunted her later in her compartment when she tried to go to sleep. She found herself going over every word he had spoken at dinner, each nuance of expression on his increasingly beautiful face. When he guided her back to her compartment, grasping her elbow, she found herself wishing he would hold her hand instead. And, worst of all, when he wished her good night in the narrow corridor outside of her door, she had to keep her eyes from pleading for a good-night kiss.

If I can just get through all this until Denver, she told herself as she tossed in her narrow bed, I'll be all right. There'll be more space between us, and Billy Beaumont will be present as a watchdog. She deeply resented Billy's presence on the trip and everything it brought to mind, but perhaps in one way it was a godsend. If Tony were only less interesting and attractive, she sighed. Mammy did not consider that she had feelings, too, when she sent such a beautiful man along with her.

She did not see Billy again until he came to collect her belongings when the train stopped in Denver. He paused for a moment in the doorway of the compartment to look back at her, and she went tight all over again in his presence. He started to speak, but Tony interrupted by appearing in the corridor behind him, smiling over the black man's shoulder, and Billy dropped his gaze and continued about his business. Teresa was so relieved by his disappearance that she did not even consider what he might have to say to her. Billy Beaumont was a witness, a specter to be avoided at all cost.

"There must be some mistake," Teresa said to the gentleman who accompanied them to the opulent suite in the Brown Palace Hotel. "This is too large. It's practically an apartment."

"There's no mistake, Mrs. Percy," he said. "This is what was requested for you and your party by telegram. I suppose the others will be arriving later?"

Teresa felt embarrassed that she was not even accompanied by a maid, and she silently implored Tony to attend to the matter. After depositing her things in the lobby, Billy Beaumont had once again disappeared, relieving her of explaining a black man's presence as well as Tony's.

"This will be fine," Tony said amiably, slipping a folded bill into the hotel employee's hand. "The arrangements were made by someone else, and Mrs. Percy was a little surprised, that's all. Please have our luggage sent up immediately and look after our colored man, too."

"Tony!" Teresa cried as soon as they were alone. "I didn't want you to do that. I just wanted nice separate rooms and a bit of privacy."

He prowled the elegant suite with curiosity, opening one door after another and turned back to her with a grin. "We have separate rooms, all we can use. I do believe you're a penny pincher, Teresa. Look, there's even a basket of fruit on the table." He removed an apple from the ribboned display and tossed it in his hand. "What's wrong with living like royalty for a few days? It's all paid for—I asked. There's even enough room for Billy here, if you like."

"No!" she said so quickly that she had to compose herself. "He's better off where he is. Mammy must have gone stark, raving mad. I don't know what's come over her. She's spending money as if there's no tomorrow."

"Maybe there isn't," he interjected with a smile, and she stared at him with surprise. "None of us know that, do we? People should enjoy everything they can today and let tomorrow look after itself."

"What a hedonistic philosophy," Teresa replied irritably as she removed her bonnet. "You and Mr. Omar Khayyam would make quite a pair."

He stared at her nonplussed. "I didn't mean to offend you. I don't know much about philosophy, Teresa. I only know how I feel. I can't see why you're so upset about this suite, or why you're taking your aggravation out on me."

"You wouldn't," she snapped, rushing for one of the bedrooms and stopping short at the masculine decoration that the open door revealed.

"That one," he said softly, indicating a room on the opposite side of the sitting room. "It's soft and feminine like you. Shall I order dinner while you're refreshing yourself, or would you prefer to dine out?"

She slammed the door behind her in reply. Why is he so charming and controlled when I'm behaving like an idiot? she wondered as she paced the ivory carpet of the coral-toned room. The suite's magnificent, and I've never quarreled about Mammy spending her money before. The intimacy doesn't seem to annoy Tony, because he doesn't know what's going on. I'm as nervous as a bride, and I want to appear ladylike. He thinks I'm a lady. It isn't as though I were saving myself for anyone else, certainly not Mr. Bell, who indulges himself with other women and shows no interest in marrying me. What really bothers me is Mammy's role in this whole thing. If she's provided me with a lover, I find that annoying. But on the other hand, I'm more concerned about Billy Beaumont being here, too. What on earth is she thinking of? She has me torn apart from trying to second-guess the workings of her mind. I'm more attracted to Tony Ward than I've been to any man, and maybe I should consider what *I* want, for a change.

She emerged from her room relaxed from her bath and wearing a low-cut, shell-pink nightgown under a matching peignoir. Powdered and lightly scented, her long blond hair tied back with a ribbon, she took her place at the table by the window, which was already set, and looked up at Tony appealingly. "I'm sorry," she whispered. "What did you order for dinner?"

He did not take his gaze from her as he took his seat. "A cold buffet and wine," he said removing the covers from the dishes. "My God, Teresa, you're so beautiful. . . ."

The rest of the trip was like a honeymoon. They explored Denver, which was still in the throes of its silver rush, and was a wildly extravagant place, to rival the San Francisco of over a decade before. They missed touring St. Louis, however, remaining instead in their hotel suite to indulge their senses. Teresa felt complete in Tony's arms, and she tried to live for the moment with no thought of the future, as he did. He even slipped into her compartment on the train on the way to Philadelphia, leaving just before the porter's wake-up call in the morning. She had never been so happy and laughed easily at the slightest provocation as the tension of the past ten years melted away.

"You have the most extraordinary eyes," he told her in bed at the hotel in Philadelphia. "I've never seen eyes so blue. They're like sapphires, darling. I love you so much. Not just for your beauty, Teresa, but because you're so gentle and affectionate. I could stay right here forever."

"So could I," she said and smiled, brushing the thick dark hair back from his forehead, "but this is Philadelphia, darling, and we have work to do. We must start by going to the Exposition."

After he had gone downstairs to get a cab, she was startled by the sudden appearance of Billy Beaumont at the door of their room. "Mis' Teresa, I got to talk to you. I don't think you know what you're doin'. You best be careful. I have a lot to talk to you about."

Teresa glanced away from him with a frown. "We haven't anything to say, Billy. I know she sent you to spy on me, and I don't care. For once in my life, I'm *living*, and I don't care about the future . . . or the past."

She brushed past him in the doorway and went to join Tony outside. Later, she wondered if that was when things began to go wrong, though she could not remember a specific incident that led to her disenchantment with Tony. Perhaps the scales fell from her eyes gradually over many small occurrences that she was too proud to censure. She remembered the first time they were together in a large crowd, when she needed Tony most. He was not interested in the Exposition's display of new technology and kitchen appliances, and she was conscious of his boredom as she followed the brochure to find the things Mammy wanted as quickly as possible. His attitude annoyed her much more than the exacting task Mammy had set for her. When Tony paused to do some gymnastics on the bars in a children's playground, she experienced a flush of embarrassment. She tried to overlook several similar instances, arguing that he was just letting off some of his natural high spirits, but she was let down by his behavior. Teresa recognized that she was more of an observer than a participant in life and cautioned herself not to be too critical of Tony. In the passion of the trip, she had overlooked his lack of education but it flashed back on her now. She wondered if she was just naive to expect a man to be all the things she expected, maintaining some tenderness and charm outside of the bedroom. Billy Beaumont's attempted warning about her behavior with Tony made her realize how much she was really risking for him, and it was perhaps only natural to question whether he was worth it.

The first time she noticed him turning to look at girls on the street was as painful as a slap in the face. She did not know whether she was angry or jealous; she only knew it hurt. She managed to set her lips and look the other way when his gaze followed a pretty girl, but she felt betrayed, suddenly conscious of her age compared to his. She was at least five years older, but it had not seemed that important until now.

She could no longer remain silent when he balked at accompanying her to the antique stores Mammy had listed so carefully in her perfect, copperplate handwriting.

"All you think of is your damned house in San Francisco," he complained. "I hate to shop for furniture and things like that. Why don't you give the whole thing up, darling? You're going to marry me, anyway."

"I'm going to . . . ?" she said, flustered. "You've never asked me, and I don't know how I'd answer if you did. I've come here for a purpose, Tony. There are things I must do, and you came along to help me." She had a sudden malicious inspiration. "Just take me to the antique broker's. I'm sure there's a nice bookshop nearby. We could meet there later."

"*Bookshop?*" he inquired irritably. "What would I do there? I want to see the city, not poke my nose into books."

"For a writer, you've an unusual blind spot about literature," she said mildly, tying the ribbons on her bonnet carefully and picking up her parasol. "It makes me wonder what sort of writer you really are. I shall go alone."

"No," he objected quickly, "I can't let you do that. As you pointed out, I was hired to assist you, though things between us have changed so much, I didn't think you'd throw that in my face."

"I don't want you to come, Tony," she said sternly. "You only make me edgy when I'm shopping. Besides, I intend to take in the museum later this afternoon, and that would probably bore you to death. You go your way, and I'll go mine. We'll meet here for dinner, if it pleases you."

Venturing into the city alone was not as difficult as she had imagined. Expensively dressed and with the manners of a lady, she was respected by everyone she dealt with. The doorman whistled for a horse cab for her, and the driver assisted her inside and drove her to an antique dealer who, in spite of his dignified manner, appeared most anxious for her account. Her experiences in Philadelphia were very different from those of her arrival in San Francisco ten years before, and she knew whom she had to thank for that. As she selected furniture for Mammy's house, she suddenly felt very lonely for her.

Tony was waiting for her with flowers and a box of chocolates when she returned to their suite. "I'm sorry, darling," he said earnestly, "I behaved like a cad. I've been out of my mind all afternoon worrying about you, Teresa."

163

"You shouldn't have bothered," she said with a pang. He really was the most beautiful man. You could have found me easily at the museum, she thought. "Shall we have dinner in the dining room this evening?"

"The dining room? Not *here*?" he said with bewilderment. "I thought you hated to be around strangers."

"I think I've overcome it," she said with her mysterious smile. "It's dreadful to have to depend on a man for everything one does. If you prefer to dine here, I shall go down alone."

His silence in the dining room was not just that of a disgruntled lover. His dark expression was desperate, and she did nothing to alleviate his anxiety.

"It's over, isn't it?" he said at last. "You know I'm a phony, and you're fed up with me."

Teresa observed him over the rim of her wineglass. "I know you aren't very interested in writing," she admitted, "but that has nothing to do with it. We just don't look at things the same way."

"If I were really a down-at-the-heel writer with a purpose, you'd probably want to sponsor me," he reflected. "I'd be more interesting then."

"It isn't that. You're a charming man, and I hope we can remain friends."

He rubbed his chin with his hand thoughtfully as he said, "Mrs. Pleasant said she'd have work for me when we return. I suppose that's out of the question now, too?"

"I never interfere with Mrs. Pleasant's plans," Teresa said with asperity, suddenly conscious that there was not much difference between her situation and Tony's. "She always keeps her word, though. I'm sure she'll find something for you to do."

"It's *him*, isn't it?" he demanded, staring at her with hard eyes. "You prefer what that old man can give you to happiness with me. I guess I can't blame you though we could have made out pretty well with the cash he entrusted to you for this buying spree."

His words hurt, but they puzzled her, too. Tony was not a cheap, ordinary confidence man like Jim Hoey, but she should have recognized his interest in the money sooner. "What old man?" she asked cautiously, "I don't know what you're talking about."

"Thomas Bell," he said sarcastically, "the Quicksilver King. You don't have to play innocent with me. Everyone knows you're his mistress and that you have a child by him."

"That isn't true!" Teresa cried, completely unnerved. "Who told you such a thing?"

"It's general knowledge, Mrs. Percy," he replied with a disinterested shrug. "As soon as your housekeeper hired me, I began hearing it on all sides. In every bar and from some journalists I got to know. They've been watching you for years, but they don't have enough on you for a first page spread. They wanted me to find out what I could about you. They even said they'd pay me. But after I met you, I forgot all about that. You're a scandal, Mrs. Percy, but I won't say anything. Everyone knows he's building that great big house just for you and his kid."

Chapter 13

They did not communicate much on the return journey. Tony kept his part of his bargain with Mammy by making the arrangements and seeing that Teresa's purchases were safely loaded on a freight car. When Billy Beaumont carried her luggage to her compartment, his eyes appraised her so directly that she turned away.

"Trouble in Eden?" he asked. "We ain't expected home until the end of the month."

"There's trouble all right," she snapped, "and I'm going to do something about it."

She locked her compartment door after him and remained there for the rest of the trip. She had been too shocked to refute Tony's accusation in the dining room that night, and she had gone up to her room to write Mammy a long, disjointed letter to inform her about the rumor, which would probably change all her plans concerning Mr. Bell. But, realizing that she could get to San Francisco as quickly as the letter, she decided to leave Philadelphia as soon as possible. The trip back was a nightmare spent pacing the enclosed space of her compartment. She felt like a messenger with lead-encased ankles, and she hardly touched the meals delivered to her. By the time she boarded the ferry in Oakland, her clothes felt loose, and she realized she had lost a great deal of weight.

Mammy was not there to greet them, but John Willis was there with the open phaeton. Teresa was almost tearfully glad to see him.

"John Willis, please drop Mr. Ward and Billy Beaumont wherever they tell you," she instructed as she took her place in the carriage, "and take me to Mammy at once."

Billy Beaumont shook his head, indicating that he preferred to walk,

167

but Tony joined her in the carriage. "I'm sorry if I said something wrong," he said nervously. "I hope we can still be friends, Teresa."

"It's all right," she reassured hm. "I was just the last to know about the rumor, which isn't true at all. I'll recommend you to Mrs. Pleasant for future employment, Tony. Thank you for your assistance on the trip."

"Friends?" he asked uncertainly, with doubt in his eyes and only a hint of his crooked grin.

"Yes," she told him with sudden empathy, "*friends*, Tony. Goodness knows, we all need them."

She hardly noticed the carefully cultivated green garden that had replaced the bare lot beside the house on Octavia Street. Anxious to see Mammy and convey to her the disturbing rumors, she hurried through the ornamented wrought-iron gate and up the steps to open the front door. To her consternation it was locked, and she had to ring the bell, which resounded musically inside the large entry hall. Mammy knew she was coming, and Teresa felt hurt that she did not answer sooner. She rang the bell more insistently, and the door was opened by a white butler in a dress suit. Astounded at the sight of him, Teresa wondered if Mammy was playing some sort of joke on her.

"Madame?" he inquired, studying her wrinkled, ill-fitting travel dress with obvious caution, and she found herself replying with some respect for his delicate sensibility.

"Mrs. Pleasant is expecting me. Please tell her that Teresa's here."

"Your card, madame," he said, proffering his well-manicured hand, provoking Teresa to a rare outburst of impatience.

"She'll know who I am," she said with heavy irony.

He admitted her reluctantly and left her sitting in one of the heavy walnut chairs that now decorated the walls of the marble hall, coordinating well with the sweeping staircase. As the butler exited in the direction of the back rooms on the same floor, Teresa noticed Mammy descending the stairs in deep conversation with a rather plump, blonde young woman, who was carrying a portmanteau. Their voices carried in the silence, and they were completely unaware of Teresa's presence in the hall at the foot of the staircase.

"Don't worry about anything," Mammy was telling the girl in words all too familiar to Teresa. "It worked the last time, didn't it? I can do it again, and you'll be paid the same amount."

"I should get more," the young woman said sullenly. "I really had to do it this time. You didn't tell me that would happen."

168

"I didn't know it," Mammy laughed shortly. "All right, you shall have a bonus, for making the outcome more believable. The carriage will be here soon to take you to—" Just then she saw Teresa and frowned slightly. "The carriage is here," she informed the young woman and then cried, "Teresa!" her face beaming with pleasure as she ignored the young woman's departure. "Why didn't Thornton tell me you'd arrived? I'm so happy to see you, my dear," she said, embracing her and looking at her at arm's length. "You've lost weight. We must do something about that right away. I was concerned by the tone of your wire. Let's go upstairs and have some tea, and you can tell me all about it."

The butler returned just as they reached the foot of the stairs and approached them cautiously across the marble floor. "I attempted to announce the young woman," he defended himself. "I thought you were in the kitchen, Mrs. Pleasant."

Teresa suppressed a giggle, "Is he *real?*" she asked. "He was so unpleasant, I thought you were playing a joke on me."

"He's real," Mammy said wryly, "and I don't know if I like him, either. Thornton, the young woman you left sitting in the hall is your employer. I think you owe her an apology."

Mammy had completely taken on her role as housekeeper and seemed to enjoy ordering people about, Teresa noticed, before the drift of what Mammy had said penetrated her mind. Employer? She had thought this was Mammy's house, and she was confused, especially since the rumors she was going to report attributed the house to her. She hardly heard the butler's apology, though she thought she nodded graciously in accepting it. She and Mammy climbed the stairs to the first landing, but Mammy did not take her to her own sitting room. She threw open a door down the hallway instead, and at first all Teresa saw was cornflower blue.

"Your rooms are ready," Mammy announced proudly, "except for the chairs you bought in Philadelphia. You did bring them, didn't you? You must tell me all about your trip over tea." She pulled a tapestry cord, and a young white maid appeared almost at once. "We'll have our tea in here, Bridget. At once, if you please."

They sat down together on the sofa, and Teresa did not speak for a moment. When she did, after taking off her hat and gloves and running her fingers through her hair to prevent the headache that seemed imminent, she did not address the subject that was really on her mind. "Are all the servants white, Mammy? After filling every house in the

169

city with colored servants, I naturally assumed you'd have them here."

"I want white servants in my house," Mammy said with a smile. "I want white servants to wait on me."

"Oh, it *is* your house, then?" Teresa said, studying her closely. Mammy was not wearing her customary white headdress, and Teresa observed that her hair was slightly wavy, though it had been smoothed with pomade. Strange that she had never noticed any curl in Mammy's hair before, she thought. Aside from that, Mammy had not changed since the day she met her; her youthfulness was phenomenal. "From what you said to the butler, I had the uneasy feeling that the house was mine."

Mammy laughed and patted her knee. "My house, your house, what does it matter? It's the same. We've both come a long way, honey. You know the way I register deeds. Lord knows, you've signed enough of them."

"Did I sign one for this house?"

"Of course. Here's our tea. I made scones this morning just for your arrival." Mammy's mismatched eyes followed the maid to the door. "Bridget," she said imperiously, "your apron isn't tied correctly. You know what I said about slovenliness. It won't be tolerated here."

The abashed maid retreated backward out of the room, and Teresa frowned slightly. "I don't remember you ever being so cross with your servants. I've never heard you raise your voice before, Mammy."

"I trained the others," Mammy said as she sugared Teresa's tea to her taste. "I don't know where these were trained, if indeed they were. The Irish ones like Bridget are the worst. They're naturally untidy."

"I'm Irish," Teresa reminded her, "and I'm sure her background's no worse than mine."

"Our backgrounds don't matter anymore. We have what counts," Mammy said slyly, touching her temple. "Now, what was that garbled wire all about?"

"I think you know," Teresa said, gazing steadily into her eyes. "You have a way of knowing everything that happens in this city. I wired you because I'd just heard that there were rumors that I'm Mr. Bell's mistress, and that Fred's our child."

Mammy was silent a moment, judging Teresa's mood. "You had to go all the way to Philadelphia to hear that one?" she asked carelessly. "Teresa, people *will* talk. If they don't have something to talk about, they make things up. I heard that rumor years ago, and I dismissed it just as quickly as you should."

"That isn't so easy. I've worked hard to make a lady of myself,

Mammy. You know how much I've tried. When I heard my reputation was being torn to ribbons, I was very upset. I still am. Don't you see how this could affect all your plans with Mr. Bell?"

"I probably see further than you think, honey," Mammy said with a faint smile. "It won't change anything."

"They think he's built this house for Fred and me," Teresa tried to impress upon her. "If I come to live here, it will confirm the rumors. Why don't you just come out and admit it's your house, for heaven's sake. Why must you always be so mysterious?"

"You want the facts, so I'll give them to you, Teresa. Mr. Bell's put a considerable amount of his money into the house. He wants his son to live properly and meet the right people. So the house doesn't belong to me alone. He wants you to live here with Fred. Honey, you're the only mother the little fellow's ever known. Mr. Bell isn't the least concerned about scandalmongers. He knows things will finally be set straight. We'd both be terribly unhappy if you refused to live here."

Teresa heaved a deep sigh. Just when things looked one way, they always turned out another. She recognized that, everything considered, she had no choice. Fred was not the most endearing youngster, but she was fond of the boy.

"Now, tell me all about your trip," Mammy requested eagerly. "I hope you had a perfectly marvelous time. Mr. Ward is a charming man, isn't he?"

"Oh, yes," Teresa said wearily, "I can't fault him there. To tell you the truth, I made an absolute fool of myself. I might as well tell you, because he probably will, anyway. I came to my senses in Philadelphia and broke off with him. But I assured him that I wouldn't stand in the way of some work you'd promised him."

"At least you parted friends. You've lost a lot of weight, and you're very pale, Teresa. You aren't pregnant, are you?"

"No," Teresa replied, shaking her head over her own foolishness. "I don't know why I'm not, though. It's some sort of miracle."

Mammy chuckled warmly, deep in her chest, in the manner Teresa had always found so reassuring. "Perhaps the trip wasn't such a bad idea, after all. You've been living like a nun. Now, do you have the catalogues I asked for? I still have one important suite to furnish."

Within a few months, the interior of the house was completed to Mammy's satisfaction, and Teresa had settled in more comfortably than she had expected. Aside from a few errors in taste, like the nude statue on the newel post at the foot of the stairs, the new house was elegant and graceful. She enjoyed dining in the large dining room with its refectory table and carved, high-backed chairs—it made her feel as if she were living in a castle. On Mammy's marvelous cooking she soon regained the weight she had lost; feeling sleek and pampered in the almost Renaissance house, she dismissed her affair with Tony from her mind. The only duty required of her was to take Fred for a ride in the open carriage on Sunday afternoons, and, safe again in Mammy's hands, she raised no objection, though she felt the outings were indiscreet, considering the gossip that was circulating about Mr. Bell and herself.

She observed with interest the installation of the furniture Mammy ordered from the antique catalogues. The suite that was furnished last was completely masculine and English from the high-posted walnut bed with its wooden canopy inlaid with box and holly to the heavy walnut desk in the sitting room. The windows were draped with crewel embroidery from India, the drapes held back by sashes with brass rings to admit the light. Teresa had learned something about antiques in Philadelphia, and she recognized the Persian carpet as one from Isfahan by its intricately woven hunting figures surrounded by an undulating patterned border of deep blue, which echoed the color of the velvet hangings on the bed. The suite had cost a fortune, she considered, and it needed a man to occupy it, a certain mild-mannered Scot with very little inclination to do so. She admired Mammy's tenacity of purpose, which endured year after year without the slightest encouragement.

"Mr. Bell and some of his friends are coming to dinner tonight," Mammy told her when everything was completed to her satisfaction. "I want to show him the house, now that it's finished. Would you care to dine with the gentlemen?"

"No," Teresa said quickly, conscious of the rumors. "If you don't mind, Mammy, I'd prefer dining in my rooms."

"He'll want to see Fred," Mammy said easily, without pressing the issue. "You can put in a short appearance with the child before he goes to bed."

Teresa opened her lips to protest, but she thought better of it. She had agreed to obey Mammy a long time ago, and very little was asked of her in return for what she enjoyed. Whether she dined with the gentlemen or appeared briefly with Fred, the result would be the same—a confirmation of the rumors about herself and Mr. Bell, if the rumors had reached as high as his friends. But Mammy had no intention of discouraging them, anyway.

Just before the gentlemen went in to dinner, she descended the stairs in a discreet gray afternoon frock, holding the five-year-old boy by the hand. When Fred saw his father, he broke away to run into his arms and proceeded to search his pockets. The gentlemen chuckled over his antics, and Mr. Bell produced a surprise for his son. Teresa stood at a distance, hovering like a governess, deploring the child's behavior while marveling at how easy it was for a man like Mr. Bell to acknowledge an illegitimate child quite openly without having any stigma attached to himself. The attitude toward the child's mother would be quite different, she knew, and she also knew that the gentlemen thought she was Fred's mother. Mr. Bell did not allow her to linger in the shadows, however. To her dismay, he motioned to her to join the group of men in dress suits, and she obeyed with quiet composure, her serious blue eyes meeting their gazes directly.

"You know some of my friends, Mrs. Percy," Mr. Bell said as he ruffled Fred's blond hair. He introduced her to the others formally, concluding, "Mrs. Percy has been kind enough to look after little Fred for me. I appreciate her gesture more than I can say."

If he thought he was discouraging the rumors, he was mistaken, Teresa observed without losing her composure. The hidden smirk of one of the gentlemen was covered quickly by his fist as he cleared his throat, and the sly, knowing glances of the others might have passed unnoticed by a more casual observer. There were other glances, too, she realized with some surprise. Several of the gentlemen were openly admiring in their appraisal of her, and more than one looked wistful, if not slightly envious of Mr. Bell, who appeared oblivious to their reactions.

"It's time for Fred to go to bed," Teresa said calmly, without any maternal pride. "His nurse is particular about bedtime. I'm pleased to have met you, gentlemen."

As she feared, Fred puckered his face in preparation for one of his tantrums, and this was something she positively would not allow tonight in front of company. She grasped his wrist more tightly than was apparent, pressing her fingernails into the child's wrist. "Come along, now, Fred," she said evenly, holding the boy's startled gaze sternly. "Say good night to your father and his friends."

"Good night!" Fred said rebelliously, but he accompanied her to the staircase without any further trouble, as the gentlemen departed, chuckling and talking, for the dining room.

"I hate you!" the child cried when they reached the landing and she released his arm. "You hurt me, and I'm going to tell Mary!"

He ran up the remaining flight of stairs to the nursery quietly

173

enough, but when he reached the third floor, she heard him bawl, "Mary! Mary! That woman's hurt me! Mary! *That woman* hurt my arm!"

Teresa wondered if the Irish nurse was an improvement over the formidable black Ophelia. She had cautioned Mammy about the change, but Mammy insisted on only white servants. Perhaps Ophelia had been too strict, but Mary was far too permissive. The child did not know how to behave. As she returned to her room, weary from the ordeal, she reflected that she had never been referred to as "that woman" when Fred was in Ophelia's care.

She did not see Mammy for several days after Mr. Bell's tour of the house, and Bridget, when she came in to make Teresa's bed one morning, indicated that Mrs. Pleasant was not in the best mood. Disregarding Mammy's warning about the lazy Irish, Teresa had become friendly with the rosy-cheeked, buxom upstairs maid, and she listened to her stories and complaints regularly while she drank her morning coffee in her sitting room.

"If you ask me," Bridget said, "she's a bit taken with herself, that one. She does give herself airs and graces, Mrs. Percy, and she behaves that badly when she's out of sorts. I don't know if she's been in the house or not most of the time in the past few days. It's positively eerie the way she leaves without anyone noticing. And appears again, when one least expects it. She gave Sheila the sack yesterday, over nothing at all. I wonder that you keep such a housekeeper, though I'm speaking above myself in saying so, ma'am."

"She's very efficient," Teresa said good-naturedly, conditioned to the servants' misconception that she was the lady of the house. "Where is she now? If she's in her room, I'll have a word with her. I haven't spoken to her for a while myself."

Bridget shrugged her heavy shoulders, "Who knows where she is? She may be in and she may be out, ma'am. And that's another thing. Her room. Not one of us has seen the inside of it, and we don't think it proper she should be on the same floor as yourself."

Teresa herself had been no farther than the baroque sitting room and secretly suspected that Mammy's bedroom was inviolate because it was as austere as her room at the convent school in New Orleans, which she had described so often. She decided that Mammy might be ill and that she should look in on her. She rose in her dressing gown to complete her careful daily toilette. Later she would call on Mammy, just down the hall. They usually saw each other daily, and Mammy's absence for almost three days was most unusual.

"There's another thing that's strange, too," Bridget continued as Teresa sat at her vanity brushing her hair, which she preferred to dress herself. "Maybe it's just because of my intuition, ma'am. I'm the seventh daughter of a seventh daughter, you know. But sometimes I feel I'm being watched, when it's impossible that anyone's around. I have the queerest feeling," she said with a shudder and then laughed. "Sure you'll think I'm completely daft if I run on like this. Forgive me. The house is that large, but it isn't old enough to have ghosts, is it?"

Bridget did not notice Teresa's hairbrush go idle in midstroke or observe the level blue eyes watching her from the mirror. Teresa made no comment on the maid's queer feeling, which she had begun to experience once again since she had moved into this house, just as she had years ago in the boardinghouse.

"I'm certain there are no ghosts," she said as she smiled at Bridget. "I suspect we have feelings like that from time to time. Will you lay out my sprigged lawn morning dress, please? It appears there'll be sunshine today. I may take a walk in the garden."

The young woman did as she was instructed, but the Irish are not called stubborn for no reason. "I've never had that feeling unless I'm really being watched," she said with determination. "And Sheila got sacked for mentioning something of the sort herself."

There was no answer when Teresa tapped at Mammy's door, and she respected her privacy enough not to try the door and enter uninvited. She took her walk in the garden, which might have been there forever in its formal green pattern interspersed by gravel walks. The rainfall and fog must nourish it year around, she considered, remembering the fields around Geneva Cottage, which were green only in the spring. Situated between the Bay and the ocean, San Francisco's climate was better for horticulture than the hills to the north and south. She watched for Mammy to return, pausing only once to pluck a dead rose from one of the bushes before returning to the house, convinced that Mammy must be away for the morning.

After touring the whole house, from the kitchen to the nursery on the third floor to see that everything was in order, she was returning to her room, thinking about what Bridget had told her, when she was startled by a figure coming out of Mammy's suite in the dimness of the hallway. Her momentary alarm turned to puzzlement when she recognized that it was Mammy in the hall; but, anxious to have a word with her, she moved forward quickly, calling her by name.

"Mammy! You're as difficult to find as a will o' the wisp," she smiled.

175

"I watched for your return in the garden, but I'd given up on you. Are you all right? I haven't seen you for days."

"Who said I'd been out?" Mammy asked peevishly with a frown between her eyes.

"I knocked on your door," Teresa replied, "and no one answered."

Mammy waved the subject aside with her long hand, but her mood did not show any improvement. "If I was in my bedroom, I wouldn't have heard you. Come in for a moment, Teresa. I think we should have a talk."

Mammy's sitting room with its painted panels and gilded cupids on the ceiling almost looked as if it had not been lived in, though she had occupied the suite for over six months, without admitting any servants. Mammy and I are alike in one thing at least, Teresa thought as she took her seat on the sofa: we are meticulous in our care of beautiful things, and our fastidiousness extends to our persons. She did not doubt that Mammy was in a worse mood than any Teresa had seen her in before, but her dark taffeta dress was tidy, as usual, and adorned with a small detachable lace collar secured at the neck by a cameo. Her hands and nails were carefully cared for, and her hair was neatly parted in the middle, without the slight crimp in it that Teresa had noticed before. It made Teresa wonder if she could trust her senses. She knew that people could curl their hair, but she was not familiar with any method for taking the curl out of it.

She shook her head slightly when Mammy offered a glass of her homemade wine—so early in the day—and she was mildly surprised to see her friend fill a glass for herself and drink it quickly before filling it again and sitting down. "We have a problem," Mammy admitted as she settled in her chair. "You don't know how upset I've been for the past few days."

She paused abstractedly, and Teresa prodded her by remarking, "You fired Sheila. She was a good servant, Mammy. It'll be difficult to replace her."

"That silly girl," Mammy breathed contemptuously. "If there's one thing, I don't believe in, it's magic and the supernatural! She thought there was a ghost in the house. These Irish servants are full of such nonsense. I let her go before she spread panic through the lot of them. Maybe I shouldn't have done it," she sighed, "but I have a lot on my mind. Teresa, would you believe that, after all the work I've put in on this house, Thomas refuses to live in it?"

Teresa would have found it more difficult to believe if he hadn't

176

refused and she studied Mammy quietly, sensing that her opinion on the matter was not being solicited. She had learned that sometimes one learned more through silence than by interrupting with questions or comments.

"That wonderful master bedroom," Mammy deplored, "and the billiard room! The very best in the city. If he thinks he can use my house as a club, he's sadly mistaken. Either he moves in and lives where he should, with his family, or he won't be invited again, regardless of how much he poured into the place for Fred."

Teresa wondered if perhaps Mammy had drunk too much of her own wine. This time the pause was so long that she attempted to clarify the matter. "But we aren't his family, Mammy," she objected, "only little Fred is."

"Oh, you haven't heard all of it!" Mammy replied with agitation. "Fred isn't to be an only child, Teresa. There's another one on the way, and he expects us to care for it too. I have to admit, he has his nerve, saddling you with another child to raise, without having the decency to marry you."

Teresa was stunned for a moment; but after thinking about it for a moment, she reacted with humor. "Why should he?" she smiled. "As things stand, he can have any woman he wants and store the results of his promiscuity in this elaborate orphanage he helped to build. I must agree with you that he has cheek," she added with a giggle. "When will the new little Bell be arriving on the scene?"

Mammy shook her head as if she did not know, but she did not join in Teresa's lightness. "Surely, he must have heard the rumors," she said sternly. "He must know how he's compromising your good name. He's behaving like a cad, Teresa—but I know a way to bring him around," she added slyly.

Until now, Mammy had always been good-natured and optimistic, and Teresa observed the new expression on her face with some alarm. There was something feline about it, so absolutely malicious, that she began to feel fear gathering in the pit of her stomach. Mammy's whole manner struck a wrong note, almost as if she wanted Mr. Bell in the house for herself. That's ridiculous, of course, Teresa thought. Mammy has always been concerned only with my future with Mr. Bell. I'm just being silly, because she's acting a little strange.

"You mustn't do anything," Teresa said cautiously, "not for me, Mammy. Either he decides to marry me or he doesn't. I guess I don't much care anymore. And as far as my good name's concerned, you

177

know very well that I'm no saint. I might not be Mr. Bell's mistress, but I've had my little fling."

"You don't understand, child," Mammy said, reaching out to touch her hand. "You don't understand at all. You know nothing about finance and real estate. Nor should you. You're a lovely lady with less worldly things on your mind. We'll get him, Teresa, I swear we will." For the first time during the conversation, she laughed slightly. "Just wait until the registration of this house comes out in the newspaper. Someone will see it, and the earth will begin to shake under his feet. Maybe it'll knock some sense into his thick Scottish head."

"What have you done?" Teresa asked weakly, not knowing what to expect with Mammy in such a mood. "Surely, you weren't foolish enough to register the house in his name?"

Mammy laughed again and gazed at Teresa with a mysterious expression on her face. "You'll see. And if that doesn't work, I have other tricks up my sleeve."

Teresa remembered Mr. Bell saying something, years ago, about Mammy's having too many tricks up her sleeve, and she grew uncomfortable at the memory. He had been trying to warn her away from Mammy at the time. "How is Billy Beaumont?" she asked suddenly, to Mammy's surprise. "I haven't thought about him for a while," she explained, "and he just popped into my head."

"He's fine," Mammy said. "He's going to marry Byna in a few months. Maggie's in fine health, too, and Ben Willard will live to be a hundred, I'm certain. Just in case you're really interested, honey."

Teresa was not particularly interested in her former maid or Mammy's occasional lover, and Mammy's health report struck her as odd until she read the newspaper the next day. She often perused the property registrations, trying to guess which ones were Mammy's under other names, and the registration for 1661 Octavia Street was in the name of *Mrs. Teresa Bell.* Her first impulse was to flee San Francisco, because the scandal Tony had predicted appeared about to break over her head. But, then, she remembered Mammy's mention of the witnesses to Jim Hoey's death. Mammy would never let her escape as long as those witnesses remained living.

MRS. THERESA BELL. Teresa crumpled the newspaper in her hands helplessly, almost physically sick with humiliation. She could not imagine Mammy doing such a thing to her, as if rubbing salt into the wound of her inability to marry Mr. Bell. She did not take a carriage ride with Fred the next day; and, during the following weeks, reporters hovered near the house on Octavia Street, watching for any activity

178

there. She peered through the curtains of her room, wondering what they would say to complete her ruin in the next edition. They did not disappoint her, because Mr. Bell retaliated. The fight was really between himself and Mammy, but nobody except them realized it. The nightmare of notoriety that followed concerned one person, the beautiful blonde woman who called herself Mrs. Bell.

Thomas Bell denied that Teresa was his wife, of course; but, he too must have found himself in an embarrassing, annoying situation. Teresa tried not to look at the newspapers, but she found herself unable to refrain from assessing her fate. QUICKSILVER BACHELOR AT OPERA WITH MISS PARSONS was the first indication of Mr. Bell's desperation to deny the marriage, and other similar indications followed quickly. She had no idea he enjoyed such an active social life. When Fred's birth certificate was ferreted out by an eager reporter, Mr. Bell was forced to face the press again. This further complicated things, and Bridget was the first to inform Teresa of the new development.

"Sure it's a bold man who'll admit a child is his and deny marrying the mother," she said as she pushed the folded paper into Teresa's reluctant hands. "Ah, you've been weepin' again, ma'am, and I don't wonder. He's a terrible man altogether. We all knew the house belonged to you from the beginning, and that you are Mrs. Bell."

"What?" Teresa asked apathetically. "You've never addressed me as Mrs. Bell, Bridget. Who on earth told you that?"

The maid was solid in her loyalty to Teresa. "Herself, that's who, your fine Mrs. Pleasant. She told us about the separation, and how you weren't in any condition to be addressed as Mrs. Bell right now. But for him to deny being married to you and you Fred's mother! Quicksilver King indeed. He should be damn well shot!"

The anger that exploded in Teresa's chest banished her weakness and trepidation. She snatched the newspaper from Bridget's hand and stormed down the hall to Mammy's room, where she pounded insistently on the door until it opened. "Damn you, Mammy!" she cried, pushing past her, "damn you! Do you see what you've done with your secrets and scheming? Now, everyone really thinks that Fred's my child, and you registered his birth just as you did this godforsaken house. What on earth do you hope to accomplish by such underhanded actions? Mr. Bell will have nothing to do with either one of us after all this. And I'll never be able to show my face in public again."

"It's caused quite a stir, hasn't it?" Mammy chuckled, putting her hand on Teresa's arm, only to have it quickly shoved away. "I know you're upset," she said, taking a more sympathetic approach, "but it's just a tempest in a teapot, honey. Everyone will forget all about it very soon. Everyone but Thomas, that is. There's more sympathy for you than there is for him. He's the one who's getting smeared. You just mark my words, Teresa. He'll be living in this house before the end of the year."

"I don't give a damn what he does," Teresa cried tearfully. "I wouldn't take him, now, with bells on! He's made me look like an adventurous whore. You've made me look that way," she corrected in confusion. "How could he do this to me? I haven't done anything to him. I've cared for his child all these years, without a penny in return. How can he do it? How could you?"

"Because I want things to turn out right for you, honey. I want you to marry one of the wealthiest men in San Francisco. You know how hard we've worked toward that end. Thomas hasn't made you look bad. On the contrary, Teresa. He's openly denied that you aren't the mother of his child and only caring for Fred, right here in this newspaper interview. He doesn't mean you any harm. He's just a little upset with me."

"To put it mildly," Teresa said, feeling completely drained. "What about that birth certificate, Mammy? Who registered that? Everyone knows I didn't have a child while I was living on Sutter. The journalists have ferreted that out, too."

"That was for future security," Mammy assured her, completely unruffled. "He just didn't realize how far I'd go." She hesitated a moment, but she could not resist revealing the full extent of her cleverness. "I suppose Byna and I are the only people who could swear you weren't pregnant, Teresa. If I remember correctly, you wore that long sealskin cape whenever you went out that winter."

"For God's sake!" Teresa cried, bursting into tears. "Is there anything you won't do to have your own way? Doesn't friendship mean a thing to you? I've never done anything to hurt you, Mammy, and you're standing by while I'm being crucified by the press. I thought you cared for me."

"I do," Mammy said softly, attempting to take Teresa's hand, which was quickly jerked out of her grasp. "You're like a daughter to me, honey . . . like my other self. I've only tried to help things along. I didn't mean to make you unhappy, you know that."

"I don't know any such thing! You have me bound hand and foot, Mammy, and you know it. I don't want anything more to do with Mr. Bell. The very thought of that man makes me sick."

"Don't you ever say that," Mammy said with an undertone of anger in her voice. "You may think you're a high and mighty lady now, but we know otherwise, don't we? You didn't always pee elegant perfume." She checked herself at the expression of shock in Teresa's eyes. "I'm sorry, I didn't mean that, honey," she recanted quickly, but her anger was still evident. "I could just shake you for driving me to say things like that! Don't you understand, Teresa, that we're in this together, and what hurts you is painful to me, too?"

"Your name isn't splashed all over the papers for everyone to see," Teresa said petulantly. "Nothing you do ever comes to the strong light of day."

"That's right," Mammy agreed with a peculiar intensity in her eyes, "and there's a reason for that, Teresa. If I'm occasionally underground in my dealings, it's because I can't walk right out in the strong light of day like you. Do you think I'd need you at all if I could? You aren't fond of recollecting your days on that upstate New York farm, are you? Has it ever occurred to you that there are things I want to forget, too? Things I've spent my whole life trying to overcome." In her anger over Teresa's rebellion, she was running on in a way Teresa had never witnessed before, pacing the rug as revelations poured from deep inside of her. "Poor little white girl! Do you think I have much sympathy about that, when I had to drag myself up from slavery to achieve what I have? Yes, *slavery!* My mother was a quadroon and my father, a white planter who didn't care anything about me. If a white man hadn't bought me when I was thirteen and put me in that convent, I probably wouldn't be alive now. Slave women like my mother died young. But I was able to set myself on a path and stick to it to get what I have, unlike you, who'd be in a brothel on the Barbary Coast if I hadn't saved you from your own weakness when I did."

Teresa was so astonished that she heard nothing beyond Mammy's admission that she was part black. It just isn't possible, she told herself. I'd have known, I'm sure I would have. Yet, there had been indications, and her mind leaped back to retrieve them. Mammy's interest in black people might have alerted her as well as the affectionate name they had for her. And her hair's beginning to curl, she thought irrationally. No one's hair starts to curl just because she's getting older. She was suddenly aware of Mammy's silence and glanced at her with alarm. She stood, tall and stately, with an expression almost of compassion on her dusky, perfect face.

"The maids didn't tell you about it, did they?" she asked in a warm, sympathetic voice. "I rather thought they had. I can see how shocked you are, Teresa. Does it make that much difference between us?"

Teresa felt numb, but she shook her head slowly. "Of course not," she murmured, "why should it? I was just taken by surprise, I guess."

"Well," Mammy considered, "now that everything's out in the open, perhaps we can combine forces effectively to get what we both want. There's no reason in the world, Teresa, why women shouldn't be in control of their lives as much as men. Even women like us, who certainly weren't born with silver spoons in our mouths."

"If your mother was a quadroon," Teresa said, pursuing her own line of thought, "and your father was white, you have hardly any black blood at all. . . ."

"You make it sound like a reproach," Mammy laughed bitterly. "Take my word for it, that doesn't mean anything in the South. Something's bothering you, Teresa."

"No," Teresa fibbed, studying Mammy's handsome face as though for the first time, looking for evidence of the quarter-blood mother there. "I'll be all right as soon as I quiet down. I won't read the papers again until it's all over, I think. It makes me feel so . . . low."

"It's just a small scandal," Mammy assured her, "one that won't hold the interest of the *Alta*'s readers very long. Everything will be back to normal in no time, my dear. Once Thomas marries you, people won't dare mention it again."

Chapter 14

As Mammy had predicted, the scandal gradually died down, and only an occasional reporter was to be seen outside the house; but Teresa continued to smart over the outrages that had been committed in her name. She did not leave the house, not even for an occasional stroll in the garden, where passers-by might point her out. She had not realized until now how much she valued her privacy, and she feared that Mammy's determination to capture Mr. Bell would violate her solitude again. Even the clucking sympathy of the servants burned her like nettles dashed across her face.

Her own suite was the only place to escape her humiliation. She spent long hours there, reading and writing in her diary. The maid, Bridget, was instructed not to speak of the scandal again, under threat of dismissal, but even the young woman's sad gaze became too much for Teresa after a while, and she made certain she was elsewhere when Bridget came to do the room. She did not see much of Mammy, and that, at least, was a blessing, because she had nothing to say to her. She did not want to know what her conniving mentor was up to, and Mammy kept her distance because she knew that Teresa was angry with her.

Teresa took her meals in her room and usually retired early to escape the depression that had settled over her. One evening she decided that she must escape San Francisco altogether, and she took out her jewelry box to count the money she had been able to save over the years, which she had concealed beneath the lining. She had only two hundred dollars—more than the five she had arrived with ten years ago, but not enough for an extended holiday. With everything provided for her, she rarely handled cash. What she had accumulated was saved a few dollars at a time, when she had been allowed to go shopping with cash in her purse. She studied the diamond earrings Mammy had given her, unable to estimate their worth. She knew she would get next to nothing if she pawned them, and anyway, she was totally inexperienced in the sale of such items. She replaced the jewelry box in the back of her vanity drawer and sat for a long time with her chin on her hand, aware that Mammy would not let her leave at this time and too impoverished to take the dangerous step herself.

A few days later, she decided without much optimism about the outcome of the request, to ask Mammy to send her somewhere for a while. She had just assembled the confidence to go to Mammy's room, when there was a crisp knock on her sitting-room door, which sent her hopes plummeting again. She was afraid to answer, wondering what new disaster might have struck; but she heard the tapping again, more insistent this time and she finally responded.

Mammy stood in the hallway impatiently, dressed in her outside clothing and poke bonnet, with a Scottish tartan shawl over her shoulders and a portmanteau in her hand. "I have some instructions for you," she said, pushing Teresa aside to enter. "I'm going to the country. I don't know how long I'll be gone. You'll have to manage the house here, Teresa. I've written everything down." She handed Teresa several sheets of folded writing paper, which she accepted reluctantly. "I'd hoped I wouldn't have to go this far, because it will hurt me financially, too. But not allowing Thomas to see Fred has shown no results, so I'm forced to take this step."

"What step?" Teresa inquired with some trepidation. "Mammy, what are you up to, now?"

"I'm withdrawing my financial advice. I'm going to the country, for as long as it takes for him to give in. If keeping him from his son isn't important to him, I know what is. I'm going after him where it will hurt most, in his pocketbook."

Teresa's eyes filled with tears, and she said softly, "All this is my fault. He just doesn't want to marry *me*. You should have given up on me a long time ago, Mammy. You still can—"

"Give up on you?" Mammy exclaimed, "never. Please don't blame yourself, Teresa. Any other man would leap at the opportunity of marrying you. You don't know how lovely you really are, my dear. My whole association with you has been a pleasure. You're my greatest success."

"I appreciate that you made me everything I am," Teresa concurred.

184

"What I'm saying is that it isn't enough for what you appear to desire."

"You're the one who improved yourself," Mammy said, embracing her briefly, anxious to be on her way. "I only saw your potential, honey. I must be off, now. Thomas will receive my letter today, and I want to be away when that happens."

Though she did not understand the financial aspect of Mammy's withdrawal to the country, Teresa was conscious of a sense of failure. It had all seemed so simple in the beginning, she reflected, especially after Jim's death had left her free. Mammy really felt that she had found the right girl for her friend, Mr. Bell. She had tutored her and trained her, and she had finally presented her to the financier at Geneva Cottage. He had been interested, Teresa was certain of that. Where had she gone wrong? she wondered, as she wandered about the stately house with Mammy's incredibly long list of her duties in her hand. If she was everything a man might want in a wife, Mr. Bell must have perceived something in her that no one else saw except Mammy. She wondered if it were possible that the little Scot with his merry blue eyes and genial manner had detected that yawning void deep inside of her that had never completely left her. She was still without cohesion, weak and dependent on others. Some men would not have objected to this aspect of her character; indeed, most men adored women who depended upon them for everything. But most men had not known Mammy the way Mr. Bell knew her; and Mary Ellen Pleasant had more strength of purpose than any woman alive. No, she decided, he probably had not detected her failings. He would never have entrusted the child he adored to her care if he had been uncertain about her character.

Without looking at the list or noting her progress, she had reached the parlor, and she pulled the tapestry bellpull to summon the butler. She was going around in circles in her mind, incapable of carrying out the simplest instruction. She must speak to someone unconnected with the household, neutral in opinion, or she would lose her mind.

"These things need attention," she told Thornton when he appeared. "I shall be going out today. Please have the carriage brought around in half an hour."

She had not been to church since she left the farm at seventeen, but she instructed the driver, Perry Cooke, to take her to the Holy Angels Church. Saint Mary's was too far away, and though her face was swathed in a dark veil and the top of the coach was covered against the fine January rain, she was still uneasy about the reporters. When she descended in front of the small church, she instructed the driver to wait for her in a side alley to avoid recognition of the carriage and ran up the steps into the dim, candle-scented interior.

Crossing herself automatically at the font, she discerned that she was alone in the church and knelt in a back pew, not so much to pray as to decide on her next move. In her confused state, she had somehow equated the church with a priest, and it took her a few moments to realize that the priest was probably in the rectory. She did not feel she should reveal herself by walking around to the rectory via the sidewalk. Blinking tears of frustration from her eyes, she said a few childhood prayers and was just on the point of leaving when a black-cassocked figure appeared in the aisle and passed directly beside her.

"Father," she whispered, too softly to check his progress, and her voice broke when she called him again, "Father!" He turned and observed her for a moment before moving toward her. He was a middle-aged man with dark eyes and a full head of white hair. "I need help," she told him. "I've been away from the church for a long time."

"Is it confession you're after?" he asked, with an Irish lilt in his voice. "These doors are never closed to a soul in need, my child."

She shook her veiled head sadly, and she could detect the faint odor of her expensive perfume more than the lingering scent of beeswax candles and incense in the church. She did not know why she had put on perfume to come here. "I have to speak to someone, Father. Perhaps later, when I'm more worthy, I'll take the sacraments again."

"The church is empty," he said gently, "we can speak here. Or, if you prefer, we can go to the rectory, Miss . . . Mrs. . . . ."

She raised the dark veil and stared at him wretchedly with her blue eyes. "Percy. Teresa Percy, Father. I'm the woman they say is married to Mr. Thomas Bell. But I'm not," she said, swallowing hard to combat the dryness of her mouth. "He's never married me."

His sudden interest revealed that he knew all about the scandal. "I'm Father Dougherty," he told her, studying her face. "If I recollect correctly, there's a child involved."

"Yes," she nodded, suddenly forgetting what she had come to say. When the words came out, she could not believe they had passed her lips. "And there's another on the way."

"And the man, Mr. Bell, refuses to marry you and legitimize the children?" he asked with more curiosity than disapproval. "The gentleman's a Scot and probably a Protestant," he considered, as though that

186

explained everything. "There must be some way to bring him around."

"He's absolutely adamant," Teresa volunteered, a vague plan forming in her mind. "He's a very wealthy man and a selfish one, too. He's a good deal older than I," she shrugged, "and perhaps he's protecting his fortune. I don't want anything for myself, but—" she put her lace handkerchief to her nose "—there are the children, the poor innocent lambs."

"Thank you for inviting me, Mrs. Percy," Mr. Bell told her awkwardly, "after all that's transpired. I've missed seeing Fred more than you know." He waited for Thornton to take his coat and leave. "You probably know that I wouldn't enter this house if Mammy were around."

"I understand that," Teresa said gravely. "I do hate to see a falling-out between old friends, though. Mammy retired to the country last week, as I explained in my letter, so you must make yourself comfortable. I'll send for little Fred."

"I'd prefer to see him in the nursery, if you don't mind," he smiled cheerfully. "I invited some friends, as you so kindly suggested, but they won't be along for a while. I'll have a nice visit with my boy before they arrive."

"It's close to his bedtime." Teresa smiled graciously. "But I think this time it will be allowed. Dinner will be served around nine. Perhaps you'd like to join me in a glass of wine before your friends arrive."

"I'd enjoy that very much," he said, marveling at her composure. "You really are an amazing woman, Mrs. Percy, and that is a very fetching gown."

She had dressed with more care than usual and knew that the pale lavender satin gown with a discreet lace insert over the bodice and flowing lace sleeves became her very well. Nevertheless, she was still rather amazed to receive a compliment from him after all the difficulty Mammy had caused. When he went upstairs to the nursery, she dismissed Thornton for the evening, as she had the other servants, except those who would serve dinner. The butler appeared dumbfounded at the suggestion that he leave during the first social function she had given, but she persuaded him that everything was quite under control.

"These particular gentlemen require very little," she said with a smile. "They enjoy relaxing together without any fuss."

All the crystal chandeliers had been lighted earlier, and she retired to the comparative intimacy of the parlor to set the wineglasses on the low *pietra dura* table and sniff the carafe of wine again. Mammy's special herbal wine, which was merely relaxing in small doses, could not be detected in the full bouquet of the French wine she had personally selected. More than once, when she had been under a strain, one small glass of Mammy's wine had tranquilized her into unconsciousness until the following morning. But prior to sleep there had been an almost euphoric, devil-may-care period during which she might have done anything if she weren't under supervision. Mr. Bell never drank just a single glass of wine, and she was depending on his habit of inbibing too much, too quickly.

She had ordered the nurse to put Fred to bed within half an hour, and soon Thomas joined her, smiling happily. "Here you are. I wasn't sure I could find you in this monumental pile. Fred's really a fine boy, isn't he? Oh, thank you, I need this. You can't imagine how happy he was to see me again. He searched all my pockets like a little ferret, and of course he wasn't disappointed."

"You spoil him," she said lightly.

"Why shouldn't I?" he asked, relaxing in a chair. "They aren't children forever, you know, and he's all I have." He considered the statement and glanced at her sheepishly. "At the moment," he added.

"Would you like another glass of wine, Mr. Bell?"

"Yes, don't mind if I do, Mrs. Percy. It's very fine. She does keep her cellar well stocked, along with her larder. I suppose you've heard nothing from her at all?"

"No," Teresa replied with a shrug. "I suspect she's putting up her relishes again. Though heaven knows we don't need them. This is hardly a boardinghouse."

"Damn nuisance," he said refilling his glass. "She isn't as responsible as she once was. She musht . . . must know we're losing money every day. I can't unnerstand why she did all that. Damn embarrassing in my poshition."

"It was worse for me," Teresa admitted with lowered lashes. "I suspect I'll never live it down."

"I'm shorry about that," he said with concern. "You're such a good, kind lady, Mrs. Pershy. You should nae ha' been brought into it. Ye've been sae gude to my boy. If there's anything I can do. . . . "

"Fred will suffer from the scandal," she suggested, observing him closely. His face, which was normally ruddy, was pleasantly flushed, and his eyes, abnormally bright. "Everyone thinks he's ours. I suppose the only way to save our self-respect is to marry, Mr. Bell."

"Fred . . . ours," he considered vaguely. "The poor wee bairn. You're

188

absho . . . you're right, Mrs. Pershy. We should marry to shave the boy."

She rang the small crystal bell from the table without taking her eyes off him. He was too befuddled to react to the sound, but Father Dougherty in the next room heard the clear, high tone and joined them at once, with a white stole over his shoulders and his missal in his hand.

Their vows were spoken and the marriage forms filled out before Thomas's friends arrived. In high good humor, they congratulated Thomas for doing the proper thing, and he accepted their good wishes. Toasts were drunk all around. Teresa marveled at his ability to stand upright; indeed, he was able to give her his arm to lead the party, along with the priest, into the dining room.

She was unable, later, to reconstruct how the events of the evening unfolded as they did, though she had drunk only a single glass of untreated wine. Quite suddenly, Mammy was standing in the dining-room door, observing the party with a tight face and an ominous stare. Teresa smiled at her to assure her that everything was all right, indicating the priest seated at her right, and Mammy moved to the head of the table quietly to read the marriage certificate, which was lying there. Teresa watched her jubilantly, waiting for her joyful reaction; she had finally married Mr. Bell as Mammy wished, and she thought Mammy would be pleased. Instead, Mammy's clear features changed subtly, and her mismatched eyes blazed with fury as she looked from Teresa to Mr. Bell and the priest. Something in her visage reminded Teresa of a picture she had seen of a panther at bay, with its ears laid back and lips snarling; and her triumph faded, turning to a stab of icy fear in her abdomen.

Somehow they got through the dinner, Mammy assisting with the serving. No matter how angry she was, she was still just the house-keeper in the eyes of Mr. Bell's friends, and she controlled herself in their presence. When Mr. Bell finally collapsed into his plate after the entrée, to the good-humored cheers of his friends, Mammy took over the situation with alacrity.

"Carry him to his room," she told two of the gentlemen and preceded them up the stairs to the suite she had prepared for him. The rest of the party rose to leave, smiling and winking at Teresa as they did, and she was left alone with Father Dougherty at the table. Mr. Bell had emptied his wallet to pay the priest directly after the ceremony, and Father Dougherty took one last sip of wine before he gathered up his paper-work carefully and reassured her, "We've done the right thing for the sake of the children, Teresa. Everything comes out the right way in the end. I hope to see you and the boy at Mass on Sunday. Good night, my child."

"Good night, Father," she whispered, wondering why she was so terrified of Mammy. Mammy had always wanted her to marry Mr. Bell; she had said so often. The scandal in the newspapers had all been toward that end. Everything had concerned this marriage, from the first time they had met on Washington Street. Why had Mammy reacted as she had? Her suppressed anger had cast a spell over the entire meal. Teresa decided that the best thing to do at this point was to lock herself in her room until the unexplained storm blew over.

Her knees felt weak as she climbed the stairway, and the coldness in her middle increased with every step. She hoped to avoid Mammy tonight; but just as she was entering her room, she heard a voice hiss at her elbow, "You stupid girl! Do you know what you've done this time?"

"I thought you wanted me to. . . ." Teresa stammered, turning to face that feline fury again. "You've always wanted us to marry, Mammy. I thought it would please you. . . ."

"*Please* me! You've understood nothing at all," Mammy continued, a peculiar rasp in her voice and a murderous expression in her eyes. "Are those my diamond earrings you're wearing?"

"No," Teresa said, her hand trembling as it touched one of them, "these are the earrings you gave me."

"When did I ever give you diamonds?" Mammy pursued with hatred in her face. "They look like mine to me. You haven't seen the last of this evening's work, believe me, Teresa. You'll never live as Thomas's wife."

Teresa dashed into her room and secured the door behind her, leaning against it until she thought there was no one in the hall, though it was always difficult to detect Mammy's footsteps. Never before had she experienced such total terror, not even when she knew Jim Hoey was looking for her. Overcome by faintness, she managed to go into her bedroom and fall on the bed without losing consciousness. She lay staring at the dark ceiling, attempting to will the panic away, but her emotions did not work that way and her fear increased in the darkness. Her mind, at least, seemed abnormally clear as it raced over the possibilities. She can't kill me, though I think she'd like to, she decided; I'm too well known in this city for that. Mammy's words had sounded like a threat, but they could be interpreted another way, and she did not relish the alternatives much more than she relished being murdered. She could say I murdered Jim; all the witnesses to his death are

190

still alive, she considered with a feeling of doom. My God, what a sensation that would cause. I might even end up being hanged. And what was that peculiar reference to her diamond earrings supposed to mean? After so recently experiencing how deviously Mammy's mind could work, how far she planned ahead, she knew she might expect anything.

I must get out of here, she decided, her fear turning to action. I must leave tonight and go as far as I can. With a feeling of déja vu, she ran to her closet and hauled the lightest leather suitcase from the rear. With no thought of her expensive gowns, she methodically began to pack a few practical items of clothing for her simplest needs. As she wriggled out of her lavender satin to put on her gray traveling dress, she knew exactly what she would do. She had considered taking this step only a few weeks before, when her motivation was not as strong. Still in darkness, she transferred the money from her jewel box into her purse and put the box in her suitcase. There was no ferry to Oakland and the railroad yard this late at night, so she would have to check into a second-class hotel to wait for daylight.

She waited until there was no sound in the house except for the chiming of the standing clock in the hall below. She doubted that Mammy was sleeping, but she must have retired to her room to pace out her rage. She slipped through the hall of the servants' quarters at the rear of the house and walked quickly down the hill from the opposite side of Bush Street, the suitcase growing heavier with every block. Her days of playing lady were over, she reflected anxiously. Now, she would have to face the world again.

The reason for Mammy's anger did not strike her until she was gazing out of the train window somewhere in Nevada; but when it came to her, everything became clear. Mammy never wanted me to marry Mr. Bell, she thought with a start—she wants him for herself. What she had planned all along was some peculiar ménage à trois with Teresa posing as his wife to lend it respectability, and so she had gone to outrageous lengths to get Mr. Bell to live in the house. Mammy and Mr. Bell, she considered with a flicker of humor that relaxed her slightly. They almost seemed too old for that sort of thing. She wondered if they had been lovers all along and she was just too stupid to recognize it. Ben Willard might have been just part of the dissembling.

Well, I didn't really want to be that old man's wife anyway, she decided with a sigh. I seem to spend my life running away from husbands of one sort or another. But she was conscious that this flight

191

was not really like the one from New York, despite the similarities. Then, she had had only Jim Hoey's jealousy to worry about, and the trains did not run regularly. This time she was fleeing the wrath of Mammy Pleasant, without knowing how far her power might extend or how patiently she might wait for her revenge.

When the train stopped in Denver, Teresa descended to the platform to stretch her legs while new passengers were being loaded. She picked up a newspaper to take back to the coach car with her. As the steam hissed along the tracks and the wheels began to click again, she perused an article about the extension of the telephone service, which had first been installed in New Haven, Connecticut, the year before. She turned to the second page, grateful to have something to distract her from her desperate journey, and she could not believe the story that met her eyes near the bottom of the page: QUICKSILVER KING AND BRIDE TO EUROPE.

Reading so rapidly that she skipped some of the words, she learned that Mr. Thomas Bell and his bride, Mrs. Teresa Percy, recently married in San Francisco, had embarked on an extended European honeymoon. The wedding had taken place in the bride's home, which was termed the House of Mystery in San Francisco, and had been attended by only a few close friends, as reported by the housekeeper, Mrs. Mary Ellen Pleasant. When asked how soon the mining magnate and his bride might return, Mrs. Pleasant was reticent at first, but finally acknowledged with a smile, "When they get back, I suppose."

Teresa leaned against the rough velvet upholstery, folding the paper over her lap. The astounding thing was that Mammy had already found some way to turn the marriage to her advantage; otherwise, she would not have allowed the reporters to interview her. The woman's mind was far more mysterious than anything about the house on Octavia Street. And what has she done with poor Mr. Bell? Teresa wondered, without much interest. But when the answer to that came to her, she had to suppress a smile. Mr. Bell had obviously fled the city, just as she had, probably to his mines in South America. She could imagine his anger whe he awakened in the thoroughly English room he had shunned for so long to find himself a married man, in spite of his efforts to retain his free bachelor status. He had probably left the house in a rage and embarked on the first vessel sailing toward his jungle holdings.

Mammy will have a difficult time gathering her happy family together again, she thought with dark humor, especially since she probably does not know where either party is. A honeymoon in Europe, indeed. Mammy's ménage à trois was down to one, and she would rattle around in that large house for a long time before she saw the bride again. Of that, Teresa was certain. The honeymoon story was one method of Mammy's handling things, but it did not reflect her true state of mind, which Teresa knew had been murderous when she had last seen her. She could never return to face that kind of Mammy again.

Chapter 15

The prospect of returning to Manhattan after ten years away did not alarm Teresa as much as her arrival in San Francisco had when she was younger. She knew New York City fairly well, from the fine shops on Fifth Avenue, where she used to window-shop, to the stately brownstones of the wealthy and the run-down hotels and cold-water flats she had lived in with Jim. She had planned her course of action while she traveled and was so intent upon it when she descended from the passenger car at the station that she did not look to right or left as she departed from the platform with the single suitcase in her hand. Conscious of her wrinkled clothing and desiring a bath more than anything else, she was bent on finding a reasonably priced hotel for her initial few days in the city. Even in this state of mind, however, she was conscious of the New York accent being spoken around her, especially in the cries of the newspaper vendor in the station.

Everything is so different here, she thought, remembering San Francisco with its mild climate and friendly inhabitants. She had observed that there was still snow on the ground as the train neared the city, and she had brought nothing to protect herself from the cold. My sealskin cape was more suited to New York than San Francisco, she thought ironically, remembering why Mammy had forced the warm, full fur on her in the first place. The woman was really a caution, she thought with grudging amusement. I think I'm going to miss her, in spite of everything. The greatest change she was beginning to experience already in New York was that she was just plain Teresa again, and no longer a lady to be treated with respect. She was jostled several times as she made her way through the station with her single suitcase, without a word of apology from the offenders; and when she checked into a second-class hotel, the male desk clerk appraised her suspiciously in her travel-rumpled clothes.

"Staying long?" he asked brusquely, swinging the register around to look at her name. "San Francisco, huh? We don't allow any visitors in the rooms."

The memory of her arrival on the West Coast poured over her with a sickening rush; but at least this time she could speak properly. "I don't know how long I'll stay," she told him primly. "I'd like to see something of the city before I return to Boston, though. I would like to freshen up. I hope you have a nice, quiet room near the bath."

"Let me see," he pondered with an abashed expression on his face. "Room two-twenty-three is in the rear, and it might suit you, ma'am. I'll have some extra towels sent up. And if there's anything else, just let me know."

"Thank you," she said wearily as she took the key. She had never been in a hotel that fit the term "shabby genteel" so perfectly. Everything was relatively clean, and her room was quiet enough, the windows looking out onto the brick wall of the adjacent building. She could not help reflecting that it was a far cry from the lavish suites she had occupied in Denver and Philadelphia, and the thought was like a grain of sand in her mind. Until it acquired several layers of nacre on its way to becoming a pearl, it would irritate something awful, she realized. I'm going to have to forget all that, she told herself, but it isn't going to be easy.

With enough money to live on for a few weeks, she did not attempt to make any major decisions at once. She spent her days going to the museums and window-shopping on Fifth Avenue, mourning her lost wardrobe at every pretty thing she saw—ready-made had become a term of derision to her. New York had not changed much. It was still an energetic, impersonal, brusque place, where she had never felt at home. A lot of things seemed to be taking place there, and everyone appeared busy, but without the relaxed enthusiasm that seemed to characterize San Franciscans. Within a week she began to experience an unexpected homesickness, and she stayed in her room a great deal, attempting to come to grips with her next move.

Perhaps I should go to Boston, she considered. I've never been there, and the very name of the city evoked gentility. But that was because of the old families on the Social Register, she realized; perhaps everyone else just serves them. She dreaded going to any new place alone. Philadelphia had been easy, because Tony had been there with her. But at least she knew New York, even if she did not like it much.

As she lay in bed one night in her quiet room, staring at the ceiling, she realized that she missed Mammy's companionship more than anything. After all, she had not gone out much when she was in San Francisco; in fact, in recent months, she had not gone out at all. The void inside her opened up for the first time in years, and she felt weak and alone. Many things that Mammy had done seemed questionable, but she was warm and charming. One never felt dull around her, even if one was trying only to anticipate her next move. And when she thought of everything Mammy had provided for her, including the voluptuous house on Octavia Street, tears began to run from the corners of her eyes.

I have not become stronger over the years, she admitted to herself, I'm still the insecure girl who stepped off the boat in San Francisco at twenty-one. The void had just been filled by friendship and activity and unexpected luxury, until she had forgotten it was there. Mammy thought that any woman could pull herself up and make a success if she tried; but Mammy was not like other women in that respect. She had more drive and ambition than most, and Teresa was certain that she had never felt weak and alone. The best a person like her could do was ride along on Mammy's flying apron strings, all the way to the top or into ruin, it did not matter.

She was too terrified of Mammy's fury to consider returning to ask her forgiveness, and she wept quietly in the darkness, wondering what she should do next. A job in a shop, which had once attracted her, was distasteful now. She did not have enough formal education to teach, though that seemed more attractive. If she had been Mammy, she could probably have bluffed her way through the formalities and done anything she liked. But Teresa was not constructed that way. She needed the added confidence of a diploma to attempt any such thing.

On top of everything else, her money was getting lower by the day. At least she would not allow herself to be penniless again. The next morning, she dressed carefully and went to one of the finest jewelry stores to find out how much she could get for her diamond earrings.

Her refined manner precluded embarrassing questions, and a jeweler looked at the stones with a magnifying glass in his eye, his face intent and noncommittal.

"They're perfect stones, Mrs. Percy," he said at last. "I'd be happy to buy them right now if you're interested in selling."

"I don't know," she vascillated, "they were a gift from a dear friend. I just wanted them appraised in the event I have to sell them later."

"He had a fine eye for diamonds," the jeweler commented, return-

197

ing the earrings to their black velvet box and putting them into her hand. "Did he buy them here in New York?"

"*She*," Teresa corrected him. "No, they're from a shop in San Francisco, I think." She waited expectantly for him to reveal their worth. After making some calculations on a sheet of paper, he gave her a good offer, enough to carry her through the year. She rose and shook his hand, expressing her thanks, and she was just turning to leave, when he cleared his throat and increased the offer.

"I have someone who's looking for some stones like yours," he explained. "I suppose you know something about the markup in jewelry, Mrs. Percy. I'm giving you a very handsome offer. If you don't want to sell them right now, please give me your address. Possibly my client will have a better offer."

She told him the name of her hotel reluctantly, because she was ashamed of its class; though she realized on the way home that she should not have been. If she were staying in an expensive hotel, she would have no need to sell a treasured personal gift.

"If there are any messages for me," she told the desk clerk when she returned, "please let me know. Someone may be contacting me within the next few days."

If the offer was much better than the one already given, she would be a fool not to take it, she had decided. She would never allow herself to get down to five dollars in her purse again.

The message came sooner than she had expected, directly to her door the same evening. No one but the hotel maid had ever knocked before, and it was the wrong time for her, so Teresa opened the door with caution, peering through a three-inch crack at the rather seedy-looking gentleman standing under the gas lamp in the hall.

"Pinkerton's," he said abruptly, holding up a badge so she could read it. "Detective Daniel Manning, Mrs. Percy. May we discuss this inside your room?"

Teresa was so dumbfounded that she allowed him to enter. He was a slight man in a pinstriped suit, with alert, observant eyes under the dark bowler squared evenly over his forehead, and Teresa had no reason to believe he was anything but what he represented himself to be. He looked too much the part.

"You had some diamonds appraised with the intention of selling them this afternoon, I believe."

"Yes. They're my own," she said, beginning to tremble inside. "They were given to me by a friend."

"That's where the difficulty comes in," he told her without emotion, his sharp eyes studying her. "One Mrs. Mary Ellen Pleasant in San Francisco has hired us to bring you back to that city, charging that you stole some diamond earrings."

"That's absurd!" Teresa cried. "She gave them to me for my birthday several years ago. Does this mean that you're arresting me?"

"No, ma'am, just returning you to the West Coast. If you aren't cooperative, it'll be in the hands of the New York Police Department. I think it will be easier if you accompany me, Mrs. Percy. If there's a misunderstanding, it can be ironed out in San Francisco. Mrs. Pleasant wants to talk with you."

"It's more likely that she wants to kill me," Teresa said helplessly, with tears brimming her eyes. "We were on very bad terms when I ran away from her. Did that nice jeweler tell you where I was?"

"We've been waiting for the gems to surface for some time, ma'am," he said, offering his handkerchief. "See here, if there's any monkey business going on regarding Mrs. Pleasant's claim, the agency will protect you. Now, get your things together, Mrs. Percy. We're leaving this evening."

Detective Manning's stories and anecdotes made the return trip seem shorter than the train ride East. He treated her like a lady and saw to all her needs, proving an altogether exceptional traveling companion. And, though Teresa revealed little of her situation to him, he picked up quickly on what she did say and confided more to her than a man in his situation should have.

"I've gone the San Francisco route before," he said lazily, settled back in his seat one evening after dinner. "I've talked to the boys out there, and this Bell fellow's name's come up somewhere. They were investigating him for something, but I don't recall the details. A city detective named Leighton took over the case, I believe."

"Mr. Bell's an important man," Teresa defended him. "I can't imagine why any detective would be interested in him. He's an important mining magnate and financier."

"I know," he nodded, "the whole thing sounded mighty peculiar. But someone hired Pinkerton's to get something on him. Only it didn't have anything to do with San Francisco, I remember that now. It went all the way back to England, and why he'd left there to begin with."

After he dozed off, Teresa considered what he had said. Any way she looked at it, everything pointed to Mammy. Mammy had hired the agency to bring her back, so she had probably used it before, probably

199

often, to obtain information on people. She could not imagine what Mammy hoped to learn about Mr. Bell, but her motivation was clear enough. Everything for years had been directed toward getting him to live under the same roof with her. Blackmail? she considered. Mammy had resorted to a lot of things, but Teresa could not believe she would stoop to that.

As he had promised, Mr. Manning accompanied her to Octavia Street on the night of her arrival, though Teresa realized it was part of his job to deliver her into the hands of her accuser, anyway. She clung to his coat sleeve as they approached the recessed entrance of the house, and her fingers bit into his arm when he rang the doorbell.

"Don't be frightened," he reassured her. "I won't leave you alone with her. I only hope that she decides not to press charges, ma'am. That would go very bad for you."

Instead of Thornton opening the door, as she expected, Mammy stood suddenly before her in her black traveling dress, and Teresa's knees nearly gave beneath her at the sight of the embodiment of her fears.

"Detective Manning reporting, Mrs. Pleasant," he companion announced crisply. "I should like to say on Mrs. Percy's behalf that she came peacefully."

"Please come in," Mammy said with her warmest smile. "Teresa, my dear, I'm so happy to see you. You mustn't worry about a thing. I've found my diamond necklace, and I finally recalled giving you the earrings."

Teresa was not reassured and clung more tightly than before to Mr Manning's arm. At least if she was murdered later for marrying Mr. Bell, the detective would know whom to accuse of the crime. Both she and Mr. Manning declined the glass of wine offered by Mammy in the parlor, but Mammy poured one for herself and settled down congenially across from them where they were seated on the sofa. "The whole thing was a terrible mistake, Mr. Manning," she said with an apologetic smile, "I'll make it all right with your agency, of course, and you shall have a special bonus for your trouble."

"A mistake, ma'am?" he asked without succumbing to her considerable charm, "or a ruse to get Mrs. Percy back here? I must confess, this isn't the first time I've encountered such a situation."

"I'm very happy to have Teresa back," she admitted, "but why should I use a ruse, Mr. Manning? I'm only acting on Mr. Bell's behalf, and he's been concerned about his wife, much more than I was about a few diamonds, I assure you."

200

"His wife?" he asked, after a short pause, and Teresa clutched his arm more desperately. "No such marriage was mentioned to me. And even if she is his wife, Mrs. Pleasant, it seems to me her feelings about the matter should be considered. Perhaps she left for a good reason. Where, might I ask, is Mr. Bell now? I think I should discuss this with him. I'm not in the business of returning runaway wives against their will."

"He was called away to his mines in South America," Mammy said easily. "He's a very busy man. That's why he entrusted his house and his dear wife to me. He was distraught when he had to leave. Teresa, my dear, you must come upstairs to see what he ordered for you before he went away."

"Only if Mr. Manning accompanies us," Teresa said tightly, unable to fathom what Mammy was up to now. Had she really come around in her acceptance of the marriage, or was she leading Teresa into a trap?

"If you like," Mammy said, rising to lead them up the stairway. "I must say, you and Mr. Manning have become good friends, haven't you?"

"Yes," Teresa assured her firmly, "he is aware of some of my doubts and fears."

He is also somewhat overcome by the magnificence of the house, she reflected as he paused to take in the grandeur of the great entrance hall. He must not abandon me now. When Mammy opened the door to Teresa's suite, allowing them to precede her, he paused again, and this time he glanced at Teresa in bewilderment.

"In the bedroom, my dear," Mammy said with a smile. Her hips were swinging in that telltale, pleased manner, Teresa observed, and her fear began to evaporate. "When Mr. Bell returns, he plans to do a good deal of entertaining. He had all this sent from Paris."

Lying across the bed were several French gowns, along with their dainty undergarments, and Teresa moved forward to examine an oyster-gray satin creation more beautiful than anything she had ever seen.

"Worth," Mammy said happily, identifying the designer, "and just look at the lovely gloves and slippers!"

Several dozen pairs of white gloves were lined up on the bureau, but Teresa was more interested in the shoes beside the bed: tiny, thin-soled shoes coordinated perfectly with the gowns. With an oyster-gray satin shoe in her hands, she stared past Mr. Manning, with his baffled, half-embarrassed expression, at Mammy, who stood demurely aside, though she was in control of the situation. If she intends to kill me, she wouldn't have gone to all this trouble, Teresa decided. She really isn't angry any more. She has another plan, of course, but she needs me to accomplish it. She was weary from all the traveling, and her beautiful suite looked good to her. All the worry about how she would make her way alone in the world suddenly left her.

"Everything's all right, Mr. Manning," she said softly. "All my fears were unfounded. Thank you for looking after me so kindly. Now, if you'll excuse me, I think Mrs. Pleasant and I have things to discuss."

He nodded uncertainly, attempting to read her enigmatic blue eyes. "If you ever need me or anyone else in the agency, we'll be at your service, ma'am. It's been a pleasure knowing you."

Mammy accompanied him through the sitting room to show him out downstairs, and Teresa overheard her saying in a low voice, "Thank you, Mr. Manning. You'll be well compensated for your work. Believe me, it was for something. Some women do peculiar things when they're in Mrs. Bell's condition. I'm sure you understand."

Teresa shook her head with amused exasperation as she began to hang her new gowns carefully in the closet. She had forgotten about Mr. Bell's new baby and that she was supposed to be pregnant again.

Mammy was full of plans for the future, dismissing Mr. Bell's flight to South America as no more than an inconvenience. "He was a little upset," she chuckled with fond understatement, "but he has to return soon. His business interests are right here. And it would cause another scandal if he lived anyplace but here. He's beaten, and he knows it. The whole world knows he's married to you. And now that everything is completely respectable, he can take his proper place in society with you at his side."

Such a leap after all the bad publicity seemed doubtful to Teresa, but she kept her opinion to herself. "Mammy, I want you to understand that I didn't marry him to live as his wife. I don't care about that. I did it only because I thought that's what you wanted. I did it to please you."

"That's all in the past," Mammy said with a wave of her long hand. "Thomas was so angry, there's no chance of your living as man and wife anyway. As long as you appear to be the ideal couple in public, everything will go very smoothly, Teresa. I think we understand each other."

"I agree to do that," Teresa said with a wry smile. "But what about this new child? If Mr. Bell and I are supposed to be honeymooning in Europe, how will its early birth here be explained?"

"Leave all that to me. You'll have to remain indoors anyway so no one will realize you've returned. The birth can be registered late, some time after his return. That's no problem."

"There's another thing," Teresa hazarded, watching Mammy closely. "Are you aware that a Captain Leighton of the San Francisco police is investigating Mr. Bell?"

There was a slight pause, but not a muscle moved in Mammy's face when she replied. "It's nothing to be concerned about. That was all a long time ago, anyway. There was nothing to investigate, really, and I know the captain pretty well." Then, almost offhandedly, she inquired, "Where did you happen to hear about it?"

Teresa's source was too obvious to deny, and she equally casual in her answer. "Mr. Manning mentioned it on the train. Mammy, these shoes are really gorgeous!"

"Did he say anything else?"

"He told me about some of his cases in New York. His job must really be quite interesting. Of course, the Pinkerton Agency will send him back to the East Coast right away, since that is his home. Why so many gloves, Mammy?"

"Because a lady wears a fresh pair every day," Mammy smiled, her suspicions dispelled. "Sometimes she changes them twice a day. In your new life, you'll need that many. Come to my rooms, Teresa. I want to show you the guest list for the party Mr. and Mrs. Bell shall give shortly after their return from Europe."

A few days later, packing crates began to arrive from Europe, and the main hall was a mass of excelsior as Mammy supervised their unpacking. Teresa noted good-humoredly that Mammy was still spending money like a drunken sailor, providing some diversion and excitement as she did so. Teresa watched from the landing on the second floor as one antique after another was removed from its box and inspected carefully for chips or warping. When Mammy was satisfied that everything had arrived in satisfactory condition, she mounted the stairs with the bills of lading in her hand, so engrossed in her activities that she did not notice Teresa until they were almost face to face.

"You shouldn't have left your room," she said cheerfully enough. "I don't want the servants to see much of you." Guiding her by the elbow to her own quarters, she confided, "All the things that arrived today were purchased by the Bells on their honeymoon. There are some papers for you to sign."

203

Teresa signed several documents in the name of Mrs. Thomas Bell for the first time, while Mammy told her about the things she had ordered. They had coffee together later, Mammy cautiously taking the tray at the door and carrying it to the table herself. "The pieces of furniture are really splendid," she said with a smile as she poured. "If you'd really sent all this from Europe, it wouldn't have had time to arrive. I ordered it some time ago, a happy coincidence. The servants won't know the difference, and they think it came from you."

"You mean that none of them realize I'm back?" Teresa asked with astonishment. "How long can we keep up such a subterfuge? My meals are left in my sitting room three times a day."

"They think one of your relatives is staying there," Mammy told her with a thin smile, "a lady with an infirmity. How long we can do it depends upon you. You can't venture out into the house as you did this afternoon. And we must continue the subterfuge, as you choose to call it, until Thomas returns. That shouldn't be too long now."

"Wouldn't it be safer if I stayed at Geneva Cottage? No one would see me there."

Mammy shook her head firmly. "I want you here, Teresa. You must be in the house when Thomas arrives. Besides," she smiled, reaching out to touch her, "I enjoy your company, honey. I missed you a lot when you were away."

Mammy changed the entire staff of servants, with particular attention to a nurse for the children. "That Irish woman turned Fred against you during the scandal," she explained. "We can't have that. I'm looking for an English nanny, because Fred needs a little discipline."

Teresa cared for little Marie from the time she was born; and her maternal instinct was finally given an outlet. She adored the blonde, blue-eyed baby enough to put up with Fred just to be near the infant. She would gladly have taken over the care of the children entirely, but Mammy would not hear of it. If Teresa told her an anecdote about the baby's development and sweetness, Mammy hardly listened.

"They're all alike," she said in the nursery one evening. "My daughter was raised by nurses, but I'm sure she'd have turned out even worse if I'd done it myself. I recognized my limitation. They're all little animals until they're four or five."

"*Your* daughter?" Teresa asked in surprise. "I didn't know you had one, Mammy."

"She was a drunk, just like her father, absolutely good for nothing. They both died a couple of years ago. She gave me nothing but trouble.

204

You really don't want to get too involved in this sort of thing, Teresa."
"I'm sorry," Teresa said softly. "I had no idea. You lost your family that recently, and I didn't know at all. Did they live in this area?"
"Neither Mr. Pleasant nor my daughter were people you'd like to know. It's something best forgotten. I only married him for his name, which was the same as my natural father's. A bastard slave girl has to be pretty clever to accomplish bearing her white father's name. I got that much out of it, at least."

Teresa remained silent, rocking little Marie's cradle. How much am I going to learn about this woman before all this is over? she wondered. Mammy's heartlessness toward her own child bothered her as much as her attitude toward the Bell children. She wondered if Mammy's daughter had done without anything while her mother was pampering her protégées. Almost as if she sensed Teresa's thoughts, Mammy leaned over the cradle to study the baby.

"You can tell she's Thomas's," she said, more gently. "She might even have his sandy hair later. Teresa, I did everything possible for my daughter, really I did. She had everything a girl wants. I received only hatred and malice in return, and more attempts to embarrass me than you might imagine. If I had my choice," she said softly, gazing across the cradle at Teresa, "I'd have had a daughter like you."

Teresa knew she must say something, but she must be cautious, too. "I didn't have a mother. Just those awful people on the farm. They told me that my real mother didn't want me, that she tried to kill me when I was born."

"There must have been a father," Mammy encouraged her quietly. "What happened to him?"

Teresa shrugged helplessly. "I don't know. They were married, I was told. He was the one who farmed me out, but then he disappeared. I used to dream that he'd come back for me, but he never did." She attempted to hold back the tears that came to her eyes. "Well, that's all in the past, too, isn't it? I don't know what sort of mother you'd have made if I'd belonged to you, but you're the only person who's ever been good to me." She studied the softly sleeping baby girl. "These children are fortunate, aren't they? They'll never have to do the hard work we did in our youth. They'll never be beaten with a stick regularly, either. Everything will be handed to them quite literally on a silver platter."

"Not silver, honey," Mammy smiled, straightening her shoulders and rubbing her hands together as if she suddenly felt cold. "Mercury, more likely. They'll have quicksilver wealth. Everything they need."

"They need love, Mammy. Even the poorest child is happy if it's

205

loved. Nurses are a poor substitute, I think. I really would like to have the children placed in my care."

But Mammy ignored her wishes. Within two days, the new nurse arrived, a thin, sour-faced woman with a British accent. The same day, Mammy appeared at Teresa's door with a gaily ribboned hat box.

'I don't need another hat," Teresa objected as the box was thrust into her arms. "You know I don't go anywhere."

"Open it!" Mammy encouraged with a smile. "Perhaps you should put it on the floor first."

Bewildered by the strange instruction, Teresa did as she was told and untied the ribbons. The top came off by itself, and a small Pekingese puppy emerged panting, its pink tongue vibrating in its flat little face. Teresa examined it without touching its long hair. "It's nice, Mammy," she said without enthusiasm. "I've never seen one like it before."

"These dogs are from China," Mammy said proudly. "She's all yours, honey. You'll have to think of a nice name for her."

"It's a queer-looking little thing," Teresa observed. "I've never considered owning a dog."

"You're closeted all alone here, and she'll be company for you," Mammy said. "The servants can walk her. But until she's trained, you'll have to keep papers on the floor. I'll get some."

When Mammy left, Teresa picked up the warm little creature distrustfully and experienced a deep sadness; she felt as if her heart might break. Mammy might think the puppy was a substitute for the children, but Teresa found the gesture meaningless. Nothing could take the place of little Marie in the nursery. She did not like the idea of papers on the floor of her rooms, either. I've never trained a dog, she thought with asperity, how on earth does one go about it? But she was sure Mammy would know all about that, too. She seemed to know everything.

That night, the puppy cried beside her bed until she finally picked it up and put it next to her in order to get some sleep.It burrowed beneath the covers and came to rest warmly against her shoulders, still whimpering for its litter mates. Seized by compassion, she picked it up and let it nuzzle against her neck. Poor little thing, she thought, you're as lonely as I am. We're really quite a pair, aren't we? You're been taken from your mother, and I've lost my little Marie.

"Come on, Baby," she pacified the puppy as she stroked its silky hair, "everything will be all right. We'll have a ball brought down from the nursery in the morning."

As it snuggled against her neck and went to sleep in her long hair, she realized she had already named it, and that Baby was probably the only baby she would ever have.

Mr. Bell's return was hardly heralded by trumpets, but somehow Teresa knew he was in the house. Perhaps it was Mammy's neglecting her daily visits or the sound of the maids scurrying in the hallways with unusual activity that first alerted her. But when she heard heavy luggage and a trunk being deposited in the English room down the hall, there was no longer any doubt. She and Mammy had discussed his return in an offhand way often enough, but she had never really considered how she would handle the situation when she met him again.

When Mammy came to tell her to dress for dinner that evening, Teresa asked her nervously, "Do you mean he actually wants to dine with me? I thought he'd never want to set eyes on me again."

"Be that as it may," Mammy told her, "you are man and wife. He's agreed to keep up appearances for the sake of the children. You will, at least, dine together."

"He's really going to live here?"

'I told you he would, didn't I?" Mammy said with a smile. "Now, hurry and dress, Teresa. He likes things to be punctual."

Nothing could have been more awkward and embarrassing than that first meal with Mr. Bell, though she gradually became inured to his silence and scowling brow. He sat at one end of the long table and she at the other, an arrangement she realized was quite sensible. They could not have spoken anyway, unless they shouted. If the wine was low in his glass, she could instruct the servant to fill it without communicating with him on the matter. The important thing at this juncture was that the servants see them together at least once a day. After dinner she would excuse herself and go back to her room and the companionship of her puppy, without even wondering how he would spend his evening. With a feeling of doom, she wondered if life would go on like this forever, but at least she was now free to walk in the garden and go shopping occasionally.

He spent the entire day away, not returning for luncheon, and when he was out of the house she enjoyed a feeling of lightness. As the lady of the house she had the respect of the servants, and it was possible for her to visit the children at least once a day; after all, they were supposed to be hers. What sort of story Mammy had spun about the Bells' arriving separately or how she had handled the birth of Marie Teresa had no idea. She did not really want to know; Mammy's schemes confused her. She found it difficult enough to keep her equilibrium without delving into what went on in the complicated maze of Mammy's mind.

The papers from Baby's training had hardly been removed from the floor of Teresa's sitting room, when she was faced with another crisis, and the entire household went into such a flurry of preparation that it was difficult for her to get her bearings. Mr. and Mrs. Bell were giving their first party.

"The new butler will announce each couple as they arrive," Mammy instructed in her in the entry hall. "Stop fidgeting, Teresa, you know what's expected of you. You've been trained for all this."

"You've invited everyone in San Francisco society," Teresa reproached her. "I haven't been trained for that. I shall come apart at the seams before the evening's over."

"Nonsense. You'll wear your oyster-gray satin Worth gown with the ostrich fan, and you'll be the most beautiful woman at dinner. You can even wear my diamonds, if they'll give you more confidence."

"No," Teresa said quickly, remembering the Pinkerton agent and New York. "Thank you, Mammy, but I'd rather not."

"I say you won't be outdressed or outglittered by any of them," Mammy declared. "You'll wear the diamonds, dear. Thomas won't be embarrassed by his wife. This will be an evening people will remember."

Though Mammy was more serious than she had been during Governor Booth's inauguration, she was every bit as excited as she had been then. "I'll do my best," Teresa said, not wishing to disappoint her. "It isn't the men who frighten me, Mammy, it's the women."

"Forget about them," Mammy advised her, "they'll be jealous of you anyway. Just be your gracious self and don't worry about what they think. One of the worst things you can do is try to second-guess anyone. It debilitates you, and you're usually mistaken in your conclusions. Unless you have the second sight, as few people do, just go your own way without attempting to read people's thoughts."

"It's odd you should say that," Teresa considered. "One of the few things I heard about my mother was that she had that ability. I haven't thought of it in years." She laughed slightly, but grew quickly serious when she observed the expression that flitted over Mammy's face. She had never before seen any indication of fear in Mammy, but for a moment that's what she had seen, and it surprised her. "You don't believe in things like that?" she asked incredulously. "I've never had such an experience myself."

"Never?" Mammy inquired, observing her closely, and only when Teresa shook her head did she appear to relax. "That's a blessing, anyway," she smiled. "I know a few people who wouldn't like to have their thoughts read. You must take a relaxing bath now and rest awhile before you dress."

Standing beside Mr. Bell in the entrance hall, Teresa experienced a sensation of unreality, as though she had suddenly been turned into a princess by a fairy godmother and was not completely in touch with reality. The chandeliers above blazed with candles whose flames were reflected in the polished surface of the marble floor beneath her feet and sent flashes of blue light from her diamond necklace when she turned her head. She felt as if she were suspended in space with stars twinkling around her, and she might have found herself falling without Mr. Bell's arm to anchor her to her surroundings.

For the first time since his return he treated her graciously, though he still did not speak much. Teresa attributed his sudden change toward her to the faint odor of alcohol around them and to his interest in the occasion. Mammy's excitement had obviously spread to him, though not her edge of desperation that everything should go perfectly. He was completely relaxed, his blue eyes shining, as he looked forward to entertaining his friends in the house he had finally decided to claim as his own. If the beautiful, elegant wife at his side contributed anything to his mood, it was only as an additional showpiece in the European interior of his mansion. He smiled when the bell chimed the first time, and she felt him straighten proudly beside her as the butler announced the first guests. They were two young men who shook his hand warmly and bowed their heads when they were introduced to Mrs. Bell. Teresa smiled enigmatically and fanned herself lightly with the white ostrich plumes, without realizing that she was a vision of loveliness in her handsome attire. Mammy was watching discreetly from the sitting-room door in her black taffeta dress, and Teresa was more conscious of her presence than of the guests'.

The third guest arrived—also a gentleman. As yet no ladies had arrived, and Teresa realized what was happening. A glance at Mammy confirmed her intuition. The black-panther appearance had surfaced in Mammy's countenance, making her face appear pointed and her glowing eyes deadly, though her expression did not really change. The women aren't coming, Teresa admitted to herself with a sinking heart; because of the scandal, the ladies are staying away. The snub hurt a little, but she was more concerned about Mammy's disappointment.

For years, Mammy had been working toward this one evening. If Mr. Bell was aware of anything, he simply did not care. He was prepared to have a good time with his friends, and he proceeded to do so, from pouring drinks in the parlor to presiding at the head of the glittering table. Teresa managed to get through the meal competently and charmingly, realizing this was all that would be required of her. As the only woman in the company, she was able to retreat to her room when the gentlemen withdrew for cigars and brandy, and she mounted the stairs with a feeling of relief instead of disappointment. She was not prepared to find Mammy waiting for her in her suite, however; rather than face her directly, she coaxed her little dog, Baby, onto her lap before speaking.

"You did everything perfectly, Mammy," she said, attempting a normal tone. "They're really having a marvelous time. The dinner was the most exquisite one you're ever prepared, too."

The sound that issued from Mammy's chest was more like a hiss than anything vocal, and Baby cowered against Teresa's bosom almost as if sensing danger. "No one will ever be invited to this house again," Mammy said through her teeth, "no one. It will not be used as a club. Those women think they're so high and mighty, but I could tell a few things about some of them."

Teresa petted the dog in silence. She understood Mammy's disappointment, but she could also understand the society matrons' point of view. A scandal was never whitewashed by marriage, and people had good memories. The announcement of the new child, though she was allegedly born in wedlock, could not erase the past. She was surprised that Mammy, with all her cleverness, had not comprehended this before. Teresa's name would never be cleared, though Mr. Bell would continue on as usual without losing anybody's respect. Perhaps it isn't fair, but that's the way it is, she thought, and I'll have to live with it. She would be the last person to point out any of these facts to Mammy in her present temper, though.

"Don't you have anything to say?" Mammy demanded in the same level, furious voice. "You're the one who's been insulted, Teresa, and you don't seem to care."

"I care, Mammy," Teresa told her softly, "but it's too late to change things. The best either of us can expect now is to bask in the warmth of Mr. Bell's prominence."

"No!" Mammy snarled, whirling on her, "you deserve the position you're entitled to. He wouldn't be anything without me, and he knows it. The ladies who sent their regrets tonight don't know what regret is yet."

"Let it drop, Mammy," Teresa said wearily, "it's hopeless. We must make some sort of life for ourselves without plotting revenge against others. Surely there must be something you want that would make up for what's been lost. Frankly, all I want is a little peace."

Her remarks had a surprising effect on Mammy, whose rage suddenly evaporated, and she became still, her thoughts turning inward. "Maybe there is something," she finally said. "I think you're right, Teresa. I lost my perspective for a while. There's something I've always wanted very much." She smiled thoughtfully as she walked toward the door. "You get some sleep, dear. You've had a grueling day. I'll see you in the morning."

Chapter 16

The household settled into a peaceful pattern during little Marie's childhood, though Teresa was constantly aware of speculation regarding her comings and goings. She did not bother to do her own shopping, because of the constant threat of reporters' attempting to interrogate her on the sidewalk. Her last encounter with them had been unnerving, but she had found it interesting, too. An eager young man had accosted her as she was coming out of a bookstore with a package of the latest French novels wrapped in paper.

"Mrs. Bell, is it true that Mammy Pleasant practices voodoo? Some of your neighbors have remarked upon strange chanting during the night," he said as quickly as he could get the words out, before she pushed past him to gain her carriage.

"I don't know what you're talking about," she said honestly. "If there were strange sounds I would hear them."

"But what about the Negroes who have been seen entering the rear of the house?"

"Nonsense," she snapped. "Our servants are all white. Thompson," she addressed her driver, "please ask this gentleman to leave me alone and drive on as soon as possible."

The neighbors' reported complaint dwelled in her mind, though she saw and heard nothing to verify it during the following weeks. The next time she went to the bookstore she searched for a book about this voodoo, whatever it was, and managed to find a chapter on it in a volume about New Orleans, which opened her eyes regarding Billy Beaumont's references so many years ago. There was no doubt in her mind that Mammy had been involved in the religion in some way when she was surrounded by her black people; but the suggestion that it was still going on was ridiculous, she decided.

The only time she was not bothered by reporters was when she took carriage rides with the two beautiful children, though she did not enjoy the outings much. Fred still did not like her, and he managed to convey his feelings to Marie almost as soon as she could talk. What appeared to be a happy family outing was difficult and fatiguing to Teresa. There appeared to be no way to bring the children around, short of spoiling them with gifts as Mr. Bell did, and this she refused to do. She regretted not being able to raise them as she wished, but she saw them so infrequently and their hostility was such that she finally gave up attempting to shape their character. Most of the time, she remained at home, pursuing her usual interests or strolling in the formal garden when the weather was fair.

As she became more reclusive, it amused her to watch Mammy's activities. Nothing seemed to bother Mammy, least of all the reporters, whom she dismissed with tart remarks that she looked for in the next edition of the newspaper, almost reveling in the attention showered on her. She had discarded her Quaker bonnet for one of pleated black satin and went everywhere in the carriage with a bright red shawl over the shoulders of her attractive black dresses in various styles and rich fabrics. She had started to wear large, gold hoop earrings that bobbed when she moved her head, and once a week she went to the Washington Street market in the carriage to haggle over prices and supply the kitchen. This activity, too, was remarked upon in the newspapers.

"You'd think they'd have something better to do than follow Thomas Bell's housekeeper around," she told Teresa, almost preening herself. "I can hardly collect the rent on my houses unless I do it at night. You'd think I was Lola Montez or someone. Hand me the scissors, honey. I want to cut this article out."

When Mammy was happy, the household ran smoothly, and Teresa had never known her to be more consistently good-humored than she was during this time. The spring in her step belied her sixty years, and her clear-featured face and good figure remained so youthful that Teresa wondered sardonically if some magic were involved. All dreams of social status seemed to have vanished, though personal notoriety had taken their place. She appeared content to be Mr. Bell's housekeeper in the House of Mystery and probably did more to earn the mansion that appellation than any of them knew.

If Teresa's little dog had not become desperately ill one night, she might never have known for certain how peculiar the relationships beneath the roof had actually become. She and Baby had been in bed for some time, and it was close to midnight when Teresa was awakened

214

by the dog's convulsions. By the time she lit the lamp beside her bed, Baby was lying, damp and twitching, on the satin coverlet. Teresa examined her with growing panic. Over the years, the Pekingese had become as close to her as the child it was meant to replace, and the thought of losing it made her behave in a way she never would have under other circumstances. Without even pulling on a robe over her sheer nightgown, she ran to Mammy's door and knocked, discreetly but insistently. When there was no answer, she turned the knob and, finding the door unlocked, rushed inside and through the sitting room to throw the bedroom door open. At first the sounds in the darkness did not penetrate. She was too concerned about her dog. But even as she called Mammy's name, her eyes adjusted somewhat to the dark and she saw two figures in the bed separate quickly.

"What in the world?" Mr. Bell's voice said testily, but Mammy was on her feet in a second, quickly covering her nakedness.

"What is it?" she cried. "Is there a fire?"

Teresa backed away as she approached. "I'm sorry, Mammy," she said tearfully. "It's Baby . . . I think she's dying."

"Jesus Christ!" She heard a groan from the bed. Though Mammy laughed, she put on a wrapper and accompanied Teresa to her room to examine the dog without remarking on the intrusion.

"She's sick all right," she confirmed, stroking the weak, panting little animal. "Hot, too . . . all over."

"She was having fits," Teresa informed her with concern, "The convulsions woke me. She's just drenched. Feel her."

"It sounds almost like poison," Mammy considered fretfully, "except she hasn't been anywhere she could get at it. The fits could have been from the high temperature, though. Wrap her in a cool towel. I'll be right back."

When Mammy's herbs had restored the dog to normal sleep, Teresa realized the magnitude of her intrusion into the bedroom. Still softly stroking the sleeping little dog, she gazed at Mammy abashed. "I'm sorry, Mammy. I didn't know. I was nearly out of my head with worry. Thank you for saving Baby."

She was surprised to see Mammy smile at her as she put her potions back into her box. "That's all right, honey. I guess it's high time you knew where things stand. You've been deaf and blind for years. Thomas will be out of sorts for a while, but he'll laugh about it later. I suppose the reason we couldn't get him to marry you willingly," she said with hidden pride, "is that it was me he wanted all along."

What she was really telling me, Teresa considered later, was that she's mistress of the house instead of I. Nothing could bother me less, since I've never been his wife anyway. She knew she should be upset, perhaps even a little unhappy, over the discovery, but she found herself viewing the affair with amusement. Just imagine, she smiled into her vanity mirror, which reflected her perfect face and garland of blond curls, at their age! What a field day the newspapers would have with this if, heaven forbid, they got wind of it. Mr. Bell's housekeeper, indeed. I really should have suspected. I realized Mammy wanted him for herself when I married him, and she usually gets what she wants. If Mammy were a less forceful person, the airs she puts on about her perpetual attraction for men would be almost pathetic at her age. As it was, Teresa found Mammy's coquettishness almost as amusing as the affair itself.

She still needs me, Teresa considered more soberly as she brushed her long hair. However tarnished my image may be, my position as Mrs. Bell keeps the whole menagerie together. For her own security, it would be well for her to keep that in mind. As long as Mammy still likes me and needs me, I have nothing to worry about.

She had finally accepted that her way of life was permanent. She knew that on her own she could never enjoy the type of life to which she had grown so accustomed, and she was determined to hold on to it, and to accept its disadvantages. Her affair with Tony had sensitized her against casual relationships. If she found living without male love and companionship difficult sometimes, she always reminded herself of Philadelphia with its disillusionment and pain. At this stage of her life, she would never be loved for herself instead of the money everyone thought she had, she recognized with a twinge, and the gallantries of a gigolo were completely distasteful to her. She had sold herself in exchange for a life of wealth and some peace of mind, but she had not bartered herself for sex and had a low opinion of anyone, male or female, who did so.

Though she did not have the second sight that, to her amusement, worried Mammy, and though she knew nothing about any such abilities her mother may have had, she had noticed that shortly after she thought about someone or something, the subject often was introduced by another person. She had not seen Tony since the day they had parted, years ago. She knew he was still in San Francisco, because Mammy mentioned him occasionally, and while Teresa assumed he was still in her employ she did not trouble herself to consider in what capacity. He was a person she did not like to think about. But several days after she had allowed herself, while standing in front of her mirror, to consider him, he walked into her life again with a suddenness that left her wondering.

She had gone to the bookstore to replenish her reading material, as she usually did once a week. The day was gray and damp, and, though reporters had not been a problem for some time, she was relieved that the carriage cover was up so she could travel in privacy. She rushed into the store to protect her hat from the rain. Her interest in the books was desultory that afternoon, her mind still preoccupied with the new development at home and how it might affect her. She picked up a book on magic and turned the pages slowly, thinking of Mammy and the accusation against her of practicing voodoo. Just as she became absorbed in reading about some tricks involving sleight of hand, a voice at her side whispered, "Teresa?" When she looked up and saw Tony, the book was still in her hand.

He was not as handsome as she remembered him; indeed, within six years he had aged prematurely, in a way that made her wonder about what had taken place in his life since the Philadelphia Exposition. His skin had a grayish pallor, and the gray eyes she had once found so attractive were empty in his puffy face. He was dressed well, as always, but he was a different man.

"I've wanted to speak to you," he said, still whispering discreetly as he studied an open book. "I have something to tell you. Something you should know."

"I don't think we have anything to discuss," she replied, lowering her voice to match his. "We never did, really."

"It's about Mammy," he said more urgently, and she glanced at him again. There was no doubt that he was in deadly earnest, perhaps a little frightened. Her curiosity was piqued, and he recognized that he had her attention, "Can we go somewhere for a cup of coffee?"

"No, that wouldn't do at all," Teresa told him. "There are always reporters somewhere. My carriage is out in front. We'll pick you up at the alley down the street."

They did not leave together. Teresa lingered for a few minutes and finally purchased the book she had been scanning. When the driver assisted her into the carriage, she observed him closely for the first time. Satisfied that the white servants did not report to Mammy, she instructed him to stop at the alley, and Tony jumped in before his face could be seen.

217

"Thank you, Teresa," he said soberly, and she realized with surprise that the rasping whisper was the normal tone of his voice. "I've wanted to speak to you for a long time. I read in the paper that you use that bookstore."

"Are you all right?" Teresa asked with concern. "You don't sound at all well."

He waved the subject aside. "We don't have much time. I'll have to get out soon. Just listen to me, Teresa, for your own sake. I know you have no idea of what's going on, has been going on for a long time. God!" he rasped. "For a long time, I thought she was just your house-keeper, but now I'm sure it's more than that. I won't have time to go into the half of it. You wouldn't believe me anyway. She's evil, Teresa, the only completely evil person I've ever known, and I don't want you to be hurt by her. At first I just collected rents for her, sometimes with a rather strong arm. She intrigued me, damn it! I went along with her, because I thought I might write about her someday. Yes," he laughed shortly, "I still want to write, but I doubt I ever will now. There are so many things. The voodoo story in the newspaper has a foundation in truth, but don't snoop around; it would be dangerous."

"You mean she's really a voodoo queen?" Teresa asked, more amused than shocked. He held up his hand against inquiries.

"It isn't a joke, believe me. I'm sure you know about the protégées. I figured that one out soon enough, at least that you were involved that way. What I must tell you about is the baby business," he said with a shudder. "The Bell children aren't really yours, are they?" When she did not respond, he nodded. "I thought as much. But he thinks they're his, I'll wager. Just as a lot of other rich men think they've fathered illegitimate children."

"I don't understand," Teresa said, suddenly completely serious. "How can they not be his children? He's accepted them completely."

"She finds a girl who's in trouble already. Then, the man either sleeps with her or someone else, and when the baby's born, it's passed off as his. She even has a house for unwed mothers, Teresa." He suppressed a shudder again. "I can't tell you what goes on there, with that doctor she has in her pocket. He's a morphine addict and will do anything she says. Some of the babies don't get born, that's all, and some of the mothers have died. The Chinese like white babies in their households, too."

"Your imagination's running away with you, Tony," Teresa said gravely. "It's like the whole underground city in the popular myth about Chinatown: it doesn't exist."

"No, that doesn't," he replied logically, "but what I'm telling you does. I've seen it with my own eyes."

"If that's the case, why are you still working for her? I assume you are, aren't you?"

'Yes," he said helplessly, "and I'll never get away now. Blackmail's the other side of the coin. That's what I wanted to warn you about. For the love of God don't ever let her get anything on you. I must get out here, Teresa. I don't want her to know I've spoken to you. Is the driver all right?"

"I think so," she nodded. "Tony, don't go yet! I want to—"

But even as she reached out to detain him, he stepped from the slow-moving carriage and slammed the door behind him. She tried to motion to him from the rear window, but he pushed his hands deep into his pockets and disappeared around a corner into the rain.

That evening in the dining room, she found herself observing Mr. Bell's children more carefully than she ever had in the past. Most of Tony's information was difficult to credit, but what he said about the substitution of children seemed quite possible to Teresa. She knew their birth certificates had been manipulated to make the babies look like hers, when she had not even given birth; from there, it was just a short step to questioning whether they belonged to Mr. Bell. The growing children had been dining with them for some time at their father's request. He enjoyed their company rarely enough, and a family dinner was a good time to be with them for an extra hour. The arrangement was a welcome one to Teresa, too, though she had become accustomed to dining in silence with him.

As a teenager, Fred was still fair-haired, but he was already taller than Mr. Bell, and his features were becoming clearer than they had been when he was a small child. He perceived Teresa's scrutiny and shot her a disdainful look from his pale blue eyes, so she diverted her attention to Marie, who, at almost ten, still retained some baby fat. They're both blond and blue-eyed, Teresa considered, but neither of them has any resemblance to Mr. Bell. In coloring they might pass for her children, if she were a natural blonde, but neither one had Mr. Bell's short, straight nose or merry blue eyes. From where she was sitting, it was difficult to study their hands closely, though even at this distance it was obvious that their fingers were longer and their hands better shaped than his. Could they have had the same mother? she wondered. That seemed extremely unlikely if any of Tony's story was to be believed. She decided on different mothers, at least, from the set of their eyes. Marie's were wide-set and large beneath her blond curls, while Fred's were narrow, like those of some Scandinavians she had known. Different mothers did not solve the problem of a lack of family resemblance, though. Surely one of the children would have inherited some trait from Mr. Bell if they were his. His sandy hair, thinning and streaked with gray now, had once been almost ginger-red, and his eyes were a distinctive, clear blue, so bright that they appeared turquoise at times. She really did not want to believe anything that Tony had told her, but she found herself starting to accept his story in spite of herself. Even if they had the same mother, the children very definitely could have had different fathers.

She had no great liking for Mr. Bell, because of his antipathy toward her since the wedding, though she had to admit she deserved it. But she experienced a deep sympathy for him as he talked happily with the children he believed to be his. He was so terribly fond of them. She tried to tell herself that he had raised them from birth; therefore, they were the same as his own. But she could accept that no better than he could, if he knew.

Lost in her own speculation, she had not been listening to their conversation, but Marie's angry voice broke through the cocoon surrounding her. Suddenly Mr. Bell was no longer smiling, and there were furious tears in the girl's blue eyes.

"I don't want to go to a convent school!" she cried. "I've told Mammy that over and over. I want to continue with my tutors here. I don't want to be with *children*."

"You won't know whether you like it until you've tried it, my dear," Mr. Bell said, attempting to reason with her. "You've never been with children your age, and it's really time you were. Only children of your class are admitted to private schools, and you'll make lifelong friends there, Marie. Besides, Fred won't be here to keep you company, either. He's off in the fall to a school of his own."

"And I'm happy to go," Fred told his sister, trying to impose his will on her as he always had. "Staying in the house with tutors is boring. It's time we saw a bit of the outside world. Anything to get away from *women*," he emphasized with a glance towards Teresa. "If it hasn't been nurses, it's been Mammy, and *that* woman with her silly dog and fancy clothes."

"You mustn't speak of Teresa that way," Mr. Bell intervened sternly. "Perhaps your stay in school will teach you the manners you would never learn from me. Teresa has shown you more kindness than you realize."

"She's never been a mother to us," the boy said stubbornly. "You'd think that, living in the same house, she'd have done that, at least. She's your wife, isn't she?"

Teresa opened her lips to explain that she had wanted to be their mother, but she surrendered with a sigh. How could she tell them anything without involving Mammy? And Fred must have forgotten how early in life he had begun referring to her as "that woman," probably after overhearing his Irish nurse refer to her that way during the scandal.

"If you ever need me," she said sincerely, "I'm here, Fred. Perhaps our relationship hasn't been the happiest one for me, either."

Sensing her sympathy, Marie turned toward her. "You don't want me to go to the boarding school, do you? Please fix it so I can stay here, Teresa," she wheedled. "I'll never call you bad names again."

Until this evening, Teresa had heard nothing of the plan to send Fred and Marie to private schools, and she was at a loss for an opinion. For their own sake, the idea seemed reasonable to her. Their lives had been anything but normal until now. "If I'd had the opportunity to go to a boarding school at your age," she said gently, "I'd have been the happiest girl in the world. I'm sure you'll like it once you're there, Marie."

Her advice was rewarded by the girl's sticking out her tongue, and Mr. Bell ordered Marie away from the table. "There'll be no more of that, young lady," he said sternly, so upset that his face went deep red. "As long as you behave like something out of the jungle, school's the only place for you."

Fred left the table without excusing himself and marched after his retreating sister with a disgusted look over his shoulder that embraced both his father and Teresa. Mr. Bell gave a deep sigh and rested his head on his hand at the far end of the table. Teresa moved instinctively to his side, fearing an attack of apoplexy after his burst of temper.

"What went wrong, Teresa?" he asked, as if they had been on speaking terms for years. "They've had everything. Everything. When I was a child, I was as poor as a church mouse. I wanted things to be better for them."

"That's a natural enough wish," she said softly, sinking into Marie's abandoned chair. "Perhaps it isn't too late, Mr. Bell. Private schools may be a very good idea, though I hadn't considered them until now.

The children are angry, and I don't really blame them, especially regarding me. I wanted to be close to them, but there were always the nurses and. . . . Well, after all that business in the newspapers, Fred wouldn't have anything to do with me, and he soon brought Marie around to his viewpoint. I'm sorry, really I am."

"You aren't to blame," he said, rubbing his face and staring into space. "Teresa, will you promise me something?"

The words startled her, but she replied softly, "Of course. Anything."

"If anything happens to me. You know. I'm not as young as I once was. Promise me that you'll look after the children. They've been through enough."

"I promise," Teresa said, frowning slightly. Why was he asking this of her instead of Mammy, his oldest friend? But perhaps that was the reason: Mammy was older than he. "I'm certain we don't have to think of such things for a long, long time," she reassured him. "But I'll see that they're treated fairly and properly cared for."

He patted her hand on the table weakly and despondently. "You're a nice woman, Teresa. Sorry I've treated you so badly. I think you understand. It's been a queer life for you altogether. I'm amazed you haven't come apart at the seams long ago."

If the fighting between him and Mammy did not begin that night, it started shortly afterward, their voices raised so high that Teresa could not avoid overhearing them. Most of it had to do with money, and she did not understand that, considering his wealth. He accused Mammy of being extravagant, to a degree that no man could bear. She replied with a high laugh, and the argument was launched for another evening.

"I'm not made of money, goddamn it!" he cried. "You, of all people, should know that things aren't what they once were. Where do you get so much to spend, anyway? I'll see that you can't draw out of our accounts."

"I have my rents!" she countered. "I have some investments of my own. If you won't let me touch my own money, Thomas, I'll simply stop advising you again, and watch the whole thing go down the drain."

Teresa put her pillow over her head, but the raised voices sometimes continued well into the night. She could not understand either of them. They had everything, including each other, and they were ruining it with their nasty squabbles. Teresa did not fancy Mr. Bell as either husband or lover, but if she had someone with whom to share all this, she would see that everything remained civilized and contented.

222

After a hectic night, Mr. Bell would stamp out of the house without breakfast, and surely that could not be good for him. Though he kept his distance from her after that one moment of confidence, she felt responsible for both him and the children now. He should enjoy the declining years of his life, instead of putting his health in jeopardy with irregular habits, she felt. She was uncertain whether he was provoking Mammy, or the other way around, but she was grateful for the serenity during the day, which was nearly complete with the children away at private schools.

When, several months later, Mammy called at her door and entered with a swing to her hips and an expression like a contented cat, Teresa realized that some complicated plan had again been accomplished, and she began to hope that peace would reign in the house once more.

"I have wonderful news," Mammy said with a smile and a wicked glint in her mismatched eyes, "and I'll need you to do some of the supervising for me. I can't be in two places at once."

Since when? Teresa wondered ironically, but she met Mammy's eyes with her impenetrable gaze, waiting for the details of this latest plot.

"I've always wanted to own a plantation, honey," Mammy said with an almost dreamy expression on her handsome face. "I've bought some land down at Half Moon Bay, and I'm going to start building there soon."

"A plantation!" Teresa exclaimed, dropping her reserve. "Like what they once had in the South?"

"Something like that. I'm going to call it Beltane. Don't you think that's a nice name for an estate? I won't be able to put in cane and cotton, of course, but I'll have a large vegetable farm. The earth's rich there, I've felt it. I'll get everything started, of course, but you'll have to spend some time down there."

"I'd be happy to," Teresa said, attempting to dispel the impression in her mind that Mammy had gone insane. A plantation . . . in California? The old woman was reverting back to her childhood and one of its most unpleasant aspects. "I imagine you won't be using slaves and all that?" she asked with a twinkle in her eyes, but Mammy disregarded the humor.

"There's a lot of itinerant labor around here," she responded, "Mexicans and Italians. They'll do just fine. They say this country's a lot like Italy, anyway. The crops aren't that important for a while. Thomas has given me a free hand to build the kind of house I want."

"I thought this was what you wanted, Mammy," Teresa reminded

223

her, realizing what all the fighting had been about and wondering how she had managed to prevail over Mr. Bell's objections. "You were very pleased when you finished this house."

"You wouldn't understand," Mammy said, dismissing the subject. "You haven't any imagination, Teresa. Some people require bigger and bigger projects to match their intelligence. They don't stand still and vegetate, they think big. If everyone were like you, there would never have been Bonanza Kings or a railroad running from coast to coast. Mr. Ralston wouldn't have built the Palace Hotel."

"And lost it to Mr. Sharon when he killed himself?" Teresa reminded her, since they appeared to be living fifteen or more years in the past. "Even Mr. Ralston didn't have unlimited funds, or he wouldn't have dipped into the bank's funds, causing it to collapse."

Mammy's mood changed so abruptly that it startled Teresa. "What made you say that?" she shot out, observing Teresa with something like fear. "You haven't been listening at my door, have you?"

"Of course not," Teresa said in bewilderment, refraining from pointing out that some things were impossible not to hear when Mammy and Bell were fighting; but that had nothing to do with her comment. She had heard no references to Sharon or Ralston during the verbal battles. "I wouldn't do that. You know I keep pretty much to myself, Mammy."

"You haven't had any dreams about Senator Sharon and the hotel, have you?" Mammy inquired cautiously, still observing her closely, and Teresa realized they were back to the subject of her possible "second sight" again. She must have said something to trigger Mammy's reaction, and she wondered what Mammy and Bell were up to regarding the hotel. A hitherto hidden sense of mischief in her almost made her report that she had experienced a dream like that, but instead she disclaimed any such dream with an enigmatic smile.

"I dream all the time," she admitted, "very vividly most nights, often in color. Do you dream in color, Mammy? When it happens, it always seems rather strange. Sometimes I'm back on the farm in the spring, and it's as if I'm actually there in the green fields with the wildflowers, beneath the blue sky. There are never any people around, though. I've never seen my foster parents in a dream, and that's peculiar, too. If I were back on the farm, I'd surely see them, even if I didn't want to face them again. I didn't know Mr. Sharon was a senator, Mammy."

"They probably aren't there anymore," Mammy responded uneasily, "they're probably dead by now. In my whole life, I've never known

224

anyone who dreamed in color, Teresa. If anything comes to you regarding Mr. Sharon, you'll tell me, won't you? If your mother had the sight, you probably have it, too. You certainly don't keep up with politics, for all your reading, though. William Sharon's been in the senate for years."

Within a few days, Teresa read about Sharon in an article in the newspaper. It gave her quite a start: could she have second sight? A young woman named Sarah Althea Hill was claiming to be the millionaire's wife, though it was doubtful that she could prove it. All the money and expensive lawyers were on the Bonanza King's side.

With the children away in school, Mammy had changed one of her rules and had started dining with the Bells every night. Teresa could hardly wait to tell her at the dinner table about what she had read. She thought better of it as soon as she took her place at the head of the table, though. She had rarely seen the aging couple in a more subdued mood, and she knew when it was expedient to remain silent in their presence. She had just decided to finish her meal as quickly as possible and excuse herself, when Mr. Bell, who had been sunk in thought, suddenly stirred, and Mammy leveled a speculative gaze at him.

"If it weren't for him," Mr. Bell said, "my friend Ralston might still be alive. Do you really think you can do it, Mammy?"

"Of course," Mammy replied with her old control and confidence. "It may take time, and it'll be expensive, Thomas, but I can do it."

Teresa could not understand the expression of pure hatred in the old man's face as he instructed Mammy in a brittle voice. "Get him, then. You can have your damned plantation as a present if you do."

225

Chapter 17

The lawsuit against Senator William Sharon dragged on for another three years. When Mammy returned from the courtroom in the evening, she would speak in cryptic sentences to Mr. Bell, who appeared pleased when things were going against his enemy. Later, she would have Teresa read the newspaper accounts to her before she retired— early, to be ready to face her adversary in court the following day.

"But this is terrible," Teresa exclaimed one evening with the paper in her hands. "It calls you a small, dark, nefarious woman with a network of 'seamy connections,' Mammy! I think you should sue the newspaper instead of Mr. Sharon."

But Mammy chuckled softly as she lay back in her chair, reveling in the publicity as much as she had before. "Some hack journalist," she commented, "no one can really call me small. Does it say anything about my fixing my eyes on Mr. Sharon during the proceedings, as it did last week?"

"Yes," Teresa said, her voice trailing off as she read, "It implies that you've put some sort of spell on him. . . ."

"Read it!" Mammy said eagerly.

As the testimony came out over the months, there was more than one reference to voodoo. Senator Sharon even found a pile of filthy rags mixed with feathers and clippings from his own hair in his suite at the Palace Hotel. When they were displayed in court, Mrs. Pleasant was asked to examine them. She did so, it was reported, and leveled her mismatched eyes at the Senator, remarking that "she just wanted to see that everything was there." Mammy cackled when Teresa read that account to her, and Teresa felt the hair rise on the back of her neck.

227

Everything she had ever suspected was coming out boldly in print, and she was so unnerved that she began to lock her door at night.

That Sarah Althea Hill, Mr. Sharon's alleged wife, was one of Mammy protégées became clear to Teresa early in the case, and she began to marvel at the convoluted plots Mammy could weave, well in advance of their being fruitful to her. That most of Sarah Althea's witnesses were Mammy's creatures was evident, too; strangely enough, considering Mammy's distrust of such things, two of the women were fortune-tellers, referred to as "seers." What on earth does Mr. Bell think of all this? she wondered, especially when there was testimony that Mammy Pleasant tried to pass a child off as his.

The reporters were in front of the house again, to Mammy's delight and Teresa's abhorrence. Once again she was confined, not wishing to face them, and between the distasteful things she had to read aloud daily and a feeling of claustrophobia, she was ready to do anything to escape. The House of Mystery was written about daily this time, and Teresa actually began to feel that there was something wrong with the house. She began to have frequent headaches that sent her to bed.

Mammy's vitality had never been greater, though. She spent her weekends at Half Moon Bay, overseeing the construction of her plantation house, and she was still full of energy for the following week's court sessions. Mr. Bell continued to go about his business as if nothing were different and was able to repel the reporters with a look. He was the first to observe Teresa's pallor, one night at dinner, about a year into the trial.

"You don't look well, Teresa," he said, ignoring Mammy's warning glance. "Perhaps it would be better if you got away for a while."

"I want to be here when the children come home at Christmas," Teresa told him. "They had to stay at school last year, and I think that was a shame."

"They won't be coming this year, either," Mr. Bell said sardonically. "It's hardly a climate to bring them into, right now. They're old enough to read the papers, and the information's being kept from them where they are."

"I don't want Teresa to go," Mammy cut in firmly. "It wouldn't look right at present. She belongs here, Thomas."

"Damn the way it looks!" he said. "No one will know if she's here or not, anyway, unless they question the servants. And they've been given their orders about speaking out of turn. Where would you like to go on holiday, Teresa?"

Teresa had not thought about it; she only knew she had to get away. Mammy solved the problem with lightning quickness, though. "Beltane. The house is coming along nicely, and there are living quarters there. I've even stocked the larder. We'll send Teresa to Beltane for a bit—but no one must know she's gone. What would people say?" The humor that rose in Teresa's chest over the remark must have been sparked by hysteria, because once she began laughing, she could not stop. Mr. Bell tried to force brandy on her, but it was Mammy's long, strong hands shaking her shoulders that finally brought her around.

"I'm sorry," she apologized, rubbing the tears from her eyes, "I don't know what got into me. Perhaps I do need a vacation."

After Teresa had packed some things to take with her and summoned a servant to carry the suitcases to the stable through the rear of the house, Mammy intercepted her in the hallway and invited her into her suite.

"You weren't going to go without saying good-bye?" she asked with a smile, as Teresa stared at a well-dressed man sitting at the desk. "You know how much I miss you when you're away, honey. Oh, this is Mr. Jennings, Teresa, and we have some business with him. Just a few papers to sign, that's all. It won't keep you long."

Teresa sat down with resignation as the papers were handed to her one at a time. She was so anxious to get away that she noticed only that they were deeds to the Octavia Street house. She had forgotten that the initial deed to this house was made out in her maiden name, Teresa Clingham, but that was so long ago that she did not pause to think about it now. She dutifully signed the transfer of the deed from Teresa Clingham to Teresa Percy, and a second sheet was placed before her.

"This one's just from Teresa Percy to Teresa Bell," Mammy explained, and Teresa sighed deeply. Good Lord, these business matters were complicated, she thought, and I think Mammy complicates them even more. The house had been registered under Mrs. Bell's name from the beginning. At least, she thought it had been during the scandal with Mr. Bell. The whole thing confused her. By the time she signed the third deed, she hardly registered what she was doing, though she noticed she was signing as Mrs. Bell to transfer the property to Mary Ellen Pleasant. She can have it, she breathed to herself, and good riddance! She'll probably have to fight Mr. Bell over it, anyway.

"If that's all, I'd like to go," she said, rising. Neither Mammy nor Mr.

229

Jennings seemed to notice her as he stamped the papers and scrawled his signature on them as notary public. "Good-bye," she said softly as she left the room.

She had only used the back entrance through the servants' quarters once before. The servants were already in bed, and the hallway was quiet and dimly lighted as she made her way to the rear door. There was a considerable number of doors there; she had forgotten how many rooms the house had. As she neared the door to the alley, the light was even worse. Aside from a single jet beside the door, she was almost in darkness. If she had not snagged her shawl on something and paused to free it, she would not have noticed the padlocked, double-doored room. She did not remember it from her tour of the house before she moved in, and it appeared to be used for storage now. Why else would it have such a heavy lock? She was so anxious to get away that she tore the edge of her shawl in pulling it free. She proceeded on her way and forgot about the door.

The gig was waiting for her in the alley, and she clambered up with the assistance of the driver. Mammy would need the phaeton to go to the courthouse, she realized: she was doing everything in style these days. Teresa did not care which vehicle carried her, as long as she got away, and the weather was mild enough for a trip in the open air. She was so distracted that she did not notice the driver until he called attention to himself after they had gone a few blocks.

"You aren't very talkative," he said in a hoarse whisper that she recognized at once.

"Tony? What on earth are you doing here?" she asked, peering into the darkness to see his face. "I didn't even notice . . . I'm sorry."

He laughed softly. "Mammy thought it might be a good idea if I accompanied you. She said it worked once before."

She was too angry to speak at first. Her emotions were strained enough without having to deal with this indignity. "Mammy made a mistake," she said tightly, "the old girl finally made a mistake. I want to be alone at Beltane."

"I can appreciate that," he said with understanding. "Living in that house must be a constant delight. The only reason I agreed to come was so I could speak to you alone. I didn't say all I had to say a few years ago."

"You mean about the baby market, the addiction of Dr. Mouser, and white slaves in Chinatown? You really should have stayed with your writing," she said with asperity. "I'm taking a vacation from Mammy before I become completely unstrung. I can't imagine her thinking I need a man right now."

"As you said, she made a mistake, probably the first one in her life. A bigger mistake than she knows." He was seized by a fit of coughing and pulled out his handkerchief. "Sorry," he apologized, "she doesn't know I'm in no condition to play gigolo. Not that the spirit isn't willing."

"You're ill," she said with a concerned frown, recalling his hoarse whisper during their previous encounter several years before. "It isn't serious, is it?"

"More than the sore throat that quack of hers treated me for in the beginning. You must never let a murderer diagnose an illness, Teresa. His motives might be slanted. But never mind that. It's a fine night, and you should be enjoying your ride. Have you been to Beltane before?"

She shook her head. The cool breeze did feel good on her face. "It can't be everything she claims," she said, smiling. "Her description's preposterous."

"So's Beltane," he told her. "You'll see. It's a pity we'll be arriving at night. You'll miss the whole effect."

The suite Mammy had furnished for herself revealed that she had not been roughing it on her weekends at the new house. Some of the furniture from Octavia Street had already been transported here, and she had fitted out a small kitchen as well for her meals. The pantry was almost as well stocked as the one at Geneva Cottage. After they had a cup of tea, Teresa gave Tony some blankets and a pillow to sleep on the sofa, and she lay down on the bed fully clothed to pass the rest of the night. She slept soundly, lulled by the muffled ebbing and flowing of the waves into the crescent of Half Moon Bay. Tony was still asleep when she arose and looked at her lapel watch. It was nearly eleven. She was tempted to take a walk to satisfy her curiosity about the mansion, but she went to the kitchen to prepare breakfast instead. Tony was not well, and he had driven long into the night. The least she could do was have breakfast ready when he woke. He stirred at the odor of the coffee, so she prepared a tray for both of them and carried it to the table in the sitting room, next to the sofa.

"Good morning," he said, blinking his eyes, "what's all this?"

"Breakfast," she said with a smile, observing his wan face in the light with a stir of compassion. He was younger than she was, but he looked at least ten years older, and there were dark smudges under his sunken eyes. She did not have to ask the nature of his illness, consumption,

231

which was all too common and needed proper treatment if a man was to survive at all. "I'm famished," she encouraged him, "how about you?"

"I'll have some of that coffee," he said, suppressing a cough with his fist against his lips. "Damn," he said, drawing out his handkerchief again and folding it quickly to conceal the bloodstain on its white surface. "This is what Dr. Morphine diagnosed as catarrh several years ago."

"Surely you've seen someone else since?"

"He wanted to send me to a sanitorium, but I told him, 'No, thank you. I'll choose my place, if not my time.' I'm onto something big, Teresa. I can't leave San Francisco now. I've written it all down," he said, patting his breast pocket. "Everything I know she's involved in. All I need is proof. I'll give her this much—she's been a busy lady. I'm actually fascinated by her devious mind."

"She's always wanted power," Teresa said, sipping her coffee. "I think I understand her a little, Tony." She did not speak of Mammy's background, because she had secrets enough in her own. "When she couldn't make a big social splash with Mr. Bell and me, she changed somehow. Instead of investing money to gain power and continuing to play the philanthropist to gain respect, she started spending money like a drunken sailor. Her extravagance was beyond belief."

"So are her methods of financing it," Tony said. "That's the key word now: money. She's scraping the bottom of the barrel, Teresa, for all this." His gesture encompassed all of Beltane, which she had not yet seen.

"How can that be?" she asked. "She has her properties, her investments. She's a wealthy woman, and Mr. Bell's financing the lawsuit—"

"Is he, now?" Tony said with a sparkle of interested amusement in his eyes. "How did Mammy manage that?"

"I shouldn't have said that," Teresa said, lowering her eyes. "I can't help overhearing things sometimes, but it isn't my place to repeat them."

"What is your place, Teresa?" he asked. "How do you fit into this crazy puzzle anyway? You're married to Bell, but she seems to be running the house."

She flushed and picked up the tray to return it to the kitchen. "You know Mammy," she tried to joke, "she runs everything. I'm anxious to have a look at the house while the weather's so fine."

232

Though the house was still under construction, the façade and one wing were completed. They climbed a small hill overlooking the house, and Teresa stared in astonishment at the pillared portico and tiled roof. The acres behind the sprawling foundations were already planted with strange, cactuslike bushes, and she saw men wearing wide-brimmed hats working in the fields.

"It'll be enormous," she breathed. "What on earth does she have planted back there?"

"Artichokes, my dear. What the Italians call *carciofo*. They aren't bad, and there may be a market for them. She must have done her homework with some of the vintners up the coast and decided against grapes. These hills aren't good for anything else. It appears she's already enlisted some of her white labor, too."

"Italians?" Teresa asked doubtfully, and he shook his head.

"Mexicans, more likely. They'll work for less, in spite of the fact that the wholestate belonged to them until a year before the Gold Rush in 1849. Ironical, isn't it? They'd hardly surrendered it to Fremont when the gold at Sutter's Mill was discovered. Now, they work in the fields."

"Well," Teresa said, "Mammy either has a culinary bonanza of her own or the greatest white elephant in history. Actually, the house is rather lovely. All it needs is a little Spanish moss hanging from the cypress trees."

"I want to show you something," he said, guiding her down the path to the stately porch. "I learned about it accidentally, when the architect asked me what it was all about."

They climbed the stairs to the resounding empty rooms on the second floor, which seemed to be built solidly enough, though Teresa stepped carefully, fearing she might fall through insubstantial flooring.

"This will be Mammy's suite when it's finished," Tony said, ushering her into the bare wooden room. "Her sitting room, her bedroom . . . and her closet. When you see this, my dear, perhaps you'll understand my fascination with the old girl."

He touched something on the inside wall of the closet, and a door sprang open leading into a passageway. Teresa gasped, several things coming together in her mind at once; and, driven by curiosity, she followed Tony through the long passage and down some steps to the first floor. They moved carefully in the semidarkness, and Teresa lost her bearings completely, until he pressed a spot on another wall, and they were blinded by sunlight as they emerged from the rear of the house.

233

"What do you think of that?" he smiled. "You think she's in her room, but she really isn't. She has her private passageway to the outside. Now, what kind of mind would dream up something like that?"

"When we walked through the passage," Teresa asked with interest, "were there rooms on both sides of us?"

"Yes."

"I finally understand," she said, torn between relief and trepidation. "Peepholes. They aren't in yet, though. She'll probably do that after the rooms are decorated. . . ."

"Peepholes?" he said with a frown. "Good God, is that what this is all about?"

"I often felt someone watching me at the boardinghouse," she said softly, "and two maids complained of the same thing on Octavia Street. I haven't sensed it there myself." She shivered in the warm sun and hugged herself with her arms. "She must have trusted me by the time she built that house."

"So, she spies on people," he considered. "Why?"

Teresa shook her head, though the possibilities that came to mind were disturbing. "Tony, let's get away from here. Will you drive me down to the beach?"

The curve of Half Moon Bay below Princeton Harbor at its upper end was not as pristine as it had appeared from the hills above. The beach was littered with bleached animal bones and the flotsam of a small industry. A number of long, flat boats bobbed in the water, attached to the shore by ropes tied to pegs driven into the sand. Teresa put her hand over her eyes to cut out the glare so she could view the small town beyond. Encouraged by her interest, Tony drove them there without speaking.

"What in the world?" she cried at the sight of men climbing over a huge body in the water, cutting strips from it with knives fixed at the end of long poles. "It smells horrid, Tony. It doesn't smell like fish at all."

"They're whalers," he told her, preparing to remain and watch the spectacle. "I've never been here when they had one before. They're stripping the blubber for oil. One usually doesn't see this sort of thing, because it's done in ships at sea. These are Portuguese whalers from the Azores, probably the only men who use those small boats for whaling just offshore."

234

Teresa found their activities revolting, even before the stench from the trying pots reached her nostrils. "Why do they let foreigners come in here to ruin such a beautiful bay?" she asked, putting her handkerchief to her nose to mask the odor. "It's horrible."

"They aren't foreigners," he smiled, tapping the reins on the horse's back, "any more than the Italians and Mexicans and Chinese are. They've all come here for a new life, Teresa, just like us."

"Perhaps their method's more forthright, in spite of the mess," she said thoughtfully. "At least, they aren't trying to get rich quick like everyone else."

"Wealth is relative, I suppose," he said, drawing up in front of a ramshackle wooden fish shop. "Jose Maria, here, considers himself a wealthy man. I'm going to get us some fresh fish for dinner."

While he bartered with the fishmonger, Teresa turned to stare at the whaling station with its smoke billowing up, blotting out the sun. Its presence cast a pall over the excursion, and she was ready to return to the house, away from the bustle and smell.

"It's very fine oil," Tony said, handing her a packet of fish wrapped in newspaper as he took his seat beside her, "but not as important as it used to be. Petroleum is replacing the need for it, though I suspect the whalers might disagree."

"Did you come to California to get rich?" she asked. "It was the farthest thing from my mind."

"I imagined myself a rich, famous writer. Remember? That was before I realized I'd have to pay my dues."

"Why did you stay on, working for her? You're a man, Tony, you had a choice."

"I don't know. I suppose I became infatuated with her, especially after I caught the scent of mystery. I wanted to get to the bottom of things to understand her better."

"Infatuated with her?" Teresa asked with surprise. "She's so much older than you are. . . ."

He laughed ironically. "Not as a woman. Though she's a lot of that, too. Her personality fascinated me. Can you understand that?"

"Yes, only too well," she nodded with grave blue eyes. "But she's been much more than that to me. She's been almost a mother and always a friend."

The fish were wrapped in pages of the *Alta California*, with death and birth announcements on the outside. Teresa scanned the obituary column as she prepared dinner, and suddenly a name leaped out from the page. She dried her hands to pick up the page and look for its date. It was nearly two months old.

"Tony," she said, walking into the parlor in her apron, "my old maid, Maggie Williams, is dead. She died two months ago, and Mammy didn't even tell me."

He observed her from the sofa without surprise. "Several of Mammy's colored friends have met their Maker lately," he said. "Were you fond of her?"

"No, not really," she admitted. "Seeing her death notice surprised me. She wasn't that old. A lot younger than Mammy. She was always rather a watchdog, and—"

She did not finish the statement. She suddenly realized that Maggie was one of the witnesses to Jim Hoey's death, and she experienced a moment of relief. If she watched the obituaries, perhaps the other two, Billy Beaumont and Ben Willard, would show up there eventually.

"And . . . what?" Tony asked, seeing the change of expression on her face. "You were going to say something else."

"Nothing, really," she said cautiously. He was too observant by far. "I always liked Byna better. She was so warm and chatty. I understand Billy Beaumont married her?"

"Yes," he said with a smile. "He and John Willis played their cards pretty well. They saved their money and built themselves some little houses near the Bay. They spend all their spare time fishing. To some men, that's wealth, too."

"Do they still work for Mammy?"

"Sometimes, but they do other jobs, too. Byna's still at the boarding-house, but she says it doesn't have any class since Mammy sold it. A lot of Mammy's colored following has drifted away. They've found themselves another religion."

Teresa did not notice the word, because her mind was dwelling on the possibilities of the obituary column. She went back to the kitchen to read it again before she served the meal. All these months she had been reading the accounts of the lawsuit without looking at the rest of the newspaper, but that was going to change. I feel freer here than I did at the house on Octavia Street, she realized, as if my mind's come out of a cocoon.

The evening breeze got chilly enough for a fire, and she and Tony sat in front of it as the fog drifted in, blanketing the world outside. The stillness was complete, except for the sound of a foghorn somewhere. She had not known such silence for a long time, and she felt herself relaxing. That was why she had come here.

"Why did you say 'another religion'?" she asked suddenly. "Do you mean Mammy was their religion, Tony? They certainly behaved as if she were. Was voodoo really involved? I've suspected it for some time."

"She's their queen. She still has some followers," he told her, "but that's kid stuff, Teresa. There isn't much harm in it, if you fancy worshipping a snake. The things she does on her own are more worrisome to me. The blackmail's something I may be able to prove. It's on a pretty grand scale or I miss my bet."

Teresa averted her eyes and folded her hands in her lap. She felt she should defend Mammy against the charge, but being one of her victims, that would be too hypocritical. And she did not like to lie to Tony, so silence was her only refuge.

"You aren't standing up for your old friend," he said with irony. "If you know anything that can help me, please tell me."

"I can't," she admitted reluctantly. "You once said she had something on you, so I guess you understand."

"Oh, no," he moaned, "I warned you, Teresa! Why didn't you listen to me?"

"It was too late, even then. It happened a long time ago, Tony. I don't want to think about it."

"You'd better. I'm in this for earnest, Teresa. I'm going to nail her if I can. I don't want you drawn into a scandal if I can prevent it. Here," he said, taking a flat leather notebook from his breast pocket, "listen to this. First I'll give you the facts, and then I'll tell you what I can't prove. Let's start with Maggie, your maid."

Teresa stared at him with alarm but masked the emotion so quickly that even his sharp eyes missed it. He couldn't know, she told herself. He wouldn't be sitting here telling me all this if he did. My secret, at least, is safe.

"Last year, Maggie invested her life savings with Mammy, who promised her a spectacular gain. Several other colored people have done the same thing. A few months ago, Maggie tried to get her money back, because she hadn't seen any of the promised interest. Ergo, Maggie is run over by a carriage on her way home one night. And who comes to nurse her with her little black bag of herbals? That's right. Maggie only had a broken leg, but she expired quietly in her sleep."

"People die," Teresa said tightly, "sometimes just from shock. You can accuse Mammy of a lot of things, Tony, most of the capital sins, but she wouldn't murder anyone. Not in cold blood," she added, considering her statement. "What she might do in a fit of anger is something else."

"Maggie isn't the only one," he pressed. "Another one of her ex-followers is missing, too. I say 'ex-followers,' because accidents don't appear to happen to those still taking active communion. The trouble is, I'm not sure who is and who isn't. Most of them claim to be good Baptists anyway. Maggie was, and she was buried by the Baptist Church, not that run-down funeral chapel Mammy uses. That's another thing," he said, counting the words off on his fingers, "a doctor, an undertaker, a huge plot in the cemetary. What kind of person needs all that? Can you think of a better way to get away with murder?"

Teresa couldn't, and the memory made her draw into herself, looking away from Tony and hugging her knees. "She wouldn't murder anyone," she whispered. "You have no proof."

"I'll find it. I just want you to be prepared, Teresa. What's going on in the courtroom is kindergarten play, believe me. And it's being done for money, too."

"No," Teresa said quickly, "it's costing money, and she's doing it for Mr. Bell."

He laughed outright. "When did she do anything for anyone but herself? Mr. Bell may think she's doing it for him, for whatever reason, but consider this: Senator Sharon has millions and the Palace Hotel. If Sarah Althea can prove she's his wife, she'll stand to inherit. He isn't well. I wouldn't be surprised if she split the inheritance right down the middle with Mammy Pleasant, who's so helpful and interested in the lawsuit. How have you remained so innocent all these years?" he asked with wonder, shaking his head.

"What about her properties?" Teresa asked. "She could sell them, if she's strapped for money, couldn't she?"

"She doesn't let go of anything, Teresa, ever. Remember that. As long as anything or anyone is useful to her, she hangs on. The properties are mortgaged to the hilt. Proof," he said, proffering his leather book, but she turned away, shaking her head. "I have these figures from the bank. Never mind how I got them. Do you know who's living in those houses, rent-free? Some of her protégées and assorted riffraff who've been of service to her. I know for a fact that a couple of them had babies that Mammy palmed off on unsuspecting men, whose mistresses—also former protégées—pretended the babies were theirs so they could trap the men into marrying them. Now, she's blackmailing them, too. I swear to God, you need a ball of yarn to get through the labyrinth! I even know how much she paid the girls for their babies."

A feeling of pain and hysteria filled Teresa's chest. She was as

238

surprised as he when she started laughing. "I'm sorry," she apologized, attempting to control the fit of laughter, "but that's hardly *murder* is it? I still say Mammy wouldn't kill anyone. As for the rest, it's just terribly confusing. It's too incredible. I married Mr. Bell without—" She checked herself and bit her lip. "Mammy didn't even suggest that I sleep with him."

"You were never his mistress, as I thought, were you, Teresa?"

"It doesn't matter," she said, wiping her eyes with her fingertips. "All that doesn't matter anymore, Tony. Let's just say that you were under a misapprehension when you accused me of that in Philadelphia. I'm married to him now."

He remained silent for some time, the only sound in the room the crackle of the fire and a log tumbling into the ashes. She felt drained. She could not sort fact from fancy out of all she had been told, but at least the suspicions regarding the protégées were probably accurate, she decided. The whole thing had too many overtones of her own experience with Mammy.

"Teresa," Tony said at last, "I think there's something else you should know. I saved it until the end, because it's something you can change. If you don't know about it, that is."

"What now?" she asked with a sigh, smiling at him faintly in the darkness. "This has been quite a vacation so far."

"I'm sorry. I can see that you need the rest. But you really must hear what I have to say. Mammy's been writing checks in your name for a long time. Sometimes even for my pay. I know she's paid for most of this house in your name. Did you ever give her power of attorney to write checks in your name?"

"What's that?" she asked without interest. The money was not hers, anyway; it belonged to Mammy. And she saw no reason to go into a long explanation about the way Mammy handled things. Tony would not understand any more than she did.

"*What's that!*" he exclaimed. "I can't believe you're that ignorant, Teresa. On the other hand, you do tend to insulate yourself from reality, don't you? Did you ever sign a piece of paper with your name and Mammy's on it? That could be a power of attorney, and she could conduct all sorts of legal transactions without your knowing it."

Teresa laughed again, this time out of real amusement. "Tony, I've signed so many papers I couldn't count them. Reams of papers that would come to here." She indicated a line just below her eyes. "I'm sure what your speaking of was probably among them. Mammy takes care

239

of everything: the house, my clothing . . . everything. She always has. The money's hers."

"Not anymore," he told her, holding her gaze. "You're Thomas Bell's wife, now, and we're talking about his money, my dear. Have you signed any papers since you've been married?"

Teresa nodded. "Lot's of them. I signed some very odd ones in the presence of a notary just before I came here. But they had something to do with the house on Octavia Street."

"You little idiot," he breathed. "As long as she has that power of attorney, your life isn't yours. What if something happened to Bell? He's no spring chicken, you know. You and those children would inherit. If Mammy has that paper, none of you will have a dime! She'll have complete control of his estate."

He had her complete attention, now. The ramifications of what he said were enormous, and they affected Fred and Marie more than her. She doubted that Mr. Bell would bestow his estate on her, but if he intended to have her manage it until Fred came of age, the prospect of what could happen was appalling.

"What can I do?" she asked.

"Find that paper and burn it," he instructed her. "Tear the house apart if you have to, but destroy that paper, Teresa. I think I'm beginning to see where all this is leading, and I don't like it at all. You must do your part, and I'll do mine."

He rose quickly with a hint of his old agility and lit a lamp. Teresa scrambled to her feet to see what he was doing, and a worried frown came over her face when she observed him getting ready to leave. He put the black leather notebook in his breast pocket and stared at her for a moment.

"I'm going back, Teresa. She thinks I'm here with you. That will give me greater freedom in the city to find what I need. Will you be all right here, alone?"

"Yes," she said hesitantly, "I'd planned it that way. What are you going to do, Tony? Will *you* be all right?"

"The less you know about me, the better," he said. "Good-bye, darling. I'll leave the gig in case you need it; but you stay put, right here. Don't return to the city out of concern for either Mammy or me. I can get transportation from Princeton Harbor. *Find that paper and destroy it*, do you understand?"

He blew her a kiss as he went out the door, walking quickly with the jaunty step she remembered, and she recalled the handsome young

240

man doing calisthenics in a children's playground in Philadelphia. She would rather he stayed here, where she could look after him for a while. But she knew he was deadly serious in his investigation of Mammy, drawn back to San Francisco by the fascination and repulsion he felt for the old woman, almost as if she were a young, beautiful mistress who had betrayed his confidence.

PART IV

THE HOUSE
OF MYSTERY

Everything seems to be
going straight to hell. . . .

—Thomas Bell,
1891

Chapter 18

Teresa remained at Beltane for the rest of the month, sunning herself on the porch and wandering through the hills. She did not go down to the beach again, though its gentle blue curve beckoned with a charm almost as strong as Mammy's. She knew that the closer one got to that beach, the more evident disturbing things became. In a way, it's not unlike Mammy and me, she thought: we are not what we seem, either, I suppose. "Whited sepulchres, which, indeed appear beautiful outward, but are within full of dead men's bones." The quotation, from the Bible, suggested by the whale bones on the beach, made her shudder. She felt terribly depressed, and that was no way to renew herself on her vacation.

Following Mammy's example when she was in the country, she cleaned the small suite thoroughly, even pounding the Oriental rug on a makeshift line. She had not done any real work for years, and she was almost gratified by the blisters on her fingers. Anything was better than sitting around, waiting out the time to return to the city. She wondered what Tony was doing. She even speculated on the outcome of the lawsuit, which had driven her away in the first place. But most of all, she felt driven to find that power of attorney and destroy it, as Tony had instructed.

She did not know why she felt so fiercely loyal to Fred and Marie. They had certainly been anything but amiable to her. She had watched them grow from infancy almost to adulthood and had stood by helplessly while they missed the things that children need most: love, companionship, a sense of really belonging. The same things she had missed when she was growing up, she realized. I really should have taken a firmer stand on their behalf. If only I'd had the courage to oppose Mammy when I knew I was right, things would be different between Mr. Bell's children and me. A chance had been lost that she would never have again.

She wished she had brought her little dog with her. She had left in such a hurry that she hadn't had time to make arrangements to bring Baby. The servants would take care of her, but she was lonely for her companion. She cleaned the kitchen in an attempt to keep busy, but she was unable to channel all her energy into putting up preserves and sorting herbs the way Mammy did. Finally, as the time to return grew nearer, she bleached her hair and began to look after her hands again. She dreaded going back to the house on Octavia Street, but she found herself looking forward to it, too.

The Mexican field hands caught the horse for the gig a week before her departure and tamed it enough for her to handle the vehicle. She nearly asked one of them to drive her to the city, because her old trepidation about managing anything herself returned at the prospect of going alone. But she could not allow Mammy to know that anyone but Tony had driven her. She must appear to have dropped him off before she arrived at the house. She had not driven anything but a farm wagon before, but with the help of the field hands, she finally mastered the gig.

She asked directions in Princeton Harbor and was fortunate enough to find someone who was going to San Francisco. She followed the slow cart as far as Market Street, and she knew her way from there without having to maneuver any of the higher hills. As soon as she turned on Bush, the course was straight—as straight, she reflected gloomily, as the trip to Laurel Hill Cemetery, though at least she did not have to follow a funeral today.

Mammy was concerned when she learned that Teresa had driven the gig into the stable by herself, but she was so beset by other matters that Teresa's simple explantion that she had dropped Tony off downtown sufficed.

"You won't believe what's been happening here," Mammy said, breathlessly eager to tell all. "I haven't had a chance to write to you. Come to think of it, you didn't write very often, either."

"It was a pleasant vacation," Teresa said by way of explanation of her few short notes, written mainly to keep Mammy from descending on her at Half Moon Bay. "You look as if you could use one, too."

Though Mammy was constitutionally immune to bad nerves, she had aged slightly since Teresa had seen her last, and she glanced often toward the hall and the door to the reception room as they stood in the parlor, her mismatched eyes darting and suspicious. "We can't talk here," she decided suddenly, "let's go to your rooms."

As Teresa followed her up the staircase, she observed that the aging woman's figure was as straight as ever, and she was more breathless than Mammy when they reached the landing. They walked down the hallway in silence, and Mammy gave the same quick, suspicious glance toward the door of Mr. Bell's room, putting her finger to her lips to caution Teresa, who wondered what he was doing home on a weekday. When they entered Teresa's sitting room, she discarded her hat casually and smoothed her hair, waiting for Mammy to reveal what was on her mind.

"I've missed you, honey," Mammy said instead, her voice soft with affection. "Your presence is the only thing that keeps this house sane. You're like the calm in the midst of a storm, Teresa."

"That's interesting," Teresa observed. "I hardly thought I was noticed."

She scrutinized Mammy enigmatically, wondering how many of the stories about her were true. Once one was in her presence, it was difficult not to fall under that charm again, but she was determined to remain as objective as possible in her search for the document. Tony had pointed out an interesting thing to her in the construction of Beltane, and she was certain the same sort of passages existed here, as they must have at the boardinghouse, where she had first felt she was being watched. She would have to watch and wait and attempt to find the passage when she was certain Mammy was tied up in the courtroom.

"You're different," Mammy said, at once sensing a change in Teresa. "You must have a secret. When a woman has a secret," she smiled cunningly, "she's much more interesting and beautiful."

"Just relaxed, I suppose," Teresa said, "thought I doubt it will last for long in this house. You were dying to tell me something downstairs, Mammy. We're safe enough here. What is it?"

The lines seemed to disappear from Mammy's face, and her eyes glowed until Teresa thought she was about to see the transformation into pantherish fury again. She trembled inside a little, in spite of herself. She can't know about Tony coming to town, she tried to reassure herself, but she's pretty angry, whatever it is. When Mammy finally spoke it was in a malicious whisper.

"That little bastard Fred's been around here," she said. "He's left

247

school, and he's trying to get money from Thomas. Sometimes I don't know if he's in the house or not, Teresa. I've never seen a more avaricious young man. I'm afraid he'll take something. Be sure to keep your door locked."

"Why isn't he living here?" Teresa asked.

"His father asked him to leave. Thomas hasn't been well, and Fred's demands were too much for him. But Fred's been lurking around ever since, as though he's looking for something. Something he can sell, I'm certain. That little bitch Marie will be turning up next. They're a dreadful pair, believe you me!"

"She's still in the convent, isn't she?" Teresa was not sure how much of this she could stand; already she was longing for the peace of Beltane. She knew that the young people were unpleasant, but she was also aware of what made them so. "I can't see why you're so upset with Mr. Bell's children," she hazarded. "I don't anticipate any real problem from them, Mammy, as long as they are treated fairly."

"You don't know them," Mammy grumbled, her anger dying quickly, and Teresa suspected more was troubling her than the children.

"I haven't seen any newspapers," she said walking into her bedroom to get out of her traveling clothes. "How's the lawsuit going?"

"It's taking so much longer than I expected," Mammy said, following her into the bedroom. "We'll win in the end, I'm confident of that. Sarah Althea has the marriage certificate. But all the legal costs are so expensive, Teresa. And I can't leave the house during the day without being besieged by newspaper people."

She's had all the notoriety she can bear, Teresa reflected as she sat down at her vanity. More has been brought out into the open than she ever dreamed. No wonder Fred had descended on his father, trying to save his share of the estate. She would have to discuss that with Mr. Bell as soon as possible. Suddenly, for the first time in weeks, she thought of Tony, and the hairbrush became idle in her hand. She could not inquire about him, because she was supposed to have spent the summer with him. Either he was still following his leads about the blacks who, he alleged, had been swindled out of their life savings, or he had dropped out of sight completely. Later, she would ask how to contact him, because she was concerned about his health.

"I'd like a long, hot bath, Mammy," she said, watching her in the mirror. "All that dust. I'll give you a report on the progress at Beltane later, if you don't mind."

248

Mammy moved to the side of the bed and jerked the bellpull almost angrily to summon a servant, mumbling, "Beltane's the least of my worries right now. It'll take a fortune to complete it. That ugly old man with his fine hotel better capitulate soon."

Teresa had reached the conclusion that her best chance of finding the power of attorney was to gain access to Mammy's room by means of the secret passageway. As the weeks after her return dragged on, she explored the house completely, but she was unable to find the exit of the passage if indeed there was one, as at Beltane. Mammy kept her suite locked, and there was only one key, which she kept on her person. Remembering the padlocked room near the back door, she went to it late one afternoon, summoning one of the maids from her quarters to accompany her. The chain and lock were still firmly in place.

"Does anyone have a key to this?" she asked the maid, Ada, who appeared to be growing more nervous by the minute, glancing back over her shoulder toward the dark hall behind them.

"No, ma'am. None of us ever comes this far. We have to leave the house by the side door, ma'am. If you'll forgive me, I don't think we should be here at all."

"You're safe enough with me," Teresa reassured her, but the young woman's eyes were blank with fright. "Who forbade you access to the back door?"

"Nobody, ma'am. But we all know that room is haunted. That's why it's kept locked. Sometimes, the most awful sounds come from it in the middle of the night. It fairly curdles the blood in my veins, ma'am, and I don't want to be here."

"Very well," Teresa acquiesced with a smile, "we'll return to your quarters. What sort of sounds do you hear?" she inquired when they were a safe distance from the back hallway. "Drum beats? Chanting?"

"I guess it could be. I put my pillow over my head, ma'am, because I'm afraid I'll hear the screeching. I've never heard it, but others have, and just the thought of it makes the hairs stand up on my arms."

Teresa looked back toward the offensive area, and what she saw caused a frisson of terror to run up her own spine. The back door, the locked room, the whole back hall had vanished behind them, and it was not an illusion of light. She wondered that she had not noticed it before, but both times she had approached the area, she had been intent on other things. The first time, she was anxiously fleeing to Beltane, and a few minutes ago, she had been engaged in conversation with the maid. The hall could not just vanish into infinity, that much was obvious. The house was constructed at a peculiar angle back here, on an incline so gradual that the area was hidden from the servants' quarters. It was also kept so dark that she herself would not have noticed the locked room if her shawl had not snagged on the chain that night.

She wished Tony were with her to explore this part of the house, because she was almost certain that the construction prevented sound from traveling far from the closed door of the room. There were probably peculiar acoustical properties to the hall's angle and the gradual incline, but she knew so little about such things that she could only speculate. She glanced at her lapel watch and was startled by the time. Mammy would be returning by the side door facing the stables at any minute, and she dared not risk meeting her coming from this direction.

"May I inspect your room?" she asked Ada courteously. "I like to think that the servants' quarters are as comfortable as possible, my dear."

"Yes, ma'am," the young woman said, somewhat taken aback, "I try to keep it tidy, ma'am, but I slept too long this morning and I haven't had a chance to make my bed."

Teresa entered the untidy room, noting that it was smaller than she remembered from seeing the servants' quarters empty on first inspecting the house. She asked a few questions about the heating and ventilation, which led to a discussion of the conditions in the house in which the maid had formerly been employed, and inquiries about her home town in the Middle West. When, without looking at her watch, she estimated that fifteen minutes had passed, she excused herself graciously and bypassed the courtyard door by walking through the pantries and kitchen to emerge in the dining room. Aside from the preparations for dinner, the house was completely quiet. She opened the double doors to the library, closed them behind her, and was sitting on the window seat deeply absorbed by a book when Mammy finally found her.

"Well, here you are!" she exclaimed, "I might have known, you're such a bookworm, Teresa. I didn't know what had happened to you, and I have a lot to tell you. Has the paper arrived yet?"

"Probably. I haven't looked," Teresa replied, putting the book aside facedown. "Has there finally been a decision?"

"Not really," Mammy said, untying her black taffeta bonnet and taking off her gloves, "but things are looking up. An expert evaluated the marriage certificate today, and he could find no discrepancies in it. And, honey, that bug-eyed old man is beginning to sweat! He kept glancing at me all day, and I didn't take my eyes off him, not for one minute. He really believes I've put a spell on him," she said with a cackle.

"Have you?" Teresa asked without interest, and Mammy dropped the ruched pouch bag she was removing from her arm.

"What sort of question is that?" she demanded with humor. "Honestly, you beat all, Teresa. I don't know how to cast a spell. That's all newspaper nonsense, you know that."

"The rags and feathers and hair clippings exhibited in court weren't put in Senator Sharon's suite by a journalist," Teresa observed. "I'll admit they'll stretch a story, but they wouldn't go that far to create a sensation."

"That old stuff!" Mammy said disdainfully. "Some disgruntled West Indian waiter probably put it there. It wouldn't do anything anyway unless old Sharon knew there was an effigy of him with a great big thorn from a black thorntree in it." Teresa observed her without speaking, and Mammy grew slightly agitated. "All right, I pretended I'd done it in court," she said testily. "It was all part of my bluff. I knew he was apprehensive about me and I just wanted to frighten him."

"For a lady who can't cast a spell, you're pretty well informed about effigies and thorns," Teresa commented and Mammy laughed warmly. "Honey, I lived in New Orleans. Everyone knows about such things there."

"The feathered object Senator Sharon found in his suite was a *wonga*," Teresa said, observing how quickly Mammy covered her surprise, "and he'd need a *gris-gris*, a charm to protect himself, wouldn't he? I wonder if West Indian waiters know how to make those, too."

"You aren't as ignorant as you used to be," Mammy said, attempting casualness. "Where in the world did you hear about such things?"

"I read a lot," Teresa said. "One can find almost anything in books."

"So it appears," Mammy said doubtfully. Then she changed the subject abruptly. "That wretch, Fred, hasn't put in an appearance here today, has he? I thought I saw him out by the carriage house this morning. Thomas is impossible enough without that scoundrel."

"I haven't seen him. Really, Mammy, Fred deserves more. He should be living here. After all, he's Mr. Bell's heir."

251

"Not if I can help it," Mammy said slyly. "I know what's in Thomas's will, you see. Thomas and I are in perfect accord."

Sarah Althea's lawsuit continued into the early part of 1884, and even the journalists appeared to be bored by it. Stories on the court proceedings moved to the second and third page of the newspapers. The hearings took place less frequently, and Teresa had difficulty determining whether Mammy was in the house or not. Since she had become aware of the existence of the secret passage—though she was still unable to find its outside exit—she recognized the danger of too much prying, and she was forced to let the matter of the power of attorney ride.

She and Mammy took their evening meal with Mr. Bell, and that was about all Teresa saw of him. He was generally morose and answered questions only if Mammy directed them at him. Teresa felt compassion for the man, whose ginger hair had turned to white. There was no more twinkle in his faded eyes, and he moved stiffly when he left the room. But she suspected that more than suspicion of Fred had brought about such a transformation. She had no ground for believing that Mammy had contributed to it. Perhaps he was just one of those people who grow old prematurely, she thought. She had wanted a word with him since her return from Beltane, but he still went to the bank every day, and by the time he returned Mammy was in constant attendance. Teresa was unable to approach him alone with the few words of encouragement regarding Fred she hoped to convey. He seemed a very lonely, discouraged man.

While Mammy perused the newspapers every evening for any reference to herself, Teresa concentrated on the obituaries, without feeling any compunction about her interest. If she could not get at the document, at least she could pursue this other aspect of her eventual freedom. It was more like a game than actually wishing anyone ill, because she did not expect to find much in the column anyway.

"What ever happened to Ben Willard?" she asked casually one evening beside the fire. "He was a very attractive man, Mammy. I haven't heard anything about him for some time."

"He's still in San Francisco," Mammy replied, tearing out a small article with her long fingers. "Still strong and handsome, too. I really robbed the cradle with that one." When Teresa laughed, Mammy was encouraged to continue. "Well, I did! But every middle-aged woman's entitled to that, as you know. Tony's a few years younger than you are, too."

So, Ben's alive and well and living in San Franciso, Teresa thought without showing any emotion. And Tony has not surfaced with anything to give substance to his accusations. "I haven't seen Tony since Beltane, Mammy. I'd like to get in touch with him. He wasn't very well when we parted."

"He's around, and he's just fine," Mammy responded. "It wouldn't be wise for you two to carry on in the city. I'll probably be sending you out to Beltane again in the spring. You can see him then."

Teresa had to restrain herself from protesting that she was only interested in Tony's health, but Mammy's view of the relationship between the sexes was too cynical for that. Teresa did not inquire as to the whereabouts of Billy Beaumont that evening, either. If she had, Mammy would have suspected what was on her mind. Her best approach in handling Mammy was to appear to accept her distorted standards without accepting those standards herself.

"You get out of this house!" Mammy screamed. "If you stay one minute longer, I'll call the police. Teresa," she said, gratefully turning away from Fred in the hall as Teresa descended the stairs hastily, "he's here again! Snooping around where he doesn't belong when his father's away at work. What are you looking for, boy?"

Teresa had not seen Fred for so long that she was surprised to see him grown into young manhood, tall and broad-shouldered, with a hard, Germanic face and the hint of a blond mustache over his thin lips.

"Hello, Fred," she greeted him politely. "There appears to be some misunderstanding. I've told Mammy you're always welcome here."

Her friendly overture only earned her a contemptuous glance from narrow blue eyes almost as cold as Jim Hoey's. "You don't make the rules around here, *Mrs.* Bell. Everyone knows that. My right to be in my father's house has nothing to do with your bounty. I've told him repeatedly to get rid of that old bitch, before she ruins him with her perpetual litigation. God knows, she's already ruined my sister and me."

"You see?" Mammy asked, her eyes blazing and her face taking on the catlike expression Teresa dreaded. "I found him in the library. He'd already rumaged through the desk, and he was shaking books and dropping them in a heap on the floor. It's pretty clear what he's looking for, and I call it downright *unfilial!*"

Teresa suppressed a smile at the word. "Fred knows his father's will isn't lying about the house," she meditated. "What are you looking for, Fred? Did you stash some money away once, when you were home on vacation?" He stared at her with withering disgust. "Perhaps, in the future, you'd better come only when your father's at home," she said with level eyes. "Your behavior isn't exactly forthright, and your manners are wanting."

Faced by two irate women, he moved with dignity toward the door. "You haven't seen the last of me by a long shot," he promised coolly. "If father doesn't throw you both out, I assure you that I will when my time comes."

"Did you hear that?" Mammy nearly screamed as the door closed behind him. "He thinks he can take this house from *me*! That nasty, pale little rabbit. He'd better watch his step, or I'll take care of him for good!"

"Don't talk like that, Mammy," Teresa said quickly, as much to reassure herself as quiet the older woman. "You should never threaten anyone's life."

Mammy swung on her with outrage in her eyes. "His life?" she cried and suddenly laughed so hysterically that the sound jarred Teresa's nerves more than Mammy's threats. "I can assure you, I can destroy the little worm more thoroughly than by killing him. His life! I practically gave him his life, Teresa. What makes you think I'd ever threaten to take it away?"

"What was he looking for?" Teresa asked, walking toward the library door. "Good Lord, what a mess! Has he done this sort of thing before?"

"Yes," Mammy said heavily, planting herself in front of the ransacked desk. "He may just be looking for something to sell. I hear he gambles a lot. You'd better hide your jewelry."

"He wasn't looking for jewelry in the desk drawer," Teresa said with a frown. "He must be looking for a document. . . ."

"The will . . . just as you said," Mammy agreed suddenly. "He must think Thomas has written a second will. He's probably seen the one on file in the lawyer's office and knows he won't get much. Only enough to live on for the rest of his life, if he oversees his father's mines. And he can't do that properly if he's dropped out of mining school. He's no good. Neither of them are. Marie keeps sending me the nastiest letters you ever saw."

"What kind of nasty letters?" Teresa asked with surprise. "That hardly sounds like the pastime of a girl who's almost ready to leave a convent school."

"Fred's been at her, too. It's obvious. What a nest of vipers we've sheltered in this house, Teresa. I told you, didn't I? There's bad blood there. I didn't want you to get too close to them, because I knew you'd be hurt."

In Mammy's present mood, it was not prudent to remind her that the children might have been different if someone had been allowed to get close to them. She found the whole episode upsetting and wished she had not witnessed it. Fred's threat that he might be able to evict both herself and Mammy was not reassuring, either. How could they be sure that Mr. Bell had not actually written a second will in favor of his son?

The winter was unusually wet and raw, and Teresa found herself dwelling on Tony's fate more than on anything else happening around her. Unable to endure the worry any longer, she finally left the house in a downpour when Mammy was at court and trudged down the hill to hail a cab. She had no idea where Tony lived, but she thought she knew someone who could find him without causing a great to-do. The Pinkerton agents were trained for this sort of thing, and they could protect their client as well. Having asked the cab to wait, she climbed the dreary stairs in an old brick building, attempting to recall the name of the agent who had brought her back from New York so many years ago. I should have consulted my diary, she thought, but if he's still here, I'll recognize him anyway. He told me to call on him if I needed help.

The men in the smoke-filled office were all younger than her agent would have been. Trying to disregard the nasty odor of cigars, she went through the line of inquiry until she found herself seated across the desk from one of them. His long face and untidy fair hair were different from her old agent's, but the expression in his dark eyes was the same: intelligent, shrewd, and a little cynical.

"My name is Mrs. Hoey," she told him, shaking the water from her umbrella. He rose to pull over a cracked umbrella stand for her and started writing notes as she explained her interest in finding an old friend who had been ill when she had last seen him. "My concern is about his health. The weather's been so terrible this winter."

The sharp, dark eyes scrutinized her, but Teresa knew her grave eyes were impenetrable. "What's your address, ma'am?" he asked her, but she was prepared for the question.

"For discretion's sake I'd prefer to call in at your office, after telephoning you beforehand, of course."

He nodded briefly. "If you'd care to wait, I can place a call to the police station, just to see if they have anything there on Mr. Ward. Just in case he's been reported as a missing person, you understand."

"Yes," she said faintly. She did not wish to become involved with the police, but she acquiesced to the formality uneasily, trying to ignore the ringing of the standing telephones on several desks and developing a headache from clenching her jaw. After what seemed an interminable time, the young agent returned with a sheet of notepaper in his hand.

"We're in luck, Mrs. Hoey. Mr. Ward's landlady reported him missing last year. Now, don't get apprehensive. The police aren't, I assure you. So many people just get up and leave for no apparent reason. Our files are crammed with them. This is a very transient city. If you like, I'll nip by the rooming house and have a word with this Mrs. Walsh, and you can contact me tomorrow to find out what she has to say."

"May I go with you?" Teresa asked unexpectedly. He glanced toward the rain driving against the window.

"Right now?" he asked reluctantly.

"Yes, please. I don't want to inconvenience you, Mr. . . . ."

"Porter. James Porter, ma'am. It's no inconvenience, really, just not the ordinary thing, that's all. If you're game, so am I."

"I have a cab waiting outside," she told him, and he reached for his coat with relief. "I really do appreciate this."

"It isn't the best part of town," he grinned, "but it isn't the worst, either. Let's just hope that the old girl's still there."

The house reminded Teresa of the hotel she had stayed in on her arrival in San Francisco with its ROOMS TO LET sign in the window, except that the curtains were not torn and the hall inside harbored no unpleasant odors. Mrs. Walsh, who occupied the first apartment on the ground floor, answered the door cradling a cat as old and plump and spotted as herself. When she learned the reason for their visit, she invited them inside and shut the cat in the kitchen.

"I've been so concerned," she said. "The police told me not to worry and all that, but I think of Mr. Ward so often. He was a consumptive gentleman, you know, not the sort to just leave without his things. He did tell me once that he'd been a sailor, but he was in no condition to go to sea, as the police seemed to think he'd done."

"Do you still have his belongings?" Mr. Porter asked. "I suppose the police went through everything?"

"One of them looked at his room. He didn't have much, the poor dear, though he dressed very well. I have everything in a cardboard box in the cellar."

"Did he have any visitors?" Teresa could not refrain from asking,

256

though she knew she should leave the investigation to the Pinkerton agent.

"Not many," Mrs. Walsh said kindly. "He was a rather lonely man, though his spirits were good most of the time. In fact, his spirits were unusually high just before he . . . vanished."

"Did anyone visit him during that time?" Teresa pursued, causing Mr. Porter to shoot a speculative glance in her direction. "I'm sorry," she apologized, "but it may be important."

"The gentlemen from the newspaper hadn't called for some time," the old woman said, responding to Teresa's line of reasoning, "but the last time I saw him he was with a tall, gray-haired gentleman named . . . oh, dear," she pondered, "he was a retired police officer, I believe."

"It sounds as if he was in safe enough company," Mr. Porter smiled, relaxing slightly. "He didn't return after that?"

"He may have. He was so quiet, I hardly knew when he was here. But that was the last time I actually saw him, several nights before I became concerned and opened his room. I really thought I might find the poor man dead," she said in justification of the action. "But his bed hadn't been slept in, and it was only eight in the morning. I called the hospitals, first, and finally the police, a couple of days later. Dayton!" she cried, "no, that wasn't the name, though I think it began with a D. The man I saw him with, I mean."

"Surely you told the police about the retired officer," Mr. Porter said, and she nodded. "May we see his belongings now?" he requested.

She lighted a kerosene lamp and led them down the wooden stairs to an earthen cellar heaped with discarded furniture. The vent from the coal furnace gave a little light, and Mrs. Walsh managed to hang the lamp on a pipe above their heads. She indicated the cardboard box. Teresa crouched in the coal dust, disregarding her clothing as Mr. Porter removed a few scant articles from the top of the box: a shaving mug and straight-edge razor, silver-backed toilet articles, and a framed picture, which he held up to the light. He glanced at Teresa sharply as he handed the picture to her. "A casual old friend?" he commented. "Things must have been different in Philadelphia, Mrs. Hoey."

She did not remember having the picture taken, but the sepia evidence was before her eyes. A young, handsome Tony smiled broadly with his arm around the slim waist of an impossibly young Teresa fifteen years ago, whose face was still dewy with affection for him. The sort of picture people have taken at fairs or expositions, posing for a full minute before the draped camera of a boardwalk photographer,

257

framed in cardboard with the name of the event embossed on it. Tony had inserted the picture in a silver frame that matched his toilet articles, using the original cardboard as a matte.

"Does it matter?" Teresa replied to Mr. Porter when she was able to control her voice. "It was before I was married to... before I was married."

The intrepid Mr. Porter probably did not hear her. He was intent on studying everything in the box, running his hands through the pockets of suits already riddled with moth holes. "Nothing," he said, "not a damn thing. I don't know what I expected, but these pockets are empty. He must have had everything on him when he... left."

"There was a small, black, limp leather notebook," Teresa told him. "Are you positive it isn't there?"

"Absolutely," he said, staring at her again. He replaced the articles and closed the box almost angrily, and then rose to brush off his clothing. Teresa still had the framed picture in her hands. "Do you want it?" he asked tersely.

She nodded and slipped it into her handbag. Mrs. Walsh was as disappointed as they, as she led them upstairs and to the front door. "If you find out anything," she said, "anything at all, you'll let me know, won't you?"

"Yes," Teresa smiled faintly, taking her by the hand. "I wish we could speak to that Dayton person, though. Perhaps Mr. Porter can make inquiries with the police."

"Leighton!" the old woman shot out suddenly with excitement. "It wasn't a D at all, isn't that always the way? His name was *Leighton*."

"Charles Leighton," Mr. Porter nodded. "Thank you, ma'am."

His hand was so tight on Teresa's arm as he assisted her to the cab that she was sure she would be bruised. He climbed in beside her in sullen silence, after ordering the cabbie to take them back to the agency.

"Mrs. Hoey," he said at last, "we run into lots of types in our line of work, but you just about beat them all. Why didn't you tell me at the beginning that the man was blackmailing you? 'A small black, limp leather book,' indeed. And that picture, very cozy."

"But, he—"

"Forget it, it happens. You could have made things easier, that's all. If Inspector Leighton took him in for questioning, as sick as everyone says Anthony Ward was, he probably just got despondent and drowned himself in the Bay. You don't have anything to worry about anymore."

On her way home in the cab, Teresa tried to put the pieces together in a more logical way. Tony must have had the book in his pocket, and he was excited about something. Evidence he was looking for against Mammy? But if he reported it to the police, why had they taken no action? Even if something happened to him on the way home, the police would have sent someone to interrogate Mammy, and probably the entire family and staff at Octavia Street. Something just did not fit. And why, she thought concentrating with her hand over her eyes, did the name Leighton echo dimly somewhere in her mind?

She knew in her heart that Tony was dead, but she could not accept that it was by suicide.

Chapter 19

By the time the judge handed down his decision in the Sharon case, Teresa had minutely searched the walls of every room in the house to determine the extent of the secret corridor, hoping that there was another entrance into it besides the one in Mammy's room and the one at the point where it exited the building. Such activities were only possible when Mammy was safely away at court. She discovered cleverly concealed peepholes in the rooms on one side of the building, which included Mr. Bell's quarters, the guest bedrooms that were never used, the dining room on the main floor, and the servants' quarters. As diligently as she tried, she could find nothing in her own rooms, and this surprised her, though it was true that she was not conscious of being watched here, as she had been at the boarding-house. Mammy must have been supremely confident of her hold over her when the house on Octavia Street was constructed; she did not appear to think that Teresa warranted watching like the others.

Teresa could not tramp around in the mud and wet outside during the winter while searching for the exit of the passageway, because such activities would surely draw comment. She was now certain that the padlocked room was not the exit, not just because it was locked from the outside, but because she had examined the area around the doors with a lamp and pressed every spot that might have held a spring. If voodoo ceremonies had been held in this house, as some of the neighbors had alleged, they probably took place in the padlocked room, though the exit of the passage must be in the rear of the house, too. She tried to recall the system she had seen at Beltane, wishing she had paid more attention to its mechanics, but she had been too amazed by its existence and too disturbed by Tony Ward's stories to heed everything

261

she should have. If she could not find the exit during the summer, she would have to try to get back to Beltane alone to take another look at the passageway there.

Her explorations ceased abruptly in late March, when the court decided that Sarah Althea Hill's marriage license was valid. The defeat of Senator Sharon's claims caused rejoicing in the house. Teresa was instructed to dress for dinner that night, and she found Mammy and Mr. Bell sipping champagne with their heads close together when she entered the dining room. He wore a dress suit with a ruffled shirt front, and Mammy displayed all of her diamonds, which Teresa had never seen all at one time before. Mammy looked like a Christmas tree. If money was as tight as she claimed, she could have completed Beltane and built another house like it just with what she had on her person.

"I told you we'd win," she said as she greeted Teresa with triumphant eyes and a beaming face. "Sit down here with us," she invited, patting the table, "we're having a party tonight."

The color had returned to Mr. Bell's face, and his eyes held some of their old sparkle. Teresa sat on his left, relieved to see him looking so well but wondering at the reason for his recovery. She had read somewhere that revenge was sweet, but she had never seen this effect demonstrated so clearly before. He held up his glass to make a toast, and she lifted hers reluctantly. She had never drunk much, and champagne on an empty stomach was not her prescription for a pleasant evening. Besides, wine tended to have the effect of depressing her.

"To William Ralston," he toasted with emotion, "whose enemy has just lost half of his holdings! I promised I'd avenge you, Bill."

Teresa took a small sip of the champagne before Mammy proposed another toast: "To the Palace Hotel, which won't be Senator Sharon's home much longer! Do you know," she reflected, "William Ralston once invited me to run that place? Now, Thomas owns it."

A few glasses of wine seemed to be having their effect on Mr. Bell, too. He excused himself from the table for a moment, and Mammy took advantage of his absence to reprimand Teresa gently. "I know you don't drink, honey, but at least try to appear happy. This means a lot to Thomas. He's always felt guilty about what happened to Ralston. You see, Thomas knew the crash was coming and saved his own fortune in time. But he couldn't tell his friend, Mr. Ralston, about the stock manipulation that was going on. He couldn't tell anyone, you understand. When the bank crashed, and Mr. Ralston drowned himself the next day, you can imagine Thomas's feelings. Sharon gobbled up

262

everything Ralston had held, including the Palace Hotel. I think he moved in that same week. But we've put things to right again!"

The confidence was aimed at raising Teresa's spirits, but it had the opposite effect. When Mr. Bell returned, she saw him in an entirely new light, as the financial shark he was instead of a kind, gentle little man. She was relieved when dinner was served so she could eat in silence without attempting a false smile. She attempted to ignore them as they divided half of Senator Sharon's estate between themselves and Sarah Althea Hill. The whole affair was slightly obscene.

"I know we need the cash," Mammy considered, "but I do want the hotel, Thomas! It's so beautiful, with all that marble and furniture and the glass dome over the carriage area. I wouldn't manage the kitchen for William Ralston when he asked, but I could really do something with that place if it were mine."

Teresa choked. Something had gone down the wrong way, and she covered her face with a linen napkin, coughing furiously to dislodge it. A blow from Mammy between her shoulder blades dislodged the obstruction, but she felt weak and shaky, realizing how close she might have been to death. Mr. Bell offered her a glass of water, studying her with concern.

"Are you all right?" he asked, and she nodded as she sipped. "Choking at table's a bad business. I knew a fellow once who fell dead right over his plate."

That terrible, uncontrollable laughter was rising in her chest again, and it would be completely inappropriate to give it free rein during this celebration. She excused herself hurriedly and ran up the stairs to her suite. As soon as she closed the door behind her, the desire to laugh, like the emotion that makes one want to laugh in church, drained away, leaving her tearful. She tried to attribute her depression to the wine, though she had not had even one full glass. This whole thing is so grotesque, she sighed, lying across her bed in her chic velvet gown and staring at the ceiling. Well, things should be calm enough around here, now that they have the money. Mammy will probably finish building Beltane, and perhaps I can move out there; at least, it was peaceful.

Something on the ceiling caught her attention, a small, dark spot between the panels of painted flowers and cherubs. She turned up the lamp as she rose, without taking her eyes off the ceiling; then, frantically, she began to pile furniture on the bed, testing the construction for stability. She climbed onto the table first and, more cautiously, onto the vanity bench, but she was still far from the fourteen-foot ceiling. She descended for the lamp and repeated her climb more cautiously, using only one hand for support.

The dark spot near the panel could be seen clearly now, and she closed her eyes for a moment with relief. A bit of cobweb, that's all, she breathed, not a peephole, as she had feared, and that was a good thing. If the holes started appearing in the ceilings, her whole mental reconstruction of the plan of the passageway would be wrong.

Only after she had come down and started to replace the furniture did the humorous aspect of her action strike her, and this time she gave in to it, laughing until there were tears in her eyes. Thank God for a sense of humor, she thought, however strangely it manifests itself. If I couldn't laugh in this house, I'd blow to bits and become part of the decoration on the ceiling.

She needed a sense of irony, if not humor, to cushion her growing uneasiness in the following months. The high-domed, bug-eyed Mr. Sharon was no fool and had not secured his immense fortune without shrewdness and less ethics than Mr. Bell. By the time for the dispersal of his money arrived, he was penniless. Everything had been transferred to his grown children by a previous marriage when the suit had begun two years before, under the stipulation that they fight Sarah Althea's claim as long as they lived. He further complicated things by dying in his suite at the Palace Hotel before the bequest could be contested, reinforcing the transfer of his assets by means of his ironclad will.

Mammy's fury was frightening even to Mr. Bell, who in an attempt to avoid her began to spend more time at his club, returning only late in the evening. If Teresa had been alarmed by Mammy's reaction when she married Mr. Bell, now she took all the precautions that would be normal for one sharing a house with a maniac. The old woman had become deadly, a state of mind manifested in her particular aversion to Teresa's arthritic old dog, Baby, who had lived far beyond the normal life span of her breed.

After the initial rages and maledictions resulting from Sharon's bequest had blown over, Teresa approached Mammy cautiously with her request to spend a little time at Beltane during the summer. She was prepared for some resistance, even a furious fit, but not for what she actually heard.

"We can't afford it," Mammy snapped as she bustled around the kitchen. "I've even had to let some of the servants go. I'll be doing all the cooking myself, until Thomas loosens up with a little money."

"My going to Beltane won't be an expense," Teresa reasoned. "Just the contrary, I should think. And no one's been there to see if everything's all right for over two years. It could be falling into complete disrepair by now."

"No," Mammy said firmly, "I need you here. Besides, the last time you went off with your lover, that old dog set up an awful howl and made messes on the floor."

"I'll take Baby with me," Teresa assured her. "I wouldn't have left her before if I hadn't been so unstrung. She whined in her sleep for months after I came back, and I felt terrible about it."

"That old dog's nasty," Mammy said with a grimace, "old and toothless and smelly. It should be put to sleep."

"No!" Teresa cried protectively. "She isn't in pain, and she still enjoys her life. She's my dog, and I'm the one who looks after her." Then, she had a flash of what she thought was brilliant reasoning. "Someday you'll be old and toothless and smelly, too, Mammy. Would you like to be considered for euthanasia?"

"I'm not a dog," Mammy said, logically enough, though her mind seemed to be on something else already. "Maybe later in the summer. You can wait that long, can't you? Someone really should see what's happening at Beltane, and perhaps things will improve by then. I want you here right now. I think Fred's sniffing around again."

Teresa had learned immense patience. She knew it would not be easy living with Mammy for a while, and she could not investigate the passageway to secure the power of attorney in Mammy's room while Mammy was in the house. The trip to Beltane to inspect the passageway there was the only way to acquire the information to finish her task, so she resigned herself to waiting. If she kept to her room most of the time, she might have some peace and quiet, like dwelling in the eye of a hurricane.

The last thing she expected was a conciliatory move on the part of Mr. Bell in the interim. He approached her one evening in the library looking unusually crestfallen. The loss of Sharon's money had not concerned him, because he had not known it was in the balance at all. For him, justice had been done and his own conscience appeased by seeing the senator get crushed publicly. It appeared to Teresa that Sharon's death had only put the frosting on the cake of Thomas's revenge. Though Mammy was difficult to live with, Mr. Bell appeared to be in better health than he had been two years earlier. Even so, he seemed more unhappy than she had thought possible when he opened the desk to take out a bundle of letters from his children.

"I won't ask you to read them," he said, slapping them down on top of the desk, "it's too depressing. The expressions of filial devotion are more than outweighed by the amount of money requested in each one of them. I love those children, Teresa, but they'll be the death of me. Have you any suggestions? I'm at a complete loss."

Teresa sympathized with the old man, as keen and ruthless as he had revealed himself to be in dealing with other matters. "I don't know, Mr. Bell," she said, approaching the desk to look down at the letters. "Is Fred living in San Jose now?" she asked with surprise at the sight of a postmark. If he was living down the peninsula, it was unlikely that Mammy could have seen him about the house so often.

"I have a mine down there," he said, tipping his chair back and putting his fingers in his vest. "Fred had a little training in mining, so I sent him there for more. It hasn't worked. I don't know how anyone can spend so much money in San Jose."

"Is Marie with him? I heard that she'd graduated from the convent school."

"No, Marie's installed in a pleasant flat of her own, here in the city. I offered her a trip to Europe after her graduation, but she disdained it. If I didn't know better, I'd think they were both waiting for me to die."

"Oh, no!" Teresa exclaimed sympathetically, "I'm sure they aren't like that. You're the only person they've ever loved, Mr. Bell. You've been very good to them. Perhaps if you invited them here for awhile and got to know them better. After all, it's been a long time since they've lived with you."

He laughed harshly. "They wouldn't come. They're adamant about that. They won't live in this house until Mammy and—"

"—and I are out of it," she said, nodding her understanding. "I'm really sorry that they feel that way. I suppose it doesn't help to dwell on the past, but I'd have done anything for them at one time. My efforts were not appreciated much, I'm afraid."

"That's why I'm speaking to you now. You didn't buy into the best of all possible worlds, Teresa. I know that. But you were always good to the children. I want to entreat you to look after their interests in the event that anything happens to me. They'll need someone with a level head to guide them. I'm not a young man. You understand?"

She did not waste time with protestations of his longevity; he was too serious for that. "I promise you I'll do everything in my power," she told him, wondering if she could live up to the promise. "They will never want for anything, Mr. Bell."

"Perhaps you could write to them," he suggested, visibly relieved, "make a friendly overture to them. When they realize what a kind, accomplished lady you are, they may change their minds about you." He glanced at the gold watch in his vest. "I must be off now. A meeting of the board I simply can't miss. Thank you, Teresa. You'll write at once, won't you? Their addresses are right here."

Wondering what sort of board meeting would take place at night, Teresa remained in the library to write the letters. He had set her a difficult task, trying to show her interest in Fred and Marie without seeming to want to get into their good graces for her own reasons. The clock in the hall chimed ten as she finished, and she tucked the letters in her bodice to hide them from Mammy's prying eyes. When she left the library to go to her room, she was surprised to see John Willis waiting in the hall with his hat in his hand.

"John Willis," she greeted him warmly, and he smiled in return. "I haven't seen you for so long. I understand you've bought yourself a house on the Bay?"

"Yes, Mis' Teresa," he nodded, "a nice little house close to the fishin'."

"Is there a Mrs. Willis yet?"

He shook his head sheepishly. "Not yet, Mis' Teresa, but soon, I hope. Do you think I'm too old to marry a gal of twenty-two?"

Teresa smiled and shook his hand. "You aren't too old if you don't feel it. Congratulations! But what brings you here tonight?"

"Got a meetin' with Mammy," he said, his manner more subdued. "Private business, Mis' Teresa. She tol' me to come at ten."

"Then she'll be along shortly," she assured him, anxious to be in her room before Mammy appeared. She'd have Mr. Bell mail the letters in the morning, and she did not want to be seen with them in her possession before then.

John Willis was still standing in the hall when she waved at him from the upstairs landing and moved quickly and quietly to her room and went to bed.

It was an overcast day. She was walking on a beach strewn with weather-whitened bones, and she could not seem to make any progress, though she knew Tony was waiting for her at the top of the hill at Beltane. Somehow, her steps took her into the back streets of a large city instead of to her destination. She did not know what city it was, because it

267

seemed to be San Francisco, New York and Philadelphia all rolled into one. She had a definite goal, but all the cobblestoned streets of the gray city came to dead ends just before she reached her goal. She was seized by frustration and helplessness. She was so unhappy she was close to tears, and that took her back to Beltane. It was not as she knew it in reality—half completed—but was instead a splendid house looming majestically in the fog, illuminated by a full moon. She entered the house, went immediately to the closet where the secret corridor began, and touched a spot on the wall with confidence. She had reached her goal, and she knew Tony was waiting for her behind the panel. It opened slowly to reveal Tony's water-swollen body leaking red from the work of the crabs.

She woke up sweating with her heart pounding in her chest and her scream still ringing in her ears. At least she thought it was her scream—though it didn't sound like her voice at all. It was deeper and farther away. Baby, awakened by the sudden motion she made to rise on her elbow and dispel the dream, was barking and whining intermittently at her side on the bed.

"I'm sorry, darling," Teresa comforted the blind little dog, her fingers trembling in its long coat, "poor little thing. I didn't mean to frighten you. Mamma just had a bad dream."

She picked Baby up and hugged her to her breast in the darkness. A strong wind rattled the windows, but everything within the house was quiet. She was afraid to go back to sleep—the ghastly dream might continue. She wondered what time it was, but she was too shaken to light the lamp and look at the clock. She walked around her bedroom for a few minutes, cradling her little dog. She thought she heard a key turn in a lock in the hallway, but the storm outside, which made the tall eucalyptus trees whistle and snap, made her uncertain as to whether she had heard anything at all. Only she and Mammy locked their doors, so if she had heard a key, Mammy was up and abroad in the night.

After she settled in bed again, still hugging Baby and staring at the dark ceiling trying to fight off sleep, she heard the large hall clock melodiously chime two.

"What a terrible night," she remarked at breakfast the next morning as she attempted to find a way to slip the letters to Mr. Bell. "I had the most horrible dream. I think I woke up screaming. I hope I didn't bother anyone."

Mr. Bell shook his head with a smile and turned the page of his newspaper. "It was that sort of night, the kind that things go bump in, as we used to say back home. I slept right through it, I guess. Didn't hear a thing after my head hit the pillow."

"What kind of a dream did you have?" Mammy asked, freshening up their coffee with hot brew from the silver pot. "Sometimes Teresa has the most peculiar dreams, Thomas."

Teresa remembered the high points of her dream, but she did not wish to relate it. "I don't remember, Mammy. I only know I was frightened. So, John Willis is getting married? He certainly waited a long time for the right girl."

"John Willis?" Mammy said with her lips at her cup. "I wouldn't know. I haven't seen him for a long time. I suppose it's time he married, though. He must be in his midforties, but it's difficult to tell with those people."

"But—" Teresa said and stopped herself quickly, astounded by Mammy's denial that John Willis had met with her last night. Perhaps it was for Mr. Bell's benefit, she tried to tell herself, but he seemed too engrossed in his newspaper to be listening to them. "I think I should take Baby to the veterinarian today, Mammy. She had a bad night, and—"

"I'll be using the carriage," Mammy told her. "Besides, there's no sense in throwing good money after bad. Only one thing will make that animal comfortable again."

"For goodness sake, Mammy," Mr. Bell said, lowering his paper, "that's a callous attitude if I ever heard one. Animals and children really aren't your speciality, are they? If the little dog needs attention, it should have it."

"Tomorrow, maybe," Mammy said, motioning to the maid to clear the table. "I have some business today. I need the carriage."

"Mind the horses don't run away and kill you," he said dourly. "They're animals, too."

Irritated by his rebuff, Mammy sniffed at him and left the room. Teresa was surprised to hear his chuckle. "All she needs is a firm hand," he said as he rose from the table. "A cat-o'-nine-tails in it might be helpful."

"Mr. Bell," she said, taking the two letters from her bodice, "would you mail these for me?"

The storm from the Pacific had passed without leaving much moisture behind it. Alone in the house, Teresa stared out the window at the garden, which was strewn with eucalyptus bark but was almost as dry as it had been before the storm. All fuss and bluster, she thought, with hardly a drop of rain. She wondered what to do with her day. Without a conveyance, she could hardly take Baby to the vet. After last night's dream, she hesitated to look for the passageway again. Her recollection of the dream made her shiver, but something else began to bother her, too. The scream. Surely, it had not been her own; Baby had reacted strangely, too. The little dog was accustomed to sudden motions, and darkness made no difference to her. She rarely barked, but she had last night before Teresa quickly comforted her. There was no reason she could think of for Mammy's denying John Willis was here for Mr. Bell's sake, but she did not know much about Mammy's business with her black friends. *Business*, she thought, drawing in her breath: the investment of money that Tony had told her about. Her hand moved to the cameo at the lace jabot at her throat. Good God, was Tony trying to tell me something through that dream? If John Willis was getting married, perhaps he would want his money back, just as Maggie Davis had.

She took Baby to the veterinarian the next day and called at the boardinghouse to see Byna, who greeted her effusively and led her to the sitting room on the second floor where Teresa had come the first time she spoke to Mammy. The furniture had changed, of course, and even the elegant wallpaper was smudged and rundown. The present owner had not even attempted to keep the place up to Mammy's standard.

"Sakes' alive, Mis' Teresa," Byna said, "you're the last person I thought I'd ever see here. I was talkin' about you to Billy just the other evening, wondering if you were happy and all. Mammy sure made a splash in that courtroom. Things like that don't look good for the folks around her."

Teresa assumed from Byna's forthright friendliness that Billy had told her nothing about Jim Hoey's death, but she decided to tread carefully in her relations with his wife. "I was in the area, and someone told me you worked here. It's been a long time, Byna. How are Billy and John Willis? I wish John Willis was still driving for me."

"Billy's just fine and as busy as usual," Byna smiled, "and John Willis is finally getting married. What do you think of that, Mis' Teresa?"

"I think it's splendid," Teresa smiled. "Have you seen John Willis today?"

Byna frowned slightly. "Now that you mention it, I haven't. He usually stops by for breakfast at our place before he goes to work, but he didn't come this morning. I hope that old boy didn't oversleep," she laughed. "We don't see him that much with all the courtin' going on."

"Where does he live?" Teresa asked, breathing shallowly to disguise her concern. "I understand you live near by."

"Not *that* near," Byna chirped. "He went and chose the best place near the water. Billy hasn't forgiven him for that. But to tell the truth, Mis' Teresa, Billy and I wouldn't have tried to buy property if John Willis didn't lead the way. Folks like us never owned any property where we come from. Do you want his address?"

"If you have it," Teresa said casually. "I'd like to send a wedding present at least." Byna wrote an address on a scrap of paper and handed it to her. "I'd like to stay and chat, Byna, but my little dog's out there in the carriage. She's old and blind, and I don't like to leave her very long."

"You come by and see us, hear? I gotta get back to work myself. It was real good seeing you again, Mis' Teresa, and Billy'll be glad about it, too."

The last thing Teresa wanted to do was call herself to Billy's attention, but perhaps that was a chance she would have to take. On the way home in the carriage with Baby on her knees, she considered her course of action. She really would have to be careful, she decided. Her reputation would be totally destroyed in Billy Beaumont's eyes if anything really had happened to John Willis and she made too many inquiries about him before it was discovered.

She vascillated for several days, approaching the telephone to call Byna and moving away from it as she considered the threat to herself if she made the calls. If only there were someone else from whom she could ascertain information about John Willis, she thought with frustration. I need someone like Tony to help me right now, and I'm completely alone. Perhaps she should call the police, she considered, but she rejected the idea at once. They were more of a threat to her than she had ever realized until now. And she dared not go back to the Pinkerton Agency after her fiasco with their agent. She had come up against a blank wall in her investigation, just as she had in searching for Mammy's hidden corridor.

A note from Marie that arrived one morning with an invitation to call on her had the virtue of providing Teresa with a diversion from her stormy thoughts. She told Mammy she wanted to do some shopping

271

and was astounded to receive not only the carriage for the afternoon, but some spending money as well. "I declare," Mammy said, "I've never seen anyone so jumpy in my life. An afternoon of shopping is just what you need, honey. By the way," she asked with a pause, "you aren't still having those funny dreams, are you?"

"I've been dreaming a lot," she reassured her. "I haven't been sleeping very well since the night of that storm. Thank you for the money, Mammy. I'm sure that shopping will be a welcome relief."

She actually stopped to buy some fabric at the lace shop before she called on Marie in the gracious brownstone building where she had her flat. A maid answered the door and led the visitor into a well-appointed parlor, further proof that Mr. Bell was taking care of his daughter in the proper style. Teresa had not seen the young woman since her Christmas holidays several years before, and she was not prepared for the sight of the tall, heavy woman who glanced up unpleasantly from her Catholic missal to greet Teresa with a belligerent expression in her calflike eyes.

"I didn't think you'd come," Marie said, waving the maid away and indicating the sofa to Teresa. "I was surprised by your letter. Perhaps astounded is a better word. I asked myself why, after all these years, Teresa was taking any interest in me."

"I always wanted to be your friend, Marie," Teresa said earnestly, without removing her wrap. "For some reason, you and Fred rejected my affection. Maybe all that can change."

Marie rolled her slightly protuberant eyes like a rebellious schoolgirl, drawing in an aggravated breath. "I doubt it. Whatever's on your mind is to your advantage and not mine. I was hoping you'd have grown old and ugly," she observed, "but I suppose women like you stay beautiful forever. You've nothing else to do with your time than take care of yourself, have you?"

It was the most oblique, resentful compliment Teresa had ever received, and she reacted to it by staring steadily at the unattractive young woman, allowing her enigmatic blue eyes to answer for her. Marie was desperately in need of a mother's training, she observed. She didn't even know how to dress her ash-blond hair, which was pulled up severely away from her broad face into a bun on top of her head, making her look closer to thirty than twenty. There was nothing of Mr. Bell in her at all, not his ginger hair nor his cornflower eyes, nor his slightness of build.

"What do you mean by 'women like me'?" she asked at last, attempting to confront the problem between them and overcome it if possible. "You know nothing about me, aside from the fact that I'm your father's wife."

"Yes, I do!" Marie said quicky, "Fred told me, years ago! You were his mistress before you were his wife, and you're not our mother. She died when I was born. That's when we were both brought to father's house, the house you're living in right now."

"Fred was very young when he came to the house," Teresa said graciously. "Perhaps he doesn't remember that he lived with me long before then. I've never claimed to be your mother, Marie. You don't have to defend yourself against that. I think you need a friend, and I'd like to be that friend if you'll let me."

The stubborn hostility in the young woman's face did not lessen. "He told me you might attempt something like this," she said, "so you'd be in our good graces when we finally get what's due us. If you want to be on our side," she smiled slyly, "why don't you help us get that old woman out of the house? She's the one who's keeping us away from father. She has him wrapped around her little finger."

Teresa arose with a sigh. "If only you'd consider that there aren't any sides involved, Marie. Your father and I want what's best for Fred and you. I don't think there's anything to discuss, my dear, until you resolve that in your mind. I'm anxious to be your friend, and that will never change. If you ever need me, you only have to write to me. Until then, I'll be thinking of you with nothing but kindness, Marie. Perhaps you might start listening to your own heart, instead of the things Fred's pouring into your ears. God knows, I was always fond of him, too."

When she arrived home at dusk and stepped from the carriage in front of the house, she noticed Mammy digging diligently at the rear of the garden. Suddenly, the horse nickered. The old woman jumped up with a start, brushed her hands against the sides of her skirt, and moved rapidly toward the side door. *What on earth is she up to now?* Teresa wondered with dismay. *Everyone in this family needs a personal attendant, including the bitter, unattractive girl I spoke to this afternoon.*

She was greeted in the hall by one of the few remaining maids, Ada, whose room she had visited when she was looking for the passage and who had attached herself to Teresa ever since. "Oh, ma'am," she cried with her lower lip trembling, "I have terrible news for you. I hate to be the one to tell you, but poor little Baby passed away this afternoon."

Teresa recalled Mammy's activity in the garden, and the first emo-

273

tion she felt at Baby's death was anger. "Where is Mrs. Pleasant?" she demanded.

"In the kitchen, I think. She just buried the poor little thing."

Teresa stormed into the kitchen, where Mammy was washing her hands at the wooden sink. She did not look up, though she was aware of Teresa's presence.

"I had a dream last night," Teresa said in an even voice. "I saw a bent old woman, who once had been rather tall. She was toothless and dressed in black with a white poke bonnet on her head, and she was clutching a ruched handbag against her bony chest. She *smelled*. She had no place to lay her head, and finally someone had to put her out of her misery. It was a very vivid dream, Mammy."

"I didn't kill your dog," Mammy said quietly, without turning to look at her. "Ask the maid, Teresa. She found her lying peacefully on your bed a few hours ago. You shouldn't say such awful things to me."

"I don't know if dreams come true or not," Teresa told her, "time will have to decide that. If you didn't kill Baby, what were you doing sneaking around in the garden the way you were? Burying a little dog is straightforward enough. Why did you wait until dusk?"

Mammy did not respond. She moved to the table to season and flour some cutlets, handling the meat gently to emphasize her calm. "I didn't want you to be upset by it when you came home," she said at last. "I didn't think of it until a short while ago. Did you know that Fred's back in town? Nothing's safe with him around."

Her reasoning baffled Teresa, or was she speaking about two different things? She had become senile if she was hiding the dead dog from Fred, Teresa thought, but Mammy certainly wasn't senile. "I don't give a damn where he is," she replied, the depth of her loss finally penetrating and bringing pain to her chest. "Maybe if we shut our eyes for a moment, he'll steal the whole damned house from around us."

She found it difficult to sleep without the warm little body nestled beside her. After she had shed all her tears, she folded a pillow beside her legs to trick herself into slumber. The bulk of the little dog was there, but not her warmth, and Teresa found herself staring miserably at the dark ceiling, as she so often did. The voices did not reach her until they were raised in anger, and she groaned at the prospect of having to endure the sound of fighting again. She reached for a pillow to put over her head, but was arrested in the action by the harshness of Mr. Bell's voice.

"Not another penny for Beltane," he declared. "You know the condition of our finances, with more going out than coming in. Someone told me Fred was gambling the other night at that casino where your old boyfriend, Ben, deals. I don't know what I'm working for anymore, for Christ's sake. I'm ready to retire."

"That's fine," Mammy challenged him, "just fine! Exactly what's needed. We'll never recoup the money we spent on the lawsuit if you do that. You have to be on the spot to make good investments, Thomas. Forget about the children, for God's sake. They're no good, anyway. Think about us for a change, the way you used to.

"I can't forget about them. They're mine, Mammy. You probably can't appreciate that. You're as maternal as a black widow spider. You ignored your own daughter until she drank herself to death."

"Don't you speak to me like that!" Mammy cried angrily. "What do you know about me, least of all how I felt about my daughter? I've given you everything you have, old man: your fortune, this house, even your family. You'd be back in England in jail, if it weren't for me. You didn't know it was I who bought Inspector Leighton off when he returned from London, did you? I had the San Francisco Police in *my* pocket!" she laughed harshly. "I know why you went to South America, Mr. High and Mighty, what you did in that London bank that you had to run away."

Teresa was stunned. She lay perfectly still to catch every word now, listening for more about Inspector Leighton. She knew she had heard his name somewhere, but she had not connected it with Mammy. She would have to figure out Tony's connection with the retired inspector later. Right now, it was more important just to listen.

"You paid him?" Mr. Bell said with a laugh. "Then we were both taken to the cleaners, because I paid him too. Christ!" There was a long pause during which Teresa could almost picture him pacing the carpet in his sitting room. Then he lashed out suddenly, "What the hell do you mean about 'giving me a family'? You told me that none of the stories that came out during the lawsuit were true. I know Fred and Marie are my children. A father can tell those things. What kind of mischief are you up to now? You want me to disinherit them, don't you, so my will will only name *you*?"

"The will's just fine, as long as I'm executor," she shot back at him. "I'd provide for the little beasts. I'm responsible for them. Thomas, for your own peace of mind, you should forget all about them. They really aren't *yours*, you know. If you don't believe me, speak to their mother.

She's married and living as a tenant in one of my houses. Do you want her address?"

Teresa had held her breath so long that she got dizzy and let it out slowly to take another breath. She felt as if she were paralyzed and, with difficulty, moved her arm to break the unpleasant spell. The voices across the hall fell silent, and she heard Mr. Bell's door close as Mammy left his room. Teresa rose from the bed, wondering if Mammy had told him the truth out of deliberate cruelty or because she was incapable of understanding his feelings. She sat at her vanity without lighting a lamp and remained there for some time with her head in her hands. Mr. Bell was not a good man, but he had tried in his own way to be a good father. Now, suddenly, in his old age, that had been taken from him.

She began to weep softly for all of them. Compassion was much closer to the surface as she grew older, and she could weep even for those who did not deserve it. Her vanity stool lurched, and for a moment she thought she was fainting. A deep rumbling sound in the earth and the tinkle of the crystals on the chandelier made her realize, almost at once, that it was not she, but the whole house, that was moving.

She ran into the hallway just as Mammy emerged from her room, wrapped in her bright red shawl. They faced each other for several moments, and there was no recurrence of the motion.

"Earthquake," Mammy explained with a smile, "just a tremor. We haven't had one for a while. It must have scared hell out of the people who've been predicting a big one for so long. It's all right, Teresa. It's over. You're as white as a sheet."

Teresa did not tell her that, for a moment, she had thought God had knocked the house clean off its foundation.

She did not know why she went back into her room and put on her clothes, but it probably had something to do with the idea of approaching doom. She had heard that people did peculiar things during earthquakes. Removing John Willis's address from her purse and looking at it under the lamp was probably the oddest thing anyone had ever done, she reflected, but he had been on her mind for too long. After everything that had happened tonight, it was unlikely that she would be missed from the house.

She had some difficulty in finding a cab and had to walk as far as Van Ness before she saw one. The horses were skittish, and the driver smiled as he tried to control them.

276

"The quake," he explained, "they started acting up even before it hit. Animals are sensitive to things like that. Are you sure this is the address you want to go to, ma'am? It isn't a very respectable district."

"I'm sure," Teresa said, feeling as nervous as the horses, but invigorated by her own boldness, too. "Some former servants live there. I'm safe enough among them."

High bushes enclosed the area around John Willis's house, and she asked the driver to wait beyond them before she opened the gate and approached the darkened house with the water of the Bay lapping beneath its pilings. The driver had offered her his lamp, and by the time she reached the lopsided, whitewashed door, she was glad she had taken it. It seemed impossible that John Willis had slept through the earthquake, but she rapped her knuckles loudly on the door in the hope of rousing him. After repeated knockings, there was still no answer, and Teresa felt her spirits plunge. Perhaps he was at Billy Beaumont's house, she tried to tell herself, though tomorrow was a workday and it was almost midnight now. He went to Billy's house after the earthquake, she thought hopefully for a moment, but would he have extinguished every light in the house before doing so? Not likely. In the terror of the moment, he'd have probably run pell-mell to his nearest neighbor's house, though it was some distance away. The Bay-front neighborhood was sparsely settled.

An instinct that was too strong to be ignored dashed that theory, too. The water of the Bay, agitated by the tremor, lapped insistently at the pilings, banging something against them. A boat, probably, she decided, holding up the lantern cautiously to survey the dark area, which drew her strongly in spite of her fear of rats. She waved the lamp over the water quickly, fearing what she might find, and turned away to retrace her steps, before she realized that her rapid survey had revealed something odd. Was it a billow of fabric that she had seen? she wondered with a rapidly beating heart. Dear God. Perhaps I should get the cabbie to take a look. I'm afraid to do it myself. But, she realized quickly, she must not be connected with whatever's down there in any way.

She had to force her feet to move along the wooden path back to the boat. She felt as if someone were holding her back physically and compressing her chest at the same time. Even before she lowered the lamp to the water beside the rowboat, she knew what she would find, but she reacted with the same horror as in her dream, when the bloated, crab-eaten body had been Tony's. I mustn't faint, she told herself, fighting off the dizziness. If I faint, I'll fall in the water with it.

277

With her eyes closed, she backed away a foot at a time, giving way her feelings only when she reached the porch again, not by fainting but by retching violently into the bushes.

"Ma'am?" she heard the cabbie's voice calling. "Are you all right, ma'am?"

"Yes," she whispered, but raised her voice with an effort to prevent him from following her. "I'm coming! I'll be right there."

Her legs were so unsteady that she did not know how she made it back to the cab. She handed the cabby his lantern quickly and disappeared inside, so that he would not smell the odor on her handkerchief.

"Your friend wasn't home?" he asked as he took his seat. "I didn't see any light but the lantern."

"No, he wasn't there," she managed. "Please take me to the corner of Octavia and Bush as quickly as possible."

The scream she had heard during the storm had not been her own, she knew it now. But could Mammy have brought John Willis back here, as old as she was? She was still very strong, and John Willis, unlike Billy Beaumont, was a slight man. She would have to think about all that later. She was shaking and exhausted. She had only one more task to accomplish tonight before she could let herself collapse.

She had left the front door unlocked, and now she went directly to the telephone in the hall. "Hullo?" she greeted the male operator, "I want de San Francisco *Po*-lice. Yes suh. Hullo? Yo' de *po*-lice? I think dere's a *daid* man in de watah at ol' John Willis place, suh. Near his boat, my chillun tol' me. I didn't give them no never mind when they tol' me, suh. But when dat earthquake woke me up, I got to thinkin' an—What? Nevah mind my name, suh. I'm a good God-fearin' Christian, and I don't want no dealin' wit de *po*-lice."

She depressed the cradle on the telephone with trembling fingers and replaced the damp earpiece on it with some difficulty. I wonder if I overdid it, she wondered. None of the black people I know have that thick an accent. She was moving toward the staircase to go to her room when everything went dark and she slumped to the marble floor.

She awoke after noon in her own bed with only a vague recollection of regaining consciousness and getting this far. The entire experience might have been one of her bad dreams, except that her head was throbbing and she felt almost too weak to rise. To distract herself from what she had seen, she tried to reconstruct the events of the night she had heard the scream, listening to the sound over and over again in her mind. If a man were shot or stabbed or clubbed, he would not make such a sound. The scream had begun in her dream, but it had become more distant when she woke; it was too far to have come from her own throat in the first place. I must take a look upstairs, she decided, rising cautiously and touching the bellpull to summon her maid.

She was still fully clothed, as she had been when she fell into bed the night before, but she put her hair into some order before Ada arrived with her breakfast tray, rapping on the door for admittance.

"I tried to call you earlier," the maid said when Teresa admitted her, "but I couldn't seem to rouse you. I guess none of us got much sleep after the earthquake, ma'am. It gave me a proper fright, I'll tell you! My bed started moving beneath me, and some plaster fell off the wall. It's the first one I've ever been in, Mrs. Bell. I felt so *helpless*. In the Midwest, at least you can see the tornadoes coming and take shelter against them."

"Yes," Teresa said quietly as she drank her coffee, "it wasn't a nice feeling at all."

She wondered vaguely what need in people was satisfied by pouring out the details of any unusual event: where they were, what they saw, how they felt. In Ada's mind, the earthquake had happened only to her. I wonder if it would help to pour out everything I saw last night? she thought with irony. To relieve the tension in myself, I'd probably make the poor girl as ill as I am.

Her investigation of the third floor disclosed nothing but the fact that all the rooms, including the nursery, had not been dusted for a long time. There was only one window that John Willis might have fallen from, under the gable of the roof overlooking the garden. Aside from the fact that the area had been dusted thoroughly, she could see no sign of a struggle, nor could she imagine how Mammy might have lured him up here.

The whole house seemed eerily quiet as she descended the stairs to look at the gravel below the suspect window. Mr. Bell was at the bank, of course, and Mammy might be in her room or anywhere in the city. With her private passage, she could move like a rat behind the wainscoting, leaving the house without anyone's knowledge. Teresa did not sense her presence, and she knelt openly to study the gravel in the area where someone pushed through the window might have fallen. She found nothing, even when she raked her hand through the tiny pebbles on the theory that the gravel had been smoothed or new stones

279

thrown on top of it. There would have been blood, she thought, thinking for the first time that perhaps her suspicion had no foundation in fact.

John Willis was dead, of that at least she was unpleasantly certain, but he might not have died here after all. The scream might very well have been part of her dream. Still, his arrival at the house and Mammy's denying having seen him gave her pause. She considered some of the things Tony had told her at Beltane about the black people investing money with Mammy and dying or disappearing afterwards. She recalled something else he had said, too, and it gave her a thrill of terror. People were safe from Mammy as long as she needed them. If that was true, then Teresa was only useful as long as Mammy had her power of attorney. Once Teresa destroyed it, she would no longer be needed.

She abandoned her search for the paper for a few weeks while she considered the prudence of destroying the power of attorney, and during this time she managed to live in relative harmony with Mammy and a very subdued Mr. Bell.

They were all at the dinner table one evening, enduring each other's company in silence over one of Mammy's particularly excellent dinners, when the incident that was to change everything occurred—too suddenly for Teresa to grasp all of its implications. She was to remember the meal for a long time, because it was the last elegant dinner Mammy ever prepared for her.

The first course was pureed asparagus soup with a spoonful of heavy cream to add to its smoothness, and Mammy carried the tureen in from the kitchen herself. If Mr. Bell was depressed and angry, he did not reveal it as he sampled the food with a gourmet's enjoyment, sometimes closing his eyes to enjoy the full effect. The main course was a scallop of baby veal and shrimp in a delicate, rich béarnaise sauce, served with an artistic garnish of colorful vegetables: tiny glazed carrots and dark green zucchini lightly flavored with garlic. The wines also were perfectly complementary to each course. Teresa realized that with this meal Mammy was trying to woo Mr. Bell back after their destructive fight on the night of the earthquake. She had just come back from the kitchen bearing a cloud-light lemon soufflé for dessert, when Mr. Bell gave a gasp—at first Teresa imagined it was of anticipation—and fell forward over his empty plate.

During the days following Mr. Bell's stroke, there was a great deal of activity in the house, with doctors coming and going, and the few remaining servants working beyond their capacity under Mammy's abrupt instructions. Teresa volunteered to help care for Thomas, but Mammy accepted the whole burden, nursing him during the day and remaining at his bedside during the night. She would allow no one else near him and appeared genuinely distraught, and this surprised Teresa after everything that had transpired. She was convinced that Mammy's revelation about the children's parentage had brought on the stroke, but she realized that there was a real bond between the old couple. They had been friends for over forty years, and lovers for probably most of that time, although Teresa was only sure of the years she had spent under the same roof with them. All that could not be erased in a few hours, in spite of Mammy's unconsidered remark, which had been made in anger.

After Thomas's condition stabilized, Mammy sent for Teresa to come to his sitting room. Teresa had not entered his suite since he had moved into the house years ago, and she noticed how worn the oriental carpet was and that the odor of his cigar smoke had clung to everything. The bedroom door was closed, and Mammy was relaxing on the sofa, her face worn and drawn, but still incredibly young-looking. She did not appear much older than Teresa, who was forty-three, although she had to be close to seventy. The strength of character she always displayed was evident in her firm lips and the slightly flaring nostrils of her straight, perfect nose. She opened her eyes, and they appeared more deep-set than usual from the ordeal she had been through. She had lost weight, and she had never carried much to spare.

"Ah, Teresa!" she said, rising to a sitting position with inherent grace. "I haven't forgotten you, honey. You know how busy I've been. The doctors are very encouraged. Thomas is paralyzed slightly on the left side, but they say it will probably go away. However, the reason I asked you to come concerns you. I promised to send you to Beltane this summer, and I didn't want you to think I'd forgotten."

"It's almost forgotten, Mammy," Teresa told her truthfully. So much had happened that Beltane was the farthest thing from her mind, and she found it remarkable that Mammy had remembered her earlier promise in such a situation.

"Well, I think you should go," Mammy said with some of the old magic warmth in her voice. "Not just to inspect the premises, but for your own sake, dear. It's been a difficult time for you. God knows, I haven't been much company, and you must have overheard something about the state of our finances. And the loss of your little dog . . ." Her

281

eyes met Teresa's directly. "I really didn't have anything to do with that, you must believe me."

Teresa nodded. She had spoken to the maid, who had exonerated Mammy. "I'm sorry I accused you," she said. "I was very upset. And you *had* suggested—"

"I'm sorry I said that," Mammy agreed, "but it's all in the past, now. We have more serious things to consider, one of them being your health."

"What about yours? You've done enough to kill a horse these past few weeks."

"I'm also as strong as one," Mammy smiled. "You're much more high-strung, Teresa. I think you should get away for a spell, honey. Take someone with you if you like. If anything's happened at Beltane, water damage or vandalism, that sort of thing, you can drop me a line. The Italians are supposed to be keeping an eye on things, but I haven't been in touch with them for some time."

Teresa noted that Mammy did not suggest that she take Tony with her this time, though she thought he had been with her before. It was almost as if she had dismissed him from the living in her mind and accidentally confessed as much by the omission.

"Oh, Teresa," she said as Teresa turned to leave, "you've probably noted all the reporters hanging around like vultures, expecting Thomas to die. You'd better slip out at night, as you did before, honey. If they saw Mrs. Bell leaving when her husband's so ill, they'd jump on the story like a duck on a June bug."

Chapter 20

Teresa had reached a point where any suggestion from Mammy made her explore the old woman's motives. As she packed her bags, she attempted to sort out what might be behind Mammy's sudden decision to send her on a trip. *She could be getting rid of me so she can accuse me of neglecting Mr. Bell some time in the future,* she thought. *But that wouldn't be to Mammy's advantage in any way I can understand.* Tony had said something about not letting Mammy care for him with her little black bag and her herbals, and that recollection gave Teresa pause. *What if she poisons Mr. Bell after I leave and has me hauled back from Beltane for murder?* The idea was frightening enough; the facility with which it popped in her mind was even more so. Her suspicions about the death of John Willis lingered. There was no way to prove or disprove anything about that now. *I'm getting a little panicky again,* she thought with a shudder. *Mammy has no reason to do away with Mr. Bell; she has no motive at all.* And there was no real proof that she had ever murdered anyone. In spite of their bickering and fights, she had no doubt that Mammy was still devoted to Mr. Bell. He was safe enough in her hands.

The wild leaps of her imagination made her abandon all second-guessing. *I'm simply and straightforwardly going away on vacation,* she tried to convince herself, *and I'll attend to Mammy's interests at Beltane at the same time. That shouldn't be too difficult to accept.* On the other hand, her own business at Beltane was not exactly straightforward, when it came right down to it. She was really going there to attack the mystery of the secret passage. She had to observe more carefully exactly where it exited to the outside of the house. *Odd,* she thought, *that Mammy would send me out through the back hall again without* considering the padlocked door. Perhaps it had nothing to do with Voodoo rites, after all; it might be nothing more sinister than a storage space. On the other hand, Mammy has probably not conducted any ceremonies for so long that she considered the room innocuous enough. Teresa realized with a sigh that she had been trying to anticipate the unexpected and explain the inexplicable for so long that it was enough to throw her slightly off-balance. The power of attorney was her one beacon of reality. And to get her hands on that, she must negotiate the secret passage to Mammy's room from the ouside of the house on Octavia Street. Why did the old woman complicate everything so much?

As she walked through the dark back hallway, she wondered who would be waiting to drive her this time. Mammy had fooled her once before, when Tony had met her, so she decided she would find out who was driving as soon as possible. The driver was a Negro, but that was all right. Mammy still hired black people occasionally, and the middle-aged man in the driver's seat was completely unfamiliar to Teresa. She remained alert for reporters for the first few blocks, but finally settled back with a sigh, glad to be out of the house, happy to be going somewhere, anywhere, as far from intrigue and suspicion as possible.

"Some kind of life you got yourself into, Mis' Teresa," the driver said in a velvety voice with a West Indian accent. "I tried to warn you, a long time ago. Now, you've got yourself a chaperone again."

"Billy?" she asked weakly, her heart tumbling in her chest, "Billy Beaumont?"

"That's right," he smiled, turning to face her. His white teeth seemed sinister in the darkness. "Your old friend."

Teresa's brain worked as fast as her heartbeat. Mammy didn't send me away to kill Mr. Bell, she thought, she's going to have *me* killed, or disposed of in some way by one of the witnesses to Jim's murder. She attempted to leap from the carriage, but he restrained her with a strong hand. "What are you doing? You'd hurt yourself on the cobbles. I don't mean you any harm, Miss Teresa."

"I don't need a chaperone," she said numbly. "You are taking me to Beltane, aren't you?"

"That's where Mammy said you wanted to go. What's the matter with you? I've never harmed anyone, you know that."

Teresa studied him in the uneven gaslight from the street lamps. She wondered that she had not recognized him at once. His face was slightly heavier, but he was still handsome with a youthfulness that belied the gray at his temples. He was not all that frightening, though she had dreaded this encounter for years.

"You speak differently," she said, trying to gather her thoughts, and he laughed warmly.

"Thanks to you, Miss Teresa. When I saw the way you improved yourself, I decided I'd do the same thing someday. I've been to school a little, and I keep working on my own, as you did.

"You shouldn't be afraid, Miss Teresa. Don't you know that's what Mammy wants? Don't let the old lady have her way. She sent me tonight to remind you that you're still in her power. That's the way blackmail works, isn't it? Voodoo, too. They both play on fear."

"Voodoo is a word you wouldn't have mentioned to me twenty-five years ago," she said, still staring at him. "I know, because I tried to get it out of you."

He chuckled deep in his chest, "I called it Vaudau, then, anyway. Actually, there ain't—*isn't* much of that around any more. Most of us are real honest Baptists, as straight as any arrow you ever saw."

"You told me you were a Baptist once before."

"Probably. But this time it's true. I came pretty close to telling you what you wanted to know, way back then, Mis' Teresa. Only I thought the blood would rise in my throat and strangle me if I mentioned Voodoo to an outsider."

"How does your throat feel right now?"

"Wide open and clear as a bell," he laughed. "She doesn't have any power over me now."

"And that's because you've become a good Christian?" she pursued.

"No, ma'am. Working for Mammy cured me of all that stuff. Jesus came to me later."

Teresa fell silent. This could be a trap; Billy might be gaining her confidence to find out just how much she knew. She had been bolder with Mammy since her last trip to Beltane, had worn her arrogant, enigmatic expression perhaps too much in Mammy's presence. She decided to move with caution and hold her tongue regarding some things.

"But you still work for Mammy," she suggested, "you're doing it right now."

"Yes and no," he said with a smile. "Mostly no. I've wanted to talk to you for a long time, ma'am. I came to that fancy house once. But I ran into Mammy and had to pretend I came to see her. When Byna said you'd looked her up at the rooming house, I was powerful relieved. I thought we'd be seeing more of you."

"You wanted to see me?" Teresa asked incredulously. "I suppose religion's made you tolerant of murderesses, too?"

She regretted the remark almost at once, though perhaps that subject, too, was better out in the open.

"No, ma'am. But I thought long and hard about all that, until my eyes were finally opened. I was all mixed up that day in your parlor, Mis' Teresa. I knew I saw what I saw, but I just couldn't believe it. I didn't sleep for a long time. The thought of carrying that corpse over my shoulder in the rug really bothered me. I didn't like nothin'—*anything* about that whole afternoon."

"Neither did I," Teresa reflected, "what I remember of it."

"That's just the point," he said with emphasis. "The fact is, you didn't *murder* anyone, Mis' Teresa. It was pure self-defense. I didn't hear about that until later, and I did some reading in the library then. That man was coming at you waving a gun like he was crazy. You shot him to save your own life. You might have shot him a little too much, but . . . you were a little crazy, too, with fear."

Teresa considered what he had said, and one portion of her mind began to clear for the first time since Jim Hoey appeared in the arch of the parlor. What Billy said was probably true. She had read of people killing in self-defense, but she had never thought of its applying to her. I must have wanted Jim dead, she thought, and perhaps that still makes it murder.

"Mammy never pointed that out to you, did she?" Billy asked urging the horse onto the dirt road to the coast. "I bet she never even suggested it."

"No," Teresa said, taking a deep breath. "Her only reference to the incident has been to remind me that there were witnesses."

"Just like I thought. You can see why I wanted to talk to you. Sometimes Mammy isn't exactly *forth*right."

Teresa found herself laughing at the description, a masterpiece of understatement. But a sobering thought crossed her mind. "What about Ben Willard? Have you any idea what he thinks, Billy?"

He shook his head in the moonlit fields and considered his words carefully. "Ben Willard's Mammy's man. He looks at things the way she tells him to. He does what she tells him, also."

Teresa looked at him sharply, "What do you mean 'her man?' Surely, all that ended a long time ago?"

"If you say so, Mis' Teresa," he said with absolute neutrality. "If ever a man was crazy about a woman, it's Ben Willard, though. He's been in her corner all the way. He'd swear to anything she told him to on a stack of Bibles."

At that moment Teresa's hatred of Mammy was strong enough to make her commit a genuine murder. She was thankful to be this far away from Mammy. Suddenly she recalled the obituary column and how she had looked for Billy's death notice; even though she couldn't tell him about that, somehow she would make it up to him. Having his friendship was a great comfort, but it had not changed her position with Mammy. As long as Ben Willard lived, she was still in the old woman's hands.

The suite she had cleaned so carefully two years ago was damp and full of mildew, and she had to scrape every surface to make the rooms livable again. The memory of Tony's short stay lingered even in the strong odor of the lye soap. Poor Tony! He had probably been right about everything he told her. As she mulled over all the mysteries in her mind, she found herself speaking aloud to him to keep her thoughts channeled on one thing. He had been intrigued by the mystery of Mammy, and he had followed his course to the end in an effort to stop her. Teresa realized she was still under Mammy's spell; nevertheless, she must try to think rationally.

Billy Beaumont was staying in a small house near the dried-up fields. She saw him only at mealtimes during the day and when they sat together in the evening on the wide porch. He had been instructed to look after the crops, but the most he could do was take a scythe to them to eliminate the overgrowth and weeds. The Italians Mammy had referred to lived some distance away and had fields of their own to work. They had taken her phrase, "Keep an eye on the place" literally, as they watched Beltane fall into ruin.

The white pillars of the porch were stained by moisture and streaks of oxidation from the iron used in their construction, and the older walls of the house, left unpainted, were already beginning to weather like driftwood. All new work had been abandoned during Mr. Bell's illness, and the second wing of the house was only a skeletal frame, a sad monument to the folly of building a large house a bit at a time, as one could afford it, with no one properly overseeing the construction.

Teresa paused only to put her suitcase in the musty suite she had occupied on her last visit before pursuing her investigation of Mammy's passageway. She mounted the stairs to the second floor and located the entrance to the passage easily enough in Mammy's quarters. When she pressed the raised decoration on the closet wall, the mechanism squeaked, but the panel opened enough for her to enter. She propped some pieces of wood against it so she would be able to get out by retracing her steps, if necessary, and held up her lantern to examine the mechanism more closely. The slightly corroded metal pieces appeared to consist of a spring and some weights. She would know what to look for if she found the outside exit at the other end of the passage.

After entering the dark maze she could feel the gradual descent of the floor as she began to approach the secret stairs to the ground floor. Even with the comfort of the lantern, Teresa felt as though she was moving through space, and had to touch the wall for support. She had the uneasy feeling that a person might be lost here forever, and felt relief when she saw the blank wall ahead, its spring mechanism clear in the dim light from her lantern. When she pressed it hard, the door groaned slightly, admitting only a sliver of sunlight from the outside. Moisture, she thought with frustration. This door is too close to ground level, and the moisture's made the wood swell. She put her shoulder against the panel to force it and discovered that a tangle of weeds had been halting its progress. Once outside, she let the panel close behind her in order to observe it closed. The location of the exit had nothing to do with the rear door of the house. It was to one side and below the level of the stairs. When it was closed, the boards of the wall and the panel fitted so perfectly the edges were as invisible as the cut of a razor. Add a green clump of foliage, she thought and no one would know it was there. There were bushes below the rear stairs of the house on Octavia Street.

She found herself almost anxious to return, but she couldn't leave until Billy had finished what he was to do in the fields. She caught up on her diary by the light of an oil lamp, pondering the two parts of her plan of action to gain her freedom:

1. *Find the power of attorney and burn it.*

2. *Ben Willard, the only witness. What to do about him?*

Unfortunately, Willard was a good deal younger than Mammy; he was not likely to drop dead for Teresa's convenience. If the thought of helping the process along entered her mind, she suppressed it before she recognized it. That might be Mammy's way, but it was not hers.

She would need something to live on once she was free of Mammy, but as Mr. Bell's wife, she realized, she would have no problem. She would not ask for much, and she was certain he would look after her. She hadn't forgotten her promise to Mr. Bell regarding the children's well-being, but she wondered if it mattered anymore, now that he knew the truth about their parentage. From what she knew of him, she thought likely that he would disinherit Fred and Marie. Mammy would eventually have everything, as she had planned from the beginning. And good riddance, Teresa thought with a sigh. *If Mammy has everything she wants, she will probably forget all about me.*

"This place gives me a bad feeling," Billy Beaumont said in one of their conversations on the porch. "I almost expect to hear the gong ringing and the slaves hallo-ing that it's quitting time when I'm out in those fields. I didn't run away from all that just to do it again here." He raised his pink palms for her inspection. "Blisters, calluses. My hands ain't— haven't been like this for a long time, Mis' Teresa."

"We won't be staying much longer, Billy. Why don't you forget about the fields? They'll be overgrown again anyway before anyone comes out here again."

"I do what I'm told," he said, widening his eyes humorously. "Mammy expects work for her money. I only have to do it for a little while more. As soon as I get the money back that I invested, I'll be going into business for myself."

"You haven't let Mammy invest your money?" Teresa exclaimed with alarm. He looked at her with surprise.

"How did you know Mammy invested it? She made it plain to me that it was just between the two of us. I wasn't to say anything, and she wouldn't either."

So, that's the way it worked, Teresa thought. No connection is made between the missing or murdered and her, because no one else knows about the investments she's supposed to have made. That's why John Willis's murder—if indeed he had been murdered—had not been connected to Mammy. She said carefully, "She mentioned she had invested some money for someone. When are you thinking of withdrawing your money, Billy?"

"Pretty soon," he said with a sigh, looking forward to being his own man. "I reckon I've got just about enough now, if the investment was as good as she said. You don't know anything about that, do you?"

"I think I'd leave the money alone for a while," she ventured. "When you want to withdraw it, allow me to take care of it. I'll get your money back for you, Billy. Just remember, I'm your friend."

"You're trying to tell me something," he said acutely, studying her face. "She hasn't lost my money, has she?"

"Nothing like that," Teresa assured him. "How much did you invest?"

"Almost two thousand dollars, my whole life savings. She said she wouldn't do it for anyone else. That was about three years ago. At the twenty percent yearly interest she promised me, I reckon I have another twelve hundred dollars by now. If there's anything I should know, you'd better tell me, Mis' Teresa."

"No, it's all right. I'll get the money for you, Billy. Please leave that to me." She hesitated a moment and finally asked, "Did you know Tony Ward?"

"Sure, I was with you in Philadelphia. Remember? He was a good-looking man, but he was in her pocket. You must have known that. The last time I saw him, he was pretty sick and asking a lot of funny questions."

"When was that?"

"I dunno," he shrugged, "a couple of years ago maybe. I figured he was one of her spies, so I didn't tell him anything."

Teresa decided not to pursue the subject. Billy obviously didn't know anything about Tony's disappearance, and she did not want to alarm him again. She did not allow for his quick intelligence, though.

"Tony dropped out of sight, you know," he speculated, "no death notice, nothing. Byna always reads things like that. I think it makes her feel good that other people die instead of her. She says she likes to pray for departed friends like John Willis. Did you know that John Willis is dead, Mis' Teresa?"

"No," she responded, attempting to stimulate shock. "How did that happen? He was my driver for a long time."

"Poor old John," he lamented, shaking his head slowly. "He was finally going to get married. They reckon he fell out of his skiff and hit his head on something. Then the waves beat him against the pilings pretty bad. He had a lot of broken bones, and he'd been in the water a few days before some children found him."

"I'm sorry to hear that," she said, and she was gratified that the story she told the police had been accepted as fact. The question of the real manner of John Willis's death began to nag at her mind again, though. If that many bones were broken, he might very well have fallen from the window.

The wire arrived the next morning: MR. BELL PASSED ON DURING THE NIGHT STOP RETURN HOME AT ONCE M.E.P. Teresa experienced some shock, but she had half expected his death since he had had the stroke. She and Billy drove back to San Francisco as quickly as they could, neither of them speaking much, each one lost in private thoughts. He offered to accompany her inside when he let her off in front of the house, but she waved him on with a gesture indicating caution. There were already other carriages in the drive behind the back garden; as soon as she ran up the steps the reporters descended on her.

"Where have you been, Mrs. Bell?"

"Is it true that he fell from the landing?"

The words echoed meaninglessly in her ears, until she passed through the front door directly into a police investigation, and her knees buckled beneath her. One of the detectives escorted her to a heavy oak chair in the main hall, and Mammy sent a maid to fetch her a glass of water.

"Mrs. Bell's had a terrible shock," Mammy told the inspector, "I'll take her to her room."

Recovering her wits, Teresa shook her head stubbornly. "I'll stay. Whatever has happened affects me."

Her eyes scanned the faces of the multitude of people gathered in the hall: the servants lined up in an uneasy row, the policemen, the detectives—to whom she paid particular attention. There was no tall, gray-haired man there. Mammy was the very picture of a devoted housekeeper in her black dress and with her hair drawn back from her brow more severely than Teresa had ever seen it. She was as emotionless as a housekeeper, too. Whatever role she chose to play, she entered completely, even if it entailed concealing genuine emotion, such as grief over Mr. Bell—if, indeed, there was any grief. Her red shawl was hanging on the landing above the staircase like a limp banner. There was an irregular outline in chalk on the marble floor, which puzzled Teresa slightly until she heard the inspector's questions.

"All right. With apologies to Mrs. Bell, we'll continue. We've established by the testimony of the servants . . . those two—you have their names, Mr. Reilly?—that Mr. Bell was confined to his bed, but was alive until nine p.m. last night, when they last saw him. When Mrs. Pleasant, the housekeeper, left him at ten, he was sleeping soundly. You were acting as his nurse, Mrs. Pleasant?" Mammy nodded. "Was it your practice to leave his rooms at night? He was pretty ill, recovering from a stroke I understand."

"Sometimes, I slept in his sitting room when he was really bad," Mammy replied. "But he's been so much better lately that I've been going to my own room. I'm not a young woman," she reminded him gently, "and my nursing chores are pretty heavy. Turning and bathing Mr. Bell, helping him regain his ability to walk. I need my rest."

Teresa's eyes were drawn back to the red shawl on the landing, and she found it as infuriating as a matador's cape must be to a bull. Why don't they just cut through all this nonsense and arrest her? she thought. It's pretty obvious what happened. She had realized that the outline on the marble floor represented a sprawled body and she felt so cold inside that she found it difficult to breathe.

"How well was he walking, Mrs. Pleasant?"

"He was coming along nicely, much better than the doctors anticipated. He just needed a firm hand to motivate him, and a strong back, for a while," she sighed.

"Nicely enough to leave his suite."

"It appears so," she said, wringing the handkerchief in her hands. "I shouldn't have left him alone, I realize that now. I didn't expect anything like this."

"What do you think happened, Mrs. Pleasant?" the inspector asked, observing Mammy with cold, neutral eyes.

"Just what I told the servants. He must have gotten up early in the morning and tried to get to the bathroom. Only it was dark and he was probably sleepy, and he turned in the wrong direction . . . toward the landing." Her voice faded, and she appeared too overcome to continue, but she managed to add, "He was a little chilly when he was reading in bed last night, and I put my shawl around his shoulders. When he dropped off to sleep, I didn't want to disturb him by removing it."

Perfect, Teresa thought with admiration. You almost have me believing it myself. A murderess would not leave her scarf hanging there as evidence, everyone knows that, including you. You're a caution, Mammy, a whole show by yourself. But you might not get away with it this time.

"You were sleeping in your room down the hall when you heard him scream. The maid, who reached the hall at the same time, saw you run to the landing in your, er, night garment, without a wrapper. Well," the inspector said, "that about ties it up here. There will be a formal inquest, of course. All of you will be required to be there. All except Mrs. Bell," he added, turning kind gray eyes on Teresa. "It's pretty well established that you weren't in the house, ma'am. We don't want to make this more painful for you than it already is. You deserve some consideration. Mr. Bell was an important man."

Chapter 21

While everyone but herself was at the inquest, Teresa finally found the outside door to the passage. She was surprised that the panel moved inward, instead of out like the one at Beltane. She lit a lamp and moved as rapidly as possible through the secret passage, resisting the temptation to glance through the peepholes, bent entirely on reaching Mammy's closet. Cold fear permeated her chest when she saw the mechanism that would bring her to her goal. What if she's in her room? she thought irrationally, and listened for several seconds before she realized that it was impossible for Mammy to be back yet. After taking several deep, even breaths, she put her hand on the mechanism, and the closet in Mammy's dressing room was revealed to her.

She worked feverishly in the close space, pausing only to brush a hand across her perspiring face from time to time. She had not realized there would be so many documents in boxes in the rear of the closet. The only thing that facilitated the search was that the boxes were dated. She finally found the box pertaining to her, but the stack of papers was much thicker than she had imagined. She knelt near the lamp on the floor of the closet, licking her finger to turn the papers, scanning each one for the words she wanted to see. It's now or never, she told herself grimly, realizing that Mammy might appear at any time. Teresa did not know how long inquests took, but she had counted on its taking the entire morning, even hoped that Mammy might be arrested and never come home.

Her eyes were so weary that she nearly missed the words "power of attorney" and had to flip back to the paper. A flood of relief poured through her, only to freeze at the sound of the sitting-room door opening. Oh, God, she's back! she thought with terror, realizing she

295

must get all the documents back into place and the boxes in order before she could leave. She pulled the closet door shut gently and, with the precious document clutched firmly in her teeth, worked as quickly and silently as possible. She heard Mammy enter the bedroom and knew she would hang up her wrap immediately. Damn Mammy's neatness, she thought desperately, as she pressed the panel and disappeared into the passageway seconds before Mammy opened the closet door.

She'll smell the kerosene, Teresa thought, she'll catch me in this dark passage, and that will be the end of me. She folded the paper and stuck it into her bodice as she scurried like a rat through the woodwork. When she burst through the exit into daylight, she did not know whether or not she was being pursued. She ran to the carriage house as fast as possible and observed the rear of the house from there while she caught her breath. Mammy did not appear, but Teresa continued to tremble as she washed the perspiration from her face in one of the horse troughs, dried herself on a gamey rag, and smoothed her hair. Now, how to get back to the house, she wondered numbly, without being seen? Mammy may not have noticed the kerosene odor, but she'll be looking for me to give me the results of the inquest.

She decided on a stroll in the garden, a natural place to go if you had a lot on your mind. She traversed the paths twice, bending to inhale the odor of the roses and waiting for her summons. If I just concentrate on the paths and plants, I'll be calm when it comes, she decided as she began her third turn around the garden. She had never walked here before without thinking of her little dog and pausing briefly near the spot where she was buried. How could she have missed doing that today, when it was such a regular habit? She walked to the area where Baby was buried and discovered that the plants and shrubs had been changed. New bushes had been put in, and even the pathway was different: its general outline was the same, but its location had shifted somehow. Mammy's new gardener must have rearranged things over the summer, she decided, dismissing the matter. Baby had never had a formal grave anyway, so it did not make any difference if it was lost. To Teresa, the whole garden was a memorial to Baby.

Mammy found her as Teresa had expected she would. She was full of the details of the inquest, which had made a finding of "accidental death." Teresa listened more calmly than she would have thought possible: the walk around the garden had done her good. All her

296

anxiety and terror had dispersed. She went to her rooms before lunch and burned the power of attorney without ceremony, before changing her dress. Everything would be settled soon, she was certain, after Mr. Bell's will was read. Mammy would have everything, and she might be benevolent again, as she had once been. She might let Teresa leave with a small annuity. She did not need her any more. The only thing that concerned Teresa was her promise to Mr. Bell regarding the children, who were no longer children now. If he had provided for them in his will, they would not need her; if he had not, she considered her promise null. It was time she looked after herself.

When Mr. Bell's lawyer, Mr. Bridges, arrived to read the will a few days later, Mammy was wearing a new black taffeta dress festooned with ribbons. She was not in mourning clothes like Teresa, because she always dressed in black, if not so exuberantly. Fred was not present, though Mr. Bridges had notified him.

"He'll probably swoop down and try to take everything," Mammy whispered maliciously as they entered the library. "He didn't come because he's afraid to face us."

It was the only vindictiveness she had exhibited all day. Her spirits were extraordinarily high; she was even swinging her hips a little, reminiscent of the way she had walked as a younger woman when she was pleased. If Mr. Bridges, a distinguished gentleman in a pin-stripped suit, noticed Mammy's absence of grief, he ignored it as he extracted a single legal-sized sheet from his briefcase.

"This won't take long, ladies," he informed them without settling into his chair. "Thomas's wishes were specific."

Mammy wriggled eagerly in the chair next to Teresa's, and Teresa tried not to look at her, lowering her gaze to the Persian carpet and following the pattern, as she had often done in the past, wondering why repeated patterns in weaving always looked like evil faces.

"The properties and assets are divided into thirds . . ." she heard Mr. Bridges' voice intone, as though from a distance, and felt slightly relieved that Thomas must have considered the children after all. " . . .between Mrs. Bell and the two children, Frederick and Marie, the estate to be administered by Mrs. Bell."

Teresa did not react at once, and when she did, her reaction was complete inaction, as if she were frozen into the chair. But Mammy grew lively enough for both of them. She rose, hissing with agitation, and nearly screamed at the lawyer, "You stupid man! That's the wrong will. I have a copy of Thomas's will upstairs. I'll get it—"

Before she could leave the room, Mr. Bridges checked her with an even voice, "Thomas made out this will in my office a few days before his stroke. Any previous will is invalid. We were personal friends, and he told me his reasons. He was of sound mind at the time."

"I'll fight it in court!" Mammy screamed. "Half of that money's *mine*."

"You'd lose," Mr. Bridges said, almost with satisfaction. "You wouldn't have a chance. According to Thomas's accounts, Mrs. Pleasant, you've spent your share of the money, and then some. Actually, you owe the estate one hundred thousand dollars. But Thomas asked me not to press you for that."

Teresa went to her rooms and locked the door. If she had feared Mammy in the past, it was only a prelude to what she felt now. The first thing Mammy would do would be to look for the power of attorney. When she found that missing, the walls might come down. She wondered how long a person could survive without food or water, holed up in a suite in a mansion in the heart of San Francisco. Perhaps, when it got dark, she could climb out of the window and flee.

No, she told herself firmly, you aren't going to fall into your old habits again. You're going to stand up and fight, for once in your life, not for the money, but your own self-respect. Mr. Bridges had informed her that the estate was not very large, anyhow, so only her principles were involved. She would keep her promise to Mr. Bell regarding the children, at least. She realized that she could not free herself from Mammy, who was furious enough at her to charge her with murder and had a witness to back her up. Teresa did not think she would really hang, but she dreaded more publicity. Damn all the webs that woman has woven, she thought, collapsing into a chair. There does not seem any way to really fight her without dreadful repercussions. Teresa felt completely drained and unable to think.

She did not know how long she had been sleeping in the armchair, when she was awakened by a scratching sound at her door that made a chill go down her spine.

"Teresa!" Mammy called softly, still scratching with her long, bony hand. "I still have the house, you know. You signed the deed over to me. . . ."

Teresa rose decisively and opened the door, bringing an expression of surprise to Mammy's face. "I think we should discuss this over a cup of coffee, instead of behaving like three-year-olds, Mammy. I only want what's due those pathetic children and enough to live on decently, but not in luxury, for the rest of my life. If the goddamn house is yours, it's *yours*. My only wish is to get away from it."

"But what about me?" Mammy asked, appearing now much older than she had during the reading of the will. "I've been good to you, Teresa. You aren't going to abandon me in my old age?"

Teresa felt the hysterical laughter rising and struggled to control it. It really was not funny. The evil old woman could blackmail her into companionship for God knows how many years. "I can look after you, if you need it," she told her, "but I don't want to dwell under the same roof with you any longer."

"You'll be sorry you said that." Mammy ground out the words through her perfectly intact yellow teeth. "You and I belong together, like two arms on a single body. We're almost the same person, can't you see? I'll never let you leave me."

Several days later, Mammy openly left the house, so intent on some business of her own that she cut across the grounds on her way to the carriage house to get the gig. Teresa took advantage of her absence to take a cab to Mr. Bridges' office, where she set up an annuity for Fred and Marie and signed Mr. Bell's quicksilver mines to Fred, his rightful heir. With Mr. Bridges' assistance, she withdrew some money from the bank and paid the back taxes on Mr. Bell's old house on Stockton Street before it was auctioned off. But the most important thing she did that morning was send a cashier's check to Billy Beaumont for three thousand dollars to prevent him from ever approaching Mammy about the investment she claimed she made for him.

She also concealed some money in her room against the day when she would be able to leave the house. Her mission was barely completed when Mammy returned in a particularly vile mood. Teresa was making herself a pot of tea in the kitchen when Mammy burst into the room, wild-eyed and furious.

"Do you know what they did?" she cried. *"Do you know what they did?"*

Teresa, who did not know what she was talking about, did not interrupt her preparations for tea.

"They filed the deeds to this house in the wrong order. I'm sure I can sue them. The deed in which you signed the house over to me was misfiled, and the damned house is still in your name!"

Teresa laughed softly. "I always knew those crazy deeds of yours would get you into trouble some day, Mammy. Why did you complicate every transaction, instead of keeping things out in the open? You'd better check your other properties. I may own them, too."

"They're all right," Mammy assured her, sitting down to pour herself some tea. "What's left of them. I sold several of them to build Beltane."

That was when you still had my power of attorney, Teresa thought, knowing that several of the properties bore her name. Mammy had never said anything about the loss of the document and obviously believed she had mislaid it, because she said no more about the misfiled deeds to Octavia Street. Teresa suspected that Mammy thought she could take possession of the house or sell it right out from under them when she found the power of attorney, but the house was actually her own to dispose of as she pleased. She felt no satisfaction over its possession. She would have preferred being released from Mammy's blackmail instead.

"Where are the servants?" Teresa inquired.

"I fired them last night," Mammy said. "We don't really need them. I can do the cooking for both of us."

"That was a move in the interest of economy," Teresa said and smiled. "If you don't mind, I'll cook for myself."

"You used to love my cooking," Mammy said, feigning hurt surprise. "I'm still as fine a cook as ever."

"I know you are. I've been gaining weight on your fancy cooking, though. On the other hand, I'm such a bad cook that I won't eat as much. All those herbs upset my digestion, Mammy."

Too many herbs, she thought to herself, in the hands of a master herbalist are bad for the constitution, and she intended to come out of all this alive.

Sitting at the tea table with Mammy, she found it difficult to believe that she was capable of such deeds, though everything pointed in that direction. Perhaps one way to handle her would be to play on her superstition, the only weak link Teresa had ever discoverd in her armor. I must pretend to be in complete control, even when I know I'm not, she decided.

"I had the strangest dream at Beltane," she said, buttering another thin slice of bread. She felt Mammy's alertness, even though she was not looking at her. "I really wasn't that surprised when I received your wire. I think I was expecting it, Mammy. I even told Billy Beaumont that morning that I thought we'd be returning to the city soon."

"Did you tell him why?" Mammy asked furtively. "I've never believed in those dreams of yours much."

"Of course I didn't tell him," Teresa said heartily. "I don't share my dreams with everyone. They're just dreams, after all. Some of them, nightmares. They're never accurate in every detail even when they do seem to come true. . . ."

"What did you dream?" Mammy asked, anxious to verify the accuracy of Teresa's dream on the night of Mr. Bell's death.

"When?" Teresa asked with a blank expression on her face, almost enjoying the suspense she had generated.

"At Beltane!" Mammy cried, "the night before you got my wire about Thomas."

"Oh . . . yes. I sensed that he was dead, but nothing was really accurate, you know. After all, I thought he was still partially paralyzed, just as his doctors did. None of us knew how far you'd brought him along. The house was almost completely dark, only the light at the top of the stairs was burning. You know, the one that's always left on during the night? I saw two figures coming down the hall, one of them leaning almost helplessly on the other, but I couldn't really make them out. Not until I recognized Thomas's face beneath that little light. The dim figure supporting him had to be pretty strong, because he was dragging his left side. And in order to hurl him over the landing that way. I'll never forget that scream, Mammy. I awoke in a cold sweat, trembling all over." She observed Mammy's face out of the corner of her averted eyes. She had made her point, though her intention was not to frighten the old woman to death. "More tea? You can see how these dreams work, can't you? Perhaps only one thing in them is true. Of course, I hoped all the way home that it wasn't—it was such an awful way to die! You can imagine why I nearly collapsed when I walked into the hall that afternoon. . . ."

"Teresa," Mammy said, swallowing hard and accepting the tea with long trembling fingers, "I think what you have may be a gift. None of those spiritualists are as clairvoyant as you."

"My dreams aren't accurate," Teresa disparaged them modestly, "and they only seem to center on the most awful events. I didn't dream of your red shawl, for instance, and it was most conspicuous, hanging from the rail of the landing."

"Just the same, you have a gift," Mammy reiterated thoughtfully. "I wonder if there's any way we could make any money with it?"

Several months later Fred and Marie filed a lawsuit to break their father's will. Teresa did not think she could face the inevitable publicity and the attention of the reporters again, and the only thing that strengthened her resolve was the promise she had made to Mr. Bell. She dressed carefully in her widow's weeds for the first appearance in court, deciding she looked respectable enough for the occasion. She had abandoned bleaching her hair long ago, but the natural color of her hair was so streaked with gray that it still appeared almost blond. She descended the stairs with a sense of resolution and calm, only to encounter Mammy in the hall, ready to accompany her in her oldest, moth-eaten dress and a bonnet with a broken brim.

"What in God's name?" Teresa breathed, staring at her in amazement. "You look like a ragpicker, Mammy."

"When the judge sees how poor we are, he won't listen to Fred's lies," Mammy confided. "Your clothes are too fine, even if they are out of style, Teresa. You have to use your head and pull out all the stops when you're dealing with the law."

"I don't want you to come," Teresa said impatiently. "This isn't going to be another spectacle like the Sharon lawsuit, though I'm sure that's what you intend. You aren't involved, and I want you to stay at home."

Though Mammy did not accompany her in the carriage, she crept into the back of the courtroom during the proceedings and caused quite a stir. Teresa did not realize she was there for a while, as she answered the judge's questions, under the contemptuous gazes of Fred and Marie, at the opposite side of the chamber, regarding her ability to administer the estate.

"Arrangements have been made with Mr. Bridges, Mr. Bell's attorney," she assured the court, "for the actual administration of the estate. My only intention is to carry out Mr. Bell's wishes, both spoken and written in his will, to the best of my ability—"

"She isn't our mother!" Marie cried, rising from her chair with hatred in her face. "She has no right to dole out our father's fortune to us, while she lives in style in his house."

The judge ordered silence in the courtroom, but he observed the brother and sister thoughtfully. "The fact that you are not the mother of Mr. Bell's children has been stated several times now, Mrs. Bell. In a rather unruly manner, too. I'd like to hear your statement regarding the parentage of Fred and Marie Bell. Are they the children of your body?"

"They are not," Teresa stated calmly. "I cared for them before my marriage to Mr. Bell, but they are not my own. I wish they were. They have rejected all my overtures of friendship, I fear. I feel I might have prevented Mr. Bell from spoiling them so much, if I had been allowed

302

more say about their upbringing. I'm casting no aspersions when I say that the young man and woman you see here today are less prepared to handle their affairs than I am, with the assistance of Mr. Bridges. At least, I have maturity on my side."

But the judge's attention was diverted. "What is that commotion in the rear?" he demanded. Mammy had freed herself from the restraining hand of the bailiff and was moving up the aisle, looking pathetic in her shabby clothes and clasping her black ruched handbag to her chest.

"I have something important to add, Your Honor," she announced. Teresa cringed inwardly, expecting her to say that the children did not belong to Mr. Bell. "I have something to say, sir."

Teresa had not anticipated the judge's astuteness. He observed Mammy for a moment with a mixture of sternness and amusement. "Mrs. Pleasant, you always have something to say," he admonished her. "I don't believe you have anything substantive to offer this court." Fred and Marie smiled triumphantly at Mammy's dismissal. "Is this woman still employed in your house, Mrs. Bell?"

Teresa flushed and lowered her eyes. "Mrs. Pleasant was Mr. Bell's oldest servant, Your Honor. One doesn't dismiss a housekeeper who has managed one's home for so many years."

"Mrs. Pleasant has managed a lot of things, apparently," he commented. "However, I am not going to have my courtroom turned into a three-ring circus, like the Sharon affair. If you'd like to sit quietly in the rear, Mrs. Pleasant, you are permitted to do so. Otherwise, I'll be forced to dismiss you from the court."

In the end, Teresa retained the administration of Mr. Bell's estate, despite the outcry that Fred raised through the press, charges that were answered with relish by Mammy Pleasant in her interviews with reporters. She did not reveal the parentage of the children—that would have required too much explanation. But she catalogued all of Fred's weaknesses and peccadilloes, even intimating that he had tried to rob Mrs. Bell's house.

"We have to keep the door locked all the time," she said, "so that terrible young man won't harm us. I'm asking you, is that any way to treat two helpless, aging ladies? In case anyone's really interested in the whole story, I'm writing my autobiography, you know. Some very arrogant heads in high places will fall when it's published."

Teresa did not know if Mammy was really writing or not. They had less and less contact with one another and, after a few years, they hardly spoke when they met in the hall. Teresa left her room only to prepare her simple meals, carefully cooking only canned goods. The only people who were admitted were the grocery boy and the iceman, who came to the rear door and did not linger to talk to either of the strange ladies in the House of Mystery. The milk and newspapers were left outside the door and were paid for with a monthly check written in Teresa's hand and stuck into the top of the mailbox.

If they encountered one another in the kitchen or the hallway, Mammy always took advantage of the meeting to make the same point: "You may have the house and the money," she would hiss, "but I have the *witnesses*. You'd hang by the neck until you were dead if it weren't for my good nature."

Mammy's hair did not gray, but every year it became more crimped. Whatever lotion she had used to straighten it had been abandoned, just as Teresa's had forgotten the ammonia and peroxide. Mammy's face did not age, either, and Teresa found that slightly eerie. She was frightened of the old woman, and she tried to avoid her. I'm no longer of any use to her, she realized, and Tony said that was when things would become dangerous. Her only defense was in the supernatural, and she got out her old book on magic and practiced some sleight of hand in her room. She did not overdo it, carefully avoiding any magician's tricks that might ruin the illusion that she had a strange, inexplicable power.

One evening, Mammy was in the kitchen when Teresa came down to prepare her own meal. Sensing an opportunity to establish her power, Teresa walked over to the stove as the old woman's gaze followed her every move. But by now Teresa's hands had grown quicker than even Mammy's eyes. She had concealed some matches under her fingers and, fussing with a pan to distract Mammy's attention, suddenly shot out a flame from her hand to light the gas burner.

"How did you do that?" Mammy rasped, her eyes widening. Teresa faced her with an enigmatic expression.

"This . . . thing . . . in me appears to be getting stronger," she confessed. "It's a bit of a nuisance most of the time, but it has its purposes." She indicated the blue fire of the burner. "I wish the dreams would stop, though. They're so unpleasant." She sighed deeply. "Sometimes I hardly sleep at all to avoid them."

"What dreams?" Mammy asked, narrowing her eyes.

"There was one during the storm the other night," Teresa reached into the past with a shudder. "In my dream, the wind was blowing the eucalyptus trees, and I heard a long scream in the night. I saw a man falling from the third floor, turning and twisting in the air, before he struck the garden." The intensity of Mammy's silence encouraged her to continue. "Then, I was someplace else. You know how dreams are. At a sort of wooden shanty near the Bay. That was the worst part of it." She hugged herself with her arms to express her terror. "There was a body floating in the water, and it had been there for some time. I couldn't tell whether it was a black man . . . or Tony. It seemed to be both."

That performance earned her Mammy's respect for some time, and she stopped threatening her with hanging. Teresa kept up her diary faithfully, recording everything she knew and had heard about Mammy in its pages, attempting to separate fact from fiction. She read the obituaries religiously every evening, searching for Ben Willard's name. Mammy did not speak of him, of course, and Teresa did not want to miss the news of his death if it occurred, because the passing of Mammy's former lover would mean her freedom.

She knew that Mammy left the house sometimes, using her secret passage, but she was never really certain that she was alone in the house or confident that Mammy was not up to some mischief when she was supposed to be behind the locked door of her rooms. The thing that frightened Teresa the most was the sound of Mammy's fingers scratching at her door at night. When she opened the door, no one was ever there, and Mammy's war of nerves was successful in that respect. Several times over the years, Teresa had reason to doubt the old woman's sanity, and that worried her, too.

One morning Teresa glanced out the kitchen window and saw the old woman digging holes in the overgrown garden, and she paused in the preparation of her breakfast to watch. If Mammy had gone mad, it was to Teresa's advantage to know it. What the devil does she think she's doing? Teresa pondered with a cup of coffee in her hands. After a while Mammy abandoned her activity with a kick at a bush that had grown completely out of control, and Teresa heard her bang the side door as she came in. Teresa was just putting the finishing touch on her breakfast by filling a chipped dish with a dab of commercial strawberry preserve that she kept hidden behind the flour bin, when Mammy passed the door, saw her, and entered the kitchen to wash her hands.

"Teresa," she said, her voice as clear as it had ever been, "do you remember where I buried your little dog?"

Teresa looked at her askance. Mammy had never seemed this irrational before. "No, Mammy, I don't," she said, humoring her, as she backed toward the door with her tray in her hands. "Whatever made you think of that?"

Mammy shrugged with her thin lips clamped together and a worried expression in her eyes. She did not communicate further, and Teresa fled to her room, trying not to spill the pitcher of milk on the tray. She made certain that her door was firmly locked before she had her breakfast.

Sometimes she watched the reporters who occasionally took their position beside one of the eucalyptus trees, though her field of vision was limited by the ivy growing over the window. They were usually young men, probably eager for a story, and she did not consider them vultures at all. In the winter they appeared cold, and she would have liked to give them the friendly advice that there was no sense in beating a dead horse. There was no news here. The House of Mystery they had created was no more than a dingy mausoleum.

Teresa heard a cry from Mammy, followed by the sound of her weeping. She rushed to Mammy's rooms, imagining she was in trouble. She might be ill, perhaps dying, Teresa thought, and an old person like her deserved some attention. The sobbing continued, and she realized it was too dim to be coming from Mammy's suite. My God, she's fallen down the stairs, she thought as she followed the sound. What shall I do? A broken hip in a woman Mammy's age was very serious, she knew, and Teresa was not strong enough to carry her.

She peered over the landing that had proved fatal to Mr. Bell and was relieved to see that Mammy was not at the foot of the stairs, but was standing beside the door with the newspaper crushed against her face. In the thirty years Teresa had known her, she had never seen Mammy cry; she was as dry-eyed as a witch. She was so immune to grief that she had not even wept when she mentioned the death of her daughter a year after it occurred. What in the world has set her off now? Teresa wondered as she slowly descended the stairs, unsure how to handle the situation.

"Mammy?" she said softly as she approached, "Mammy, what is it, for goodness sake?"

In answer, Mammy thrust the newspaper into Teresa's hands and turned away with a sob. Teresa scanned the front page, but found nothing in particular that would elicit Mammy's reaction. Then, as she looked once more, she noticed a small article at the bottom of the page:

GAMBLER SHOT DEAD IN BARBARY CASINO. She read the brief account, finding it difficult to understand Mammy's grief. She herself felt elated, every vein in her body tingling with relief; she had waited for this day for a long time. But Mammy's emotion was loud and heartfelt, and Teresa turned her attention to her.

"Come, Mammy, I'll help you to your room. Do you have the key? What you need is a sip of your homemade wine. I didn't realize Ben meant so much to you. . . ."

The old woman was so much taller than Teresa that she found it difficult to ascend the stairs under the weight of the leaning body, which did not have an ounce of excess weight on it anywhere. She's all muscle, Teresa thought, like a jungle cat, and it would be well to remember that fact.

She sat Mammy on the sofa and began to look for the wine. This is a miserable turn of events, she considered. I'm free, now, but how can I evict her from the house in this condition? She's eighty years old. Heaven knows she has enough to live on, but she may be right about our being bound until death. In spite of everything, I still feel something for her.

Mammy sipped the wine like a bird, one tiny drop at a time, darting her pathetic tear-stained eyes at Teresa, who attempted to fight back any feeling of compassion. "Are you all right now?" she asked. "I really think we should have a doctor look at you. I've never seen you so shaky before. You stay right there, Mammy. I won't be long."

"Don't you leave this house," Mammy ordered in a level, threatening voice, her whole aspect transformed into her former unyielding strength. "You aren't going anywhere, do you understand? I still have one witness to your husband's murder, and don't you forget it! If you leave, you'll hang."

During the following week, Teresa attempted to expel Mammy from the house, but all her efforts were fruitless. The old woman locked herself in her room, and Teresa did not know whether she went out through the passage or not. When Mammy learned that Billy Beaumont would not appear as a witness against Teresa, and realized that she no longer had any control over her former protégée, she retreated like a beast into its cave and sulked. The old woman knew she could not bring a charge of murder against Teresa, recognizing that her own credibility was legally nil after all her appearances in courtrooms, but she would not give in. Teresa realized that they were facing the ultimate crisis in their long associati⌄n, and though she was resolved in her purpose, she was growing frightened again, too. She had reached a point where she could not take any more, and she was in a position to do something about it. But Mammy was strong, both mentally and physically, a bundle of long, strong muscles and hatred, and Teresa knew the old woman was capable of murder, so she stayed in her room to avoid her.

Finally, early one morning, she gathered all her courage and slipped downstairs to the telephone. She had thought about the call all night: she could either contact Mr. Bridges, who would evict Mammy legally, but in a highly public way; or, she could call Byna at the boardinghouse to seek Billy Beaumont's help. She decided on the latter, and Byna informed her that Billy would be there with a carriage within the hour.

The hour might have been the longest in her life, but it turned out to be a blessing. Bolstered by the knowledge that Billy was on the way, she entered the passageway at the rear of the house to gain entrance to Mammy's closet and spy on her as Mammy had so often spied on others. When she opened Mammy's closet door a crack, she was astonished to discover that no one was in Mammy's suite. She would never have such an opportunity again, she realized, and she dragged both the sofa and a heavy cabinet to block both of the entrances.

By the time Billy arrived, she had packed all of Mammy's belongings, and he helped her carry them down into the hall. He removed the lock from the hall door of Mammy's suite and moved the cabinet away from the closet. Then, they both sat down in the hall to wait.

"That secret passage sure explains a lot," Billy said thoughtfully during their vigil. "She knew everything that went on at the boardinghouse, Miss Teresa. *Everything.* And we were fools enough to think it was because she was a Voodoo queen. Why, I bet she even listened to all those financial gentlemen that dined there. I remember looking for her once, after they settled down to dinner, and no one was allowed into the dining room. I couldn't find hide nor hair of her, but a few minutes later, there she was right there on the main floor with us. It was pretty spooky at the time."

Recalling the financial advice Mammy gave Mr. Bell in her presence, Teresa did not question Billy's assessment of the eavesdropping at the boardinghouse. What a warped, avaricious mind that woman had! But she was intelligent, too, and Teresa began to wonder if they were waiting in vain.

Billy's thoughts must have been running parallel to hers, because he remarked, "Maybe she flew the coop on her own. You know, Miss Teresa," he chuckled, "when that old lady dies, they're going to have to *screw* her into the ground!"

Mammy did not spare them the unpleasantness of evicting her bodily, though. Within an hour, she appeared on the landing above them with her head held high and her lips compressed with anger. "What are my things doing down there?" she demanded, moving down the stairs to reclaim her belongings. *"No one touches what belongs to me."*

Billy Beaumont rose to his feet, tall and strong, and the sight of him brought her up short. "What are *you* doing here? You're no longer in my employ, you turncoat!"

When comprehension of her situation penetrated her understanding, she turned her threatening gaze on Teresa, who simply shrugged her shoulders and said, "This is it, Mammy. Billy will take you and your belongings wherever you wish to go. I'm closing the house. Remaining here is no longer an issue."

Apparently, someone had witnessed Mammy's eviction and seen her fighting in Billy's arms until he deposited her in the carriage. A small crowd, including reporters, had gathered by the time Teresa came out of the front door an hour later. She realized her departure from the house would not be free of scrutiny, either. But it was a small price to pay for freedom.

Everyone turned to watch the fifty-year-old woman in a rust-colored traveling dress leave the House of Mystery, but all, even the reporters, were gracious. She carried only a small suitcase, enough things to last her until she was settled in at the Stockton Street house, and one of the reporters offered to carry it for her.

"Thank you so much," she said, turning the full charm of her enigmatic blue eyes on him. "I prefer to carry it myself, though. I shall be doing everything on my own in the future. What better time to start than now?"

When Mr. Bridges had an inventory made of the items in the house preparatory to putting it up for sale, it became clear that several valuable items were missing. In the week during which she had balked about leaving, Mammy had somehow managed to abscond with the entire silver service from Shreve's and the most elegant pieces of furniture. Teresa was not sure how Mammy had managed it, but she was not particularly upset—in fact, she could not refrain from admiring her old adversary's cunning, which was not completely dulled by age.

"But those items are part of the estate!" Mr. Bridges fumed. "How could she have taken them without your knowing it, Mrs. Bell?"

"I had to sleep sometimes," Teresa said with a faint smile. "Mr. Bridges, let her have them," she coaxed. "Mammy's completely devoted to *things*. Perhaps it will keep her away from me."

The sale of the house brought new disturbances. People streamed through the doors just to look at it. Few of them were potential buyers, though there were several promising offers. Teresa expected to have the house on Octavia Street out of her life forever very quickly. That was when the first letters began to appear in the newspapers. No one knew where Mammy had holed up, but she used her time to dip her pen in vitriol regarding anything in which Teresa was involved. "The mystery house is haunted," the first letter claimed,

> *anyone who buys it does so at his peril. Murders have been committed there by a certain party. The ghosts of the victims roam the halls at night, moaning and scratching at the doors. It is my opinion that anyone who enters that house is in some danger. I am almost certain that one of the ghosts has attached itself to me: there is no ridding oneself of the horrors.*

The line of curious people on the porch evaporated when the letter was published as rapidly as it had appeared. Any prospect of selling the house vanished and after about a year, Mr. Bridges had the windows boarded up to protect the furniture, though Teresa teased him that he had taken the action to keep the ghosts inside.

"Perhaps some charitable organization would brave the threat of ghosts," she suggested in his office one day. "If we're really lucky, maybe we can give it away."

"How can you be so tolerant of that woman's actions?" he asked. "Why in the world do people listen to what she says? That house is worth a good deal of money, Mrs. Bell. You really shouldn't be facetious about such things. You behave as if you hadn't a care in the world, and you don't have that much to live on, either."

Teresa was building a new life for herself. She had ignored the invitations of the curious rich who had had a sudden change of heart about Mrs. Bell and were anxious to show her off at parties as a celebrity, to enliven the social season. She was not interested in taking a position of any kind in society, though that was what Mammy had wanted so long ago. Teresa acquired a circle of friends with interests similar to her own by participating in the meetings of a literary group that held meetings once a week. She even met a kind, scholarly gentleman who liked her for herself and who, in his single-minded devotion to books, had somehow missed all the adverse publicity in the newspapers.

Her income was not large, but she had enough to live on respectably. She replenished her wardrobe, buying a few fashionable clothes: skirts were narrower and hats were larger than she was accustomed to wearing. At first she deplored the new fashions as being less gracious than the kinds of things she had worn when the fashion clock stopped for her after Mr. Bell's death. But once she became accustomed to the narrower line and fewer petticoats at the turn of the century, she found the garments more practical for her present mode of life. She did not employ any servants, not even a personal maid, and it was easier to care for her clothes now than it would have been ten years before.

If anyone had asked her, she would have said that she was happy, though not a day passed without her thinking of Mammy—not the Mammy of Octavia Street, but the Mammy who had befriended her thirty years before. If any problem arose regarding the house, she immediately thought, "Mammy would know how to handle this," and she was particularly wistful when she finally had to learn how to cook. Over the years she had almost forgotten the basics, and she found herself attempting to create dishes for which she had no recipes, for Mammy had guarded hers to the end.

"I think she'd have put some thyme in the veal," she considered late one afternoon as she was preparing food for a dinner party. "She'd also have given this dish a French name. I can do without the thyme, but it really does need white wine in the sauce."

There was none in the house, so she shed her apron and walked to the nearest store to get some, returning in less than fifteen minutes to add a little wine to the dish, shortly before her company arrived. She tasted a spoonful of the sauce critically, and she was just considering complimenting herself on it when she became so ill that she nearly died.

"It wasn't food poisoning," the doctor told her. He had come to her hospital room after her stomach had been pumped and the effects of the emetics she had been given had run their unpleasant course.

311

"You were fortunate that your friend, Mr. Powell, arrived at your house early, Mrs. Bell. Has anyone had access to your kitchen besides yourself?"

She shook her head on her pillow. "What was it?" she asked quietly.

"The only thing I can think of that would accelerate your heartbeat to that degree and cause such a total collapse would be a large dose of digitalis. You don't have any foxglove in your garden, do you? Usually it grows wild, but some people transplant it in ignorance of its properties."

"I don't grow any poisonous plants," she said, a terrible suspicion forming in her mind. "I don't even cultivate my own herbs. . . ."

"Many plants are poisonous," the doctor said. "The alkaloids from common flowers like daffodils are enough to make a person pretty sick. But this wasn't anything like that. I'm certain it was foxglove, but it had to be very concentrated, perhaps distilled by someone familiar with herbal medicine, to make you this ill after you tasted only a tablespoon of the sauce."

"Where does it grow?" she asked, no longer able to deny her worst fear. "Would it be in the fields outside of the city?"

"Indeed, it would. Have you any idea how it got into your food?"

She turned her head and gazed through the window at the dark city streets, illuminated only slightly by their gaslights. "I left my door unlocked for a few minutes when I went to the store," she said faintly.

Billy Beaumont and Byna visited her in the hospital with a bouquet of flowers, and she asked him if he knew Mammy's whereabouts.

"I don't have any idea," he said, shaking his head and observing her with an expressionless face. "Byna, honey, why don't you go buy Mis' Teresa a newspaper? That's a good girl." As soon as they were alone he said, "You think she did it, don't you?"

"I know she did it," Teresa said with conviction. "The thing that bothers me most is that she must have been watching my house for the opportunity. I'm almost afraid to go back."

The newspapers got wind of the story at once. MRS. BELL POISONED, the heading read, and Teresa was once again the center of publicity. She had stopped reading the papers during Mammy's rash of anonymous letters; now, she felt she must build a wall around herself to protect her privacy. She had three locks installed on the doors, she never left the house without securing everything completely, and she kept the doors and windows bolted when she was inside. Her hopeful new life was in

312

danger of withering before it came into full bloom. She was a prisoner again. No one in the city seemed to know where Mammy was hiding, though Teresa had not charged her and did not cooperate with the police regarding the poisoning. She would rather risk a repetition of the episode than see Mammy Pleasant in court again, generating publicity as only she knew how to do.

A few weeks after her recovery, she invited Billy and Byna to dinner. She was preparing the meal when someone pounded the knocker on the door. She glanced at the clock; Billy and his wife were not expected for another hour. Once before, however, an early-arriving guest had saved her life, she reflected. The knocking became more insistent, and she finally took off her apron and went to the door to peer through the curtain cautiously before unlocking it. The young reporter who had once offered to carry her suitcase was standing on the porch, his impatient breath steaming in the cold air. She hesitated. He was a nice young man. He had not been aggressive when she walked away from Octavia Street several years before. He was obviously agitated, and her curiosity overpowered her caution toward the press. As soon as she opened the door, he began speaking rapidly, ignoring preliminary greetings.

"Have you heard the news, Mrs. Bell? Everyone will be descending on you shortly. I thought I'd better warn you, ma'am. I know how much you dislike that sort of thing."

"Come in, please," she said and locked the door behind him. She led him into the warm parlor and poured a glass of sherry for him. "Now, what on earth are you talking about?" she asked.

"Mammy Pleasant's dead. She died in a run-down hotel this morning, and all hell's broken loose in the newsroom. I beg your pardon, ma'am," he apologized for his language, "but there isn't much time. Is there any place I can take you to avoid the news hawks?"

Teresa sat down on the arm of the sofa. "What was she doing in such a hotel?" she asked, unable to take the whole thing in. "She was a wealthy woman. . . ."

"That isn't the way it looks, ma'am. A woman down the hall was looking after her. Apparently she had pneumonia. But that isn't the strangest part, Mrs. Bell. She'd been carrying a black handbag and never let it out of her hands. She was clutching it when she died."

"Her black ruched pouch," Teresa considered, "she's had it for years." Mammy couldn't bring herself to part with her diamonds, Teresa thought. She held onto them until the end.

313

"I think the woman who was caring for her must have thought she'd get whatever was in the bag," the young man continued. "And that's what Mrs. Pleasant wanted her to think. Do you know what was inside?"

"Diamonds?" she asked, wondering why Mammy felt she had to buy assistance in such a devious way. Why didn't she just hire a nurse during her illness? She felt her old impatience with Mammy's complicated dealings rise again.

"I imagine that woman thought something of the kind," the young man grinned. "The bag was full of strips of newspaper, torn to the size of bills."

Teresa stared at him in stupefication for such a long time that she finally realized what she was doing. "I'm sorry, Mr. . . ."

"Morgan, ma'am. John Morgan."

"I don't understand," she said softly, shaking her head. "She was rich. She had a fortune in diamonds, all the silver and antiques from the house. She told me she'd sold some of her properties, and I thought she was . . ." Suddenly, she did understand, though: The episode of the braided handbag was so like Mammy, conning someone until the end. Was it possible that she had put everything into Beltane? Over the past few weeks, Teresa had started suspecting that Mammy might be living there. "She never registered anything under her own name," she said aloud. "If anything's left, it will be a real headache to sort out. It could take years. But maybe that's what she wanted, too. The woman was an enigma, Mr. Morgan. If she knew she was approaching death, there's no explaining what she might do. . . ."

Such as taking me along with her, Teresa realized with a shock, all regret over the old woman's passing evaporating as quickly as it had come. "We're one person," Mammy had told her, "like two arms on a single body." Apparently she had really believed that and had prepared for death by attempting murder. The pitiful black ruched handbag would not leave Teresa's mind, and a tickle of amusement in her chest made her smile.

"That woman was a caution," she remarked, "manipulating people right to the end."

"We really should leave," Mr. Morgan said, glancing toward the window. "You won't have a prayer if they all come at once. I'm not after any kind of story, Mrs. Bell. I've admired you for a long time, and I just want to save you further distress."

"No," she said, pouring herself a glass of wine and refilling his glass, "we'll lock the doors against them and remain here. You're right about my not wishing any more publicity. But Mammy loved it so much. I have a story to tell you, if you'll just leave my name out of it. Some people are arriving soon who can tell you even more, perhaps. You said nothing else was found in the room?"

"That's right, ma'am."

"Then she didn't actually write her famous autobiography," Teresa breathed with some relief. "She really was an amazing woman, Mr. Morgan, more than anyone knows. If a life can be measured by what one spends, instead of leaves, hers was probably unique. She pulled herself up from slavery in the South to manipulate some of the best financial minds of our time. Her story includes a governor, a senator, the board of the Bank of California, and more elite families than even I know about. She once promised the press that some heads would roll when she revealed everything. What I have to tell you might only make them bow, but I think Mammy would consider even that a fitting tribute. First, let me tell you how she got her inside information about the stock market. . . ."

She had not felt this relaxed in years. She was anxious to speak about Mammy now, to get the whole burden off her shoulders forever, so she could get on with her life. She was finally really free: Mrs. Thomas Bell, a respectable widow with less of a fortune than most people realized, but with a circle of friends of her own choosing and a kind, decent man interested in her.

The future held nothing but promise for Teresa on the brisk California evening of January 11, 1904.

Epilogue

On April 18, 1906, the great earthquake and three-day-long fire demolished most of San Francisco. Many people claimed the catastrophe was retribution for the sinfulness of the city. Teresa survived the disaster and increased her inheritance with careful investments. Her Stockton Street house was destroyed, so she moved into another one, where she spent the rest of her life quietly.

The House on Octavia Street survived the earthquake and fire, but it was demolished later to make way for modern construction. The address has changed, because the hill is so heavily populated now, but a few of Mammy's eucalyptus trees still survive on that corner.

Mammy's buried diamonds were never found.